"Okay, so I'm a vampire," Leigh acknowledged. *"I gather this means I'll live forever?"*

"Probably not forever," Lucian told her. "But you won't age, or get sick, or even get cavities."

She grinned. "At least there are some perks with this deal."

He noticed her eyes seemed preoccupied with roving over his bare chest. He found himself straightening, his chest puffing up like a male peacock preening for her admiration. Disgusted with himself, he leaned against the counter and crossed his arms self-consciously over his naked chest. She blinked as he ruined her view. She glanced at his face, flushing guiltily on realizing she'd been caught ogling him.

His gaze slid over her in the over-large terrycloth robe. She was almost a foot shorter than he.

She was also a bundle of luscious curves...

By Lynsay Sands

BITE ME IF YOU CAN
A BITE TO REMEMBER
A QUICK BITE

LYNSAY SANDS

Bite Me
If You Can

AVON BOOKS

An Imprint of HarperCollins*Publishers*

AVON BOOKS
An Imprint of HarperCollins*Publishers*
10 East 53rd Street
New York, New York 10022-5299

Copyright © 2007 by Lynsay Sands
Not Another New Year's copyright © 2007 by Christie Ridgway; *Bite Me If You Can* copyright © 2007 by Lynsay Sands; *Warrior Angel* copyright © 2007 by Margaret Weis and Lizz Baldwin Weis; *The Secret Passion of Simon Blackwell* copyright © 2007 by Sandra Kleinschmit
ISBN: 978-0-06-077412-7
ISBN–10: 0-06-077412-6
www.avonromance.com

First Avon Books paperback printing: February 2007

Avon Trademark Reg. U.S. Pat. Off. and in Other Countries, Marca Registrada, Hecho en U.S.A.
HarperCollins® is a registered trademark of HarperCollins Publishers.

Printed in the U.S.A.

10 9 8 7 6 5 4 3 2 1

For Dave.
Next road trip you drive (grin).

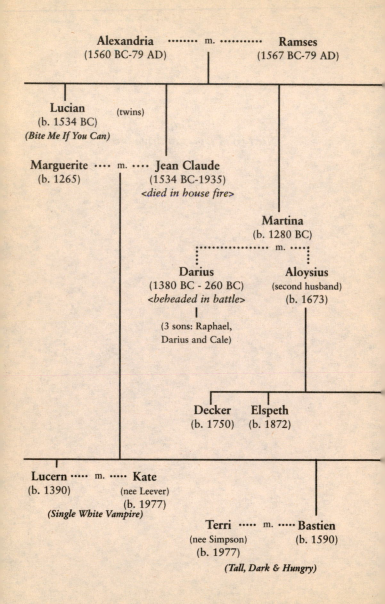

Arøeneau Family Tree

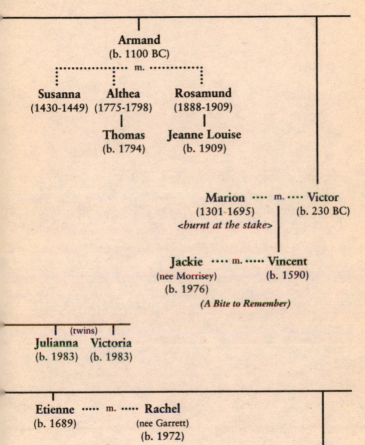

Armand
(b. 1100 BC)
m.

Susanna
(1430-1449)

Althea
(1775-1798)

Rosamund
(1888-1909)

Thomas
(b. 1794)

Jeanne Louise
(b. 1909)

Marion ···· m. ···· **Victor**
(1301-1695)   (b. 230 BC)
<burnt at the stake>

Jackie ···· m. ····· **Vincent**
(nee Morrisey)   (b. 1590)
(b. 1976)

(A Bite to Remember)

(twins)
Julianna   **Victoria**
(b. 1983)   (b. 1983)

Etienne ····· m. ····· **Rachel**
(b. 1689)   (nee Garrett)
(b. 1972)

(Love Bites)

Gregory Hewitt ····· m. ····· **Lissianna**
(b. 1965)   (b. 1798)

(A Quick Bite)

 One

Leigh was only a block and a half from home when she noticed the footsteps echoing her own. At first she didn't think anything of it. This was Kansas. Nothing ever happened here, especially not at five in the morning. Even Dorothy and Toto had to get picked up by a tornado and dropped somewhere else for adventure to come their way.

Of course, this was Kansas City, not some backwater town. There *was* crime in the city. It was also five o'clock in the morning, and she was a lone woman walking down a dark street that—while a residential area of old houses with families—was also only a couple of blocks from the downtown core where the homeless and druggies tended to concentrate.

A shiver of unease crept up Leigh's spine as she became aware that the footsteps behind her had picked up speed and were drawing nearer. She'd walked this route hundreds of times over the last five years and never once felt uncomfortable . . . and didn't like that she now was. Telling herself to stay calm, she tried to recall what she'd been taught to do in self-defense class, but, of course, now that she needed it, her brain was blanking on her.

Wasn't that always the way?

She felt her muscles begin to tense as the footsteps continued to draw nearer, and feared if she didn't do something soon, it might be too late.

The thought spurred her into action. Changing direction, Leigh cut toward the curb to cross the street, casting a nonchalant glance back as she did, as if looking for traffic. The look didn't reassure her. The person approaching was a man; tall, slender, and dressed in dark clothes. She couldn't see his face, however; it was in shadow, thanks to the hood of his jacket. All she'd managed to do with her quick glance was make herself more uncomfortable, more on edge. More scared.

Acting as if she weren't troubled by his presence, Leigh started across the street, her mind now considering and discarding possibilities of what she should do. A glance around the dark house-lined street ahead told her she was on her own, there wasn't a car or pedestrian to be seen. No help there.

She really should have taken a taxi home, she acknowledged, but had never had a problem before, why should she have thought this morning would be any different? Besides, it was too late for regrets, they weren't going to get her anywhere.

Leigh felt her heart squeeze tight as the footsteps followed her across the street. Now her gaze was sharp as she scanned the houses she passed, searching for any sign of life, trying to deduce which she should approach for help. This was a quiet residential street, the houses in darkness, people having long retired for the night and not yet rising. She appeared to be the only person in this area who worked late and was still up.

Coco's, the restaurant/bar she owned, closed at 3:00 A.M. Well, the bar closed then, the restaurant area closed much earlier. Leigh managed the bar at night. Once the last customer trundled out and the cleaning crew set to work, she retired to her back office to do paperwork; filling out the work schedules, checking time cards, writing up orders, checking the day's receipts, and so on. She was usually done about the same time as the cleaners. Otherwise, she waited for them to finish, saw them out, locked up and headed home . . . always between 5:00 and 5:30 A.M., that dark predawn time when most criminals were tucked in bed.

Just as everyone on this road appeared to be, Leigh thought, her heart sinking. Then she spotted a porch light pop on several houses up. A moment later the front door opened and an older lady in a housecoat appeared. The woman didn't notice her coming up the street, her attention on the German shepherd who slipped past her to pad eagerly down the steps onto the front lawn.

"Waking me up before dawn." The woman's annoyed mutter carried clearly in the near silence. "You should have gone when I took you out for your walk earlier."

Leigh's heart lifted. A safe port in the storm. She could seek shelter from the woman and call the police, or maybe just a taxi. Surely the dog's presence would discourage the man following her from making a nuisance of himself?

She put on a burst of speed and opened her mouth to call out, but that was as far as she got. She never heard the man behind her pick up speed, never realized he'd rushed forward. Suddenly he was there before her, forcing her to an abrupt halt.

"Hello, Leigh."

The sound of her name made her pause with confusion, then the man shrugged the hood off his head, revealing his face.

"Donny?" She said with surprise, relief coursing

through her. Donny Avries had worked the bar at Coco's for a year. He was always eager to please and a hard worker. Milly—Leigh's friend, and her day manager in the restaurant—claimed he had a crush on her and had begged for steady night shifts to be near her, but Leigh thought that was nonsense. They just got along well as friends. She'd been terribly upset when he'd gone missing more than a week ago.

Usually prompt, and often even early for his shift, Donny simply hadn't shown up on Monday night. Leigh had tried calling his apartment, but there'd been no answer. When he hadn't shown up the next night, she'd called again, then grown concerned and called his landlady to have her check on him.

The woman reported that while everything looked fine in his apartment, his cat was obviously hungry and the litter box had been overflowing, suggesting he hadn't been home for a while. While there were no signs that he'd left on a planned trip, she'd talked to people in the neighboring apartments, and no one had seen Donny since he'd gone out Saturday night with some friends. They'd decided to call the police.

Now, a week later, the police had been to the restaurant twice, asking questions and admitting that he appeared to have disappeared. They told her to contact the station if she heard from him.

"Where have you been?" Leigh asked, anger replacing concern. She'd been worried sick about the man, and here he stood, apparently fine and well.

Donny hesitated, then said simply, "You'll see."

Leigh blinked at his answer, not finding it acceptable after all her concern. And frankly, the words—as well as the odd smile on his face—were creeping her out. There was also something strange about his eyes.

"No, I won't see," she said firmly. Her fear had now fully turned to anger, and she was no longer in the mood to hear what he had to say for himself. Turning on her heel, she continued in the direction she'd been heading. "You can explain yourself tomorrow when you come by to pick up your severance pay."

She'd taken only a few steps before, unaccountably, stopping, her body going limp. She heard the soft thud as her purse slid from her lifeless hands and landed on the grassy verge along the sidewalk, then found herself slowly turning back. Donny was no longer alone; another man stood beside him. He was tall and lanky, with long, straw-colored hair that hung in greasy strips around a thin pale face. He also had yellow-brown eyes that seemed to glow.

If her sudden lack of control over her own body hadn't been enough to scare her, one glimpse of this man's dead eyes was enough to make her blood turn to ice.

"Hello, Leigh. Donny's told me a lot about you." He smiled, and she saw his two canine teeth slide down and forward to form two pointed fangs.

Some part of her mind shut off at the sight, telling her it wasn't real, that it wasn't ready to accept it as real and it was going to sleep now. But she snapped back with horror when the man abruptly swooped forward, enveloping her in the darkness that seemed to surround him. She felt a pinch on her throat, then excitement and pleasure rushed through her like a drug.

"Ah," Donny complained from somewhere beyond the shoulder blocking her view. "I wanted to be the one to bite her."

Leigh blinked at the whiny sound to his voice, even as the pleasure invading her faltered and the man before her muttered something against her throat.

"What?" Donny asked. He moved into view as he tapped the man's shoulder. "What did you say?"

The man muttered again, something that came out sounding like, " 'Huh-uh!" Then he lifted his head with an impatient tsk and glared over his shoulder at Donny.

"Shut up!" he snapped, and some part of Leigh's mind thought, *Ohhh, that's what he'd said.*

"*I* am the master vampire," he went on. "*I* am the one who sires new children of the night."

Leigh's eyes widened at his words. Vampires?

She supposed it was hard not to accept that when the guy's fangs were flashing with every word and there was blood on his tips. Hers, she presumed. She could feel warm liquid running down her throat and dampening the front of her white blouse. It was coming from the spot where he'd nipped her, and she suspected it was blood, so . . . a vampire? Okay. But "children of the night"? That sounded a bit corny and too late-night-movie to her.

That's when she realized that she might have lost it. Having such thoughts in the midst of this situation didn't seem all that healthy. Unfortunately, she realized it wasn't just her body she couldn't control. Her mind felt woozy, as if she'd been given a tranquilizer. Her thoughts were her own, but she couldn't seem to work up much concern over what was happening. While her mind was urging her to scream her head off, she couldn't seem to work up any fear, or the energy to even yell.

"That is because you are under my control," the man holding her announced, as if he'd read her thoughts, and Leigh supposed he had. Weren't vampires supposed to be able to control their victim's minds? Of course, they were also supposed to be irresistibly attractive and suave.

Unfortunately, Donny was just your average red-haired, freckle-faced guy, and Mr. I-Am-the-Master-Vampire wasn't particularly handsome . . . or charismatic either, for that matter. Really, it was all rather disappointing when she thought about it.

A low growl drew her attention to Mr. Master Vampire, and she noted with some concern that he looked kind of pissed off.

"You *will* change your mind," he growled, staring into her eyes. "You will want me uncontrollably, desire me beyond all others, obey me without question."

It was the obey thing where he lost her. Leigh wasn't big on the word. It had been her ex-husband's favorite order . . . usually just before he tried to use his fists to convince her. It was the main reason he became an ex.

"Hey, Morgan," Donny protested, his voice again whiny. "What are you doing? We're supposed to be turning her for *me*."

"Shut up, Donald," Morgan snapped. His eyes were narrowed on Leigh, and she suspected he was beginning to realize she wasn't completely under his spell. She knew for sure she was right when he asked, "How can you be thinking? You shouldn't be thinking, but I can hear your thoughts."

Leigh had no idea why, either. If she'd been able to, she would have shrugged in response. Unfortunately, while her mind was somewhat her own, her body was not.

A growl distracted Morgan and he glanced down to the side. Leigh still couldn't move her head, but her eyes did angle down and she caught a fuzzy glimpse of a dog. She recognized it at once as the German shepherd she'd seen come out of the house up the street. For a moment she thought the animal might yet save her, but then Morgan flashed his fangs in a sort of half hiss, half growl, and the dog backed off, head low, teeth bared, but his own growl losing some of its strength.

"Morgan," Donny began nervously, eyeing the German shepherd, who was still close enough to be worrisome.

"Oh, do shut up, Donald," the Master Vampire said with exasperation. Then, to her surprise, he scooped her into his arms and started back across the street.

Donny followed. He was muttering under his breath with resentment, Leigh noted, glancing over the shoulder of the man carrying her. Then her view was obstructed as Morgan carried her around the back of a black van. She'd crossed the road just two car lengths before the van earlier, and now suspected it was where Morgan had appeared from. She was sure it had only been one set of footsteps following her up the street. Donny's. Morgan, she supposed, had been waiting in the van, and if she hadn't crossed the street, the side door of the van probably would have opened as she passed and she'd have been dragged inside.

Leigh suspected she'd forced them to change plans when she'd crossed the street.

"You're a clever girl," Morgan said as he set her in the back of the van. "That's exactly what happened."

He'd obviously read her mind again, Leigh realized as he climbed in after her. Donny closed the doors behind them, and a moment later she heard the driver's door open. The van shifted a bit on its wheels as he got in the driver's seat.

"I don't know why you still have control of some of your faculties, but it intrigues me," Morgan announced, lifting her into his lap so that she leaned back against his right arm as the van's engine roared to life.

Woo-hoo, she thought dryly. *She'd impressed a blood-sucking vampire.*

Morgan seemed amused by her thoughts. At least, a smile curved his lips, but his voice was deadly serious as he announced, "And *you* shall be a blood-sucking vampire, too. Will you like me better then, I wonder? Once I am your sire?"

Leigh was trying to decide if he meant from the bite he'd given her or if he'd have to bite her two more times, like in the books and movies, when he abruptly raised his left wrist to his mouth and sliced open a vein with one of his fangs.

Oh, that is so totally gross, she thought.

"Yes," Morgan agreed as if she'd spoken aloud. "And it hurts like a bugger, believe me. However, it *is* necessary, I'm afraid."

Leigh was still trying to sort out why it would be necessary when her mouth suddenly opened of its own accord and he pressed his bleeding wrist to her lips. The tinny liquid poured over her teeth and across her tongue. She was forced to swallow or choke on it. She swallowed.

Dry grass and dead branches crunched under Lucian Argeneau's boots as he approached the van parked in the trees at the edge of the property. Two men stood by the open back doors, choosing and checking weapons in the gray predawn light. Like himself, they were dressed all in black and were over six feet tall. Both were also muscular and had short hair, but one was a brunette and the other a blond.

"Are we set?" he asked, running one hand through his own short ice-blond hair.

"Set," Bricker—the brunet—said calmly as he leaned into the van to grab two cans of gasoline. "How do you want to do this?"

Lucian shrugged, unable to find any real enthusiasm for the task ahead. He'd done this so many times over the years that there was little challenge to it anymore. He found it more interesting to track down the nests than to clear them out, but even that was less challenging than it used to be.

It didn't help that this was Morgan they were going after. He had been a best friend to Lucian's twin brother, Jean Claude, right up until the other man's death a few years earlier. The two men had been thick as thieves for centuries, and because of that, Lucian had counted the man as a friend as well. So much so that when the first whispers and rumors that Morgan had turned rogue started, Lucian ignored them, sure they couldn't be true. The rumors had persisted, however, and he'd had to look into the matter, though not enthusiastically. Now, here he stood, the rumors confirmed and Morgan marked for death.

"Here comes the sun," Mortimer murmured, and then repeated Bricker's question, "How do you want to do this?"

Lucian blinked away his thoughts and took in the first rays of sunlight creeping up to drive away the night. This was the best time to hit. Everyone would be returned to the nest by now and settling in to sleep the day away.

Because—of course—vampires didn't walk during the day, he thought dryly as his gaze slid over the surrounding trees, then finally to the decrepit house where Morgan had holed up with the pack of rogues he was creating. It looked bad in this light, but was worse—he knew—in daylight, when the sun baked down cruelly on the flaking paint, the boarded-over windows, and the weed-tangled lawn.

How the rogues chose to live never failed to amaze him. It was as if—once their mind snapped and they decided to become the scourge of the earth—they believed normal, civilized homes were beyond them. Or perhaps they were simply living *down* to what mortals thought they were, hoping to lure and hold their pack members in thrall that way. After all, if mortals knew how little magic immortals truly had, they might find it less attractive to be one, or at least to be their servants.

Shaking off these cynical thoughts, Lucian glanced toward the other two men and finally gave his answer. "The same as always."

Nodding, Mortimer closed the van doors, took the larger gas can from Bricker, and the three of them moved to the edge of the woods. They paused, their gazes sliding over the windows once again. There was no sign of movement from the house, but half the windows were boarded up so that didn't mean much.

"Do we give them a couple more minutes to settle in, or—" Mortimer's question died, and they all glanced around as the sound of a vehicle disturbed the silence. They watched in silent surprise as a dark van turned into the driveway and crunched up the gravel lane.

"Hmm," Lucian said, with his first real spark of interest. This was different. Usually the "vampires" would have been in-house by now, if not already snug in the coffins they seemed to favor.

They moved back a bit into the trees to be less visible. As they watched, the van parked close to the house, then the driver jumped out and ran around to open the rear doors. Lucian stiffened as Morgan swept out of the van, a brunette in his arms. Dressed in a short black skirt and a bloodstained white blouse, her eyes shot over the house and yard as if seeking an escape, but the way she lay limp in Morgan's arms told him that the rogue immortal had taken control of her body. There would be no escape.

"That's Leigh," Mortimer murmured with a frown.

"She works the bar at Coco's. The restaurant we've eaten at all week," Bricker explained, and Lucian grunted. Justin Bricker was young enough that he still ate, and Garrett Mortimer went along to keep him company and sometimes picked at food.

Lucian didn't bother with food, but he'd heard a lot this week about the "pretty little thing" who'd served them their late meals in the bar. They both seemed taken with her charm and sense of humor, and he supposed this Leigh was the "pretty little thing" in question. Certainly, neither man seemed pleased to see her being carried up the porch steps, obviously about to become Morgan's latest victim.

"We have to help her," Bricker said.

Mortimer nodded in agreement. "Yeah."

"She could be willing," Lucian pointed out, though there had been something in her eyes that suggested she wasn't.

Both men were silent, their gazes locked on the woman Morgan was carrying into the house.

"No. She isn't," Mortimer said with certainty as the door closed behind the trio. He sounded grim and angry. Mortimer rarely got angry.

Bricker agreed, "No, she isn't."

Shrugging, Lucian turned his gaze back to the house. "We should give them ten minutes or so to settle in for the night."

"But the longer we wait, the worse it could be for Leigh," Bricker protested.

"He's already bitten her and given her his own blood," Mortimer pointed out, obviously having gained the news from her thoughts when he'd read her. "There isn't much more he'd bother doing to her before she finishes turning."

Bricker frowned and glanced at Lucian. "We're taking her out of there, right?" When Lucian hesitated, he argued, "She hasn't bitten anyone yet, and doesn't want to be there. Leigh's a nice lady."

"We'll see," Lucian said finally.

Realizing it was all he'd get for now, Bricker fell silent, but he looked worried.

Lucian ignored him and proceeded to examine his equipment. He gave his crossbow a once-over, then counted the specially made wooden arrows in the quiver strapped to his leg. Satisfied that all was in order there, he retrieved the gun from his pocket, checking to see that it was fully loaded and the safety was on before putting it back.

Lucian glanced toward the house, impatient to get things going. Then he forced himself to wait the full ten minutes, but the moment the digital face of his watch said that time had passed, his hand tightened on his crossbow and he started forward without a word.

Mortimer and Bricker fell into step on either side of him as he emerged from the trees and approached the dilapidated house. They mounted the front porch as silently as possible.

"Careless," Mortimer murmured when Lucian turned the knob and the door opened. The red-haired guy hadn't bothered to lock it. Lucian wasn't terribly surprised. If he was newly turned, the man would see himself as invincible, and none of Morgan's followers should be more than a month or so old. That was when the first whispers that Morgan had gone rogue started.

The three men eased into the house, eyes alert, ears straining for any sound. As expected, the upper floor appeared deserted. After setting the cans of gasoline in the kitchen, they separated to make a thorough, silent search of the top two floors, just to be sure. Once finished, they regrouped in the kitchen and approached the door they knew led to the basement.

Lucian was thorough by nature and had trained anyone who worked with him to be so, too. They always sought out all the information they could on a nest before approaching it. Knowing the layout made things much easier, and this time they'd managed to track down the daughter of the previous owner. The woman had sold the house when her mother died, but had grown up there and knew it well. From her, they'd learned all they could and even got a crude drawing of the layout before erasing all memory of their visit.

Now, Mortimer and Bricker moved to the left-hand side of the door while Lucian moved to the right. Once situated, he nodded at the other two men, raised his crossbow and reached for the doorknob with his free hand. That hand froze an inch away when the knob began to turn on its own.

Lucian jerked his hand back and waited. The door only opened halfway before the brunette named Leigh slid through and took a cautious step into the kitchen.

As Lucian stared in amazement, her head slowly turned and she blinked at the sight of him. He saw fear leap into her eyes, and moved quickly, clasping one hand over her mouth and drawing her silently away from the door so that her back was pressed hard to his chest.

Her body briefly tensed, as if preparing to struggle, then she abruptly went still. When Lucian glanced down, he saw that her wide eyes were on Mortimer and Bricker on the other side of the door. Both men were giving her what he supposed were reassuring smiles. To him, they just looked like a pair of idiots, but it apparently worked on Leigh. As he watched, Bricker placed one finger to his mouth to warn her to be quiet, while Mortimer stared at her with a concentration that suggested he was sending her reassuring thoughts and perhaps also the same, silent warning. The woman relaxed against Lucian, and he found himself responding as her body molded to his, her bottom unintentionally nestling his groin.

"I just fell asleep, Donald. I don't appreciate being woken up for this."

Lucian stiffened as that voice floated up the stairs, aware that Leigh had gone still. She was actually holding her breath, he realized, and found he disliked that she was so afraid.

"I'm sorry, sire," someone—presumably Donald— responded, but in truth he sounded more resentful than apologetic. "But I've searched the basement and she—"

"Because she's not going to hide in the basement. She's going to run, you idiot!" Morgan's angry voice snapped back.

"But why? Why isn't she willing?" Donald's voice had turned frustrated and even whiny.

"Not everyone wants to be a child of the night. I warned you of that. I told you, you couldn't turn your back on her for a moment until we have control over her. Not for a damned moment! I *told* you that! She isn't a willing turn. Until she accepts me as master, she'll try to run."

"I just left her alone for a minute. I—"

"You shouldn't have left her alone at all. Get her back and—"

"But what if she's outside? The sun's coming up!"

"You wanted her. She's—"

The words stopped short and Lucian felt himself stiffen further. The voices had drawn closer with each passing moment, and by his guess the speakers were at the bottom of the steps now. The sudden silence seemed to suggest something had given away their presence.

Lucian glanced at Mortimer and Bricker, but he was sure neither man could be seen from below. Then he let his gaze drop over the woman before him, and spotted the problem at once. Lucian hadn't pulled Leigh back far enough. She was short, the top of her head barely reaching the base of his throat, but she was generously proportioned and part of her generous proportions were protruding past the edge of the door in her bright white blouse.

"Is that a boob?" he heard Donald ask, and Lucian closed his eyes.

The ensuing silence was so long, he knew that Morgan was seeking out Leigh's mind and searching for information on the situation at the top of the stairs. Lucian supposed it would have been too much to hope that the man would just assume she was a bimbo bartender too stupid to leave the house and was standing up here contemplating her navel. No. Morgan suspected something was up.

Knowing their surprise approach was now over, Lucian shifted Leigh so he could lean forward and peer around the edge of the door. On the other side, Mortimer did the same thing, and they found themselves staring at two men frozen at the bottom of the wooden steps. Then all hell broke loose.

Morgan and Donald suddenly spun and sped up the dark hall below, breaking into a run as they slipped out of sight. Bricker and Mortimer charged after them, and Lucian pulled Leigh away from the door and pushed her into a chair at the kitchen table.

"Stay," he hissed, his gaze sliding over her face as he got his first close-up look at her. She was a beautiful woman, glossy chestnut waves of hair framing large, almond-shaped eyes, a straight nose, and high cheekbones in an oval face. She was also terribly pale and swaying in the chair, leaving him to wonder just how much blood she'd lost.

He would have asked, but a burst of gunfire from below recalled him to more urgent matters. Leaving her there, Lucian turned away and hurried downstairs after his comrades.

 Two

"Where's Leigh?"

Lucian paused on the top step. He and Mortimer had finished clearing out the nest and trailing gasoline through the basement and up the stairs to the kitchen, the first time either man had been there since rushing downstairs. Bricker had been the one to run up to retrieve the cans of gasoline they'd left in the room. He'd brought the smaller one down to them, then taken the other up to the second floor to drop a trail of the flammable liquid there and down to the main floor.

"I left her seated at the table," Lucian said. "Maybe Bricker already took her out to the van."

"Maybe," Mortimer agreed wearily.

Lucian turned back to continue splashing the gasoline on the tile floor, but he, too, was tired. It had been a lot of work.

There had been more vampires in the nest than expected. Morgan had managed to turn upward of thirty-odd followers . . . and they hadn't all laid around accommodatingly for Lucian and his men to put out of their misery. It had taken quite a while to take care of them all.

It was only after they'd gone through the rooms in the

basement that they realized Morgan had gotten away in those first moments of chaos after they charged downstairs. So had the man he'd called Donald. The pair had slid out through a pair of cellar doors that opened into the backyard. The daughter of the previous owner had apparently forgotten this detail.

Moods grim at what they considered a failure, they'd started to lay the gasoline down. Lucian now trailed it into the hallway, following Mortimer toward the front door. They met up with Bricker coming out of the living room, splashing his own can around.

"Did you take Leigh to the van?" Mortimer asked.

Bricker's eyebrows flew up. "No. I thought Lucian did before following us downstairs."

"No." Mortimer shook his head. "He left her at the table in the kitchen."

Lucian shrugged and returned to splashing the gasoline along the hall toward the front door. "Morgan must have taken her. We catch up to him, we'll find her."

Neither man looked pleased, but moved quickly toward the door to stay out of his way. Bricker emptied the last of his can as he went, then tossed it aside and stepped out of the house. Mortimer followed and Lucian continued with his own gasoline until it ran out two feet short of the door.

Tossing his can to the side, Lucian pulled a Zippo from his pocket. He flicked it open, struck the wheel with his thumb to light it, then tossed it over his shoulder as he stepped onto the porch. He pulled the door closed just as the fire whooshed to life behind him.

It wasn't until he'd started down the steps that Lucian saw the woman. She was on her knees on the gravel where Morgan's van had been parked. Her arms were wrapped tight around her waist as she swayed weakly where she knelt. Her pain was obvious, as was the fact that a combination of determination and the desire to survive were all that had helped her make her way out of the house.

Mortimer and Bricker were on their haunches, one in front of her, one beside her, both of them peering at her worriedly.

"She's turning," Mortimer announced as Lucian paused beside them.

Of course she was, he thought wearily. He had hoped she hadn't yet been given blood. Then they could have erased her memory and sent her on her way. However, that wasn't possible anymore. She was now an immortal and would have to be taken care of and trained.

The only good news was that unlike those in the house, Morgan hadn't had her long enough to turn her into a heartless, killing machine.

"We'll have to take her back to the hotel and take care of her," Mortimer announced, the words bringing a grimace to Lucian's face.

"We don't have time to nurse a baby vamp," he said dryly. "We have to catch up to Morgan before he starts another nest."

"Well, we can't just leave her here," Mortimer pointed out. "Bricker and I will take care of her."

"What about Morgan?" Lucian asked.

The two men exchanged a glance, then Bricker said, "The plan was to go back to the hotel, get some sleep, and then start out fresh tonight, right?"

"Right," Lucian allowed, his gaze flickering to the sky and the bright white orb of the sun. It was nearly mid-morning, and the sunlight was getting stronger by the minute. He bent to unstrap the quiver from his leg as Bricker made his case.

"Well, the turn doesn't usually take more than twenty-four hours. Eight hours while we sleep, then one of us can stay and watch over her while the other two go after Morgan and the Donald guy. There are only the two of them; all three of us aren't really needed."

"And who's going to stay awake today to give her blood?" Lucian asked as he straightened with the empty quiver in hand.

"Bricker and I will take turns."

Lucian wasn't pleased, but he supposed there weren't a lot of choices. Besides, he was growing uncomfortable under the direct sunlight and wanted an end to the discussion.

"Fine, but she's your responsibility," he said abruptly, and headed for the vehicles they'd parked on a small, unused dirt lane beyond the trees surrounding the house.

Lucian released a small breath of relief as he slid into the safety of the rental car. There was still sunlight coming through the windshield, but it was better than being out in full light. He placed the crossbow and quiver back into the large duffel bag on the passenger seat, then straightened and glanced out the window again. Bricker was carrying the brunette toward the van a car's length up the lane, while Mortimer rushed ahead holding both weapons.

Lucian shook his head as he watched Mortimer open the van's back doors and Bricker jump inside with the woman. The men, he knew, hadn't thought it through. The woman was going to be a problem. She was moaning and writhing in obvious pain as the turn began, her white blouse bearing a large rust-colored stain that could be mistaken for nothing other than blood. And it was after 10:00 A.M., so the hotel lobby would be busy. Yet, *somehow*, they had to get her into the hotel.

When Mortimer closed the van doors and hurried around to get behind the wheel, Lucian started the rental car and backed out of the lane. He retrieved the cell phone from his shirt pocket as he started slowly up the road. He punched in the first number on his speed dial and glanced in the rearview mirror to watch the van back onto the road behind him as he waited to be connected.

"Hello?"

Lucian smiled faintly at the sleepy snarl, knowing he'd woken up his nephew. "Good morning, Bastien."

There was a pause, then a suspicious, "Uncle Lucian?"

"That's right. I didn't wake you, did I?"

Bastien grunted in reply. "How did it go? Did you get Morgan?"

"No. He got away with another man. Someone named Donald."

"I'm going to need more information than that if you want me to trace this Donald guy—" Bastien began.

"That's not why I'm calling," Lucian interrupted. "How long would it take for one of the company planes to get here?"

"A company plane?" Bastien echoed.

"Yes."

"Hmm. We only have the one available at the moment. The others are all booked today," he said thoughtfully. "I'd have to call the pilot and co-pilot. They'll have to get up and around and get to the airport, gas up, file a flight plan, fly down to Kansas. That's a what? Two hour flight? Two and a half hours?"

"Closer to two and a half hours," Lucian guessed. He hadn't paid close attention when he'd flown down.

"Two and a half," Bastien murmured. "I'm guessing

it would be at least four to five hours, probably more, before the plane could get there. No, definitely more," he added suddenly and explained, "The only pilot we have available at the moment lives an hour from the airport."

"So, six hours, maybe more?" Lucian asked with a frown.

"I *did* offer to keep one there at your disposal until you were done, but you said—"

"Yes, yes," Lucian interrupted impatiently. He hated hearing *I told you so.* "Just send the plane down. Have them call me at the hotel before they leave and I'll head to the airport to wait."

"Okay. Anything else?"

"No." Lucian clicked the button to disengage before realizing he hadn't said good-bye, or even thanks. Living on his own had made him a rude bastard. Fortunately, his family members—including Bastien—were used to it.

Returning the phone to his pocket, he took the turn that would take them back to the hotel. He'd hoped to head right to the airport with the girl to wait for the plane, but six hours was a long wait when you were already tired. It looked like they were going to have to take Leigh to the hotel after all.

"How are we going to get her to our room?" Mortimer asked as he slid out of the van and met Lucian getting out of his car. Apparently, he had considered the problem during the drive.

Lucian's gaze moved around the hotel parking garage. They might be able to get her to the elevator without anyone seeing her, but the elevator would certainly stop in the lobby, and possibly at other floors. He already knew from their short stay that the elevators were always busy, jam-packed in fact. Chances were they would encounter anywhere from twenty to sixty people between the elevator and the hall to their room. He didn't like the idea of having to erase the memories of so many people.

Lucian's ruminations were interrupted by the purr of a car pulling into a parking spot. Both men glanced over as a woman got out, walked around to the trunk, opened it, and struggled to pull out a huge black suitcase.

Before he'd even thought about it, Lucian found himself walking to the woman's side. He flashed his best smile, but when that just made fear curl to life in her eyes, he gave up the smile and slid into her mind instead. Controlling one was better than having to control sixty.

"You can't be serious?" Bricker gasped minutes later when Lucian opened the back doors of the van and the man caught sight of the large, now empty suitcase.

"You come up with an alternate method to get her inside without having to erase the memories of half the hotel clients and I'd be happy to go along with it," Lucian said as he set the suitcase on the van floor. He didn't know what all the fuss was. It was a huge suitcase, lots of room. It had wheels that would make it easy to maneuver, was cloth so she wouldn't suffocate, and she wouldn't have to be in it long. It was a short walk to the elevator, a quick ride up, then a stroll to their suite of rooms . . . *and* she wasn't even really conscious. It wasn't like she would ever know.

Mortimer finally gave a helpless shrug. Letting his breath out, Bricker peered down at the woman writhing in his arms, then glanced up at Lucian. "Okay, open the case."

Lucian flipped the lid open, then glanced around to be sure no one was in the parking lot to see as Bricker set

Leigh into it. The only person around was the woman who owned the suitcase, and she was asleep in the driver's seat of her car. Mortimer would bring the suitcase back when they were through with it and erase the whole episode from her memory. Lucian had already slipped a fifty dollar bill into her purse for the use of the suitcase. She would recall it as a fifty she'd found on the floor of the parking garage. Lucian hated being beholden to people, whether they remembered it or not.

"Maybe I should leave it unzipped a couple of inches to make sure she gets enough air," Bricker said thoughtfully.

Lucian turned back to the interior of the van to see that Leigh was already in the suitcase and Bricker had it half zipped up. As he'd thought, there was lots of room. With her seated at the bottom, knees pressed close to her chest and head resting against them, there had to be six inches of space above her head.

"I'll take the bottom to lift her out," Mortimer said once Bricker had the zipper closed except for an inch at the top.

Lucian moved out of the way to give the men room, then glanced at his watch. It had only been twenty minutes since he'd called Bastien. If they got through this quickly, he could catch a good four or five hour nap before he had to wake up to head to the airport. He grimaced at the idea. He'd rather get eight hours, but five was better than the none the other two men would get.

"All set." Bricker followed the suitcase out of the back of the van and slammed the doors closed.

Nodding, Lucian turned to lead the way to the elevator. He pressed the call button, then glanced back to see that the men were only halfway there. Bricker was pulling the suitcase, but both he and Mortimer were moving slowly, fussing over bumping it too much.

Lucian bit his tongue on the reminder that she was unconscious, and turned back as the elevator arrived. He nodded at the couple who stepped out, then stepped on board and pressed the hold button as he waited for Mortimer and Bricker to reach him. He thought he showed amazing patience by not commenting when they finally reached the elevator. Lucian remained silent as they lifted the suitcase over the small crack at the door to prevent unnecessary jarring. The moment they were inside, he let the elevator doors close and pressed the button for their floor.

"Do you think she's okay in there?" Bricker asked as the elevator started upward.

"I don't know," Mortimer murmured. "Maybe we should check on her."

Before Lucian could snap that they were being idiots, the elevator suddenly gave a ding and slid to a stop. The doors opened, revealing the lobby and about two dozen people all waiting to crowd in.

Mouth tightening, he moved to the corner of the elevator where Bricker and Mortimer stood, positioning his body in front of the suitcase to prevent anyone from bumping it and discovering it held something more than clothes. Mortimer stood to the side of the case, protecting it from that angle, Bricker stood behind it, and the other side was against the back wall of the elevator. It was the best they could do.

Lucian ground his teeth together as body after body crowded into the small contraption. When not one single person more could squeeze in, those still waiting in the hall sagged and moved away from the doors. They closed, and the elevator finally continued upward.

One floor up it stopped again. Two people got off, one got on. At the next floor, one got off and two got on. But after that it was a slow, steady stream of people getting off, until by the eighth floor there were only themselves and two other couples. The others all eased a little away from each other, taking advantage of the extra space, but Lucian stayed right where he was. Leigh had begun to thrash about inside the suitcase, and the last thing he wanted was to step aside and let them see the cloth case bulging and shifting about.

He should have moved forward, though, he realized a moment later when he got a good whack in the back of the knees that nearly sent him to the floor. Grabbing the rail that ran around the elevator, he caught himself and ground his teeth as he was repeatedly pummeled through the bag. Distracted by the beating he was taking, it wasn't until Bricker began to whistle loudly that Lucian realized Leigh wasn't just thrashing about, she was moaning, too.

Noting that the other two couples were now looking around with confusion, searching for the source of the moans, Lucian began to whistle as well. Unfortunately, he had no idea what tune Bricker was whistling, so started an entirely new one. When that didn't wholly drown the sounds Leigh was making, Mortimer joined in with a tune of his own.

It was a great relief when the elevator dinged, the door opened, and the last two couples rushed out. Lucian moved away from the suitcase as the doors closed, relieved to note that the next floor was their own.

He rolled his eyes as Mortimer bent to rub one hand soothingly over the part of the suitcase that kept bulging outward, and murmured, "Its all right, Leigh. We're almost there."

"Don't do that," Bricker said. "You don't know what you're rubbing."

Shaking his head, Lucian turned away as the door opened onto their floor. Mortimer and Bricker were two of the toughest hardasses he knew, but they had been acting like a couple of old women ever since Leigh appeared. It was almost painful to watch.

Leaving the two men to bring their burden at their own speed, Lucian strode down the hall to the door of their two bedroom suite. He was seated on the side of his bed, kicking his shoes off, when he finally heard them enter.

Pushing his shoes aside, Lucian stood and began to undo his shirt as he walked to the door. He arrived just in time to see them finish unzipping the suitcase. Before they could open it, Leigh had thrown it open and tumbled out. Both men immediately let the suitcase drop and rushed to her side. It only took one look for Lucian to see that she wasn't conscious. She was pale, sweat was pouring off her, and she was now thrashing around on the ground, almost appearing to be in convulsions.

Lucian watched Mortimer and Bricker move her to the couch, but when they began to flap over her like a couple of useless old women, he decided it was time to step in and take control.

"One of you has to take the suitcase back, then head to the nearest hospital and get a portable IV set up and more blood."

"I'll go." Mortimer took the suitcase, zipped it up, then headed for the door. "How much blood?"

"Lot's of it. And another cooler, too," Lucian added, then glanced at the screaming woman and added, "And some drugs to kill the pain and make her sleep."

"What do *I* do?" Bricker asked as Mortimer hurried out of the room.

Lucian shrugged. "Watch her to be sure she doesn't hurt herself."

"Shouldn't I try to give her some blood, or something?" Bricker asked, concern on his face. It was obvious he was desperate to do something of use.

"You can try, but she'll probably just choke on it and vomit it back up at this stage."

"What?" Bricker asked with amazement. "Well, how the hell did people go through the turn before IVs and stuff?"

Lucian grimaced. "They suffered through it until their teeth finished changing, then we *carefully* allowed them to feed."

"How long will it take for her teeth to change?" Bricker asked.

Lucian shook his head wearily. "It's different with each person, Bricker. It depends on size, age, how much blood she got, how fast her natural metabolism is . . ."

The man looked so forlorn that Lucian nearly walked over to pat his back reassuringly. Instead, he turned back into his room. "I'm going to take a nap. Wake me if anyone calls."

Lucian woke up reluctantly a short time later, scowling as his consciousness was assaulted by a cacophony of sound.

Leigh was now obviously well into the throes of turning. She was shrieking long and hard and *nonstop*. The sound was desperate, grating, and nearly drowned out someone hammering at the door of the suite.

Growling under his breath, Lucian turned on his side,

punched his pillow and closed his eyes determinedly, but when a man's shouting joined the screaming and banging, he cursed and rolled out of bed.

Irritated to have what little sleep he was going to get disturbed, Lucian strode to the door to the living room and jerked it open, stepped out, then simply stood there gaping.

Leigh was no longer on the couch where the men had first put her. She was now on the floor in the middle of the cleared room, thrashing, kicking, writhing, and rolling. But it was Bricker who had shocked Lucian. At first glance one could be forgiven for thinking he was mauling the girl. The large, dark vampire was lying sprawled sideways across her torso, one hand stretching up to try to hold both of hers, the other reaching down to try to keep hold of her ankles as he bounced, jerked, and jolted around on her undulating body.

"What the hell are you doing?" Lucian finally asked, having to shout to be heard over Leigh's screams.

"Trying to keep her from hurting herself!" Bricker yelled back, grabbing at the hand that got loose and began to hammer anything in its way; the floor, the couch, Bricker himself.

"Well there's someone at the door. Didn't you hear the knocking?" Lucian asked with exasperation.

Bricker turned a disbelieving look over his shoulder. "Yeah. But I'm a little busy here."

"Jesus Christ, Bricker! You're stronger than the woman. Restrain her," he snapped impatiently.

"I don't want to hurt her trying to keep her from hurting herself," the man snapped back.

The pounding at the door got louder, and the shouting now sounded like more than one voice. Sighing, Lucian moved toward it. "I'll get the damned door, then."

"Gee, thanks a lot." Bricker sounded less than appreciative.

Lucian opened the door to find himself staring at three men: a diminutive man in a suit, who was obviously the manager; and two large beefy guys in security uniforms. He forced them all backward as he stepped into the hall, then pulled the door closed behind him to shut out the screaming. It didn't work very well—the screams were muffled but still voluble.

"We've had some complaints about the noise," the manager began, his voice trembling with outrage, then he gave up all pretense at polite inquiry and snapped, "What the hell is going on in there, Mr. Argeneau?"

Lucian didn't even bother to try to explain. It was impossible to explain anyway. Instead, he slid into the mind of the manager and took control, blanking his thoughts. He then turned his attention to each of the security guards. Within moments the men were on their way back to the elevator, the entire incident removed from their memory. Lucian watched them onto the elevator, then turned to open the door to the suite and found it locked. And he hadn't thought to bring the keycard with him. He knocked, but knew it was a useless endeavor. There was no way Bricker would hear him over the racket going on inside.

He slumped against the door, giving up any hope of getting back inside any time soon.

Lucian was nodding off outside the suite door when someone shook his shoulder. Blinking his eyes open, he lifted his head and jumped quickly to his feet when he saw Mortimer standing over him, holding a large cooler.

"What are you doing out here?" Mortimer handed him the cooler so he could pull out his own key card and slide it into the lock. The light turned green and he opened the door.

Lucian just shook his head and moved past him. He was too tired to bother with explanations. As Mortimer rushed over to help Bricker restrain the woman, Lucian set the cooler on the coffee table, which had been moved across the room, probably to prevent Leigh from slamming her head into it.

The first thing Lucian looked for were the drugs. Spotting the syringes and ampoules, he took them out, selected the one most likely to silence and hopefully still the woman, and inserted the needle. He drew the liquid into the syringe as he crossed to where both men were now wrestling with Leigh, and knelt to jerk the sleeve of her blouse up her arm. Holding her arm firmly with one hand, he used the other to inject her. She went silent and still almost before he removed the needle from her arm.

Grunting with satisfaction, Lucian stood and walked back to the coffee table. He set the syringe on it, then reached into the cooler for one of the bags of blood. Slapping it to his teeth, he dropped into one of the overstuffed chairs and let his head drop wearily back and his eyes close.

Lucian stayed like that, ignoring the murmur of Mortimer and Bricker's voices until the bag was empty. Then he lifted his head and opened his eyes as he pulled the empty blood bag from his mouth.

The two men had moved Leigh back onto the couch, he saw. They'd situated her with pillows and a blanket, set up an IV of blood that ran down into her arm, and were now both fussing over her. Bricker was wringing out a cool cloth and using it to wash the sweat off her neck, hands, and lower arms, while Mortimer placed another cloth over her forehead, left it for a minute, then took it, dipped it in the water, wrung it out, and placed it back on her forehead again.

Lucian found himself just gaping. He'd never seen anything like it. These two were hard, heartless hunters. What had gotten into them?

The phone on the table beside him rang, and he reached over to pick it up. Relief coursed through him at the sound of Bastien's voice.

"You got lucky," his nephew announced. "One of the directors was supposed to fly from Lincoln, Nebraska, to California today, but business is keeping him another day, so he doesn't need the plane. It's coming to pick you up in Kansas."

"Hmm," Lucian murmured. "What time will it get here?"

"If you leave for the airport now, you might just get there first."

Lucian sat up abruptly. "That quickly?"

"It's on the way now, and Lincoln's a hell of a lot closer than Toronto," Bastien pointed out.

"Yes, but, I have to—"

"I already ordered a limo for you," Bastien interrupted soothingly. "It should be there any minute, and I arranged with the rental company to pick up your car from the hotel parking garage."

Lucian opened his mouth to say he'd still need it. He had no intention of getting on the plane. He was going to put Leigh on it, have Thomas pick her up at the airport and deliver her to Marguerite's for his sister-in-law to look after. However, he changed his mind and let the order go. They didn't need two vehicles. He could ride in the van with Mortimer and Bricker. They'd only ended up with both the car and truck because the boys had flown in the day before him. Since they were busy gathering information on Morgan, he'd rented a car rather than take a taxi to the hotel. Lucian hated taxis. As far as he was concerned, taxi drivers all drove as if they had a death wish . . . and they talked too much. How could they claim to be concentrating on traffic, traffic lights, and pedestrians with their mouths constantly flapping?

"Is there anything else you needed?" Bastien asked.

"No," Lucian said abruptly. "That's fine."

"Good, then you'd better get moving."

Lucian thought Bastien might have said good-bye, but wasn't sure. He was already setting the phone down.

Three

"No."

"What do you mean no?" Lucian stared with amazement at the pilot, Bob Whitehead. They were standing on the tarmac between the limo and the waiting plane, a cool breeze and cold rain spitting down on them. Bob was the only one with an umbrella and wasn't in the mood to share.

"Just what I said. I'm a pilot, not a babysitter. I'll be too damned busy to look after the girl. Either you arrange for someone to accompany her or she doesn't go."

"The co-pilot can . . ." Lucian's words faded as the pilot firmly shook his head.

"I need Ted in the cockpit. There's a reason there are both a pilot and co-pilot, and it isn't in case a passenger needs their blood bag changed or their hand held."

"Do you know who I am?" Lucian asked shortly. He wasn't used to being told no, and didn't like it.

"I know who you are," Bob assured him grimly. "And it doesn't matter one damned bit. I am not taking an unattended woman who is in the middle of turning onto my plane. What if she attacks me or my co-pilot?" He shook his head. "No way."

"I'll accompany her," Mortimer offered. "It's only

two hours or so there, two hours back. I'll be back before you two wake up."

"Fine," Bob said abruptly. "As long as there's someone with her."

Mortimer reached for Leigh as the pilot turned to walk back to the plane, but Bricker stepped forward in protest.

"No, I want to go with her. I've never seen a turning before. It will be good experience."

"That's the perfect reason why *I* should go," Mortimer argued. "I *have* seen a turning. I know what to expect and how best to help her."

Lucian rolled his eyes as the two men began to argue. They'd come to blows in a minute. There was obviously only one way to resolve the matter.

"I'm taking her," Lucian announced. "You two go back to the hotel and get some rest. I've had at least a little sleep. I'll ride there with her, then sleep on the flight back."

Ted was waiting just inside the door of the plane. He stepped back out of the way, and greeted Lucian as he boarded.

"I put the blood in the refrigerator in the seating area," the man said, pulling the steps up and the plane door closed as Lucian carried Leigh toward the sleeping section in the back. "I didn't set up the IV, though. There's a hook for the bag on each wall above the beds. There are intercoms in each section. You can use it to reach us in the cockpit if you need anything."

Lucian grunted an acknowledgment.

"Bob said to remind you to shut off your cell phone if you have one, and to tell you to get the girl settled, then buckle yourself in. We'll be taking off in about five minutes."

Aware the man was already moving away to return to the cockpit, Lucian didn't bother to respond. He'd reached the sleeping section, a small room with an upper and lower bed on either side and a narrow aisle down the middle. He set Leigh in the bottom bed on the left, then quickly hung the blood bag from the hook in the wall. Her bag was almost empty, and he slipped back through the plane to the small refrigerator where the blood had been stowed.

Lucian grabbed two bags and hurried back to the sleeping section. He had the empty bag switched for the new one and settled himself on the bed across from Leigh with the second bag pressed to his own mouth when the plane began to taxi out to the runway.

It wasn't until they were up in the air that he remembered his cell phone. Lucian pulled the blood bag from his mouth and tossed it in the garbage bin by the bed. He then reached into his pocket, only to frown on feeling the empty space there. His cell phone was on the bedside table back at the hotel, as were his wallet, keys, and everything else he'd taken out of his pockets before lying down. He hadn't thought to grab any of it before leaving, but simply picked up Leigh and headed for the door.

More important than any of that, he hadn't thought to call Marguerite.

Lucian leaned his head back against the wall and closed his eyes, hardly able to believe he'd made so many mistakes in such a short time. He was generally a very organized man. He was organized, his life was organized, his plans were well thought out and . . . well . . . organized. To the point where it was boring, really, but he didn't like surprises.

It seemed to him, however, that he'd had nothing

but surprises and chaos today. Ever since Morgan had stepped out of the back of that van with Leigh in his arms.

Lucian opened his eyes and scowled at the woman. She was beautiful when she wasn't screaming, he noted, and that just made him scowl harder. His life had taken a sharp turn off its predictable street with her arrival, and now he found himself babysitting a turning vamp.

Not for long, Lucian assured himself. He'd take her to Marguerite, leave the girl in her care, then turn around and fly right back to Kansas to continue the hunt for Morgan.

Satisfied that his life would soon be back to normal, he closed his tired eyes. He'd just rest until Leigh's blood bag needed changing again, he told himself as he drifted off to sleep.

"Jesus Christ! How can you sleep through this racket?"

Lucian blinked his eyes open and stared blearily at the man glaring down at him. It took a minute for his sleep-fogged mind to pull itself together enough for him to realize where he was and that the man was the co-pilot, Ted. Then he also realized that the horrible high-pitched whistle of the teakettle in his dream was in fact screams. Leigh was in need of another shot. Her blood bag was also empty.

Scrubbing his hands over his face, he forced himself to his feet.

"We could hear her all the way up in the cockpit," Ted growled as Lucian stumbled past him into the sitting area. "We thought you were killing her."

"Not yet," he said dryly as he opened the cooler.

"Yeah, well Bob says— What are you looking for?" the man interrupted himself to ask as Lucian closed the cooler and turned to search the refrigerator instead.

"Her drugs and syringes. They were in the cooler."

"The only thing in the cooler was the blood," Ted informed him.

Lucian stiffened, his head shooting up. "You're sure?"

"Of course I'm sure. I emptied it."

"They must have put them in the refrigerator at the hotel while they were getting her settled," he realized, then grabbed a bag of blood and straightened. "In which case, you'd better get used to her screaming, because without the drugs, it isn't going to stop."

"You're joking," Ted gasped with horror.

"Do I look like a man who jokes?" Lucian asked as he headed back to the sleeping section to change her bag again. "How long until we land?"

"An hour," Ted admitted, then asked, desperately, "What about mind control?"

"What about it?" Lucian asked as he removed the empty blood bag from the hook where it hung.

"I thought you guys could keep us mortals from feeling pain?"

"Sure," he agreed, throwing the empty bag in the garbage. "And if this was just a bite, or cut, or maybe even a gunshot wound, I could, but not this."

"Why not?"

Lucian frowned. The truth was because the nanos were scrambling her brain, her body, her everything. It would be impossible to blank her out. Their attack was overwhelming, every nerve on fire. But he didn't say that, he'd already explained more than usual.

"Because no one can," he said simply, and saw the man's shoulders slump in defeat. "Are there any earplugs on this plane?"

"Yeah, in the drawer above the refrigerator, but Bob and I can't use earplugs."

"But I can," Lucian said with a smile full of teeth as he finished with Leigh's IV.

The co-pilot's mouth snapped shut and he whirled away. "Try to keep her quiet. We have to concentrate."

Lucian found the earplugs where Ted had said they'd be, slipped them into his ears and let out a pleased little breath as Leigh's caterwauling was reduced to a low hum. These were the superduper model of earplug, for passengers who wanted to sleep. Lucian had never bothered with them before, but they worked well.

Feeling his tension begin to slip away, he returned to the sleeping section to watch Leigh. There wasn't much to watch, however. She was an attractive woman, but thrashing about on the bed with her mouth gaping on screams of pain did nothing to show off that attractiveness. He was relieved when they landed forty-seven minutes later. Lucian didn't know if they'd just gotten lucky and hit a good tailwind, or if Bob and Ted had put on a little speed in an effort to bring an end to the trip and Leigh's shrieks. He didn't care either way, but was just glad to have this half of the journey over with. It meant that in about half an hour he'd be free of Leigh.

Originally, Lucian had thought arriving at the airport would be the end of their acquaintance, but that was before he'd realized he hadn't called Marguerite and didn't have his cell phone to do so. Even he wasn't rude enough just to send the girl to Marguerite's with Thomas like a couriered package. He'd ride over, talk to her in person, and *then* dump Leigh and head back.

Lucian felt rather than heard when the engines were shut off. His gaze slid to Leigh to see that while she was shifting restlessly about, her mouth was closed. It had been for the past fifteen minutes or so, and he figured she'd worn herself out. Still, he took out his earplugs cautiously, relieved that the only sounds coming from her were quiet moans.

Slipping the earplugs into his pocket, he stood and unhooked the blood bag. He set it on her, then scooped her into his arms.

A less than pleased looking Ted was coming out of the cockpit as Lucian started up the aisle with his burden. The man nodded grimly and couldn't move quickly enough to get the plane door open for him.

"Has someone taken care of the airport officials?" Lucian asked. He had no desire to deal with airport and customs officials himself.

"Thomas," Ted answered tersely, and stepped out of the way for him to disembark. "He should be here with a car at any moment."

Lucian nodded at the mention of another of his nephews and turned to peer out of the plane. It was just past three in the afternoon, and he'd worried that the sun would be a problem. However, while it wasn't raining as it had been in Kansas, it was a cool, damp day. The sun was hiding behind rain clouds that had obviously already spilled some of their liquid on the area, but were threatening to drop more.

Shoulders relaxing, Lucian eased his way through the door, turning and shifting his burden to avoid banging her into the walls of the plane. By the time he descended the steps to the tarmac, a car was pulling to a stop several feet in front of him.

Thomas seemed to be out of the car almost before it came to a halt. He hurried forward with a loose-legged walk and a bright smile. It was one of the things that drove Lucian nuts about the lad. Thomas was *always* smiling and cheerful. It was his youth, he supposed. The man was only a couple hundred years old. Thomas hadn't seen as much of life as he had, so could be forgiven for not knowing there was little to smile about in this world. He would learn soon enough.

"How was your flight?" Thomas greeted him.

"Fine. Carry this." Lucian hefted his burden toward his nephew, who quickly raised his arms.

The younger man caught Leigh to his chest with a grunt, eyes wide as he peered down at her pale face. "Who is she?"

"Mr. Argeneau?"

Ignoring his nephew's question, Lucian glanced back to find Ted holding out the portable IV stand. He took the stand with a nod, then ordered, "Have the plane refueled. I'll need to fly back to Kansas when I return, which shouldn't be more than a couple hours."

"Yes, sir." The man's face was grim as he backed into the plane, presumably to pass on the news to the pilot.

"Who is she?" Thomas repeated.

"Leigh."

"Leigh who?"

"How should I know?" Lucian asked with irritation. "Open your fingers."

Thomas looked confused, but uncurled the fingers that rested under the girl's outer thigh. The moment he did, Lucian slid the folded portable IV into them, then turned to walk to the car.

"What do you mean *how* should you know?" Thomas demanded.

Lucian smiled faintly to himself as he heard Thomas scurrying after him with his burden, but merely shrugged with disinterest and opened the front passenger door. "Just what I said. I don't know who she is."

He slid into the front seat and pulled the car door closed, leaving Thomas to deal with getting the woman into the backseat. He'd done his bit by taking her away from the house in Kansas and changing her blood bags for the last two hours. He now fully intended on delivering her into his sister-in-law's tender mercies and never giving her another thought.

Marguerite would see her through the turning, then help her learn all those things she needed to know to live as one of them. And Marguerite—or one of her brood—would also then see the chit set up with an identity and probably even a job. It was what Marguerite did. She took in all the strays. Thomas and his sister Jeanne Louise were two of several the woman had mothered over the ages.

Lucian settled back in the front passenger seat, fully satisfied that—once again—he'd proven he wasn't the complete bastard everyone seemed to think he was. He'd spared a life and seen to her well-being, or would have within the hour. Then he could get on with business, he assured himself, ignoring the muffled curses and grunts through the car window as Thomas struggled to get the back door open without dropping either the woman or the IV.

"You could have at least opened the door," Thomas muttered as he got into the driver's seat a moment later.

"Why? You managed fine on your own," Lucian pointed out mildly.

Shaking his head, Thomas started the engine and began to steer the vehicle away from the plane. "Your place?" he asked moments later, as he negotiated the car onto the highway.

"Marguerite's," Lucian corrected, aware that the answer drew a sharp glance.

"Does she know you're coming?" Thomas asked warily.

Lucian frowned at the expression on his face. "Why?"

"No reason. Never mind," he said quickly, then muttered under his breath, "This ought to be good."

Lucian opened his mouth to ask what he meant, but before he could, Leigh began to scream and thrash about on the backseat, her legs kicking at the door by her feet. Startled, Thomas jerked and the car swerved, crossing over the center line before he regained control and pulled it back. Fortunately there was no one in the lane beside them at the time.

Lucian didn't comment, but was aware of the sharp glances Thomas kept sending his way.

"Can't you do something for her?" his nephew finally asked, when several moments passed and her screaming and thrashing didn't stop.

"I already have. I didn't kill her," Lucian said dryly, then added, "Slow down. You're as bad as taxi drivers."

"And you're a backseat driver," Thomas muttered, then cursed under his breath. "Surely there are some drugs or something we could give her to settle her down?"

Lucian glanced at him with interest. "Do you have any?"

Thomas blinked. "No."

"Hmm." He sat back in his seat. "Neither do I."

Thomas stared for a moment, glanced back at the woman in the back of the car, then said, "Her screaming is rather loud, don't you think? Just a bit distracting for those of us trying to concentrate."

"Yes, it is," Lucian agreed, and reached into his pocket for his earplugs. He popped them into his ears and closed his eyes, the shrieking in the car considerably muffled. He'd have killed the woman before the plane had landed without the earplugs. They were a blessing.

The rest of the ride to Marguerite's was uneventful as far as Lucian was concerned. He opened his eyes once or twice to see Thomas talking to himself. Most likely cursing him, Lucian thought with amusement, and closed his eyes again, only to open them several moments later as the car slowed and turned into Marguerite's driveway.

Relieved to see an end to this chore, Lucian cautiously removed the earplugs, to find the screaming from the backseat had been reduced to a hoarse cry and the thrashing to restless twisting and turning. The girl had worn herself out for now. Thomas parked as close to the front door as he could get, which was right behind one of the company vans in the drive that curved around the front of the house. Lucian glanced at the other vehicle curiously as he got out of the car.

He thought that it might be delivering blood, then realized that it was one of the Argeneau Enterprises vans, not one of the Argeneau Blood Bank trucks. Besides, it appeared to be full of luggage . . . as well as Marguerite's housekeeper and groundsman, he saw as he walked past the open side door.

"Bring the luggage in, Thomas," Lucian ordered with a frown as he approached the front.

"What about the girl?" Thomas asked with irritation.

"That's what I meant." Lucian stepped through the open front doors of the house.

"Oh, thank goodness!"

The cry drew his gaze to the stairs to the right of the door, and he smiled faintly as Marguerite came rushing down. She was a beautiful brunette with classic features and laughing eyes, and looked no more than twenty-five, which was damned good for a woman of seven hundred plus years. Her youngest son, Etienne, was hard on her heels, a suitcase in each hand. Tall, blond, and equal in good looks to his mother, the man smiled at him over her head.

"I was afraid you would not get here before we left, Lucian." Marguerite reached his side and leaned up to kiss his cheek.

He stiffened under her greeting. "You knew I was coming?"

"Yes, Mortimer called both Bastien and myself after you left Kansas City. How was your flight?"

"Fine," Lucian answered absently, nodding in response to Etienne's smile of greeting as the man rushed out the door with the suitcases. "What's going on? And what do you mean *before* you left? What about the girl?"

"I took care of everything," she assured him. "As soon as I got off the phone with Mortimer, I immediately arranged to have blood delivered, then set up Lissianna's old room for her."

"What about drugs?" Lucian asked with concern.

"On the bedside table."

He nodded.

Marguerite patted his arm, then pressed something into his hand and turned to head out the front door. "I'm so glad you got here before we left. I didn't want to leave the keys under the front mat. I was afraid you wouldn't think to look there."

Lucian glanced down and opened his hand to reveal the keys she'd pressed into his palm. Her keys. To the house, the car, the— Snapping his hand closed, he hurried after her, pausing to step out of the way as Thomas struggled through the door carrying the girl and the IV. He waited impatiently for him to move off up the hall, then hurried out the door, toward Marguerite, who was fussing over the way Etienne was placing the last two bags in the back of the van.

"What do you mean before you left?" Lucian asked again as he reached her side. "Where are you going?"

"That'll do," Marguerite decided, apparently now satisfied with the placement. "Thank you, Etienne."

She patted his shoulder as he closed the side door, then turned to answer Lucian, only to pause, her gaze shooting past him. "Thomas! Get over here and give me a kiss good-bye."

Lucian shifted impatiently and glanced over his shoulder as the younger man rushed over to kiss and hug her, saying, "Have a good trip."

"I will, thank you. And you stay out of trouble while I'm gone," she ordered lightly.

"I'll do my best," Thomas assured her with a grin, then turned to step out of the way as Lucian glared at him.

"Marguerite—" he began as she turned to open the front passenger door. "Where do you think you're going?"

His sister-in-law stepped up into the van and reached for the seat belt as she answered. "To Europe. Don't you remember? I have a job there. I told you about it last week."

Yes, she had, Lucian realized, but he'd forgotten all about it. "But who's going to look after the girl?"

She finished snapping her seat belt into place, then glanced at him with surprise. "Why, I thought you were going to, Lucian."

"Why would I have brought her *here* if *I* was going to look after her?"

"I did wonder about that," Marguerite admitted. When he opened his mouth again, she added, "I knew you weren't arrogant enough to expect me to change all my plans and neglect the first job I've had in seven hundred years, in order to handle a problem you chose to take on."

Lucian snapped his mouth closed.

Marguerite smiled and leaned out to kiss his cheek, then pulled the passenger door closed and leaned forward in her seat to smile at him through the window. "She's very pretty."

"Yes," he agreed, distracted.

"I did wonder what had moved you to help her. You don't generally collect strays, and aren't known for your mercy, but now I see. Congratulations, take good care of her."

Lucian scowled and was about to protest, but she'd turned to glance at Etienne as the younger man started the van.

"Let's go, Etienne," he heard her say, then she turned to peer out at him again as she added, "By the way, Julius is still here. The woman from the kennel was supposed to be here about ten minutes ago. She's late. Julius and all of his things—along with the special instructions for his medicine—are in the kitchen. Just send her in there when she gets here, won't you?"

Lucian nodded, his heart sinking as he watched the van pull away. It had nearly reached the road when he recalled Thomas. He turned toward where the car should have been, eager to enlist his aid, and frowned when he saw the car was gone. The lad had snuck off while he was distracted, probably hoping to get away before he could be recruited for the chore ahead.

Well, his dear nephew thought wrong. Lucian strode into the hall and snatched up the phone, then stared blankly at the ridiculous number of buttons and symbols on the huge dial pad. It was as bad as an airplane cockpit. Shaking his head, he began to punch buttons randomly until he got a dial tone. He'd barely heard the blessed sound before a scream rent the air from the living room.

It was Leigh again. *Great.*

Lucian ignored it and punched the button with Thomas's name beside it. Marguerite had all of her brood on speed dial, and she counted Thomas and his sister Jeanne Louise among them. By the time the phone began to ring, a dog's howl had joined the chorus of shrieking.

Julius, Lucian thought, closing his eyes as he listened to the phone ringing and willed his nephew to pick up. He let it ring until it cut out then dialed again. After three tries he cursed and slammed the phone down impatiently.

"Julius, shut up!" Lucian roared as he stormed up the hall. The dog obeyed at once, cutting the cacophony of sound in half. He only wished the woman could be silenced so easily.

Lucian followed the screams into the living room and surveyed the scene. The blood bag was empty, which was a good thing because the girl had thrashed about enough to dislodge the IV from her arm, leaving it to leak onto Marguerite's snow white carpet. Fortunately, there were only a couple of drops to worry about. Not that he would.

Marching across the room, Lucian glared down at the woman and opened his mouth to order her to silence as well. But he knew from prior experience that wouldn't work. Grimacing, he pulled the earplugs out of his pocket once more and popped them in his ears, decreasing the noise to a faint roar.

Feeling a little more composed now that his ears

weren't assaulted by her high-pitched screeches, Lucian bent and scooped her into his arms, then carried her out of the living room. He'd almost reached the stairs before he noticed the woman standing, gaping, in the open front door.

"Oh, you must be here about Marguerite's dog, Julius!" he said, his voice rising to a shout because of the earplugs and the muffled shrieks of the woman in his arms. Lucian glanced back over his shoulder toward the kitchen door at the end of the hall, adding, "He's in the kitchen. Marguerite said all his stuff is in there, too. As well as some instructions . . ."

Lucian's voice faded away and he tilted his head with a frown as he realized a second noise had joined the muffled shrieks of the woman in his arms. It took a moment for him to realize it was Julius barking again. He grimaced, but supposed the dog had heard him shout his name and was now excited. Lucian shrugged. Not his problem anymore, the dog-lady could deal with it.

He turned back and opened his mouth to shout again, only to pause as he noted the dog-lady was staring at the woman in his arms with abject horror. Lucian glanced down. Leigh's hair was damp with sweat, her face deathly pale, her white top bloodstained, and she was flopping around in his arms like a fish landed on a boat with a hook in its mouth. And speaking of mouths, hers was open on the screams she didn't seem able to stop at the moment, shrieks of combined agony and horror.

Oh yeah, Lucian thought dryly, *this couldn't look good.*

Sighing inwardly, he raised his gaze to the dog-lady,

planning to do the mind zap bit, only to find himself staring at blank space. The woman was gone. Frowning, Lucian stepped up to the door, arriving just in time to see a white van screech off down the driveway.

"Hey!" he roared. "What about Julius?"

The van didn't even slow down. Lucian scowled after the vehicle with impotent fury as it careened out onto the road, then he turned back into the house. He'd just kicked the door shut with one foot when the kitchen door at the end of the hall burst open and a mass of black fur exploded up the hall toward him.

Apparently, Julius had heard his name being shouted and worked frantically to get to him. And succeeded, Lucian realized with alarm.

Julius was a Neapolitan mastiff. He was black as night, thirty inches tall, and weighed in at a little over two hundred pounds. He was also presently dragging a gutted bag of garbage that he'd obviously attacked and somehow gotten caught around his back left leg. Empty cans and various bits of debris were spilling out every which way as the dog charged toward him, and the large jowls of his ridiculously wrinkly face swung to and fro, drool flying every which way as he ran.

Lucian instinctively bared his fangs and hissed at the oncoming dog. Rather than lunge up to plant his paws on Lucian's chest—which would have done further damage to the woman he carried—Julius skidded to a halt, his hind end sliding out from under him on the marble floor. He nearly crashed into Lucian's feet, but fortunately managed to regain his footing at the last moment and turned to charge up the stairs, away from Lucian's wrath, dragging the garbage bag with him.

Lucian watched the dog disappear along the upper

hall. He then let his gaze drop slowly over the trail of discarded newspapers, cans, leftover food, and other detritus Julius had left in his wake, and felt a headache begin somewhere behind his right eye.

 Four

Leigh's head was throbbing. It felt like someone was crushing her skull. Slowly. She'd never experienced pain like this. It was accompanied by a bad case of cotton mouth and stomach cramps like she'd never known. Basically, she felt like hell.

A groan started to slip from her lips, but the pain it caused in both her dry throat and her head made her abruptly cut it off. She tried to blink her eyes open, but the sudden assault from the light made the pain in her head roar and she quickly closed them again.

This was bad. Very bad. She hadn't felt this bad since . . . well, ever, she realized. She'd had broken bones, colds, flus, chicken pox, and every other childhood ailment, but didn't recall feeling anything like this.

After several moments of lying still didn't do anything to ease her pain, Leigh decided she'd have to get up and find some aspirins or something. And water. She was so dehydrated her tongue felt like sandpaper. It would also—she hoped—help remove the nasty taste in her mouth.

Mentally bracing herself against the coming pain, Leigh eased her eyes open, only to close them again as the pain in her head ratcheted up a notch.

Aspirin, she reminded herself. And water. Just a dozen steps to her bathroom and she could have both. Maybe she could manage getting there without opening her eyes. She'd lived in her little house for two years, surely she could find the bathroom without opening her eyes? *If I can walk*, she added, as worry claimed her. As bad as she felt, it was possible she might be too weak to get around.

Leigh took a deep breath, then managed to sit up on the bed. The small action left her panting and breathless. *Oh, this can't be good*, she thought vaguely, then became aware of a tugging on her arm every time she moved it and forced one eye open to peer down.

Spying the tape wrapped around her arm, she blinked her other eye open in surprise and stared with confusion, then noted the tube sticking out of it and followed that up to an empty bag hanging from a stand beside the bed. The bag was empty, but there were traces of a red liquid pooled in the bottom, and a label on the bag with a large *O* and *Rh positive* under it.

Blood?

Her head turned slowly as she examined the room, and she realized with dismay that it wasn't her cozy bedroom in the home she'd purchased and decorated so lovingly. This was a room she'd never seen before—a large blue room with a sitting area to one side that included a couch, a coffee table, and chairs. There were a set of double doors, obviously to a closet, and two other doors besides.

A prickly sensation of fear crept up the back of her neck, and she began to recall some of what had happened the night before. Donny stopping her on a dark street. Her anger with him. Turning to walk away, then losing control of her body, and then . . . *Morgan*.

Leigh stiffened as she recalled him biting her and giving her blood in the back of the van. The van had stopped at an ugly old house that seemed about to collapse in on itself. Morgan carried her inside and downstairs into a cold damp basement. She'd stared in horror at the coffins there, and the pale, hard-faced people, then he took her into a tiny room that held just a cot. Then Donny was leaning over her, telling her everything would be all right. He'd chosen her. They would live forever.

She remembered shaking her head, trying to get past the pain throbbing in her temples as he'd gone on about vampires and eternal life. She hadn't listened to most of it; her mind had been fixed on only one thing: she knew she had to get out of there.

And she had, Leigh recalled. With Morgan gone, she'd had control of her body once more. She'd managed to stay conscious despite the pain and weakness that assailed her, and suspected Donny had unintentionally helped her. He'd been as solicitous as a lover, covering her with a blanket as he promised a happy ever after and an eternity of wonderful nights in their own little coffin built for two.

Every word he'd said had fueled the fury burning in her, so that when he finally left the room, she somehow managed to gain her feet and stumble to the door to make her escape. She'd made it all the way upstairs and into the kitchen without interference.

But what happened then? She had a vague, fuzzy dreamlike memory of three men in the kitchen. She'd recognized two of them, since they were at Coco's every night that week, eating at the bar because they showed up so late. The third man was blond with chiseled features, as gorgeous as a Greek god come to life.

It must have been a dream, she decided. No man could be that good-looking.

She glanced around the room again. Had she escaped from that house? Perhaps she was still there, but in a different room. She had no idea, except that this wasn't her own room in her own cozy home.

Shifting her feet off the bed, Leigh started to rise, only to pause at another pull on her arm. Turning, she grabbed the tube and tape and gave an impatient tug, wincing as the tape ripped hair from her arm and pain shot through her. Gritting her teeth against the sting, she managed to gain her feet, but found herself swaying alarmingly. In the next moment, she crumpled to the floor, her legs folding under her.

"Dammit, Julius! Get down! You'll make me drop the tray."

Stiffening, Leigh raised her head to peer over the bed and at the door across the room. It was closed at the moment, but she heard a man's exasperated voice clearly through the wood. Ignoring the pain in her arm, she ducked instinctively to hide behind the bed, her body seeming to make the decision before her mind had processed her options. In the next moment she was sliding under the bed on her stomach. Once in the center, she stilled and held her breath, her eyes finding the door through the crack between the floor and the ruff around the bed.

A pair of bare feet and the bottom hem of what looked like black jeans appeared as the wooden panel swung inward.

"Stupid dog," the man muttered as the bare feet moved into the room. Then, four black paws followed and Leigh bit her lip. A dog. Her hiding space suddenly didn't seem such a good idea.

"Well hell! Where did she go?"

Leigh glanced to the side as the bare feet stopped beside the bed, then moved forward to the headboard. There was the clatter and clink of glass as something—the tray he'd mentioned?—was set down on the bedside table, then the bare feet moved away, toward one of the other doors in the room, this one on the same wall the headboard was against.

"As if I don't have enough to do with you wrecking the house at every turn and my constantly having to run up here to change the blood bags," the man was muttering.

Leigh wasn't paying much attention to him, however. Her focus had turned to the dog. Rather than follow the man, the four black paws were approaching the end of the bed, and she had a sinking feeling her hiding spot wouldn't last long.

Ignoring her various aches and pains, she glanced around wildly, looking for some sort of weapon, any weapon at all, but she saw nothing, not even a dust bunny under the bed. If this were her room and her bed, there would have been clothes, shoes, possibly a hanger or two. Shoes, or even a hanger, made a better weapon than the nothing under this bed. The space was as barren as a desert.

"When I get my hands on Thomas," the man was muttering now. "He's deliberately not answering his phone because he knows I want him here to help with this mess."

Leigh glanced to the side, to see that he'd moved away from the first door and was now moving to the closet doors. Curiosity got the better of her then and she reached out with her sore arm to lift the side ruff enough to see him.

Her eyes widened. He was barefoot, as she'd known, but also bare-chested, or mostly bare-chested. The flowered apron he wore covered part of a very muscular, very naked chest and skirted over his black jeans. A kerchief was tied around his face, covering his mouth and nose like a bank robber of old. Another covered most of the short blond hair curling in waves away from his face, and he wore rubber gloves on his hands, then her attention was diverted as he opened the closet door.

Leigh grimaced at the sight of the shoes lining the bottom of the large wall closet. They were women's shoes, maybe half a dozen, and every one sported a pointed heel. A lot of good they did her there, she thought irritably, then glanced sharply toward the end of the bed as a rustle caught her ear.

Much to her horror, the dog had found her. He was now on his stomach at the end of the bed, snuffling as he began to scooch his way forward under the bed. Eyes widening, Leigh scooted back as far as she could until her feet hit the wall at the head of the bed, but the dog just followed, dragging himself forward on his belly and making little whimpering noises that she thought might be meant to reassure her that his intentions were friendly.

Leigh's eyes widened in growing amazement as his size became apparent. The animal was beyond large, his head a big square that could have passed for a small television, his body lifting the bed each time he bumped it. He was a bloody monster. *Huge!* He could eat her for dinner and probably still manage a snack afterward.

"I don't need this. I— Julius? Where the hell did *you* go now?"

Leigh tore her eyes away from the dog who was now almost completely under the bed and glanced toward the bare feet as they moved to the door where they'd entered. The man was obviously looking out in the hall for the dog, and for a moment she hoped he might leave the room in search of them both. Then she was distracted by a wet tongue sliding up her cheek.

Blinking, she turned to discover that the dog had reached her. Fortunately, his intentions didn't seem vicious. Unless he was just taking a taste before he bit, his greeting seemed friendly enough. Relieved that she needn't fear having her throat ripped out—again—she eased one hand forward and patted the dog awkwardly in greeting. Leigh knew it had been a bad move the moment she heard the thump of his tail on the floor as he tried to wag it in greeting.

She squeezed her eyes closed, hardly aware of the tongue slapping wetly across her cheek this time, though it was hard to ignore the doggy breath.

"I should be out helping to hunt down Morgan."

That mutter caught Leigh's attention and she stilled under the dog's tongue. Hunting down Morgan? Then he wasn't a cohort of Donald and the man who'd bit her?

"Instead, I'm stuck here babysitting a—" There was a pause as the man apparently became aware of the thumping sound of the dog's tail. Leigh raised her hand to her face to block the dog's tongue and opened her eyes in time to see the feet by the door turn slowly back to face the room. Just as she noted that the tip of the dog's tail was sticking out from under the bed, the man snapped, "Julius! What the hell are you doing under the bed?"

Leigh groaned inwardly and watched the bare feet move closer. They stopped beside the tip of Julius's protruding tail, then a pair of knees and the skirt of his apron came into view as he knelt at the foot of the bed.

A bare arm followed, then his face appeared, still hidden behind the kerchief. His eyes, however, were not hidden, and she felt her stomach clench as she stared at the silvery blue as he glared under the bed. It took her a moment to realize he was glaring at the dog, then his gaze shifted to her and he blinked in surprise.

"Oh. There you are." The glare softened, but there was still irritation in his eyes. "What are you doing out of bed? Don't I have enough to do?"

Leigh had the most ridiculous urge to apologize, but bit her tongue to keep it back. She had no idea who he was, or where she was, or—

Her thoughts scattered as the dog gave her face another lick. Either he believed she was a doggy popsicle or they were going steady now, she thought, her sense of humor returning as the ridiculousness of the situation sank in. Her hiding spot had been a decided failure, yet she was still in it. And she wasn't even sure she needed a hiding place. If the man was hunting Morgan . . . "The enemy of my enemy" and all that.

Leigh was about to roll out from under the bed when her hand was suddenly caught in a rubbery grip and she was dragged out. She managed a gasp of shock, then found herself scooped up into strong arms and carried to the bed she'd struggled out of just moments ago.

"You shouldn't be up and about yet. You're too weak," the man scolded as he straightened, his kerchief billowing against his lips with each word.

"I—" Leigh began, but he'd noticed her arm and interrupted.

"You've torn out your IV. Now I'll have to put it back in."

Leigh watched wide-eyed as he grabbed the tube from the IV, found the end of it, and began to remove the tape to examine the tip. Most of her fear was easing away. He seemed harmless. A little batty, she decided, taking in his eccentric costume, but harmless. She barely had this thought when her gaze was drawn to the dog. He was finished dragging himself out from under the bed and leapt up onto it to settle at her side.

Leigh eyed him warily, afraid he would start licking her again. Now that she could see all of him and tell how big he was, she was very, very grateful that he seemed a friendly mutt, but not so grateful that she wanted to be covered in doggy spit from head to toe. Fortunately, it seemed he was done with that. He spread out on the bed beside her, dropped his head onto his front paws, closed his eyes and appeared to go to sleep.

A discouraged sigh drew her attention back to the man in time to see him send an irritated glance her way. "You broke it."

Leigh blinked. "I did?"

"Yes. Snapped the needle tip in half," he announced, then glanced over the bed. Leigh glanced down as well, her gaze skimming the surface of the white bed for the tip of the IV needle.

Muttering under his breath, he bent to run his hands over the linen surface, presumably in search of the needle tip. Leigh drew her legs up, pulling them in closer to her body to avoid his hands, but the increased pain in her arm as she started to wrap it around her knees made her still. Raising the arm, she turned it over and peered at it, grimacing as she noted the tip sticking out. It almost seemed to push farther out of her body before her very eyes. She'd been so distracted by her fears, she hadn't paid attention to the pinching pain in her arm.

"Oh, there it is." Taking her hand, he drew her arm out straight and then plucked out the bit of metal.

He peered at it closely and scowled, his gaze sliding from the broken needle to the IV with irritation. "How am I—"

His question ended abruptly as the phone rang. Scowling, he tossed the needle tip on a tray now on the bedside table. Presumably, this was what she'd heard him set down when he first entered, because she was sure it hadn't been there earlier. Her gaze slid over the contents with interest. It held a pitcher of water, a glass, and a plate of something vaguely resembling dog food . . . except that it was steaming. Leigh eyed the water greedily as the man reached for the phone.

"Hello?" he said into the receiver, and she eased closer to the bedside, her tongue slipping out to lick her lips as she drew closer to the water.

The phone rang again.

Leigh glanced back to see the man's eyebrows draw tight together until they almost became one. He stared at the buttons on the phone and pushed another one. "Hello?"

The phone rang again.

"Bloody, newfangled—" He began pressing button after button, repeatedly saying, "Hello?"

"Lucian?"

The dog beside Leigh shifted in his sleep, ears twitching at the sound of the voice that came through the telephone speaker.

"Marguerite." The man's relief was palpable, Leigh noted curiously as she eased a little closer to the side of the bed. She could almost reach the water jug now.

"Why do you sound so far away, Lucian?" the woman asked.

The man, Lucian, snorted with irritation. "You're in Europe, Marguerite. I *am* far away."

"Yes, but you shouldn't *sound* far away." Her voice was exasperated. "Are you on speaker phone?"

"No," the man said quickly, and Leigh bit her lip to keep from smiling at the lie when he sent a warning glare her way. Apparently, he didn't want to fuss with any more buttons, but didn't want to admit he didn't know how to use the phone either.

That thought made her frown. Why didn't he know how to use his own phone?

"Hmmm." The disbelieving murmur distracted Leigh from her thoughts, and she glanced toward the phone, her gaze stopping on the water instead. She was close enough to reach the pitcher, she noted, and started to pick it up, only to have her hand knocked away.

"Well," Marguerite announced. "I called because it seems Vittorio forgot to take out the garbage. He apparently collected it all in a big black garbage bag and set it by the back door in the kitchen to take out before we left, but in all the excitement, he forgot."

Leigh lost interest as soon as she heard the word garbage, but then her attention was focused on the pitcher as Lucian picked it up and poured a glass of water. Then he set the pitcher down, picked up the glass and handed it to her.

She felt relief course through her. She took the glass in both hands, then opened her mouth to thank him only to find her lips covered by one rubber gloved finger as he shook his head. He wasn't supposed to be on speaker phone, she recalled. No doubt he didn't want the woman to hear her, as it would give away the game.

Mouthing the words "Thank you," she raised the glass to her lips and took a swallow, just managing to restrain a murmur of pleasure as the clear, cold liquid filled her mouth. God, it was good.

"I'm sure it's fine," Marguerite continued. "I was just worried because we put Julius in the kitchen and he has a tendency to nose through the garbage and—"

"Nose?" Lucian asked dryly, his tone drawing Leigh's gaze. He was glaring at the sleeping dog on the bed. "Don't you mean claw through it, rip it open, and drag it around the house?"

"Oh dear," came faintly from the phone. "I take it Julius got into the bag before the people from the kennel got there?"

Lucian hesitated, his gaze shifting from the dog to Leigh, before he simply said, "Yes."

Leigh glanced at the dog, wondering how they'd come by his name. Julius seemed a pretty powerful name for a dog. On the other hand, she supposed he was a powerful dog, and names like Spot and Fluffy just wouldn't have cut it.

"But you got Julius off all right?" Marguerite asked. "There was no problem with the kennel people? I've never put him in a kennel before, but I couldn't leave him alone there at the house. I don't know how long I'm going to be gone. You did make sure they got his medicine and instructions? He has an infection and has to have his pills."

Leigh took another sip of water as she waited for Lucian to answer. Obviously, there had been some sort of problem, since the dog was still here, but Lucian just turned his back to her and said, "Look, Marguerite, I'm glad you called. There *is* a problem."

Despite the fact that he was actually talking to this Marguerite through the speaker phone, Lucian still held the receiver to his ear, and Leigh found herself smiling faintly. There was just something about the man that made her want to smile. Despite what had happened, and the fact that she hadn't a clue where she was or who he was, she didn't find him the least bit threatening. It was hard to find a man in such a weird getup threatening, she supposed, her gaze sliding over him again and seeming to get caught on the ripple of muscle in his back as he shifted the useless phone receiver to his other ear.

"What problem?" Marguerite asked as Leigh's eyes dropped over his tapered waist to his behind. Her eyebrows lifted a little as she saw that he didn't have the flat ass that so many men were cursed with, but a pert rounded one that just made her want to reach out and give them a squeeze.

"The girl broke the needle ripping it out of her arm."

The irritation in his voice drew her gaze back up as he turned to give her an irritated glance.

"I need to replace the needle. Where do I find them?"

"Oh dear." This comment was followed by a long silence, then the woman said, "I'm afraid I don't have any replacements."

"What? But—"

"Lissianna doesn't need them anymore so I've never bothered to— Call Thomas," she interrupted herself suddenly. "He can pick up one at the blood bank and drop it by."

"Yes, well that's another problem. I can't reach Thomas." There was steel in his voice now, and Leigh didn't envy this Thomas person. He was obviously not on Lucian's list of favorite people.

"You can't?" Marguerite asked with surprise.

"No. I've tried calling him several times tonight and he isn't answering his phone."

"Hmmm. That's odd. Maybe it's his night off. He shuts off his cell phone on his nights off."

"Maybe," Lucian muttered, not sounding convinced. "Is she awake?"

"Who?"

"The *girl*," Marguerite said, then made a sound of annoyance. "What is her name, Lucian?"

"It's Leigh. Leigh . . ." His expression went blank, then he glanced at Leigh. "What's your last name?"

"Gerard." It tumbled out before she could think better of giving it.

"I heard that. You *are* on speaker phone," Marguerite said sharply.

Lucian's eyes looked annoyed above the kerchief on his face, but before he could admit or deny it, the woman went on, "And why didn't you tell me she was awake? For heaven's sake, Lucian. Just teach her to use her teeth to feed until you can get hold of Thomas. It's faster anyway."

Lucian heaved a sigh that sent his kerchief billowing.

Wondering absently what the woman was talking about, Leigh reached out absently and petted Julius. The action roused the animal from sleep, and his whole body went stiff under her hand as Marguerite began to speak again. He was suddenly very much awake. Awake, alert, and stiff and quivering as he searched the room for the source of the voice.

"Try calling Jeanne," the woman was saying. "She'll know where her brother is and how to reach him. He always gives her a number in case of emergencies."

Lucian rumbled something that might have been an agreement to her suggestion, and the woman went on. "And thank you for waiting for the kennel people. I don't know what I would have done if you hadn't arrived. We probably would have had to drop Julius off at the—" She stopped abruptly as Julius barked in response to hearing his name. "What was that? Was that Julius?"

Julius barked again despite the glare Lucian had turned on him, and Leigh bit her lip at the frustration on his face as he clutched the phone to his ear.

"Why is Julius still there?" Marguerite sounded alarmed. "I thought the kennel people came to collect him!"

"They did," Lucian answered. "A woman came by."

"Then why is he still there?"

Lucian opened his mouth, closed it again, then reluctantly admitted, "She didn't arrive at an opportune time."

Silence seeped through the room. When Marguerite finally spoke, her voice was terribly calm, even a little cold, as she said, "Explain."

Lucian's eyes shifted to Leigh, and her own widened in surprise at the accusation in his gaze. It seemed obvious he blamed her for whatever had happened.

"I'd left the front door open and gone in to check on . . . er . . . Leigh," he said, grasping for the name. "She was back to her screaming and thrashing so I decided to take her up to Lissianna's room."

He ignored Leigh's startled gasp at the announcement that she'd been "back to screaming and thrashing" and continued, "I picked her up to carry her upstairs, and when I got into the hall there was a woman in the doorway. I started to explain that Julius was in the kitchen, but the sight of Leigh covered in blood and in a fit must have upset her, because she . . . er . . . took off."

"She saw Leigh covered in blood and in the midst of turning?" Marguerite said carefully.

Leigh glanced down, noting the large red stain on her blouse, and supposed the sight of it might be somewhat distressing. She certainly found it distressing.

"I believe Julius may have been barking rather frantically at the time as well," Lucian announced.

"You *believe*?" Marguerite asked dryly.

"I had my earplugs in to drown out the screaming," Lucian explained.

Leigh gaped at the man. Geez, he was all heart.

There was a long drawn-out sigh across the phone. "She probably thought you were some mad killer."

"That's what the police said," Lucian agreed.

"The *police*?" Marguerite squawked.

"Everything is fine," he said shortly. "I explained everything."

"You explained *what*?" Marguerite sounded almost hysterical. "You couldn't tell them the truth."

"Don't be ridiculous, Marguerite, of course I didn't tell them that." He released a long sigh that sent his kerchief fluttering again. "It's obvious you're on edge from your long journey. Don't worry. I'll take care of everything here. Get some rest."

"You'll take care of everything?" Marguerite sounded a bit stressed, but Lucian wasn't listening. He'd set the receiver back in its rest and was pushing buttons, trying to disconnect as she went on, "I've known you for seven hundred years, Lucian, and in all that time you've—"

Her rant was cut off as Lucian finally succeeded in finding the button to end the call. Leigh was almost sorry he'd succeeded. She would have liked to hear more. Marguerite had known Lucian for seven hundred years? She must have misheard her, Leigh thought. She'd probably said seven *hungry* years or something, though that didn't make any sense either. Anyway, she had a feeling that whatever followed would have been interesting.

Relaxing as silence drifted through the room, Lucian

straightened his shoulders and turned to Leigh. He stared at her for a while, then gestured to the tray. "I made you something to eat if you're hungry."

Leigh peered at the steaming pile on the plate on the tray, then asked uncertainly. "What is it?"

"Prime cuts in gravy."

"Prime cuts in gravy?" she echoed slowly. "Did *you* cook it?"

"I opened the can and heated it up in the microwave for one minute. Someone named Alpo cooked it."

Leigh stiffened, her head shooting up, eyes wide with disbelief. "Alpo?"

He shrugged. "That's what the can said."

Leigh shook her head with bewilderment. "You can use a microwave, but not a phone, and don't know that Alpo isn't the *chef*, but the brand name for *dog* food?" There was something seriously wrong here.

"I *can* use a phone," he snapped. "I'm not an idiot. It's just Marguerite has these stupid fancy phones with more buttons than a plane cockpit and . . ." He paused and seemed to regain his temper, then added, "As for a microwave, I have one of my own. I occasionally like to warm . . . beverages before I drink them." He scowled, then added, "And what's wrong with dog food? Food is food, and it smells pretty good."

Leigh stared at him as the vague, dreamlike recollection of stumbling into the kitchen returned to her. Her eyes narrowed on Lucian as she wondered if he'd been the blond with Morty and Bricker in the kitchen, the one who'd covered her mouth and pulled her out of the door and against his chest. Had that really happened? Was Lucian that man?

Leigh supposed he could be, but it was hard to tell without seeing his face.

"Do you want it or not?" Lucian asked, and she turned to him with disbelief.

"You're kidding, right?"

He shrugged and repeated, "Food is food, and I didn't find anything else in the kitchen."

Leigh shook her head. She wasn't that hungry and hoped to God she never was. "No, thank you."

Shrugging again, he picked up the plate and set it on the bed in front of Julius. The dog immediately began to lap it up.

"See. He likes it," Lucian said, and Leigh bit her lip against the rude comments that sprang to mind as she watched him bend to the bedside table and open the door.

Curious, she leaned forward and found that it wasn't a bedside table at all. It was actually a small refrigerator and it was presently stacked half full with bags of blood.

"Open your mouth."

"What?" Leigh asked. It was such an unexpected order, and his head was in the refrigerator and half-muffled. She was quite sure she'd misheard him.

"I said open your mouth." Lucian straightened from the refrigerator with a bag of blood in hand.

Leigh eyed it with confusion. "Why?"

Apparently not the most patient of men, rather than repeat himself again, he reached out, clasped her face in one hand and dug his fingers into her cheeks. She was forced to open her mouth to avoid pain. Lucian paused and frowned as he peered at her teeth.

"Of course not." Shaking his head, he glanced around, then back to her, his gaze pausing on her blouse. "Right."

Leigh frowned, wondering what on earth he was

thinking, then gasped in surprise as Lucian caught the bloody front of her blouse and raised it to her nose. She tried to pull her face away from the crusty cloth, but he simply followed with the stiff material, and she stilled as she breathed in the scent of her own blood.

Normally, her reaction would have been to wrinkle her nose with distaste at the tinny scent wafting up her nostrils. However, Leigh found herself pressing her nose closer into it, her stomach rippling with cramps as she breathed in the distinctive smell. After a moment she became aware of a shifting sensation in her mouth.

Startled, she jerked her head away, her hand rising to her mouth. Her fingertips brushed against the sharp tip of a tooth that was suddenly protruding past the others, then Lucian brushed her hand aside and slapped the blood bag to her mouth.

Leigh heard the pop of her teeth piercing the plastic, then felt something cold slipping up through her teeth as the bag quickly began to deflate. Her eyes shot to Lucian, scared and bewildered as she tried to understand what was happening.

"Right," he said firmly. "I'm going to explain a few things to you. In the meantime, you just sit there and hold onto this."

Lucian caught her hand in his free one and raised it to hold the bag in place. Once he was sure she had a grip on it, he straightened and considered her, apparently trying to decide how to go about explaining what he had to tell her.

"I don't know how much you remember of last night."

" 'Onny," Leigh muttered around the bag, then paused, thinking there was no way he would understand anything she said. Much to her surprise, however, he seemed to grasp it.

"Donny?"

"Unh," Leigh said, nodding.

"The red-haired guy Morgan was talking to?"

Leigh nodded quickly again and spoke around the bag once more, " 'Or'an 'it 'e."

"Morgan bit me—you?"

Leigh nodded again.

"Right. Then you do remember. So I don't need to explain that vampires really do exist, one bit you, and—apparently—gave you blood?"

Leigh grimaced around the bag against her lips, vividly recalling choking as the tinny liquid poured into her mouth. The same liquid apparently presently being sucked up by her own teeth, which had grown decidedly fangish.

"And now you're turning, too," he continued. "You're a vampire."

"O' 'it," she muttered around the nearly empty bag. That so wasn't what she wanted to hear.

"Oh shit, indeed."

 Five

"So, Morgan really *was* a vampire?" Leigh asked as soon as the first bag of blood was empty and she could remove it from her mouth. She then frowned at the lisp to her own words. It was odd trying to speak with a mouthful of fangs. Her tongue instinctively tried to avoid the sharp incisors, and as a consequence some of her words were mangled.

Lucian didn't seem to have any trouble understanding her, however. He merely opened the refrigerator door again and said, "You remember Morgan biting you and giving you blood. What did you think that meant?"

"It could have been the result of drugs dropped into my soda at work," she pointed out almost hopefully.

"No."

"Are you sure—" Leigh stiffened as he cut her off by popping a fresh blood bag to her open mouth. She instinctively pulled it away to finish her question, only to gasp as blood shot everywhere, springing into the air like a red fountain from two puncture holes.

Cursing, Lucian snatched the bag from her. Spinning away, he strode to the door against the wall the bed rested against and slammed it open to reveal a bath-

room. He tossed the bag into the sink, grabbed a towel
off the rack and whirled to return to her.

"Sorry," Leigh said quietly as he swiped at some of
the blood that had sprayed over both her and the bed.
Not that his effort did much good. The blood had already soaked into the sheets, and probably into her
shirt, though it was hard to tell with the bloodstain already covering it.

Lucian didn't respond to her apology other than to
grunt, then—giving up on any hope of mopping up the
blood—he turned to retrieve another bag of it.

"Open," he ordered firmly.

Feeling guilty about the mess she'd made, Leigh sighed
and opened her mouth for him to pop the fresh bag
there. She then sat there with questions rushing through
her mind that she couldn't ask. The moment this second bag was empty, she ripped it impatiently from her
mouth.

"Do—"

"I know you have questions," Lucian interrupted,
"but they will have to wait until we get through feeding
you."

"No. I . . ." Leigh paused and growled in her throat
as he popped another bag to her mouth. The man was
fast, managing to pick the moment when her mouth was
open just wide enough. She hadn't even seen the bag
coming, it was just suddenly there, stuck to her mouth
and blocking her speech.

Leigh glared at him over the bag, and Lucian glared
right back, then his eyes shifted to the center of her forehead and narrowed in concentration. Frowning, she
looked upward, wondering what he saw there.

"I can't read you."

Her eyes shot forward to find him looking stunned,

almost horrified. Frowning, she thoughtlessly pulled the bag away.

"What?" she asked, then cursed as she realized what she'd done. Fortunately, the bag had nearly been empty and it simply sagged, dribbling onto her upper legs and black skirt. "What do you mean, you can't read me?" she asked as he began to mop up her legs.

Lucian stiffened, then handed her the cloth to clean herself and straightened. "Nothing. I'm just tired. I'll try again later."

"Try what later?" she asked with confusion.

"Never mind. How's your stomach?"

"My stomach?" Leigh echoed with bewilderment.

"Any cramps, queasiness, or anything?" he asked, the question just confusing her more.

"No, I'm fine. My stomach's fine. But—"

"Good. Go take a bath."

"But I want to know—"

"After you bathe," Lucian insisted. "You reek of blood."

"Probably because I'm covered in it," she said dryly.

"And whose fault is that?"

Leigh's mouth tightened, then she heaved out an exasperated breath. Fine, she'd go clean up . . . if she could walk, she thought, recalling her earlier weakness, when she'd been flopping on the floor beside the bed. She stood carefully, and blinked in surprise. Her strength appeared to have returned. Her legs were shaky, but held her up as she walked into the bathroom.

"What do—" she began, turning back toward the door, only to see Lucian pushing it closed.

"Bath!" he snapped as the door slammed shut.

"I don't want to take a bath. I'm going to shower," Leigh said in rebellion, and childishly stuck her tongue out at the door. She hated being told what to do.

Silence was her only answer.

Sighing, she turned away, but paused as she caught sight of her reflection. If she had thought about it, she would have guessed that she'd look like hell—she certainly felt like hell—but the woman peering back from the mirror looked pretty okay. Her skin glowed, her eyes were bright and the color of...

She leaned closer.

"Gold," Leigh breathed with awe. Her previously boring, brown eyes were now a golden bronze. They were beautiful, she thought with amazement.

"Cool," she breathed.

Cheered by this, she briefly forgot all about her questions and concerns. Quickly stripping out of her clothes, she faced the mirror, then stared at herself for a long time. She turned this way then that, then faced the mirror straight on again, before leaning in to examine her neck closely.

She'd been sure Morgan had bitten her, and yet there was no mark. At first she thought it was simply because the blood staining her neck obscured it. She grabbed a washcloth that had been left neatly folded beside the sink, wet it under the tap, and quickly scrubbed the blood away in search of the bite. All she found was perfect, unbroken skin.

Yet her neck and chest and blouse were stained with blood.

Leigh peered at her body again, then her hands, looking for the little nicks from shaving and the burn she'd received the other night at work, but that skin was perfect, too. Even the cellulite on her hips and thighs was gone. And her figure was a little different as well. Not much, but her hips were a bit smaller, as was her waist.

Unfortunately, her breasts weren't, though they seemed higher than they had been, defying the gravity that had pulled at them as she turned thirty. Maybe they would still shrink some, she thought hopefully.

Her gaze slid back to the mirror and she wrinkled her nose as she acknowledged that she was also still short. She supposed it was too much to hope that becoming a vampire would make her suddenly shoot up a few inches.

Leigh's smile faded as the word vampire slid through her mind.

Leaning forward, she opened her mouth to peer at her teeth, but they seemed no different. And yet they'd popped holes in the blood bags. Recalling Lucian lifting her shirt to her nose and the feel of pressure and shifting, she bent to grab her shirt off the floor where she'd dropped it and pressed it to her nose. The moment she inhaled, she felt the same pressure and shifting along her upper jaw.

Dropping the shirt, Leigh leaned toward the mirror and opened her mouth again to see two sharp fangs slipping out.

"Wow," she breathed, her stomach fluttering.

Reaching up, she poked and prodded at the two canines, trying to see if she could push them back up into her jaw. No go. They seemed firmly in place.

"Huh." She stared at them, then leaned toward the mirror and tipped her head back to see the tips, looking for the holes that the liquid slid through, but she couldn't see any.

"Huh," she said again, then just stood there, unsure how to get them to go away.

Staring at her new teeth—fangs, really, she admitted reluctantly—and waiting for them to go away, she began to consider other concerns she would now have. Like daylight. Obviously, she'd now have to avoid sunlight. Considering she'd worked nights for the last six years, she supposed she shouldn't mind, but she did. She had *chosen* to work the night shift all this time, but now it appeared she no longer had that choice. Vampires could not go out in daylight without bursting into flames. She'd seen as much in the movies.

Then there were other things . . . She'd have to stay out of churches and avoid crosses. She was now cursed and soulless. She didn't much care for that. Deep in her heart, Leigh believed in God, but often felt like God had forgotten her. He'd taken her parents, took her grandfather . . . and then there was Kenny. Though she didn't suppose she could blame Him for her marrying Kenny.

Leigh peered at herself, trying to see if she could see a difference now that she had no soul. She didn't feel any different. There was no sudden urge to go ripping the throats out of poor, unsuspecting humans. Maybe she still had her soul. Maybe you didn't lose it unless you actually bit someone, she thought. She'd had only bagged blood up to now . . . and would continue that way, she decided. If there was a way to do it, she'd rather keep her soul. It might have been a long time since she'd gone to church, and she often felt as if God had forgotten her, but she had never forgotten Him and spoke to Him each night before sleeping. She intended to continue doing that, whether she was a cursed, soulless vampire or not.

Leigh searched her mind for other ways life would now change, and her first thought was garlic. Never having cared much for garlic anyway, it wasn't of great concern. Then she blinked at herself in the mirror as she recalled that vampires weren't supposed to have a reflection.

Hmm, well that one's obviously wrong, she thought. Unless she wasn't done turning. Or maybe it was something that happened over time. She'd have to ask about that.

"I don't hear the bathwater running." Lucian's voice boomed through the door, and Leigh rolled her eyes.

"I'm taking a shower," she reminded him.

"Then take it."

Muttering under her breath, Leigh moved to the bathtub, opened the glass door and reached in to turn on the shower.

Lucian was most definitely a bossy man, she decided as she adjusted the temperature of the water. Kind of like her grandfather, who had been a crusty old soul with a heart of gold underneath.

But not like him at all, she decided in the next moment, as she recalled watching the play of muscles over his back and ogling his butt. She'd never lusted after her grandfather, but Lucian . . .

Leigh smiled as she stepped into the shower and pulled the glass door closed.

Though she would never have told him, she could admit to herself that Lucian was a very sexy man. At least, what she'd seen of him was. She found a new bar of soap in the soap dish, unwrapped it, then rubbed it between her hands under the spray.

Lucian had nice wide shoulders, a sculpted chest and back . . . and that ass! Leigh shook her head as she turned her back to the water to work a lather from the soap and admitted to herself that she'd wanted to run her hands all over his body; caress those muscles in his back, squeeze the taut muscles in his bottom and press herself naked against his chest. It was an unusual reaction for her. She didn't generally run around lusting after men she'd just met. Especially when she hadn't seen their face.

Although, Leigh thought, he could be the third man from the kitchen, the one who had pulled her back against his chest. He'd felt strong and sturdy there, reassuringly so. And he'd been very handsome. Lucian was the right height and size and also had the same ice blond hair.

Picturing the face of the man in the kitchen on Lucian's body, Leigh dropped the soap in the dish and began to run her hands over her body, spreading the lather. Somehow in her mind they became his hands, smoothing the soap across her stomach and then up over her breasts . . . caressing them . . . rolling the nipples between soapy fingers.

Leigh shuddered and moved to lean against the tile wall as her legs went a little weak. It was so real . . . She could feel the rough calluses and heat of his hands, even smell him. He smelled spicy and musky in her mind, and she inhaled deeply, despite knowing she couldn't actually be smelling and feeling this.

Unless it was something to do with being a vampire, she thought absently. Perhaps her imagination was somehow stronger. The thought drifted away as one of his hands moved from her breast to slide down over her stomach, running the soap over her trembling skin, then down over her hip.

In her imagination—if it was imagination—she pressed lightly against his chest, her sensitive, erect nipples scraping through the hair there. Then she pressed closer, transferring some of the lather.

A small sigh slid from her lips, and she pulled back slightly to run her hands over the smooth plains of his chest, spreading the lather around as she curved her hands over muscle and velvet-covered bone. He felt warm and solid under her hands, and so big and wide. He had the body of an athlete, or a warrior, and she wanted to lick every inch of him.

Leigh moaned in protest as his soapy hands dropped away, but then they caught her by the bottom and kneaded lightly as he urged her closer again. She caught her breath and clutched at his upper arms as she felt him press against her stomach. Like the rest of him, he was hard and big . . . at least he *seemed* big. Curious, she reached between them to grasp him in one soapy hand, and a little sigh slid from her lips as she felt his size.

Damn. Fantasies were wonderful, she thought as her dream man bucked at her touch, and then her fantasy lover took on a life and mind of his own and suddenly bent to kiss her. His tongue thrust into her mouth in time with her slow strokes; once, twice, three times, then he let go of her behind.

For a brief second Leigh feared he would end their embrace, but instead he tangled one hand in her hair, using it to shift her head slightly to the side as his mouth ravaged hers. Her dream Lucian was suddenly both demanding and commanding as he used the other hand to press her tighter, sliding her soapy body against his until he'd shifted her enough so he could slide one leg between both of hers.

Leigh moaned into his mouth as his upper thigh pressed against her, rubbing insistently. She found herself bearing down into the caress, her mouth becoming more demanding in turn as her excitement mounted. When the leg suddenly slid away, she nipped at his lower lip in protest, then gasped as his hand replaced his leg and his fingers slid over her slick skin.

Her body heavy and achy, Leigh arched into his touch, urging him on until she couldn't stand it anymore and broke their kiss. Letting her head fall back, she cried out with need.

In answer to that cry, he knocked her hand away from his erection, then spun her briefly under the water, rinsing away the soap. Just as quickly, he spun her back out and lifted her.

The bathroom tiles were cold against her back as he pulled her legs around his warm body. His mouth traveled down her throat, then farther, until he caught one nipple in his hot, wet mouth. He drew on it, teeth grazing the tip and her body arching to offer him more, unintentionally making her lower body rub against his erection.

Growling deep in his throat, Lucian straightened abruptly and claimed her lips in a searing kiss as he shifted and drove into her hot and hard. Her cry this time was caught in his mouth as he pinned her there against the wall.

Leigh had been holding his upper arms, but now shifted her hands; one to his shoulder, where it dug into the hard flesh, the other to tangle in his hair and tug demandingly.

Tension strung through her body, becoming thinner and more brittle with each plunge of his body into hers. They were both panting, both gasping, both striving toward release . . . and then the line of tension suddenly snapped and Leigh ripped her mouth free of his and screamed with release.

That's when her legs gave out. Her eyes shot open as she slid down the tile wall to sit on the back of the tub.

She was alone.

There was no warm Lucian, no hands holding her, no demanding lips claiming hers . . . No body had possessed her . . . yet her own body still trembled with release. She stared at the water shooting down from the shower head with bewilderment as she realized it all; scents, touch, caress, passion . . . It had all been in her imagination.

My imagination, Leigh thought weakly, and pressed her hot face against the cold tile. It was hard to believe . . . and yet probably for the best since it had ended before her dream lover found his own release.

Shaking her head, Leigh got carefully back to her feet. She eased forward until the water shot down over her flushed skin. Her legs were still weak.

Gad, she thought with sudden consternation. She'd never had such a realistic wet dream in her life, and while awake!

A small embarrassed laugh slipped from her lips, and she ducked her head under the water, thinking that—if nothing else—it had done wonders for her stress level. She wasn't quite as upset about things as she had been. In fact, other than a little bemusement, Leigh was feeling pretty relaxed and happy at the moment. She could deal with this. So her life had changed. She was used to change. It seemed that's what her whole life had been about. She'd deal with it one day at a time, one matter at a time.

She'd try to think of it as an adventure, Leigh decided, and reached for the shampoo on the side of the tub.

Lucian woke with a start and jerked upright on the bed. He'd just had the most incredibly erotic dream . . .

Frowning, he peered around Lissianna's room. He'd grabbed a bag of blood and sat down on the side of the bed to feed, but had lay back while his teeth drained the bag. He'd lain there, eyes growing weary, listening as Leigh turned the water on in the bathroom. Much to his surprise, he'd then found himself imagining her stripping that blouse from her pale shoulders and slipping out of her short skirt before his eyes drifted closed and he fell asleep.

He supposed those last thoughts were what had brought about the dream, for the next thing he knew he was naked in the shower with Leigh, running soapy hands over her soft, pale skin, catching her breasts in his palms and rolling the nipples.

He'd kissed her, their soapy bodies gliding together, then she caught hold of him, and her hand had been warm velvet gloving his erection. He'd kissed her as she stroked him, one leg sliding between hers, then replaced it with his hand before taking her right there against the wall until she cried out with release.

Her release.

Unfortunately, that's when he woke up. If he'd just stayed asleep a couple more minutes...

Glancing down, Lucian lifted the apron he still wore to peer at the erection straining his black jeans. Just one more minute and he was sure he would have found release, too.

Shaking his head, he let the apron drop back into place. He supposed he should be glad. At least he now knew he could still *get* an erection. It had been so long since he'd had one that it might have been in question. He hadn't been interested in sex in a hell of a long time. Though no mortal would believe it, even that got boring after a couple of millennia.

It seemed his interest in sex was back, however, Lucian acknowledged, and his gaze slid to the bathroom door. He stared at it thoughtfully as he recalled trying to read her earlier. He'd intended to slip into her thoughts to silence her questions and control her. However, he hadn't been able to pierce her thoughts, perhaps because he was tired—and he'd been very tired, as his falling asleep while feeding attested to. But his sudden reawakened interest in sex suggested otherwise. It was possible Leigh was his life mate.

Lucian frowned at the thought.

Over the last couple of years, he'd watched his niece and nephews find their own life mates, and he'd been happy for them. He'd also been envious, yearning for someone of his own again. He'd had a life mate once before in Atlantis but had lost her during the fall. Part of him was excited at the idea of finally having someone to share the passing years with. But another part was anxious, reluctant to love and—possibly—lose again.

She might not even be my life mate, Lucian told himself. He would know one way or the other after he'd had some sleep and tried to read her again. He really was tired. So tired that if he sat here much longer he'd fall asleep again and Leigh would come out to find him passed out on the bed. Unfortunately, he had things to do. He would sleep later.

Sighing, Lucian pushed himself off the bed, then froze as he caught sight of himself in the mirror over the dresser across the room. He was bare-chested, wearing a flowered apron, rubber gloves, a bandanna over his hair and another over his lower face . . . He looked like an ass.

Shaking his head, Lucian yelled at Leigh to find something clean to wear in the closet when she was done, then headed for the door.

The moment he opened it, Julius leapt off the bed to follow. Lucian waited for him, then pulled the door closed and headed for the kitchen. One step into the room and he paused abruptly. Julius had managed to spread garbage from one end of the house to the other before he'd caught up with the dog and untangled the garbage bag twisted around his back leg. The kitchen was the worst. Julius had managed to dump most of the wet garbage there before escaping and dragging the shredded bag through the house.

His initial intention last night had been to ignore the mess and let Thomas look after it when he got ahold of him—if he ever got ahold of him. However, that was before he'd gone down to the kitchen to get some water for Leigh when she woke up. Stepping into the room, his foot had landed on some slippery muck and went out from under him, and he found himself lying in the gooey, rotting leftovers that coated the tile floor. Marguerite had apparently decided to empty the refrigerator before she left. Spread across the floor was spaghetti, some sort of stew, a rice dish or two, and what he'd assumed was some sort of chili.

He had rolled in the disgusting mess as he repeatedly tried to regain his feet and failed. Everytime he got halfway to his feet and found them sliding out from under him, he cursed his niece, nephews, and their mates. Marguerite didn't generally eat. However, her children had done so since finding their mates. He wasn't sure why, but it was one of the first signs of a lovesick immortal. He himself hadn't eaten since the death of his wife and children during the fall of their homeland. However, it appeared Marguerite had been having her children over and feeding them when they visited, hence the leftovers.

Once he'd finally managed to get himself up out of the mess, he had stripped off his shirt, shoes, and socks. He'd washed the muck out of his hair and off his hands, and then—rather than risk getting anything else dirty while he cleaned—had simply kept his already filthy pants on, donned the apron, the rubber gloves, and then found and wrapped a kerchief around his hair to prevent anything from splashing into it while he worked. After catching a whiff of the rancid garbage he was about to clear away, he had to fetch a second bandanna to wrap around his face in the hopes it would block the worst of the smell.

The better part of the evening and night had passed as Lucian divided his time between cleaning up the mess Julius had made and running upstairs to change the blood bag in Leigh's IV. He'd also checked in with Mortimer and Bricker, to learn they were working with Bastien to track Morgan and the Donny fellow. They'd checked the ID on everyone in the house that day, and Mortimer made a list for the council records. It was standard procedure. Now, Mortimer had given that list of names of rogues and victims to Bastien, who'd immediately set people to work watching the bank accounts and credit card activities of all the individuals.

Lucian hadn't been surprised to learn that there was activity on one of the credit cards. It belonged to a Bryan Stobie, one of Morgan's victims who had been dead when they'd arrived. He hadn't been a turn, but someone whom several of them had apparently fed on, killing him in the process. Yet his credit card was still being used. Whenever a new charge came through, Bastien called Mortimer and Bricker and reported it, and the men were following that trail. So far there was a rental car and several restaurant and gas charges on it. Morgan had moved up through northern Kansas and into Missouri, apparently heading north toward Canada.

Lucian's instincts told him the man was heading their

way. The protective way Morgan had cradled Leigh in his arms as he carried her out of the van and into the house made him think the rogue's interest in her was more than that of a sire who had turned her to please Donny, as the conversation they overheard in the house suggested. If he was right, it meant Morgan might become a problem. However, he knew they were still far enough away that it wasn't an urgent issue. The smelly and dangerous mess in the kitchen had held more import at the time, and he'd turned his attention to that.

After several more attempts to contact Thomas, Lucian had been forced to wash the hall floor, and finally the kitchen. He was halfway through when he recalled his intention to take water and perhaps some food upstairs to leave for Leigh in case she woke, which was why the floor was only half cleaned. Cleaning the other half wasn't an attractive prospect.

Julius shifted beside him and whined when Lucian bent a glare his way.

"Yeah, you know you messed up, buddy," he muttered, and walked over to kneel by the pail. Reaching into the cold, dirty water, he retrieved the sponge, wrung it out and bent once again to the tiresome business of cleaning the floor. He was still at it ten minutes later when the dog walked over and began to nose the pail.

"Julius," Lucian said in a warning tone.

The dog paused, glanced at him, then nosed the bucket again, as if telling him he should empty it and get fresh water. Lucian wasn't in the mood for criticism.

"Keep it up and I'll put you outside," he threatened.

Julius peered at him with his big brown eyes, then nosed the bucket again.

"That's it." Dropping the sponge in the bucket, Lucian stood and moved to open the door that led out to the backyard, then pushed the screen door open as well.

"Come on. Out you go," he said firmly, and Julius nearly knocked him over in his excitement to get outside.

"Stupid dog," Lucian muttered as he returned to his knees on the floor. He'd just wrung out the sponge and begun to swipe it over the floor when the door to the hall opened behind him, slamming into his butt. Jerking forward with surprise, he knocked the pail with his arm and sent it tipping onto its side.

"Oh, sorry," Leigh gasped behind him as Lucian stared at the dirty water running in a large wave across the floor.

 Six

"Are you still angry, or can I ask questions now?"

Lucian raised his head slowly from the wet mess he was mopping up and eyed the woman seated on the table. It was where he'd put her. It kept Leigh out of his way, kept her feet from getting in the way as he'd mopped up the spilled water, and kept her from causing any more havoc. If he could have, he would have put her out in the yard with Julius. Fortunately for her, even he wasn't that much of a bastard.

His gaze slid over her, taking in her damp, slicked-back hair, her clean face, and the overlarge terry-cloth robe she wore. One such robe hung from a hook on the back of every bathroom door in this house, he knew. Though whether she'd donned it because she hadn't heard his shout to borrow clothes from Lissianna's closet or had just refused to do so, he couldn't say. He hadn't asked. He'd been a little put out since she entered the kitchen.

Lucian turned his attention back to the mop, lifting it to dip it in the bucket. He swished it around before shifting it into the wringer now hooked onto the bucket's side.

Leigh had found the mop and wringer in the kitchen

closet while he knelt in the center of the flooded floor, clenching and unclenching his fists as he stared at the mess with exhausted disbelief.

She'd even started to mop up the mess, but then he stood, picked her up by the waist, set her down a little roughly on the table, and took the mop from her.

In truth, the mop was a godsend, and Lucian wished he'd seen it before he started cleaning. It made the job much easier and faster.

The knowledge minimized some of his anger, and he growled, "Ask."

A relieved little sigh slid from Leigh's lips and she asked, "Am I really a vampire?"

Lucian's hands froze on the mop and he glanced at her with surprise. "You doubt it? You haven't noticed anything different?"

Understanding struck him when Leigh looked away, and he said, "It's tempting to deny it to yourself, but it won't change anything. It just delays your coming to grips—and learning to live—with it."

"I suppose you're right," Leigh acknowledged unhappily as he went back to mopping. He glimpsed her sitting up, straightening her shoulders, and raising her head, then she said, "Okay, so I'm a vampire."

"Yes." Lucian said solemnly, and added, "But we dislike that name."

She shrugged that aside with a little movement of her shoulders. "I gather this means I'll now live forever and never age?"

Lucian rung out the mop again as he considered how to answer her question.

"Probably not forever," he said finally, as he slapped the mop to the floor. "But so long as you aren't decapitated or trapped in a fire, your life has been greatly prolonged and you won't age, or get sick, or even get cavities."

"Yeah?" she asked with interest. "No cavities?"

Lucian shook his head.

"Hmm." After a pause to consider that, she asked, "What about a reflection?"

Lucian glanced over with confusion. "Reflection?"

"Will it fade now? And if so, how long will that take to happen? I don't wear much makeup, but I do wear lipstick, and I don't want to walk around with it lopsided, or on my teeth." She frowned. "And what about spinach?"

"Spinach?" He had just grasped her concern about a reflection, but she lost him again with the spinach bit.

"Well, you know how when you eat a spinach salad? Or cooked spinach? And a bit of it gets caught between your teeth? And you walk around all day looking like an idiot until you see yourself in a mirror and see it caught there?"

"No, I don't know about that," he said dryly, but her eyes had already widened with thoughts of a new horror.

"Without a reflection you could walk around with that bit of spinach caught in the corner of your teeth for years, even decades, or—"

"Your reflection won't fade," Lucian interrupted before she worked herself up further.

"Oh . . . good." She looked relieved. Lucian shook his head and went back to what he was doing, only to have her ask, "Can I turn into a wolf, or a bunch of rats, or bats or—"

"No," he interrupted, wondering where mortals got these ideas. Unfortunately, he knew where. Movies and books, all of which could be traced back to that damned Bram Stoker. *If Jean Claude hadn't—*

"Can we fly?" Leigh asked, interrupting his musings.

"No."

Leigh was silent long enough that Lucian glanced her way. Her expression was disappointed.

He cared less that she was disappointed than that he finally had respite from her questions.

He pushed the mop absently around as he peered at her. She was swinging her legs back and forth like a child as she considered what she'd learned so far, and her terry-cloth robe was parting at the knees, revealing her thighs halfway up her legs. It was sexy as hell, and for some reason that irritated him. Scowling, Lucian turned back to his mop, telling himself his irritation was because she was driving him crazy with her questions. He was starting to recall why it had been so long since he'd helped initiate a new turn. He simply didn't have the patience for it.

"What *can* we do, then?" Leigh asked finally. "I mean, I know the downside; no sunlight, stay out of churches and avoid crosses, because I'm now cursed and soulless, but—"

"We are not cursed," Lucian said shortly. "We can go in churches without bursting into flames and we can touch crosses. We can also go out in sunlight, we just have to drink more blood to make up for it."

Leigh blinked in surprise, then frowned. "Are you sure? I mean it's not that I believe every movie I see or anything, but until Morgan bit me, I didn't believe in vampires either, and the movies all seem to suggest churches and sunlight aren't healthy for vampires."

"Immortal," he corrected automatically.

"And Morgan and his people all slept in coffins," she went on, as if he hadn't spoken. "If the rest of it isn't true, why the coffins? Do I need to keep a bit of the soil of my homeland in the coffin with me?"

Lucian grimaced at the memory of the more than twenty coffins in the basement of the house, resting places for Morgan and his turns. It had been a long while since his people slept in coffins to avoid exposure to the sun. Some had done it as a protective measure in the days when homes were drafty edifices with cracks that allowed the sun in, but that was long ago. Still, it was common for one of their kind who had gone rogue to use the old mythology brought about by books and movies to control their followers. They usually claimed they were their sire, could read their minds, and know whether they were faithful or not. All of which was true, actually.

However, they also let them think they were now one of the soulless, walking dead, and didn't tell them they could walk in daylight and enter churches and such. Rogues and their followers usually lived the life of a vamp in a bad movie; shunning sunlight, feeding off the living, and making slaves and sycophants of their followers.

Lucian had no idea why some went that way while others didn't. It was as if they just snapped after living so long and witnessing so much. He had known immortals who were fine for a thousand years and then suddenly went rogue. Others had turned after only a couple of centuries, but however long it took, they snapped and became the darker version of their kind, using and abusing mortals, and ultimately turning as many as they could to create their own cult of worshippers. Lucian didn't understand the whys of it, although he'd noted that they were always single immortals who had either lost or not yet found their life mates. Since he fit into that group, he found it all rather worrisome. He didn't want to turn that way. He had Marguerite and the kids to worry about. Someone had to keep an eye on them now that Jean Claude was gone.

Wringing out the mop one final time, Lucian carried it and the wringer to the closet to hang them up, then collected the bucket and carried it to the sink to empty.

"Movies and books are just that—fictional tales meant for entertainment," he said tartly. He hated to repeat himself or have the validity of what he said be questioned.

"So we really aren't cursed and soulless and we can go out in sunlight." She said the words slowly, and he suspected she didn't believe him.

A little put out at her still doubting him, he turned, lifted her off the table, then caught her hand and led her to the back door. Pushing open the screen door, he walked outside, tugging her behind him.

"There," he said firmly as Julius rushed over to them. "It's morning and you're outside and you haven't burst into flames."

Leigh shifted on her bare feet in the grass, her gaze dropping to Julius as she petted the beast, then up to the sky overhead.

"Yeah, but it's not really morning yet, the sky is mostly dark," she pointed out.

Flapping his hands in exasperation, Lucian turned to march back into the house. He paused at the door and called out to Julius, but the dog simply ran off to the back of the yard. Apparently he wasn't ready to come inside. Shrugging, Lucian entered the house, and was back at the sink, rinsing the bucket out, when he heard the door open and close as Leigh came back in.

"But I do believe you," she announced as if he needed reassurance. "And it's . . . well, it's good."

Lucian felt his mouth twitch at the understatement, but killed it. Then he gave in to the offered olive branch and said, "You *can* go out in sunlight, but I do not recommend you do so again for a while."

"Why?"

"You are still in the turning and will be for a while. During that time you'll already need a lot of blood. There's no need to add to it by going outside."

"Why do I need a lot of blood?" she asked.

"While you're turning, your body uses up more blood than it will once it's done."

"Why?"

Lucian frowned. It was like talking to a ten-year-old. Why? Why? Why? Repressing his impatience, he explained, "Because the blood is needed to repair any damage incurred over the last—" He paused to glance at her, then guessed. "—Twenty-six years."

"Thirty," Leigh corrected with a grin. "But thank you for the compliment."

Her grin made Lucian want to smile. He scowled instead and turned back to the sink as he continued, "Your body will be busy repairing any damage to your skin, liver, kidneys, lungs, heart . . ." He shrugged. "It will also be using the extra blood to improve your eyesight, hearing, strength, speed—"

"Improve?" she interrupted with interest. "You mean I'll be able to hear and see better and I'll be stronger and faster?"

"Yes."

"Hmmm. Kind of like Superman. I guess that's cool. At least there are some perks with this deal."

Lucian set the bucket in the sink and glanced over his shoulder with disbelief. "*Some* perks? What part of never aging, never getting sick, and living hundreds—

possibly thousands—of years, didn't you understand?"

A smile pulled at the corners of her mouth, but all she said was, "You're cute when you're grumpy."

Lucian was still blinking over the comment when she asked, "So it will improve me and needs the extra blood at first to do so?"

He stared for another moment, trying to figure out if she really found his grumpiness cute or if she was teasing him. Unable to tell from her expression, he muttered under his breath and turned back to the sink. Tugging the bandanna off his head, he tossed it on the counter.

"Is that right?" she persisted.

"Yes," Lucian said shortly as he removed the bandanna that had covered the lower part of his face. The rubber gloves and apron followed, leaving him clad in only the muck-covered black jeans.

"Okay. But why does that mean I should stay out of the sun?"

"Because any exposure to sunlight causes damage," he explained, jaw tight. Turning his back to the sink, he added, "Your body will use extra blood and resources to try to repair that damage, which will slow down your turning. It's better to avoid it until your turning is done."

"Oh, I see," Leigh said slowly, and he noticed her eyes seemed preoccupied with roving over his bare chest. She thought his grumpiness was cute and seemed fascinated with his chest. Lucian found himself straightening, his chest puffing up like a male peacock preening for her admiration. Disgusted with himself, he leaned against the counter and crossed his arms self-consciously over his naked chest. Leigh blinked as he ruined her view. She glanced quickly to his face, flushing guiltily on realizing she'd been caught ogling him. In the next moment that expression was replaced with recognition.

"You *are* the third man from the kitchen," she said.

Lucian merely grunted an acknowledgment and turned to finish rinsing the bucket, then put it away in the cupboard under the sink. The floor was streaked from the dirty water, but he'd done enough. He'd call in a service to clean it properly when they opened . . . which was only in a couple hours he noted, glancing at the clock on the kitchen wall.

Lucian supposed that meant he'd have to stay awake awhile yet. The idea wasn't a pleasing one. Other than two short catnaps, he'd been awake since six o'clock the night before last. It was now just after six o'clock in the morning, almost twenty-four hours after they'd hit Morgan's house in Kansas, thirty-six since he'd slept. He desperately needed sleep. He also wanted a nice long soak in a tub to remove the grimy feel coating his skin.

"If this isn't some curse, what is it?" Leigh asked, slipping off the table to follow when he headed out of the kitchen.

Lucian heaved a sigh as he pushed through the kitchen door. He understood she had questions, but he was too tired to be bothered with them. It was time to try again to find someone else to deal with her. He began running through a list of people in his head, trying to decide whom to enlist.

There was Thomas, but the little shit still wasn't answering his phone. Marguerite was in Europe. Lucern and Kate were in New York, as were Bastien and Terri. That left Etienne and Rachel, Lissianna and Greg, and Thomas's sister, Jeanne Louise.

Lucian frowned over his choices. Lissianna would have been his first choice if she weren't pregnant. Very pregnant. Lissianna was his favorite. She'd proven her-

self less prone to being cowed by him than her broth-
ers. The girl had even yelled at him a time or two. He
respected her for that, and smiled to himself now at the
memory.

No, he wouldn't bother Lissianna this close to giving
birth to his first grandniece or -nephew. As for Etienne
and Rachel . . . well, Rachel still hadn't forgiven him for
threatening to have her terminated when she refused to
do what they asked when she'd first been turned and
got involved with Etienne. Anytime he found himself in
the same room as the volatile redhead, she glared at him
like he was the devil incarnate. He'd rather not have her
filling Leigh's head with nonsense about him.

That left Jeanne Louise.

"Lucian?"

He paused on the stairs and glanced back with surprise. It was the first time Leigh had spoken his name.
He hadn't even known she knew it, but supposed she
overheard it while he was talking to Marguerite on the
speaker phone. Her soft voice speaking his name caused
an odd fluttering in his chest. Pushing away the sensation, he raised his eyebrows in question.

Leigh paused several steps below him and rephrased
the question he hadn't answered. "What are we if not
cursed?"

His gaze slid over her in the over large terry-cloth robe.
She was short, almost a foot shorter than he. She was
also a bundle of luscious curves, he noted with an interest he hadn't experienced in quite a while. Disturbed by
the effect she was having on him, he turned and continued upstairs. "Immortals," he told her again.

"Immortals," Leigh echoed, her mind wrapping itself
around the word. It was the second time he'd said it.

She didn't think he meant immortals like in the movie *Highlander*, but it didn't really answer her question. It didn't explain what she now was. Or how they were the way they were if it wasn't a curse.

Leigh glanced up, mouth open to ask for clarification, but Lucian had continued upstairs and was now disappearing along the hall. Scowling, she hurried after the half-naked man, catching up as he entered the room next to the one she'd woken in.

"But *how* are we immortals?" she asked as she caught the door before it swung shut in her face. She took several steps into the room before stopping, her gaze jumping nervously to the big bed against the wall, then away.

Lucian didn't seem surprised that she'd trailed him into the room. He just shook his head and moved to the phone.

"Well?" she asked, growing impatient.

"I'm getting you the answer." Lucian picked up the phone and pressed several buttons until—presumably—he got a dial tone. This time it wasn't over speaker phone, she noted, as he punched in a number from memory. They both stood waiting as he pressed the phone to his ear, but after enough time had passed for a couple dozen rings to have sounded without it being picked up, he hung up and punched in another number, then waited again.

Leigh shifted impatiently, but made herself wait. It seemed to her that he should *know* the answer to the question, but it was obvious he wanted someone else to do the explaining. Perhaps there were some embarrassing issues to it, she thought, then glanced to Lucian as he hung up again and tried once more.

"Marguerite?" Lucian said finally, sounding terribly relieved.

Leigh peered at him with surprise. From the earlier conversation she'd listened in on, she knew that this Marguerite was in Europe. Why was he calling her?

"No, no, Julius is fine." Lucian scowled with irritation. "No I— Marguerite, I just called because the girl is asking questions . . . Well, I thought you could explain things to her."

Lucian pulled the phone away from his ear as Marguerite's irritated voice buzzed back through the phone loud enough for Leigh to hear. His mouth tightened, then he turned away from her, put the phone back to his ear and said, "I know it's not like explaining men's knees to a teenage daughter . . . Menses," he corrected quickly. "Whatever, but—"

He paused and slapped his hand impatiently against his leg as he listened, then said, "Yes, of course I know you're in Europe, *I* called *you* remember . . . Yes, yes, I know it's long distance. I'll pay for the damned call."

Lucian stiffened as he listened to whatever Marguerite was saying, and Leigh found her gaze traveling over the tensed muscles of his naked back. The moment he'd removed the bandanna from his face in the kitchen, she had recognized him as the third man from the kitchen. It had been a relief, actually. At least she'd put the right face on the man in her fantasy.

Leigh rolled her eyes at her own thoughts.

"There are more important issues here than your waking wet dreams in the shower," she reprimanded herself under her breath. Really, her thinking seemed terribly scattered since she'd woken up. She had to wonder if it was a side effect of the change. She still had no idea where she was, or who he was . . . Why was he helping her? Or was he even trying to help her? How would all of this affect her life now? Would she find herself suddenly biting waiters instead of tipping them?

That thought gave her pause. She couldn't imagine biting *anyone*, and briefly considered she might, instead, be reduced to biting someone's little fluffy white dog like the character in the Anne Rice movie, but she couldn't imagine doing that either. Dogs were so cute . . . and what if they had fleas? And, really, they rolled around in the grass and dirt, who knew what they had in their fur?

Leigh heaved a sigh. The questions running through her mind were endless. She knew now that she wasn't cursed, couldn't do anything cool or freaky, like fly or morph into a wolf, but she wanted to understand *what* exactly she was now. Was she still human? And if so, how could she now live so long, and not age, and not get sick, and not get cavities and so on?

A small sound from Lucian drew her attention back to him. He no longer had his back to her, but had turned to face her, a stunned look on his face, the hand holding the phone forgotten at his side.

"What?" she asked warily.

"You had a wet dream in the shower?" he asked.

Leigh immediately flushed and cursed herself for muttering under her breath. If he had been anyone else, he never would have heard her. But Lucian wasn't anyone else, he was an immortal like she was becoming. He'd said her senses would improve . . . including her hearing. So his was obviously superior. Great.

There were only two options here, she realized. Either she lied and denied it, or brazened it out. It wasn't like he knew he had played a key part in the shower action.

Shoulders straightening, she took on an uncaring expression. "Sure. What? You've never had a wet dream?"

"Was I in it?"

Leigh's eyes went wide and she gasped with horror, "What?"

A squawking from the phone drew his attention back to it, and he lifted it to his ear, listened for a minute, then sighed. "I don't *want* to explain it myself, Marguerite. I haven't slept in thirty-six hours. I've spent all night cleaning up your house. She wants answers but I'm filthy and want a shower and— What?"

The way Lucian stiffened made Leigh's eyebrows rise, then he said, "*I* haven't done anything to your house, Marguerite. I was cleaning up the mess *Julius* made when he broke out of the kitchen." He listened for another thirty seconds, then shifted uncomfortably. "Marguerite, I don't want to have to spend the next hour explaining—" He tsked impatiently. "No, I can't control her mind and make her wait. I can't get into her thoughts." He paused, then gave a snort. "No, Marguerite, that *isn't* what it means. It means I'm tired." Lucian made an impatient gesture, then said, "I'm going to take a shower, Marguerite. Here's Leigh."

Her eyes widened in surprise as the phone was suddenly shoved into her hand. Before she could protest, Lucian had turned, walked into the bedroom's adjoining bathroom, and slammed the door. Leigh stared at the closed door for a moment, then raised the phone to her ear and said uncertainly, "Hello?"

There was a moment of silence, then a long sigh, and Marguerite said, "Leigh?"

"Yes."

"He's impossible, isn't he?"

Leigh hesitated, all her protective instincts coming to the fore. For some reason, she wanted to defend the man. "It sounds to me like he's just tired."

"Hmmm." Silence buzzed along the line, then Marguerite asked, "What do you think of him?"

"Well . . ." Leigh hesitated. Her first thought was that she hardly knew him, but then she realized she did know a thing or two. She knew he had taken on the burden of taking care of her during the turn when he needn't have bothered. She knew he was brave enough to go after the rogue vampires rather than relax and enjoy the good health he had.

"Leigh? Are you still there?" Marguerite asked, and Leigh cleared her throat.

"Yes. Sorry. Er . . . he seems strong and brave and caring and concerned."

"Excuse me?" Marguerite asked, sounding surprised. "Caring and concerned, did you say?"

Leigh frowned as she recalled his reaction when he'd found her under the bed, his pulling her out and putting her back in bed again. He'd said she was too weak to be up and about. And he'd brought her food . . . well, dog food, but then she was getting the distinct impression that he didn't eat much.

"Yes, caring and concerned," Leigh said firmly, then tried to think what else she knew about him.

She knew he wasn't afraid to look like an idiot in odd getups, so she supposed he wasn't vain. He seemed well-spoken—when he spoke—and he tended toward grumpiness, or seemed to.

Leigh suspected it was just a shield, a way to keep others from getting too close. She knew how that worked. When she was on the run she'd had to pull on a mask to keep anyone from getting too close. She'd always had her guard up, and to keep people at arm's length she acted cold and what some would have said was bitchy, though that wasn't in her nature. It had been fear-driven, and it made her wonder why Lucian felt he needed a shield to keep people at a distance.

Pushing these thoughts aside, Leigh tried to think what else she could say. The only thing that came to mind was that he looked damned good half-naked.

"Half-naked?" Marguerite asked with interest, and Leigh blinked. Had she spoken aloud? It was a bad habit she had. Usually, she muttered and no one could hear what she was saying, but—like Lucian—Marguerite was an immortal with exceptional hearing.

"Leigh?" Marguerite said after a moment of uncomfortable silence had passed between them.

"Yes?" she asked warily.

Marguerite hesitated, then said, "He may seem grumpy and miserable, but he's a good man. My husband, his twin brother, always said that before Lucian lost his wife and two young children, he was always smiling and laughing. I think the grumpiness is just his way of keeping people at a distance."

Leigh blinked. It was exactly what she'd thought moments ago, except that she hadn't known about his wife. She asked, "His wife and children?"

"Yes." Marguerite said quietly. "It was a very long time ago. Before I married his brother."

Leigh considered this news, then asked, "Why are you telling me this?"

"Because he can't read you," Marguerite said simply.

"I don't understand," Leigh said warily.

"I know." She sighed. "There is so much you have to learn about us; too much for me to explain over the phone. But don't worry. I'll take care of everything. I'm going to call my daughter and she'll help you understand everything. It's probably better this way anyway. Lucian could never understand what we women would think is important to know."

"Okay," Leigh said slowly.

"I'll call her as soon as I hang up, but in the meantime just know you are safe and everything will be fine. All right, dear?"

"Yes," Leigh murmured. "Thank you."

"Okay, I'm going to hang up and call Rachel. You should hear from her shortly after that. You might want to put a pot of coffee on. She's a big fan of coffee."

"Okay," Leigh murmured again.

"Welcome to the family, Leigh," she said, and while Leigh was still blinking in confusion over that, Marguerite hung up.

Leigh listened to the dial tone for a moment and then she, too, hung up. She stood for a minute, unsure what to do. Lucian had told her to find clean clothes in the closet. She'd felt self-conscious about using someone's clothes without their permission, so had chosen to don the terry-cloth robe she'd found hanging from a hook on the bathroom door. Now she felt she would be more comfortable being dressed when this Rachel arrived. On the other hand, she would hardly be comfortable if it turned out to be Rachel's clothes she was borrowing.

Grimacing, she hurried to the closet. Relief coursed through her when she opened the door and saw the row of men's clothes. She'd feel better borrowing something of Lucian's. She would rather be swimming in clothes far too large than meeting Rachel in the woman's own clothes, borrowed without permission.

After rifling through the clothes, she chose a pair of jogging pants, then turned to the shelves on the side of the large closet and pulled a t-shirt from the stack. Leigh knew she'd swim in anything of Lucian's, but at least the joggers had a drawstring she could pull tight to keep up. Taking the clothes with her, she hurried to the room she was beginning to think of as her own, where she doffed the robe and donned what she'd selected. As she'd expected, they were far too large, but she pulled the drawstring tight, and decided it would have to do as she headed for the kitchen.

Leigh had no idea how long she had until Rachel arrived, and she wanted to get the coffee going before then.

The cupboards in the kitchen were mostly empty. There were things like salt, pepper, flour, and sugar, and there were some condiments in the refrigerator, but there was little real food other than that. She wasn't surprised.

It wasn't until she checked the stainless steel storage jars on the counter that Leigh found what she was looking for. They were unlabeled, but one held powdered milk, one held tea bags, another sugar, and the third and largest held coffee. Just enough for two pots by her guess.

Leigh made the coffee, then paced the room as she waited for it to finish dripping. Questions were lining up in her mind like soldiers in formation, one after the other marching across her thoughts. If they weren't cursed, what were they? How would her life be affected now?

Her gaze lifted to the ceiling several times as she paced, and each time a scowl claimed her lips. She understood that Lucian was tired, but it was hard not to be impatient with the lack of answers and the need to wait for this Rachel when he could easily answer her questions.

When the coffee machine buzzed, announcing that the coffee was done, she moved out of the kitchen and up the hall to peer out at the driveway that circled in front of the house. There was no sign of Rachel yet and no sign of a car approaching up the road that she could see. Leigh clucked her teeth impatiently, then glanced toward the stairwell.

Surely Lucian was out of the shower by now? Perhaps cleaning up had refreshed him, made him feel more like talking. She could always go see . . . maybe take him a cup of coffee to sweeten him up.

Biting her lip, Leigh peered out at the driveway and the road beyond again. There was still no sign of an approaching car. She'd just pour a couple coffees, and if Rachel hadn't arrived by then, she'd take a cup to Lucian and ask a question or two until the other woman did arrive.

 Seven

Leigh considered it a good sign when there was no sound of running water coming from the bathroom as she slid into Lucian's room. She was sure it meant he'd finished his shower, as she'd hoped. It was only as she pushed the door closed with her foot and surveyed the empty bedroom that she realized she was lucky she hadn't entered to surprise Lucian in his towel . . . or even naked. That could have been embarrassing. Well, for him at least. The idea was filling her mind with images that made her face flush, but not with embarrassment. *Really, the man is dangerous, walking around with that muscular physique,* she thought, recalling him standing half-naked in the kitchen.

Forcing away the memories and the thoughts they invoked, Leigh crossed to the bedside table to set down the tray she carried. It held two cups of coffee, a bowl of sugar, and a bowl of powdered milk. Having no idea how he took his coffee, she'd brought the fixings with her.

It was bribery, and there was no denying it. She was hoping the coffee might make him look more kindly on her pestering him with questions. Leaving the tray for the moment, she walked to the bathroom door and paused to listen. There was no sound at all coming from beyond the door; no movement, no rustle of material, nothing.

Leigh bit her lip. Perhaps she'd missed him and Lucian had already dressed and left the room. Her gaze slid around the bedroom, but it looked the same to her as when she'd left earlier. Perhaps he'd fallen and hit his head getting out of the shower. That was more worrisome than the first possibility, and she immediately raised a hand to knock sharply at the door.

"Hello? Lucian? I brought you coffee," she announced. When silence was her answer, Leigh frowned and shifted her feet uncertainly. What should she do? Her hand moved uncertainly to the doorknob, but hesitated.

"Lucian?" she tried once more. When there was still no answer, she drew her shoulders up and turned the knob. She had to be sure he was all right.

"Lucian?" she whispered, her voice dropping as the door slid open to reveal the neat, white marble countertop with the sink in it, then a toilet, and finally the tub itself. Her eyes widened in alarm when she saw Lucian lying, seemingly unconscious, in the large clawfoot tub. His eyes were closed, his long eyelashes fanning over the marblelike skin of his cheeks.

Gasping with alarm, she rushed to his side and dropped to her haunches as she reached instinctively to grab his shoulder, though what she'd intended to do, Leigh couldn't say. There was no way she could lift him out of the water by herself. Fortunately, there was no need. The moment she touched him, Lucian's eyes shot open. He stabbed her with a glance that went from sleepy to sharp in a heartbeat, then sent the water roiling and splashing from the tub as he abruptly sat up.

"What's happened?" His voice was harsh, his expression dark with concern.

Leigh stared, suddenly unable to speak as her gaze slid over his wide chest and dropped of its own accord down to where he disappeared below the bubbles that filled the tub. She was surprised that he would have bubbles in his bath, and also disappointed at how it blocked her view of what they hid.

"Leigh?" he snapped, reaching for the towel on the floor beside the tub.

"I— Oh!" Shaking her head back and forth with a jerky repetitive motion, she stood from where she'd been kneeling and abruptly turned her back to him. Then she gave herself a mental slap and forced herself to speak. "There's nothing wrong. I just—I called out, but you didn't answer, and I was worried you'd fallen and hit your head or something."

When her only answer was the soft slosh of water in the tub as the water slowly settled, Leigh risked a glance backward. Lucian had the towel in his hand, but was still seated in the tub, his expression blank.

"You were worried about me?"

She frowned at the surprise in his voice and the bemused look on his face. Surely anyone would have been worried. Turning away before she could be tempted to ogle him once again, she shrugged.

"You said you were taking a shower but there was no sound of running water and no answer when I called out to you," she repeated.

"I decided to take a bath instead. I guess I fell asleep."

"Yes, I saw," Leigh muttered, then cleared her throat

and forced away the image of him naked in the water. "I thought I'd surprise you with a cup of coffee."

"Hmm."

She bit her lip at the skeptical sound to that grunt, and wasn't terribly surprised when it was followed by the sarcastic comment, "And no doubt to take the opportunity to ask some questions."

There was a soft splash as he shifted in the tub, then he said with exasperation, "You're going to hound me until I answer, aren't you?"

"No, of course not," Leigh said quickly, then belied the words by adding, "But if you could just answer a few questions . . . ?"

His snort of disgust wasn't encouraging, and Leigh sensed her chance to get answers slipping away.

"I'm not trying to be a pest," she said apologetically. "It's just that this is my life. And I have no idea what's happened to me, or how it will affect my future, or . . . anything," she finished weakly.

The silence following her words seemed to spin out for a very long time, then she heard a soft curse.

"Oh, very well," he said with resignation. "Ask your questions."

Leigh felt relief course through her, started to turn in her excitement, caught herself, then asked, "Would you like your coffee? How do you take it? I'll fix it and—"

"I don't drink coffee," he interrupted.

"Right." She frowned. He didn't drink coffee. Should she offer to make him tea? Or—

"Ask your questions before I change my mind."

"Yes, of course. Thank you," she murmured, then blurted the first question on her mental list. "If we aren't vampires because of some curse, how are we vampires?"

"Nanos," he answered promptly, and Leigh couldn't help herself, she glanced over her shoulder in surprise.

"Nanos?" she asked uncertainly.

"Yes. I'm afraid it's due to plain old science, not some romantic curse that would leave you soulless."

Leigh grimaced, aware that she actually *was* disappointed to learn it was science, not a curse. Really, how stupid was that?

"I'm going to give you the short explanation," Lucian announced, distracting her. "If you want more in-depth answers, you'll have to talk to my nephew Bastien. He's the answer man. In future, if you have any questions or problems, he's the one to go to. Understood?"

"Bastien," Leigh murmured, nodding.

Seemingly satisfied, Lucian shifted again in the water. Leigh turned quickly away when she realized that her eyes were drifting away from his face, to more interesting bits.

"The short version is I come from a people who were very advanced scientifically. In search of a way to repair wounds and attack diseases such as cancer without invasive surgery, our scientists combined nanotechnology and bioengineering to create bionanos. These were shot into the bloodstream of the ailing or injured person, where they were programmed to make repairs and regenerate cells from the inside.

"It was quite a breakthrough when they succeeded," he acknowledged. "Or seemed to be at first. Several people were treated with it, my mother among them. She was pregnant with myself and my twin brother Jean Claude at the time, which is how we came to be infected."

"Infected?" Leigh queried softly, and glanced back to see him shrug.

"As I say, it seemed to be a miracle cure at first, but

it wasn't long before they realized the nanos did more than intended. They were supposed to repair the wound, or attack and kill the disease and then shut down and disintegrate, for the body to flush out. What the scientists hadn't considered was that the nanos were programmed to search out and find any ailment or injury in the body. While they may have been introduced to a person to attack a cancer, once that was done, they didn't shut down, but turned to other repairs needed in the body."

"And this was a bad thing?" Leigh asked with confusion.

"As it turned out, yes. The human body is in constant need of repair. It's attacked daily by sunlight, age, environmental factors . . ." He shrugged again. "The nanos turn their attention to those things, constantly regenerating themselves and making repairs and helping to generate new cells in their host."

"So the host never gets ill, never ages," she realized.

When he nodded, Leigh considered what he'd said. In effect, his people had found the fountain of youth. She blinked as a question occurred to her. "But why the fangs and the need for blood?"

"The nanos were developed to live in and travel through the body via the blood. They also use the host's blood to make the repairs and regenerate cells as well as themselves. Unfortunately, human bodies don't create enough blood to support all their activities," he explained quietly. "The nanos use up the blood at an excelerated rate and then attack the organs in search of more blood. This problem was dealt with through transfusions before Atlantis fell, but—"

"Atlantis?" Leigh interrupted with disbelief. Some part of her mind had been assuming Lucian and others like him were from another planet or something. It was just what she'd automatically assumed when he said he came from a people who'd been highly advanced. But now he'd referred to *human* bodies not creating enough blood and . . . Atlantis?

"Yes, I am from Atlantis," Lucian acknowledged.

Leigh couldn't help it, she whirled to gape at him. "But Atlantis was . . . that was . . ." She shook her head with bewilderment, not even sure how long ago in history Atlantis was rumored to have existed.

"Eons ago," he acknowledged, sounding weary.

God, she thought, staring at him with a fascinated horror. He'd said his mother was one of the ones the nanos had been used on . . . and she'd been pregnant with him and his twin brother at the time, which meant he and his brother were original Atlanteans. "But that would make you . . ."

"Older than you," he acknowledged dryly.

"Older than me?" Leigh echoed with disbelief. "Lucian, you're older than America. England, even. You're—" She cut herself off abruptly when she saw the closed look that came over his face and realized how rude she was being.

"Sorry," she muttered. An uncomfortable silence filled the room, and then she cleared her throat and forced herself to recall what he'd been explaining before she interrupted him.

"So, before Atlantis fell, this problem was dealt with by transfusions," she prompted.

Lucian frowned, his gaze dropping away as he apparently tried to find the thread of his explanations again. The moment he wasn't looking her way, Leigh found her eyes drifting down over his wide chest and flat stomach. Damn, the man sure looked good for his age. And now she supposed she understood why he was as crusty and grumpy as her grandfather. He certainly came by it naturally. The man was *ancient*.

"Yes, the transfusions." He cleared his throat. "They used transfusions in Atlantis, but when it fell—"

"How did it fall?" she interrupted, curious.

His face darkened briefly with memories that were obviously painful, but then cleared, leaving his expression flat. "A double whammy of a volcanic eruption and an earthquake. Atlantis was on the tip of the continent, separated from the rest of it by a high mountain range. We were an insular society, never looking outward to see what was beyond our mountains. An earthquake changed that. It split the mountain, cracked it open, bleeding the volcano onto the city, then a second earthquake—or the aftershock—swallowed it up. It just sank into the water."

He shook his head. "The few of us who survived were all immortals, and we were suddenly left without our technology. While Atlantis had been advanced technologically, the world we now found ourselves forced to join was peopled by far less advanced societies; hunters and gatherers, for the most part. There were no more transfusions, no more science, but the nanos were still doing what they did and using up our blood to keep us alive and in peak condition. Most of us had never known the hunger for blood until then and were consumed by it, but the nanos were programmed to see to our survival, and on some the nanos made the necessary changes to see to that survival."

"The fangs," Leigh breathed, understanding.

"Yes. The nanos made us evolve into beings able to get the blood they needed . . . we needed. They made us stronger and faster to be more efficient at the hunt, they improved our night vision so we could hunt at night and avoid the damaging rays of the sun that would increase our need for blood, and they gave us fangs to get the blood we needed."

"They made you night predators," she realized.

"Yes. And you are now one, too," Lucian said quietly.

Leigh stared at him with dismay. "But other humans are our prey."

"It's not as bad as it sounds," he assured her quietly. "Especially now that there are blood banks again."

Leigh felt relief rush through her. Of course, there were blood banks. She wouldn't be expected to run out and attack poor unsuspecting people and suck on their necks.

"Despite popular lore, we do not have to kill our prey," Lucian said quietly. "In fact, it's better if we don't. As my nephew Lucern likes to say, that would be like killing the cow that gives the milk. It also would draw attention to our existence. Before the advent of blood banks in this society, we fed a little here, a little there, and did our best not to do anything that would increase the need to feed; hence the reason we avoided sunlight."

"But we *can* go out in the sun," Leigh said, wanting to be clear on that point.

"Yes, but it means consuming more blood," he reminded her. "And the less we had to feed back then, the better if we wanted to avoid detection. Of course, now we can go out in daylight when necessary with little problem so long as we have a supply of extra blood with us."

"I see," Leigh said slowly, then asked, "How much stronger and faster will I get?"

"Really strong and really fast."

Leigh considered his words, recalling how swiftly Donny had moved last night, if it had been last night. She wasn't sure how much time had passed since then, but now that her thoughts had shifted to her attack and turning, other questions crowded into her thoughts.

"Why didn't you kill me along with the others in that house?" she asked. Leigh's memories were becoming clearer as time passed and her confusion lifted. She'd heard the shouts and sounds that broke out once the men left her in the kitchen and hurried down into the basement. She'd understood at once that Morty and Bricker and the third man she now knew was Lucian had been killing the vampires she'd seen in the basement. It was the impetus that had given her the strength to get out of the house and try to escape. By that point, she'd been fleeing them as much as Morgan and Donny.

"There was no need to terminate you. Morgan hadn't had a chance to convince you that you were one of his ghouls, and get you to feed off mortals and so on."

Leigh nodded in understanding, thinking she was lucky in the timing of her attack and when Lucian and the others had made their approach.

"They were rogue. You weren't. So you were spared," Lucian said simply.

Leigh frowned at the answer. "What is a 'rogue'?"

He paused, considering before answering, "There are rules our kind have to live by. If you break these rules you'll be considered a rogue and go up before the council. If you can defend your actions, fine. If not, or if you don't show up, you'll be marked for termination."

"And Donny and the others were rogue?"

"Yes."

"Why? What are these rules?"

"The first rule is that you can turn only one mortal in a lifetime. The second is that you can only have one child every hundred years."

"One child every . . . *hundred* years?" Leigh stared at him with horror. Spacing kids out was one thing, but one every hundred years? Dear God. "Why?"

"Population control," he answered promptly. "It wouldn't be good to let our population outgrow the blood source."

"Oh, I see," she murmured, and did. "So, no turning more than one mortal in my life and no more than one child every hundred years."

"Yes. The other rule is we are restricted to bagged blood except in cases of emergency."

"Okay," Leigh said. It seemed like a good rule to her. She had no desire to go around chomping on neighbors and friends anyway, but just to be clear on things she asked, "What kind of an emergency?"

"If you're in a car crash, or an airplane accident away from blood banks and unable to call in help," Lucian said as an example. "You could feed on a human then if necessary."

"If I survived," Leigh said dryly.

"Unless you're decapitated, your heart's ripped out, or you're trapped and burnt up, you *will* survive," he assured her. "And even with the burning, you quite literally have to be *burnt up*. You'll survive third degree burns all over your body. You basically have to be cremated."

Leigh grimaced at the thought, but said, "I'm guessing the biting is what made Morgan a rogue. He bit me."

"He did more than that, he turned you," Lucian pointed out. "He's turned a lot of mortals, and all of them are feeding on other mortals. He has to be stopped. He's turning people willy-nilly and he's turning them rogue as well."

Making a face, Lucian shifted unhappily in the tub. "The man had them living in that dump, sleeping in coffins, letting them think they had to hide from the sun, and feeding off other mortals and only mortals, and not nicely."

He made a sound of disgust and added, "He, like other rogues before him, is churning out some heartless, bloodthirsty immortals that think they're living a really bad vampire movie. *From Dusk till Dawn* and so on."

Leigh tilted her head curiously. "Do many of your kind go rogue?"

"*Our* kind," Lucian corrected, reminding her she was one of them now. He paused and seemed to consider her question, then said, "Even one going rogue and turning innocent mortals into monsters is one too many."

Leigh supposed that was true. "What makes them turn?"

"What?" He seemed surprised by the question.

"Well, why is Morgan doing this? I mean, Donny was an okay guy, but from what you're saying, he probably thinks he *is* a soulless, cursed creature of the night." Or rather, *child of the night*, as she recalled Morgan using that term. "Why is he doing this?"

Lucian shrugged. "Madness, boredom, who knows?"

Leigh arched an eyebrow. "You have no idea? All these years and no one has noted even one similarity between those who go rogue?"

Lucian considered the matter, then said reluctantly, "They're usually older immortals."

"Older like you?" she asked. When he stared at her blankly, Leigh pointed out, "Well surely you're one of the oldest, aren't you?"

Lucian scowled. "I said *usually* older. Sometimes they aren't. They . . ." He stopped to glare at her, then said, "What made Jack the Ripper suddenly start killing prostitutes? Or what made Charles Manson do what he did? Or Jeffrey Dahmer? Who knows why they suddenly turn? It could be a loss of hope, or anything. Many of them are alone, without families or loved ones or anything to keep them grounded."

"You have family," Leigh said with quiet relief. It wasn't that she'd feared he would suddenly go rogue and take her down with him, finishing what Morgan had tried to start, but still, she found the fact that he had Marguerite and the others reassuring.

"Yes, I have family," Lucian said quietly, then asked, "And what of you?"

Leigh stiffened. "What about me?"

"Do you have family?" he asked. "It can be something of a problem if you do, Leigh. You can't reveal what you are to them and—"

"That won't be a problem," she assured him solemnly, then explained, "My parents died when I was ten. My grandfather raised me, but he died while I was away at Harvard. I'm alone now."

"I'm sorry," he said gruffly, and Leigh shrugged.

"I've been alone a long time. I'm used to it," she murmured, but even as she said the words, she knew they weren't true. She doubted if she would ever get used to being wholly alone in the world.

Lucian cleared his throat, but his voice was still gruff when he said, "If you're finished with your questions, I suggest you leave. My bath is growing cold and I'm going to get out now."

"Oh, yes of course." Leigh stood abruptly and moved toward the door. She still had questions, but the more urgent ones had been answered and the rest could wait. At the door she paused and murmured, "Thank you, Lucian. I know you're very tired and I've been a bit of a pest disturbing your bath and everything, but I—"

"Leigh," he interrupted.

"Yes?" She glanced back wide-eyed.

"I should have answered your questions as soon as you woke up. I should have realized you would—" He shook his head and sighed. Apparently giving up on trying to give her what she was sure was an apology of his own, he simply said, "Just go on. I want out of this bath. Besides, I hear a car coming up the drive and need to see who it is."

Leigh's eyes widened. She couldn't hear anything, but had no doubt that he could, and she was suddenly reminded of Marguerite's promise to send her daughter over to explain things.

"Oh, that will be Rachel," she said, hurrying to open the door. "Marguerite said she'd send her over to help answer questions."

"Rachel?" Lucian sounded more alarmed than relieved to hear someone was coming to help him out like this. Leigh didn't stop to ask why, however. She hurried out of the room, barely noting Lucian's curse as she rushed to answer the doorbell that was now sounding through the house.

As it happened, Marguerite's daughter didn't wait for the door to be answered, Leigh arrived at the top of the stairs and glanced into the hall below to see a man and woman kicking off their shoes and removing light fall jackets by the front door.

The man bore a pronounced resemblance to Lucian, though his hair wasn't quite the same quality of blond. It was more a dirty blond to Lucian's icy, almost white blond. And while he seemed about the same height, his build was a little less muscular and more wiry in the t-shirt and tight jeans he wore. The woman was a redhead; slender, pretty, and confident looking in black dress slacks and a white blouse.

"Leigh?" the man asked, spotting her as she descended the stairs to meet them.

Forcing a smile, she nodded and paused on the last step, but her gaze moved to the woman. "Marguerite's daughter, Rachel?"

"Marguerite's daughter-*in-law* Rachel," the girl corrected with a smile, and then explained, "I was just fortunate enough to gain her as a mother through marriage. My husband, Etienne here, is her son."

"Hi," Etienne said as Leigh's gaze shifted to him, then he added, "I must say you look better in my clothes than I do. But you could have picked a more appropriate t-shirt. I must have left something more suitable than that in my old room."

"These are yours?" Leigh asked with embarrassment, then glanced down at the t-shirt saying and blanched. It read, I'M THE TEENAGE GIRL YOU HAD CYBER SEX WITH IN THE CHAT ROOM.

"It's funnier when a guy's wearing it," Etienne said wryly.

"Etienne is a computer geek. He makes PC games," Rachel said dryly, as if that explained everything.

"Oh," Leigh said lamely.

"Is that coffee I smell?" Rachel asked, glancing toward the kitchen door.

Leigh stared at her wide-eyed, amazed that she could smell it from the front door, but then relaxed as she recalled all she'd learned about their state. Shaking her head, she muttered, "Oh yes, vampires senses."

"Exactly," Etienne said lightly. "Kind of like spidey senses, but with more bite."

Rachel groaned, then smiled at Leigh. "I did mention he was a computer geek, didn't I?"

Leigh merely smiled. Despite the woman's teasing, there was a look of open love and affection on her face as she glanced at her husband.

"Come on. We may as well enjoy a cup while we talk," Rachel said, moving up the hall toward the kitchen.

Etienne picked up a bag off the hall table and followed, then glanced back with a smile. "Come on, Leigh."

"You two sit," Rachel instructed as they followed her into the kitchen. She moved to a cupboard and began to retrieve cups. "You made the coffee and Etienne bought the doughnuts, so I'll pour."

"Doughnuts?" Leigh glanced toward the bag the man held, noting the Tim Horton's name and logo on it as they both settled at the table. "We can eat real food?"

"I wouldn't call doughnuts real food," Rachel said with a laugh. "At least not real healthy, but yes you can still eat food."

"Oh." Leigh's gaze slid to the doughnut bag again, her mouth suddenly watering. She supposed she should have guessed she could still eat by the fact that Lucian had brought her food earlier, but . . . well, it *had* been dog food. And perhaps she could only eat during the change, but wouldn't be able to after. However, if Etienne and Rachel still ate...

Rachel grinned as she carried three coffees to the table. "Guess what the best news you'll hear today is?"

Leigh raised an eyebrow in question as the redhead turned away to retrieve the canisters of sugar and powdered milk. "What's the best news I'll hear today?"

Rachel settled in a seat, then reached into the bag

Etienne had set on the table. She pulled out a jelly-filled doughnut, held it up and announced, "You can eat all the doughnuts you want and won't gain an ounce of weight."

Leigh watched blank-faced as Rachel smiled and took a bite, then chewed with relish.

"Really?" she finally asked with disbelief.

Rachel nodded and swallowed. "No matter what you eat, or how much, your body will work to keep you at peak physical fitness." She let that sink in for a moment, then added, "Of course, it means you have to increase your blood intake."

"Oh." Leigh frowned over this news and Rachel shrugged.

"There's always a price, isn't there?" she said dryly. "Unfortunately, anything you do that causes damage to your body means an increase in the blood you have to consume; overeating, exposure to sunlight, consumption of alcohol . . ." She made a face. "All mean you have to suck back more blood."

Leigh nodded slowly as she accepted this.

"So," Rachel said a tad sharply, after chewing and swallowing another bite of doughnut. "According to Marguerite, Lucian is being his usual pain and refuses to explain things to you."

"My wife isn't too fond of Uncle Lucian," Etienne explained, a hand moving to cover his wife's where it had fisted on the table. "I'm afraid they didn't get off to a very good start."

"I— Oh," Leigh said lamely. She was curious about this claim, but since Lucian had just spent his entire bath explaining things to her, she felt moved to defend him. "Actually, he did answer my questions in the end. In fact, we just finished talking when you arrived."

Rachel seemed more irritated than happy about this news, but Leigh hardly noticed. Her attention was taken up with what Etienne had said before she'd spoken. "I'm sorry," she said with a frown. "Did you say *Uncle* Lucian?"

He raised his eyebrows. "Yes."

"But—" She shook her head. "He doesn't look any older than you."

"Ah." Etienne sat back with a smile. "And how old do you think I am?"

Leigh stared, taking in his youthful skin and demeanor. He wore hip-hugging jeans and a t-shirt that said GEEKS DO IT BETTER. He could have been anywhere between twenty-five or thirty . . . but he was a vampire, she recalled, and Lucian had told her she wouldn't age and her life would be prolonged so long as she didn't get trapped in a fire or decapitated. He could be any age, she realized, and she shouldn't be surprised that Lucian was his uncle, though they looked about the same age.

"Exactly," Etienne said, and Leigh blinked in confusion.

"Exactly?"

"We don't age and we all look about twenty-five to thirty years old . . . well, once we reach twenty-five or thirty," he added.

"Are you— Did you just read my mind?" she asked with amazement.

"I'm afraid so," he said apologetically. "Rude, I know. I'll try not to in future, but it's difficult because you're broadcasting your thoughts at the moment. It happens to everyone when they first turn. You'll learn to tone them down and keep them to yourself eventually."

Leigh shrugged his apology away and asked, "Can I read minds, too?"

"Probably not yet, though you'll gain that skill in time. However, you'll probably never be able to read the minds of the older of our kind unless they're distracted or upset."

"But you can read me?" she asked with interest.

"Yes."

Leigh glanced to Rachel. "And you?"

Rachel nodded.

"Can you control me, too?" Leigh asked, recalling the way she'd found herself unable to move, or struggle, or even yell, while Morgan had bitten her.

"Probably," Etienne acknowledged. "But I wouldn't."

Leigh considered that, her mind slipping back to something Lucian had said on the phone to Marguerite: *No, I can't control her mind and make her wait, I can't get into her thoughts.* She hadn't understood it then, but did now.

"Lucian can't read you?" Rachel asked, her voice sharp with interest.

Leigh blinked, taking in the fact that her mind had been read again, or she was broadcasting her thoughts. Letting it go, she said, "No," then added, "But then he's tired. He thinks that's why."

Rachel turned to her husband with dismay. "He can't read her."

"No," Etienne agreed, a slow smile spreading his lips. "Damn . . . Uncle Lucian's finally met another mate."

Leigh stiffened, but before she could ask what they were talking about, Rachel asked, "Do you have any family down in . . . Kansas, was it?"

"No, I'm all alone and . . ." Leigh paused as the meaning behind the question sank in. "What do you mean *down* in Kansas? Aren't we *in* Kansas?"

"Sorry, but no, you're not in Kansas anymore, Toto,"

Etienne said lightly, then seeing the dismay on her face, said more solemnly, "You're in Canada, Leigh."

"Canada?" she squeaked with disbelief.

"Toronto, to be exact," Rachel informed her, then asked with irritation, "Didn't Lucian tell you *that*?"

"Why am I in Canada?" Leigh asked instead of answering her question.

"Because that's where we live," Etienne said simply. "I gather he brought you up here for my mother to look after, but Mom was on her way to Europe, so he had to look after you himself."

"But how did I *get* here?" Leigh asked. "I wasn't even conscious. Surely they don't just let people drive through the border stops with unconscious women? Or did we fly? They certainly wouldn't have let him carry me on the plane unconscious and covered in dried blood as I was."

"I think he used the company jet," Etienne said soothingly. "There would have only been Lucian and the pilot and co-pilot to see the state you were in."

"Even so, the airport officials—"

"Would have been handled," Etienne said quietly.

"Oh yes, the mind control thing," she said faintly, then asked, "So he just carried me on a plane? Without my purse? I don't have ID, or credit cards, or *anything*."

"It's all right," Rachel said quietly. "You're safe here. And we'll see what we can do about getting your purse with all your credit cards. Where did you leave it?"

Leigh blinked. "I'm not sure. I had it when I was walking home. I think I dropped it, though." She grimaced. "Yes, I did drop it. I remember it hitting the ground."

"I doubt they would have left it lying there in the street," Rachel assured her. "I'm sure they would have taken it when they took you to the house. If so, we can get it back."

Rather than feel relief at these words, Leigh's shoulders slumped with defeat.

"What's wrong?" Rachel asked. "If it's at the house, we can just have someone go out and pick it up." She glanced at Etienne. "Can't we?"

"I'm pretty sure they burnt the house to the ground," Leigh admitted, then added, "Unless that part was just a dream."

"It wasn't." The announcement made all three of them swivel sharply to the open doorway, where Lucian now stood. His hair was still damp from his bath and he was wearing soft, pale blue jeans, and a tight, plain white t-shirt that lovingly hugged his muscular chest. He looked delicious, Leigh acknowledged, as he said, "We set the house on fire before we left."

"Why?" Rachel asked with amazement, then understanding donned on her face. "To remove any evidence of the pack and what they were."

Lucian nodded, then glanced at Leigh and said, "That's another rule; you avoid hospitals, the police, and all other mortal authorities at all costs. Don't go to a hospital, or the doctor's, if you're somehow injured. *Do not* call the police if you have a break-in. Call Bastien. We handle all our problems ourselves. We can't risk anyone in an official position seeing, hearing, or finding something that might give away our existence."

Leigh nodded her understanding, then glanced to Rachel when the other woman patted her hand.

"It's all right, ID and credit cards can be replaced," the redhead said.

"Yes, but in the meantime I'm without," Leigh said quietly. She hated the idea of being dependent on the kindness of these people, who were really—nice as they seemed—strangers. She'd been independent too long to be comfortable with it.

Rachel sighed, then turned a glare in Lucian's direction, obviously blaming him for it. But he merely shrugged and revealed just how much he'd overheard by saying, "I'm not the one who left it in the house."

Leigh made a face at the man as he moved to lean against the kitchen counter. It wasn't as if she'd forgotten it in her rush; she'd been weak and sick and escaping kidnappers, not worrying about her purse.

"Don't worry, Bastien will take care of it," Etienne assured her. "He deals with stuff like this all the time."

"We'll call him in New York as soon as we get home," Rachel added to his reassurance as she got to her feet. "Or actually, later in the day. He'll be asleep by now," she added, glancing at the clock on the wall as Etienne stood up beside her.

"Where are you going?" Lucian asked with a frown as Rachel led Etienne to the kitchen door.

"Home," Etienne said, following his wife out of the room.

Leigh glanced from the closing door to Lucian as he suddenly sped across the floor. He moved fast. Super fast. It was like watching a video on fast forward, and she was left blinking at the closed door with both surprise and curiosity, wondering why he seemed in such a panic over their leaving.

Eight

"Wait!" Lucian hurried up the hall. He caught up to Rachel and Etienne as they stopped to don their shoes and coats. "What about the girl?"

"You mean *Leigh*?" Rachel asked pointedly.

"Yes. Leigh."

"What about her?" She shrugged into her jacket. "Marguerite asked us to come explain things to her, but you already have."

Lucian waved that away impatiently. "She needs training. She has to learn to control her teeth and all those other things a new vampire needs to know."

Rachel arched her eyebrows with amusement. "That's *your* problem. What's the matter, Lucian? Scared of her?"

He stiffened and stared at her coldly. "I've been alive too long to be afraid of anything, or anyone, in this world."

"Hmmm. Yeah, you've seen and done a lot in your life, I suppose," she agreed, then added, "Accept live."

"Rachel," Etienne said in warning tones.

"Explain yourself," Lucian snapped.

"Have you loved anyone in your whole life besides that pitiful excuse for a man who was your brother?"

"I gather someone's been telling tales about the dead," he said, sending a glare at Etienne.

"Are we talking about you or your brother when talking about tales of the dead?" Rachel shot back. "Jean Claude was the only person you've cared about in several thousand years, and he wasn't worthy of it. Well, now you have a woman in that kitchen you can't read, or control, and we all know what that means."

"It means I'm tired and need to sleep so that I can read and control her," Lucian said shortly.

She gave a snort. "Yeah, you tell yourself that."

Rachel turned to the door, then paused, and suddenly turned back. "Try to read me."

"What?" Lucian blinked in surprise at the challenge.

"Let's find out if it's just tiredness."

"No," he said at once, but despite himself, his mind instinctively sought out hers at the suggestion. Lucian stiffened at the one thought that drifted to him.

Coward.

Spotting his reaction, Rachel smiled. It was a wide, satisfied smile. "You *can* read me . . . despite being tired."

Lucian neither denied nor acknowledged it, but his mind was in an uproar. He *had* read Rachel and he'd barely been trying.

"But you can't read Leigh," Rachel continued, obviously enjoying herself. "She's your life mate . . . and you *should* be scared silly."

Lucian's eyes narrowed. "And why is that?"

Rachel smiled. "Knowing what a cold bastard you are, you'll probably mess this up and drive her away. Then you'll miss out on the best thing that might have happened to you."

Lucian ground his teeth together but didn't fight back.

He was hoping once Rachel had vented her spleen, she might be able to get past her anger with him. It would make things easier on everyone.

Reaching out, she patted his shoulder and smiled. "Let's hope the loss doesn't turn you rogue so that we have to hunt you down and terminate your ass. I wouldn't want to upset Marguerite or Lissianna, who—despite everything—both seem fond of you."

Rachel then walked out, leaving Etienne frowning after her. Shaking his head, he turned to his uncle to offer lamely, "It's past our bedtime and she's tired. I'm sure you'll do fine with Leigh. Give me a call if you want any advice."

Lucian stared after the departing man with disbelief. Etienne was the last person he'd go to for advice. Dear God, he had nearly messed up his own relationship with Rachel, and would have lost her if it weren't for the intervention of his mother. *Besides*, Lucian told himself as he closed the door behind them, *Rachel was wrong. Leigh wasn't his life mate.*

He leaned his forehead on the cool wood and closed his eyes, Rachel's words playing through his head. The young woman disliked him, and it colored everything that had to do with him, but—despite his denial of it—everything she'd said might be true.

One of the signs of a life mate for their kind *was* an inability to read their minds or control them. Except for his long-dead wife, Lucian had never encountered that problem before—not with a mortal or a newly turned individual—and this wasn't the first time he'd been tired in his life. Added to that, he suspected their minds had connected while he'd slept on Lissianna's bed. He suspected he'd not had his own wet dream, but shared Leigh's. That was another sign of a life mate.

If it was what happened, he told himself.

Either way, he was suddenly feeling confused and unsure, something else he very rarely felt. He didn't know what was happening, and didn't even know what he wanted to happen.

A life mate. A companion to live out eternity with. Someone of his own to love and greet the sunset with. It was what most immortals seemed to long for, but caring and loving meant being vulnerable to pain if that person was injured or died. Lucian had already suffered that once. He'd lost his wife and two young daughters in the fall of Atlantis. That loss wasn't something he wanted to experience anew.

Straightening, he shook his head and told himself to take it one problem at a time. Right now he couldn't read or control Leigh. If it was a simple matter of exhaustion weakening his abilities, that was fine. After he rested he'd be able to read her. But if it wasn't that, if he couldn't read her even then . . . Leigh could be a life mate for him, and that meant being faced with the possibility of loving . . . and the chance of losing that love once more. Was he willing to give her up now, rather than suffer the pain of losing her later? Probably not. A life mate was a rare and wonderful gift. Having experienced it once, Lucian knew that, and he also knew—if she was his intended life mate—he'd do whatever it took to keep her.

Sleep, he told himself. Despite being able to read Rachel, he was sure he just needed to rest and then would be able to read Leigh. All of this worry might be for nothing.

But he couldn't sleep right away. He had to contact Bastien, or Mortimer and Bricker to see how the hunt for Morgan was going. He also needed to arrange for cleaners to give the house a proper going over.

Lucian supposed he'd also have to arrange for groceries for Leigh. She was newly turned so would still want to eat. And he had to find someone to teach her how to control her teeth and those other things she needed to know to survive as one of them. He simply didn't have the patience for it. Unfortunately, Etienne and Rachel obviously weren't willing, and he still didn't want to trouble Lissianna and Greg with it. Lissianna wasn't just close to giving birth, she was also in the midst of moving. The couple had sold their apartment and bought a house outside the city where they could raise their son or daughter. But that still left Jeanne Louise, or Thomas.

"Lucian?"

He turned slowly, almost reluctantly. Leigh had come out of the kitchen and now walked down the hall toward him. And she looked tired, he noticed. "Would it be all right if I went and lay down for a while? I seem to be tired again."

"Of course," he said quickly, relieved not to have to deal with her at the moment. Between his exhaustion and the business he had to take care of, he didn't have time to handle her, too.

Nodding, Leigh moved past him to the stairs, then hesitated. "I appreciate you bringing me here and taking care of me. I'll try not to be too much of a burden." She paused, then added, "I know you'd rather be out hunting Morgan. It's important he's stopped before he turns some other unsuspecting human. I'll understand if you want to go. I'd muddle through somehow. I mean, you guys had to learn it all on your own after the fall when the nanos changed you. I'm sure I can figure it out as I go along."

Lucian felt his heart soften. She looked so small and

lost as she made that offer, he knew she was hoping he'd reject it. He found himself with the unexpected urge to take her in his arms and make everything better. Instead, he simply said, "Go to sleep, I'll find someone to help me help you. I'll make some calls while you rest."

Lucian sensed her hesitating at the foot of the stairs as he picked up the phone to, yet again, dial Thomas's number. It wasn't until the phone began to ring in his ear that he heard her quiet footsteps move upstairs. He let the phone ring several times before hanging up, then moved into the library to settle at the desk and use the phone there to make his calls.

First, he called the cleaning service that took care of his own home. Unfortunately, it would take a while for them to get a crew together on such short notice and the best they could do was promise they'd have someone at the house later in the day. He then called Mortimer's cell phone. He woke the man from a dead sleep, only to learn that Morgan appeared to have dropped off the face of the earth, as had the Donny that had escaped with him. There had been no more charges on the credit card since his last call. Morgan had apparently holed up somewhere, so Mortimer and Bricker were taking the opportunity to rest.

He called Bastien next, waking him up as well. Lucian didn't apologize, but simply asked him to get to work on getting replacement credit cards and ID together for Leigh when he could, a task he realized was impossible the moment Bastien asked for her full name. Lucian couldn't believe it, but he had no idea what her full name was. Frustrated, he promised to get the information when she woke up, and then tried to call Thomas again . . . and again without success.

Jeanne Louise was his last hope at that point, and

Lucian dialed her number with his jaw clenched, then almost sagged with relief when the phone was answered.

"Hi! This is Jeanne Louise."

"Jeanne Louise?" Lucian said quickly. "This is—"

"If you're calling, you must be one of the few people in the world who hasn't realized I've gone on vacation with Mirabeau," her voice continued, and Lucian slumped in the desk chair as he realized it was an answering machine message.

"If it's urgent, page me, but otherwise I should be back from Europe in two weeks. See you then!"

He set the phone back with a sigh. Lucian considered paging her, but realized if she was in Europe, she wasn't much use to him. It appeared the universe was against him. A situation he wasn't used to at all. He liked to get his way, and worked to make sure it happened. He wasn't doing so well at the moment, however.

Despite the possibility that she might be his life mate, or perhaps because of that, Lucian was more determined than ever not to train her himself. It was as bad an idea as a husband training a wife to drive, in his opinion, but it looked like he had no choice. He'd be training Leigh . . . unless he went over and hunted down Thomas in person. He was considering doing just that when he became aware of scratching at the French doors behind him. Standing, he moved to the door and shifted the curtain to see Julius on the other side, looking pathetic in the early morning fog drifting around him. It seemed he was ready to come in now.

Lucian opened the door to let the dog back in, then ignored him and moved to the leather couch against one wall to lay down. He would take a nap there until the cleaners arrived, then figure out whether he should hunt down his nephew or not.

* * *

Leigh slept for four hours, but was still weary enough when she opened her eyes that she might have rolled over and gone back to sleep if her conscience had let her. However, she was very aware that she'd done little more than sleep during the forty odd hours since escaping the house in Kansas, and felt guilty for such sluggardly behavior.

A hard worker by nature, Leigh normally slept no more than six hours and filled the other eighteen hours of the day with work. Turning or no turning, sleeping this much didn't feel right. She forced herself to get up and went into the bathroom to splash cold water on her face, then went downstairs in search of her host.

After a quick walk through the main floor, she found Lucian in the library. He was fast asleep on the sofa with Julius curled on the carpet before him. Leigh's gaze moved curiously over Lucian as she approached.

He was a handsome man while awake, but his features had a cold, hard cast to them. In sleep, Lucian looked much different. His features were softer, as innocent as a child's, and she found herself smiling as she paused beside the couch.

Leigh petted the dog absently when Julius lifted his head, then bent over Lucian and brushed a stray lock of pale hair away from his cheek. When he murmured in his sleep and turned his cheek into her touch, she felt her heart give an odd little kick in her chest.

Smile fading, she withdrew her hand and simply stared at Lucian. It had been a long time since she'd had such a reaction to a man. Not since escaping the disastrous marriage she'd fallen into at twenty, a mistake it had taken her three years to flee. Once she had, however, she'd sworn to never again put herself in a position where a man had power over her. She'd taken her independence back and liked it. Even now, seven years later, she wasn't ready to risk it on another man. She'd been there and done that, thank you very much.

Straightening, Leigh glanced around the room. Her gaze landed on the phone and paused there. It was noon according to the clock on the desk, which meant it was more than a day since Donny and Morgan had kidnapped her. Her absence would definitely have been noticed by now and people would be worried. She should really call Coco's and assure Milly—her day manager and best friend—that she was fine. She would also have to make arrangements for someone to replace her as night manager at the bar until she returned.

Her gaze slid back to Lucian and her mouth twisted. Even without asking, she suspected he wouldn't be pleased if she made the call, but Coco's was her business, her responsibility. Turning away from the sleeping man, she headed for the door.

Julius immediately got to his feet and lumbered after her. The dog followed her out of the room and along the hall to the kitchen, where he dropped to lay by her feet while she made coffee. There was just enough to brew one more pot, and she was still weary enough to need it.

Leigh's gaze slid repeatedly to the telephone on the wall by the door as she worked, her thoughts distracted by the call she would need to make. Her staff at the restaurant were the closest thing to family she had. A motley crew of runaway wives and abandoned men, they seemed drawn to Coco's and considered her family in return . . . which could be something of a problem at times.

Leigh smiled to herself faintly as she poured water

into the reservoir. Troublesome as their affection and attitude could be, she wouldn't have it any other way. They worked together, played together, and celebrated the holidays together, closing off the restaurant to share a big meal and to open gifts. More important than all that, they cared about and looked out for each other like a family would. Which was rather ironic, she thought now. She hadn't been looking for family when she'd arrived in Kansas, she'd been fleeing the only family she had left—Kenny, her abusive husband.

She'd actually chosen Kansas City because Kenny had always denigrated it, but in the end she loved living there. With a population under 450,000, it was big enough to have everything, but small enough not to be as dangerous as New York and the other really big cities. She'd found the people warm and welcoming.

Switching on the coffeepot, Leigh turned away, her eyes landing on the doughnut bag sitting in the center of the kitchen table. Crossing the room, she peered inside to see that there were still a couple of walnut crunches left.

When the coffee was ready, she doctored it with sugar and the powdered milk they'd used that morning, then carried the mug to the table and pulled the bag of doughnuts toward her. Julius was immediately at her side, and Leigh smiled faintly at the dog.

"Hungry?" she asked.

Julius inched closer and sat on his haunches as he licked his chops. A sucker for the big-eyed, begging look, Leigh shared the doughnuts with him and decided he was a nice dog. He was a little silly looking with his wrinkly face, was as big as a small horse, and seemed to drool an awful lot, but he was also friendly and well-mannered.

"That's it," Leigh announced as she gave him the last bite of doughnut.

Julius accepted the offering, then immediately dropped to lie on the floor as he consumed his last bit of food.

Leigh watched him, then glanced toward the phone, knowing she couldn't put off the call any longer. Moving to the telephone, she wiped her hands nervously on her borrowed joggers, picked up the receiver and dialed the number to the restaurant.

While eating, she had tried to come up with an excuse to explain her sudden absence and being in Canada. She could hardly leave Canada out of it when she'd have to leave this number with Milly in case there was an emergency, and it was obvious this wasn't a Kansas number. Since Milly knew she had no family left, claiming she'd been called north by a family emergency wouldn't work, so she'd settled on the lie that her best friend from Harvard had been in a terrible car accident and she'd rushed up here to offer her support. She hated to lie to Milly, but couldn't think of any other way to explain her sudden absence.

Unfortunately, when the phone was answered and Leigh told her tale, the silence that followed was so long she knew her lie hadn't passed muster. She didn't understand why until Milly finally announced, "The police came to the restaurant with your purse yesterday."

Leigh felt her heart lurch. Her purse hadn't burned up in the fire. Donny and Morgan had left it where it fell. The idiots.

"Some lady a block over from your place let her dog out to relieve himself, and when he came back, he brought your purse with him," she continued. "The woman called the police."

The German shepherd, Leigh recalled. He must have

found it just moments after she was knocked out. He must have carried it home like Lassie. Great.

"Leigh?" Milly sounded concerned.

She forced a laugh and lied. "It was stupid of me. I got the call on my cell phone and was so distressed I guess I dropped my purse when I hurried home. I didn't even realize it was missing until I got inside, and then I thought I left it at the restaurant and didn't want to take the time to go back for it."

Silence echoed down the phone line until Milly finally asked, "How did you buy a ticket to Canada without your credit cards?"

Leigh stiffened, but had always been a quick thinker; living with Kenny had taught her well.

"I have a backup credit card at home. An old habit from when I was on the run from Kenny," she said. While she'd been on the run, no one had known her circumstances, but Milly now knew all about her past. The woman shared a similar one.

"Uh-huh," Milly said. "And how did you get in your house? Your keys are still in the purse."

Leigh licked her lips nervously. "I keep a spare under the flowerpot on the front porch."

"Your cell phone was apparently in your purse, too. Hard to be distracted by a phone call if your phone is in the purse you leave behind in your haste."

Leigh sighed and rubbed the bridge of her nose. Milly was smart. It was why she'd promoted her to manager after buying Coco's.

"And just how did you cross into Canada without some form of ID?" Milly asked.

Game, set, match, Leigh thought unhappily. Releasing her breath on a sigh, she let her hand drop to her side and straightened her shoulders. "Milly, I'm fine. Really.

And I *am* in Canada, and I'd appreciate it if you'd over-night my purse to me here."

"The police have it," Milly said quietly, the tone of her voice saying she was still worried and wasn't happy.

"The police?" Leigh echoed dully.

"They seemed to think it was all pretty serious. First Donny went missing, then you disappeared and your purse was found lying in the middle of a sidewalk in the early morning hours. Everyone here's been a bit shook up, wondering who would be next."

"Of course," she murmured, her mind racing.

"In fact, the police told us that if you or Donny made contact, we were to find out where you were and have you call them . . . then we were to call them ourselves," Milly informed her.

Leigh clenched her fists, hardly aware of the way her nails were digging into her palms as panic crept up on her.

"Do you want the officer's name and number?"

"Just a minute, I need to grab a pen and paper," Leigh said, then pressed the phone to her chest. Her mind bounced wildly around inside her head as she tried to figure out what to do. It wasn't until her gaze landed on the labels beside the speed dial buttons on the phone that her thoughts cleared. The first button was labeled BASTIEN, the second read BASTIEN NY and she distinctly recalled Lucian saying that Bastien was the man to go to when there was a problem.

Well, she couldn't wait until later in the day. Breathing out slowly, she snatched up the pen that hung from a cord attached to a message board beside the phone, then put the receiver back to her ear.

"Go ahead, Milly. What's the officer's name and num-ber?" she asked, then wrote it down as the woman read it out. Leigh made her repeat it once, then told her she'd call her back and hung up. She then lifted the receiver again and immediately pressed the speed dial number for Bastien in New York.

The phone began to ring at once, and Leigh took a deep breath to steady herself, then winced when a sleepy male voice growled, "Hello." She'd woken him up.

"Hello. Bastien?" she asked.

A grunt of acknowledgment was her answer, and Leigh took another deep breath then plunged in, "I'm sorry I woke you, but it's important. My name is Leigh Gerard. I'm . . . er . . ." She paused, at a loss, then asked, "I don't suppose you've heard of me?"

"I have if you're the Leigh my uncle brought back from Kansas," Bastien answered, sounding suddenly awake and alert. She heard the rustle of material and suspected he was sitting up in bed to take this call.

"Yes, that's me," Leigh said, relieved she wouldn't have to explain who she was.

"Has something happened, Leigh?" Bastien asked. "Are you or Uncle Lucian hurt?"

"Oh, no," she assured him quickly. "I mean something *has* happened, but no one's hurt." Feeling guilty for waking him and then making him worry, Leigh explained about her phone call and what she'd learned, as well as the unfortunate events she'd set into motion.

"So you see," she said at the end, "whether I call the police or not, Milly will, and I'm not sure what to do. If I call, they'll ask all the questions she asked, and I just don't know how to answer them. But if I don't call, she'll no doubt tell them what I said and—"

"I understand, Leigh." Bastien sounded soothing, then cleared his throat and asked, "Can I ask you how you knew to call me?"

"Oh . . ." She hesitated. "Well, Lucian said you were the one to go to if there's ever a problem. So when I saw your number on speed dial, I . . . well, I called. I thought you might know what I should do."

"I see." There was a pause and then he asked, "Where's my uncle?"

"Asleep on the library couch," she answered.

"Right." She heard more rustling, a lot of it, and suspected he was getting up and getting dressed. "You did the right thing by calling me, Leigh. I'll take care of this."

"Oh." She blinked at the phone. Just talking about it had calmed her and made her feel more in control. Frowning, she said carefully, "I appreciate that, Bastien, but I didn't mean for you to solve this for me. I was just hoping you might have some idea how *I* should handle it. I didn't expect that they'd have left my purse behind so I wasn't prepared for the questions and—"

"It's all right, Leigh. Lucian was right when he said I handle these kind of situations all the time."

"Not for me," she said quietly. "I'm used to handling my own difficulties."

Bastien was quiet for a moment, then said, "Leigh, I don't want to take away your independence, but this is not a situation you're equipped to deal with yet. A phone call won't handle this. The officer and Milly and probably several other people at your workplace are going to have to have personal visits. Their memories will have to be altered and partially erased, and your purse retrieved. You're just starting to turn and can't do that. I'm afraid you're going to have to let me help you this time."

"But—"

"This isn't just for your sake, but for all of us," Bastien

interrupted. "Anything that draws attention to one of us, draws attention to all of us. Do you understand?"

Leigh let out a slow breath. "I understand."

"Good." The tension left his voice at her assent. "Now, you just relax and let me deal with it, and have my uncle call me when he gets up. All right? I may be in transit so have him call my cell phone."

"All right," Leigh said quietly, and wrote down the number he rattled off to her, writing *Bastien's cell* beside it. "Thank you, Bastien."

"You're welcome, Leigh. Keep a copy of that number yourself in case you need me again, okay?"

"Okay," she agreed, then said good-bye and hung up.

Leigh then stood there for a moment, frowning to herself. She really *was* used to handling her own problems, and wasn't terribly comfortable passing this one on to someone else. On the other hand, she knew he was right and she wasn't yet equipped to deal with it.

She considered the phone for a minute, recalling that she'd told Milly she would call her back, then picked up the receiver and dialed the restaurant again.

"Did you call the police?" Milly asked the moment Leigh identified herself.

"I . . . Yes, but he was on another line when I called," she lied. "He must have been on the phone with you."

"Not me. I was caught on the phone myself," Milly told her. "Donny called."

"Donny?" Leigh asked sharply.

"Yeah. He called and asked for you."

"What did you say?" Leigh asked.

"I said you weren't here, you were visiting a friend in Canada, and then told him to call the police just like I told you."

"You're sure it was him?" she asked with a frown.

Leigh had assumed that she'd heard the last of Donny.

"As sure as I can be. He's got a pretty distinctive voice, Leigh."

She nodded to herself at that comment. Donny wasn't originally from Kansas City either. He was a transplant from New Jersey with a thick Jersey accent. He'd never told her why he'd moved, and she hadn't asked. She'd learned during her time hiding out from her husband that it was best not to ask questions of others that you didn't want asked of yourself. It was a habit that was hard to break now that she was no longer on the run.

"He's not with you, is he?" Milly asked, and Leigh stiffened in surprise, her hand tightening around the phone.

"No. What would make you think that?" she asked with amazement.

"Well, he went missing, then you did—"

"No, he's not here. But he's obviously fine. Don't worry about him, Milly," Leigh said, then shifted the conversation to the restaurant. She gave her instructions on who should fill her position as night manager while she was away, discussed expected deliveries and bill payments, as well as orders that would need to be put in over the next couple of days.

It was a long call, made longer by Milly's constant attempts to pin her down on when she'd be returning. Leigh was evasive and just kept steering the conversation back to business. She had no idea how long this would all take. She hadn't thought to ask either Lucian or Rachel and Etienne how long a turning took. In the end, she told Milly she'd call her back the next day with a date for her return, then said she was getting off to call the police and hung up.

A glance at the clock told Leigh she'd been on the

phone for more than an hour, and she grimaced to herself. She was in Canada, it had been long distance. She'd
have to make arrangements with Lucian to pay for the
call. She had no intention on sticking them with the bill
when these people had rescued her from Morgan's house
and were caring for her through the turn.

Making a mental note to herself not to forget about
the two calls to Milly in Kansas City, or the call to
Bastien in New York, she ripped off the top page of the
phone pad. Leigh copied Bastien's number from it onto
the fresh sheet of paper left behind, then folded the original and slid it into the tiny front pocket of the joggers
she wore. He'd said to keep his number in case she had
any more problems, and she intended to do that.

A whimper from Julius drew her attention then, and
Leigh glanced to where he sat on his haunches, staring
at her from across the room. The moment she looked
his way, the dog stood and nosed the door beside him.
It was wood with a window in the top half. Fortunately,
the sunlight outside was blocked by a dark blind.

When Julius whimpered again and continued to nose
the door, Leigh raised her eyebrows and walked toward
him. "What's the matter, fella? Do you have to go outside?"

Pausing at his side, she used one finger to lift one of
the flaps on the blinds and found herself looking out on
the backyard bathed in sunlight. Releasing the blinds,
she glanced down at Julius.

"Are you a mortal dog, or an immortal?" she asked,
then felt stupid. Not once had anyone mentioned the
possibility of turning a dog. He was most likely mortal.

Shaking her head at herself, Leigh unlocked the door
and pulled it open, relieved to see there was an awning
outside the door that kept the sun from creeping in to

touch her. Reaching for the handle of the screen door, she opened it as well and held it while Julius slid outside.

Once he was clear of the door, she let the screen close again and watched him run around the yard, sniffing here and relieving himself there. The backyard was huge, stretching the distance of a small football field, but Julius didn't move more than twenty or thirty feet away from the door at any time. Even so, he spent a long time jaunting about the yard, and she leaned against the door frame and simply watched, her thoughts drifting over the events of the last day or so and how her life had changed.

When a scratching at the door caught Leigh's attention, she shook her thoughts away and focused on the dog standing on the other side of the door. It seemed Julius was finished relieving himself on every available bush and was ready to come back in.

Smiling faintly, Leigh opened the door, then closed and locked both the screen door and the wooden inner door behind him. She then crossed to the cupboards to take another look for food. Her stomach was actually beginning to cramp with hunger. Leigh supposed she'd need more food than usual as her body adjusted to all the changes it was going through.

She'd just opened the cupboard doors when the doorbell chimed. Leigh stiffened with her hand on the cupboard door, briefly frozen. When the sound came again, she recalled Lucian sleeping in the library. Afraid the noise would wake him, she turned away from the cupboard and hurried out of the kitchen.

Nine

Julius stuck by Leigh's side as she hurried up the hall to answer the doorbell's summons. She patted him gratefully as she reached the door. Her recent experiences had made her somewhat nervous, and she appreciated whatever support she could get.

Leigh shifted the curtain aside and peered out. Two women stood on the front stoop; a full-figured blonde who couldn't have been more than twenty or so, and a thin, older woman with faded red hair, speckled with gray. The redhead was reaching to press the doorbell again, but paused when she spotted Leigh looking out and offered an encouraging smile.

"Hello, Mrs. Argeneau," the woman greeted her as soon as the door swung open. "I'm Linda and this is Andrea. We're from Speedy Clean. Mr. Argeneau called to have someone sent out to clean up the house."

"I'm not Mrs. Argeneau," Leigh said. She forced a smile before glancing uncertainly back up the hall to the closed library door. Should she wake Lucian up?

"Oh." The redhead's voice drew her gaze back. "Is Mr. Argeneau in, then?"

Leigh bit her lip and briefly considered the matter, then stepped back out of the doorway for them to enter and explained, "He's asleep in the library at the moment and I'd rather not wake him. I'm sure he'll wake up before you leave, though."

"Well, that's all right then." The redheaded Linda led the younger Andrea into the house. "He told our dispatcher that he wanted—" She stopped abruptly as she spotted Julius. Her eyes widened at the size of him.

"It's okay. Julius is friendly," Leigh assured her, reaching out to slip her hand under the dog's collar just to be sure.

Both women nodded, but she couldn't help but notice they didn't look all that convinced.

"I'll just take Julius in the living room while you clean. I don't think he got in there with the garbage so you probably don't have to clean that room."

"The garbage?" Linda echoed, and the two women exchanged a glance.

"Yes. I'm afraid Julius was in the kitchen with the garbage and tore it apart. He somehow got the bag tangled around his back paw and dragged it through the house," she explained, frowning as the women exchanged alarmed glances.

"It's all right," she said quickly. "Lucian cleaned up the worst of it. I think he just expects you to go over what he's done."

When the women didn't look much reassured, Leigh gestured to the hall floor, which wasn't as streaky as the kitchen floor but showed signs of a less than perfect cleanup job. "He already washed the floors and picked up the garbage, as you can see. It all just needs a proper going over."

"Okay," Linda said, looking a little more relaxed. "So what does he want cleaned?"

Leigh hesitated, then asked, "Didn't he say when he called?"

"He said a complete run-through," Linda replied.

"Right, well then that's what you should do," she said with a nod, then added, "Just bypass the library until he wakes up."

"All right, if you'll point us toward the kitchen, we'll get started."

After a hesitation, Leigh opened the door beside her. It led into a games' room, she saw, as she urged Julius inside. She'd just leave him there until she got the women started, then find somewhere out of the way for both of them to wait.

Pulling the door closed, Leigh started to move past the women to show them to the kitchen, but slowed as she slid by the older woman. The redhead was standing so close, she could smell her perfume and found herself slowing to a stop and inhaling deeply. It was intoxicating.

Realizing Linda was staring at her wide-eyed, Leigh flushed and said, "Sorry, but that's a lovely perfume. What is it?"

"I'm not wearing perfume." The redhead sounded amused.

"No?" Leigh murmured, but hardly heard her answer. She was having trouble concentrating on much more than the smell taunting her nose. Her vision grew fuzzy and she found herself leaning forward, inhaling again as her stomach cramped and reminded her of its hunger. For some reason the redhead's perfume made her think of food.

"Uh, ma'am?" Linda's voice intruded on her thoughts. "Ma'am, the phone's ringing."

Leigh blinked as she became aware of the strident sound of the telephone. Frowning, she straightened away from the cleaning woman and peered around with confusion, then moved to the phone on the hall table.

"The kitchen's through that door," she said distractedly as she picked up the phone.

"Leigh?" a man said as she watched the women move off into the kitchen.

"Yes?" She frowned at the receiver, not recognizing the voice. "Who's this?"

"Bastien."

"Oh." Leigh relaxed and even smiled, her hunger temporarily forgotten. "I'm sorry. I didn't recognize your voice."

"That's all right. I just called to let you know that everything has been taken care of."

"Already?" she asked with surprise. "Surely you couldn't get from New York to Kansas City and handle everything this quickly?"

"No," Bastien said. "I'm still in New York. I had one of our men in the area do it. My man went to see Milly and the others at your restaurant. He altered their memories. As far as everyone there is concerned, Donny quit work a week ago and you're on a well-earned vacation in Canada."

"Oh, I see," Leigh said.

"He handled the police, too. He got your purse back, removed all files pertaining to you and Donny, and completely erased the two of you from their memory. As far as they're concerned, they've never heard of either of you."

"Wow," Leigh breathed, impressed with the speed and efficiency used in dealing with the matter. It hadn't been that long since she'd called him. Had it?

Her gaze dropped to the digital face of the phone and she saw with surprise that it had actually been almost three hours since they'd talked, then she recalled that she'd been on the phone with Milly for more than an hour, and stood by the door lost in thought for a good while as Julius ran about outside. The time had passed swiftly.

"I'm having your purse couriered to you," Bastien informed her. "You should get it tomorrow morning. My man says there are a couple of credit cards and even cash in the wallet, so he doesn't think anything was taken before it was handed in to the police."

"Oh good, thank you." Leigh twisted the phone cord around her finger, her gaze drifting to the kitchen door. She could hear the tap running; the women were obviously setting to work.

"He said your ID appears to all be there as well, but if there's something else you think you'll need during your stay, he can use your keys and go to your house and collect it before he sends you your purse."

Leigh briefly considered asking to have some clothes packed and sent up, but the idea of someone she didn't know pawing through her closet and panty drawer wasn't an appealing one. She'd rather go shopping tomorrow when her purse arrived. "No. Thank him, though, for offering."

"Okay." There was a pause, then Bastien said, "I heard you talking to someone as you picked up the phone. Is my uncle awake?"

"No, that was the cleaners," Leigh explained.

"The cleaners?" Bastien asked, and much to her surprise, he sounded concerned.

"Yes. Julius broke open a garbage bag and dragged it through the house. Lucian cleaned up the worst of it, but called a service to have someone come and do a more thorough cleanup job," she explained.

"My uncle cleaned?" Bastien sounded stunned. Leigh smiled faintly at his reaction. She opened her mouth to respond, then paused as he said, "Er . . . wait. Uncle Lucian is sleeping?"

"Yes."

"And there are cleaners there with you?" he asked carefully.

Leigh's eyebrows rose. His tone seemed to suggest this was a bad thing, though she couldn't think why. They seemed a perfectly nice pair of women and hardly a threat.

"Maybe you should wake up Uncle Lucian," Bastien suggested, and a disbelieving laugh slipped from her lips at the idea.

"There's no reason to wake Lucian. I'm perfectly capable of overseeing a couple of cleaning women. Although I suppose I'll have to wake him before they finish, since I'm not sure what arrangements he made to pay them." She frowned as she considered that, then added, "But I see no reason to wake him up before then. I don't think he's had a lot of sleep in the last couple of days."

"Yes, but—"

"Bastien, I appreciate your helping out with the police and Milly and I'm quite impressed with how quickly and efficiently you handled it, but please don't make the mistake of thinking I'm some defenseless little twit who needs to be sheltered and taken care of. I'm perfectly capable of directing a couple of cleaning women on my own. I'm also safe. Linda and Andrea seem perfectly nice, and even if it turns out they aren't, Julius is here with me and Lucian is only a shout away."

"Yes, but—"

"No buts," Leigh interrupted firmly. "Everything is fine and I thank you very much for your help. Now, you should go back to sleep. I know I woke you up when I called the first time. I'm going to go grab something to eat. I'm having hunger pangs like crazy."

"Oh, damn," Bastien breathed, then said urgently, "Leigh—"

" 'Bye, Bastien." She hung up and shook her head with mingled amusement and exasperation. While it was nice of him to worry, she'd taken care of herself, and even run a business, for years all on her own. This experience had temporarily left her off kilter, but that was to be expected. Being kidnapped, bitten, force-fed blood, and then finding out you'd been turned into a vampire—a creature you previously thought was mythical in nature—would knock anyone off balance. However, she was starting to feel more like her old self again.

Leigh thought it was probably the second phone call to Milly that had done it. Talking shop and giving instructions had returned some of her self-confidence and made the world feel more its old self. It had reminded her of who she was, who she'd fought to become—a strong, independent woman with her own business.

Moving away from the phone, she headed for the kitchen in the hopes that another look around would turn up some food. She already knew the cupboards and refrigerator were bare of anything edible, but she hadn't checked the freezer and was hoping there would be something in there, even if only a microwavable meal. Otherwise, she would be forced to do what she could with the flour and sugar and other staples in the cupboard and make some cookies or something. Not a very wholesome meal, but filling enough to stop the cramps in her stomach, she hoped.

The blonde, Andrea, was on her knees scrubbing the kitchen floor when Leigh entered, but Linda was nowhere to be seen. Leigh supposed the redhead had gone upstairs to start cleaning there. She'd apparently been so distracted with her telephone call from Bastien, the woman had slipped by without her even noticing. Leigh hoped she hadn't been saying anything the woman might have found questionable when she'd passed.

"Sorry," Leigh said when the blonde glanced her way as she entered. "I'm just a little hungry. Actually, I'm starved," she corrected herself with a laugh. "I wanted to see if there was anything in the freezer to heat up."

"Go ahead," the girl said with a smile. "I'll just do this side of the kitchen floor until you're done."

"Thanks." Leigh moved to the refrigerator and opened the small freezer door, her disappointed gaze sliding over the empty shelves inside.

"Nothing?" Andrea asked as she closed the door.

"No," Leigh admitted with a sigh. "There isn't a thing in this house to eat unless I want to bake cookies or something."

"Mmm, cookies. My favorite." The blonde grinned.

Leigh smiled wryly in return and moved to the cupboard to survey the dry goods available. There was flour, sugar, oil, nuts, chocolate chips, and various extracts, but she just stared at them with frustration as she said, "Mine, too. Unfortunately, I don't know any recipes by heart."

"No recipe books here?" Andrea asked, her gaze sliding across the countertops as if she might spot an errant cookbook lying around.

"I don't know. This isn't my house, I'm just visiting," Leigh admitted.

"Maybe there's a recipe on the flour bag or something." Dropping the sponge in her bucket, Andrea got to her feet and joined Leigh at the cupboard.

Leigh stepped back automatically to make way for her to reach in to pull out the flour bag, but then stopped and found herself inhaling deeply as she caught a whiff of the blonde's perfume. While she'd been impressed with Linda's perfume, Andrea had on a great scent, too. One with a sweet edge. Leigh closed her eyes briefly as she inhaled again. Canadians really had some exceptional perfume, she decided, breathing in deeply as the girl turned the flour bag in her hand, searching for possible recipes.

"Nothing here." She set the bag of flour on the counter, then reached in to retrieve the chocolate chip bag as she added, "These *always* have recipes."

"Yes," Leigh murmured, taking a step closer . . . the better to smell her.

"Ah ha! Just as I thought, they do have a chocolate chip recipe on here," Andrea said with triumph. "Let's see, flour. Got that. Brown sugar and white sugar?" She paused to peer in the cupboard, then nodded. "Got that. Baking soda?"

Leigh moved closer, ostensibly to look over her shoulder and into the cupboard for baking soda, but really to get a better sniff of Andrea's perfume. It was the most incredible scent she'd ever smelled. Tantalizing . . . sweet yet pungent . . . yummy.

She felt her stomach ripple as if in agreement, little biting cramps stinging at her. When Andrea bent slightly to check the lower shelves, Leigh found herself following and leaning in closer until her nose was a bare inch away from the back of the blonde's neck. She inhaled again.

"There it is!" Andrea jerked suddenly upward and the back of her head slammed into Leigh's face.

"Ouch!" both of them said at once, and Leigh stumbled back several steps, her hand going to her nose as pain exploded there.

Grabbing the back of her own head, Andrea turned to her with surprise.

"Sorry, I was trying to help you look for baking soda and got too close," Leigh muttered, closing her eyes to hide the confusion now swirling through her thoughts. Just before Andrea had straightened, Leigh had felt her teeth slip out and had been consumed by the oddest urge to sink them into the girl's neck. A bad instinct, she knew. Immortals were *never* to bite a mortal except in case of emergency. It was one of their few rules, and one she could be killed for disobeying. She had no desire to go rogue.

"Are you all right?" Andrea's voice was full of a concern Leigh didn't understand until the blonde added, "You're bleeding."

Making sure to keep her mouth tightly closed to hide her teeth, Leigh took her hand away from her nose and stared at the blood on it. She could feel more blood dripping down over her upper lip and instinctively tightened her lips to keep any from getting into her mouth.

She suddenly understood why first the redhead and then Andrea had smelled so good to her. It wasn't a *perfume* she'd smelled on them, it was their *blood*. She seemed to be drowning in the scent at the moment and her stomach was going crazy, rippling and cramping and urging her to lick the blood from her own hand. Fortunately, she retained enough good sense not to do that. At least not in front of Andrea.

"Boy, I really cracked you one." Andrea's eyes crinkled with concern as she moved closer to peer at her now throbbing nose.

Leigh closed her eyes against temptation as the blonde

drew nearer. She was *hungry*, and Andrea was the food her cramping body wanted. Her mind was screaming, *Just do it. Just bite the girl and draw her warm, sweet blood into your body. It will nourish you. You'll feel better. The pain will end.*

Gritting her teeth to keep from acting on these urges, Leigh realized she had completely misunderstood Bastien's concern about her being alone with the cleaners. It hadn't been *her* welfare he'd been worried about. She probably wasn't the first newly turned immortal to mistake her need for blood for a need for food and let it carry on until she was ready to take a bite out of the first likely mortal to come along.

And it *had* been a mistake. If she had realized the hunger pangs she was suffering were for blood, she would have gone straight upstairs and raided the small refrigerator in the room she'd woken up in. But she hadn't known, and now was standing in the kitchen, unable to make herself move away from Andrea and the temptation she represented, yet unwilling to do what her body was encouraging her to do and bite her.

"Here."

Leigh blinked her eyes open as Andrea's hand urged her own away from her face. The blonde had grabbed a paper towel and moved in close to try to help. The only problem was, her proximity made it harder for Leigh to control the desire to bite her. She was drowning in the smell of blood, both her own and the more subtle scent of Andrea's as it pulsed through her veins. And—Leigh realized suddenly—she could actually *hear* the blood pulsing through the woman, a steady throb of the nourishing red liquid that she knew would be warm and would chase away the cramps eating away at her stomach.

Realizing she wouldn't be able to find the strength of will to move away herself, Leigh started to open her mouth to say something, *anything*, to make the girl move away instead. She'd barely started to open her mouth, however, when she recalled her teeth and snapped it closed again. She was quick enough that the girl didn't seem to notice her fangs, but the moment her lips began to part, the blood that had been dripping over them slipped into her mouth. It dripped straight onto her tongue, where it seemed to explode full and sweet through her mouth, bringing her taste buds to roaring life.

Lucian woke up with a stiff neck and aching back. That was his first hint that he'd slept longer than intended. The couch in the library obviously wasn't made for long snoozes, he acknowledged, peering around the dim, book-lined room.

Forcing himself to sit up, he slumped against the back of the couch and raised a hand to rub the back of his neck, massaging the sore muscles until some of the pain eased. He then let his hand drop back into his lap and glanced toward the clock on the desk. His eyebrows jerked upward when he saw that it was now late afternoon. He had definitely slept much longer than intended.

Shaking his head, he knuckled the sleep from his eyes, his mind now crowding with all the things he had to do. There were at least three phone calls he had to make. First he wanted an update from Mortimer and Bricker on the hunt for Morgan, then a call to Thomas was in order. The man had to answer his phone eventually, and when he did, Thomas was going to get an earful. There was no way he would believe his nephew wasn't deliberately avoiding his calls, and that simply wasn't acceptable.

He was a member of the council and deserving of respect. There had been a time when he could have had Thomas flogged for less. Of course, that was long ago. Immortals, like the mortal world, had softened over the centuries. They weren't as soft as today's society, which still believed in capital punishment but no longer held with the barbaric torturers of the past.

Pushing aside his irritation with Thomas, Lucian considered that before those other calls, he should see about the cleaning service. He was surprised they hadn't yet arrived, but was sure the doorbell would have woken him if they had.

Standing, he moved to the phone on the desk, picked it up, then paused as he recalled that he also needed to call Bastien back with Leigh's full name so he could take care of the ID problem. Unfortunately, he didn't yet *know* her full name. Deciding he'd rather make all the calls at once, Lucian set the receiver back in the phone. He really should go check on her before he started making his calls, he supposed, although it was surprising that she hadn't already awakened and come to find him. Leigh should be starved by now.

Lucian headed out of the room, thinking he could do with a bag of blood or two himself. He was halfway upstairs when he became aware of the sound of a car racing up the driveway. Pausing, he turned back and glanced to the front door.

It was probably the cleaners, he realized, and supposed he should let them in and get them started before checking on Leigh. Raising his hands, he ran them over his face to scrub away any last remnants of sleep, then ran his fingers through his hair in an effort to make sure it wasn't standing on end as he started back down the stairs.

By the time he reached the door, the approaching car had come to a halt in front of the house with a squeal of tires. The sound came to him muffled through the door, but his hearing was exceptional and he had no problem distinguishing the slamming of two car doors that followed. It seemed obvious the cleaners were in a hurry to set to work, though he couldn't imagine anyone being *this* eager to clean.

Reaching for the door, he pulled it open before they could ring and found himself staring not at a pair of anonymous cleaning women, but at Rachel and Etienne. He blinked in surprise at the couple, his weary mind slow to understand why they would be at the door at this hour of the day. They had left after daybreak that morning, and he would have expected them to still be sleeping at this hour in the afternoon. Before he could ask why they were there, Rachel pushed past him into the house.

"Where is she?" she demanded sharply, pausing several feet past him and turning back to spear him with angry, bloodshot eyes. It seemed he was right, Rachel obviously needed more sleep.

"Where is who?" Lucian asked as Etienne followed his wife inside and closed the door.

"Leigh," she said impatiently. "Bastien called and woke us up. He was concerned about her."

Lucian's eyebrows flew up on his forehead. "Why?"

It was Etienne who answered. Moving to his wife's side, he took her hand, the action seeming to soothe her temper at once as he said, "Bastien said you were asleep."

"I was," Lucian acknowledged. "I just woke up a minute ago. I was heading up to check on Leigh when I heard your car. She's still sleeping."

"No she isn't." Rachel's voice was so certain that Lucian narrowed his eyes.

"How do you know? You just got here."

"She called Bastien around noon," Etienne informed him, and Lucian blinked.

"Why?"

Rachel and Etienne exchanged another glance.

"I'll explain," he said to his wife. "Why don't you go find Leigh."

Nodding, Rachel leaned up to kiss him, then hurried upstairs. Both men watched her go, then Etienne quickly explained about Leigh's calls to her restaurant in Kansas City, her call to Bastien, and what his brother had done to take care of the matter.

"When he called her back to tell her everything was taken care of, Bastien was a bit alarmed when she said you were sleeping and the cleaners were here," Etienne explained.

"The cleaners?" Lucian said with surprise. "They're here?"

"Apparently," Etienne answered, and glanced to the stairs as Rachel appeared at the top and jogged quickly down.

"The only person up there is a redhead vacuuming the room you're using, Lucian," Rachel announced as she reached the bottom of the stairs and joined them. "She said there was another cleaner downstairs in the kitchen."

They all turned to glance toward the kitchen door.

As if on cue, it suddenly burst open and Leigh rushed out. She hurried halfway up the hall, then stopped abruptly at the sight of the three of them standing there.

Lucian stared at her with growing horror. It seemed Bastien had been right to worry. There was blood on her face and hands, her teeth were fully extended, and her face was covered with horrified guilt.

"Ooops," Etienne muttered, and Rachel whirled on Lucian, her face a picture of fury.

"How could you?"

"Me?" Lucian blinked in bewilderment. "I haven't done anything."

"Exactly," she snapped, and turned to hurry after Leigh, who rushed past them and raced upstairs.

 Ten

"And then I straightened and unintentionally slammed my head into hers. I'm afraid we hit pretty hard. When I turned around, her nose was bleeding."

"A nosebleed," Lucian said with disbelief.

With Rachel attending to Leigh, he and Etienne had headed straight into the kitchen. They'd expected to find either a dead cleaner or a hysterical bleeding one. Knowing Leigh wouldn't yet have been able to control the woman's mind, they'd expected a bloody mess. What they found instead was a completely intact blonde, calmly scrubbing up drops of blood from the kitchen floor.

Spying them, she sat back on her haunches and asked if "the lady" was all right, then proceeded to explain what had happened.

"A nosebleed," Etienne echoed, and Lucian peered his way. They exchanged a relieved glance.

"Yes." The blonde was still looking worried. "Is she all right? She was pretty upset when she ran out of the kitchen. I tried to help, but she pushed me aside and hissed at me to stay away from her, then charged out. I didn't mean to hurt her."

"I'm sure she knows that," Etienne soothed, and

Lucian left him to it. He had never been good at the touchy-feely handholding of emotional women.

"She has a . . . er . . . phobia," Etienne said, lying to explain away Leigh's odd actions.

Leaving him to his good-intentioned lies, Lucian slid from the room to go check on Leigh. While he'd rather have bamboo shoots shoved under his nails than willingly put himself in the same room as Rachel in the mood she was in, he suspected not going up there would just give her something else to criticize him for. Besides, he found himself oddly concerned about Leigh's well-being. She'd shown surprising strength by not biting the cleaner, especially at this point in her turning and with the scent of blood probably driving her wild. Most wouldn't have had such control. But then, she'd shown an incredible amount of character already.

Lucian had seen a lot of newly turned immortals down through the ages, and the majority didn't take it as well as Leigh had . . . at least not if they were turned unwillingly. But she appeared to have accepted what she'd become, and seemed determined to just get on with learning all she could about her new status and how to function as an immortal.

A pang of guilt nipped at Lucian as he realized he'd been of little help so far. Tired and dismayed to find himself burdened with her, at first his only concern had been to find someone to dump her on. He'd answered as few questions as possible, even going so far as to call Marguerite long distance in Europe so he didn't have to explain things to her himself.

Actually, he realized, every accusation Rachel had thrown at him over the last day had been true. Not that he'd admit that to her, he thought as he reached Leigh's room and opened the door.

The two women were seated on the side of the bed. While Rachel was rubbing her back soothingly, Leigh had a blood bag stuck to her mouth, tears were streaming down her face, her eyes were red and puffy, and her nose swollen and still bloody. She looked just adorable to him.

Pushing that thought impatiently away, Lucian narrowed his eyes and concentrated on slipping into her thoughts . . . and concentrated . . . and concentrated . . . and—

"She didn't bite the cleaning girl."

Lucian blinked at that announcement and glanced down to find Rachel now standing at his side. He'd been concentrating so hard on Leigh, he hadn't noticed when Rachel stood up and moved to join him by the door.

"I know," he said calmly. "The cleaning woman explained everything."

Rachel nodded and tilted her head, considering him with a solemn expression. "You still can't read her."

Lucian's mouth tightened but he didn't say anything. She was right, but he hadn't yet had time to come to grips with the issue himself, and certainly didn't want to discuss it with Rachel. Rather than address the subject, he asked, "How is she?"

For a moment he thought Rachel might ignore his question and pursue the matter of his not being able to read Leigh, but then she heaved a sigh and said, "She's upset. I think she's scared of herself now, of what she'll do."

Lucian relaxed a little and nodded. "I'll talk to her."

"You?" she asked with surprise, and he felt irritation flicker through him.

"I have been an immortal a long time, Rachel. I do know *something* of the matter."

"Yes, but this isn't— This is—" She grimaced, then simply said, "It's not about how many pints of blood she'll need a day, or what the change will do to her physically. It's emotional stuff, Lucian, and somehow I don't think that's your strong suit."

He glared at her for a moment, furious, mostly because she was correct. Emotional garbage wasn't really where he was at his finest. However, he was the one who had brought her here, and he was the one who couldn't read her. She might be his future life mate. It seemed to behoove him to learn how to deal with Leigh, and understand her emotional perspective so he could help her through this difficult landscape. Besides, how hard could it be?

"Etienne is down in the kitchen," he announced meaningfully, then left her to make her exit and walked to the bed.

Lucian heard the door close softly as he paused in front of Leigh. His gaze slid over the two empty bags on the end of the bed beside her, and he found himself smiling faintly. Leigh was binging. Consuming bag after bag of blood, in the hopes she'd fill herself up so she couldn't *possibly* be interested in biting again, he realized, then congratulated himself for being so insightful. Maybe this emotional stuff wasn't as hard as he'd thought.

His gaze shifted back to her and he noted that she'd stopped crying. Thank God! He hated weeping women. There was nothing so difficult to deal with as a weeping woman. They didn't listen, made no sense, and left a man feeling guilty and helpless. He hated that.

Feeling awkward just standing there, he settled himself on the bed where Rachel had previously sat, then turned to peer at Leigh. She met his gaze and they simply stared at each other as she continued to feed. Her eyes were huge and luminous after her tears, their color a beautiful golden brown now swirling with emotion. They were sad, but there was also shame, anger, hurt, and loneliness there. Lucian felt a twinge in his chest as he recognized the loneliness. It was something he often saw in his own eyes on looking in the mirror.

He reached out to pat her hand awkwardly, then cleared his throat before speaking, and still his voice came out gruff as he said, "It's all right."

When Leigh's eyes widened over the shrinking blood bag in her mouth, he added, "You didn't bite her. That was very strong of you. Not everyone could have resisted, but you did."

Lucian patted her hand again and said reassuringly, "You did good. I should have warned you about the hunger. This was not your fault. It's my fault for sleeping when you needed me."

Feeling he'd said what needed to be said to soothe her, he would have stood then and left, but found his gaze sliding over her again. She was wearing the same god-awful outfit she'd had on earlier; the overlarge joggers and a t-shirt she was swimming in. His gaze paused on the writing on the front of the t-shirt and his eyes widened incredulously: I'M THE TEENAGE GIRL YOU HAD CYBER SEX WITH IN THE CHAT ROOM.

Lucian blinked several times, one part of his mind telling him that as she had no clothes of her own here, the t-shirt was borrowed, and probably from Etienne. He was the computer geek in the family. The other part of his mind was wallowing in wholly inappropriate ideas. He wasn't sure what cyber sex was, but he did recall good old-fashioned sex, and while he hadn't been moved to indulge in it in . . . well, a period too long for any self-respecting man to admit to—his mind had no problem throwing up image after image of himself naked and sweaty and entwined with an equally naked and sweaty Leigh.

Lucian closed his eyes and almost groaned aloud. He had a problem. He couldn't read Leigh, couldn't control her, and he was lusting after her. And that was rather startling. He was an old man. An *old*, old man, and she was so young compared to him. He didn't look old, but he sure as hell felt old sometimes . . . most of the time. All right, *all* of the time. And she was like spring, fresh and sweet and innocent to the ways of the world, as proven by the bruised, wounded look in her big wet eyes.

"Dammit!" Leigh snapped, pulling the now empty blood bag away from her mouth.

Well, she was mostly *sweet and innocent*, Lucian corrected as he opened his eyes to find her leaning to the side to retrieve yet another bag of blood from the refrigerator.

"I could just kill Donny!" she growled.

Okay, forget the sweet and innocent, he thought. It was overrated anyway. She was still young, Lucian thought wryly as she continued her rant.

"I nearly bit that girl. Why couldn't Donny have had a crush on someone else?"

Lucian stiffened. "A crush?"

"Well, why do you think he dragged me off the streets?" Leigh asked with exasperation. "He was rambling on about how he'd chosen me for his own, and we'd be together forever, eternally happy in our coffin built for two, blah blah blah. As if I'd want to be with *any* man forever."

"You don't?" Lucian asked with a frown.

"Hell no!" Leigh exclaimed firmly. "I've already been married once."

Lucian's eyebrows flew up. This was news to him.

"Three years of that was more than enough for several lifetimes," she informed him grimly.

Lucian pondered that, then asked, "Not a happy marriage, I take it?"

Leigh snorted. "Not if you don't like waking up bruised and battered every morning."

"He *beat* you?" Lucian asked, eyes narrowing. If there was one thing he hated, it was bullies and cowards, and a man who beat a woman was the worst kind of cowardly bully. "Give me his name and I will hunt him down and kill him for you."

Leigh paused and blinked at him in surprise, then shook her head. "Too late, he's dead." She smiled faintly and added, "Thanks for the offer, though."

From her tone of voice and expression, Lucian knew she thought he'd been joking. He hadn't, and opened his mouth to tell her so, but the sound of a throat being cleared drew his gaze to the door.

"Lucian, can I speak to you?" Rachel said, her eyes wide and eyebrows flying about in a manner that suggested to him she felt it was important. He glanced back to Leigh to find she'd popped a fresh bag of blood to her mouth. With no excuse to avoid it, he reluctantly joined Rachel by the door.

"You didn't leave," he accused her, and glared.

Rachel waved that away as unimportant and ushered him into the hall.

"You can't tell her you were serious about killing her husband," she said firmly as soon as the door was shut.

"Why?" Lucian asked with surprise.

"Because killing is wrong," she said, as if speaking to a particularly dull-witted child.

Lucian snorted at the suggestion. "Rachel, once you've

lived a couple hundred years, you'll come to realize that some people just need killing. For those people, killing them isn't wrong, it's the *not* killing them and leaving them to hurt others that is."

"Lucian—"

"Should we leave Morgan to go around ripping the throats out of unsuspecting mortals—like Leigh—willy-nilly?" he interrupted.

Rachel blinked, hesitated, then said, "No, of course not, but . . ."

"But?" Lucian arched his eyebrows.

"But Morgan's an immortal."

"Ah." He nodded with sudden understanding. "I see."

"You see what?" Rachel sounded annoyed.

"You're a racist."

"What?" she cried with shock. "How could I be racist against immortals? I *am* one."

"That may be, but if you believe it's all right to kill off immortals who hurt and turn unwilling people, but not humans who hurt and kill . . ." He shrugged. "Perhaps you haven't fully embraced your new status."

"That's not it at all. It's just . . . It's not the same thing," Rachel argued, but there was little heat behind her words, and he could see she was considering the matter. That was enough for him.

"Very well, I won't tell Leigh that I wasn't joking about killing her husband. He's dead anyway, so it doesn't matter. However," Lucian added, his voice becoming irritated, "I would appreciate it if you'd stop reading my damned mind."

"I—"

"Don't even try to deny it, Rachel," he interrupted. "The only way you could have known what I was about to say was if you'd been reading my thoughts."

She shrugged, a guilty smile curving her lips, then tilted her head and asked, "Why can I read your mind all of a sudden, Lucian?" When he just frowned, she added, "I've never before been able to do it."

He remained silent and avoided her gaze.

"Though, as I recall," Rachel went on. "Etienne had a problem controlling his thoughts, too, when we were first together. It annoyed him no end that everyone could suddenly read his thoughts and he couldn't block them as usual."

Lucian's mouth twitched.

"Is it something to do with the life mate thing?" she asked curiously.

"She isn't my life mate," he ground out stubbornly and Rachel shook her head with disgust.

"I know, you know it's true. You just want private time to adjust. I can read your mind, remember?"

"And you've taken full advantage of that," Lucian responded grimly. He'd been subconsciously aware of a ruffling of his thoughts several times earlier that morning and this afternoon while Rachel and Etienne were there, but was too distracted to pay it much attention. Now he realized that while he'd been fretting over Leigh, Rachel—and perhaps Etienne, too—had stolen in and been rifling through his thoughts like a couple of thieves.

"Yes, I have," she said without shame. "And I'm glad I did."

His gaze narrowed on her warily. "Why?"

Rachel hesitated, then chose to ignore the question and said instead, "She *is* your life mate, Lucian. Even you have acknowledged that in your subconscious, if not consciously."

"That doesn't mean I have to do anything about it," he pointed out.

"No, I don't suppose it does," she agreed quietly. "You can ignore it and dump her on someone else to deal with and then avoid her, I suppose. But tell me one thing."

"What?" Lucian asked warily.

"In all your years of living—and there have been many I know—how many other people, mortal or immortal, have you come across that you could not read or control?"

"Easily a hundred," Lucian answered promptly.

Rachel's eyes narrowed and he felt the ruffling in his head, then she said dryly, "I mean those who haven't been insane." She shook her head. "And don't bother lying again. I already know that Leigh is the first sane woman you've met since the fall of Atlantis whom you couldn't read or control."

Lucian stared over her shoulder, not responding.

"Are you willing to wait several more millennia? Alone?"

Lucian frowned at the suggestion. In truth, he was already tired of living. When he was home alone, he was bored. When he was out working for the council, he was bored plus angered, depressed, exhausted, and saddened by the cruelty and uncaring he saw around him. People could treat other humans—whether mortal or immortal—worse than the cruelest master would treat a dog, and sometimes he just...

He ran a frustrated hand through his hair as he let those thoughts go. The truth was, ever since pulling Leigh out of the doorway in that kitchen in Kansas City, his life had been altered. He'd been annoyed, exasperated, curious, excited, and interested by turn. His life was actually more interesting at the moment than it had been in centuries, perhaps millenia. Had he not taken her from that house, he would now be in Kansas hunting Morgan. Once that was over, he'd be at home, watching all the latest releases on the movie channels, reading the latest releases of books, then dipping into old movies and old classics to fill time once those were caught up on . . . Or he'd sit alone in the dark, staring at the walls, trying not to think of the things he'd done and seen in his life.

But since arriving here with Leigh . . . well . . . he had done none of that. Between cleaning up after Julius and caring for Leigh during the turning, he hadn't had time for anything else.

To be honest, he had no idea what to expect next. From anyone. Rachel, who normally just glared and glowered at him, seemed to be trying to help. Thomas, who normally would have jumped around at his beck and call, was avoiding him. And Leigh . . . well . . . he didn't have a clue what to expect from her. First, she'd taken this all much better than he'd expected, and now she was having fits over *almost* biting someone.

"Lucian," Rachel said quietly, drawing his attention back to her. "When I first met you at Lissianna and Greg's wedding, I thought you were the meanest, coldest son of a bitch on the planet."

"Thank you, Rachel. I *do* try," he said drolly.

Her lips twitched with amusement at his sarcasm, but she reminded him, "You threatened to have me killed if I didn't toe the line and lie about what Pudge had done."

"He tried to kill Etienne and nearly killed you instead," Lucian began impatiently. "All we wanted you to do was—"

"It doesn't matter." Rachel waved it away with some impatience of her own. "The point is I've been angry with you ever since then."

"Yes, I did notice," he said dryly.

"But," Rachel continued determinedly, "not so angry that I haven't seen your position in this family."

Lucian's gaze narrowed. "What do you mean?"

"I mean, you are the strength and backbone. Everything you do—including threatening me that day—you do for your family and your people. I've seen it," she argued, as if expecting him to deny it. "They all look to you for answers and strength, and you give them both in spades. You do whatever it takes—hard, mean, or just plain nasty if necessary—to keep them safe and protect them."

Rachel shook her head. "And you do it alone. It must be a heavy burden. Don't you think you deserve someone to share that burden with at the end of a long day?"

Lucian looked away, touched by her words and the sadness he saw in her eyes. It was unexpected from Rachel.

"And this isn't just about you, is it?" Etienne asked, making his presence known.

Lucian and Rachel glanced sharply to the side as he moved up the hall to join them. He stopped and put a hand on Lucian's shoulder, his expression solemn as he said, "Think of Leigh, Uncle."

When Lucian stilled, he continued, "Leigh doesn't realize how long a long time can be alone. We do. You more than I." He looked sad. "I only had three hundred years alone, but you've had ten times that. I've never understood how you've stayed as human as you are so long without a mate. But you have. I don't know if Leigh's that strong. I know you can't read her, but we can. She's lonely already."

"But she doesn't have to be," Rachel said.

"Okay, you can stop," Lucian said dryly. "You had me convinced already without bringing on the guilt of leaving Leigh without a life mate."

The couple beamed at him, and Lucian rolled his eyes, then narrowed them when he noticed that Rachel's smile was fading, concern taking its place.

"What?" he asked, wary again.

"I just—I'm worried that Leigh might prove a bit resistant."

"What?" he asked with amazement. He had been so wrapped up in his own reluctance to acknowledge Leigh as his life mate, he hadn't considered that she might be less than enthusiastic herself. "Why?"

"When her grandfather died and Leigh was suddenly alone in the world, she married a man who turned out to be an abusive jerk. Leigh blames herself for that. She feels she was weak in needing someone and is determined to prove that she can be strong, that she doesn't need anyone. She's afraid of making another mistake."

Rachel had obviously done a lot of digging in Leigh's head . . . and—since he couldn't do it himself—he was grateful for it, Lucian acknowledged, then frowned. "How do you suggest I convince her otherwise?"

Rachel bit her lip. "I think you'll have to prove to her that you're trustworthy, that you aren't someone who is going to hurt her, and aren't a mistake."

"How?"

Etienne raised his eyebrows at his wife expectantly even as Lucian asked the question, but she remained silent for so long that Lucian felt sure she didn't have a clue until she said, "I think your best bet with Leigh is to sneak up on her."

Etienne peered at her with disbelief. "You just finished

saying that Uncle Lucian had to prove himself trustworthy. Now you're saying the best way for him to do that is to sneak up on her? What kind of logic is that?"

"Women's logic," Lucian said wryly, and received a glare from Rachel for his trouble.

"I don't mean—" Rachel began, then shook her head. "I—"

"I think the easiest thing to do," Etienne interrupted when she floundered again, "would be for us to explain to her about life mates and then tell her that Uncle Lucian can't read her, or control her, and so"—he shrugged—"he is her life mate."

"I think that would be a mistake," Rachel said at once, her voice firm. "I think a straight on approach would be a mistake with Leigh. I think she'd run from that, raise her defenses and back off emotionally."

"Then what do you suggest?" Lucian asked dryly.

Rachel pursed her lips as she thought, then said, "I think you have to approach her in a nonthreatening manner, as a friend, or a teacher."

"Hmmm," Etienne murmured. "The teacher idea's good. She has to be taught to control her teeth and so on. That would be a good approach."

"Okay." Lucian nodded. He could do that, he could train her in her new abilities and skills, and teach her to differentiate between food hunger and hunger for blood. Teaching her how to control and read minds and how to feed on a living human was also necessary. If an emergency cropped up, the immortal had to know how to do it properly without causing pain or injury. They also had to know when to stop feeding so they didn't accidentally kill their host. He wouldn't necessarily *like* it, but he *could* do it. "And then what?"

Rachel and Etienne exchanged a glance, then she

sighed. "I'm not sure. I'll think about it, though. You start with that and I'll come up with something else."

Lucian nodded slowly. The training would take a while, he supposed. And he'd think, too, see if he couldn't come up with some way to approach her as well.

"I guess we should leave," Rachel said. "I have to head to work soon."

"I have some work to do myself," Etienne said with a nod, then glanced at his uncle. "We'll think about this and—"

"Greg!" Rachel blurted, and both men glanced at her with blank expressions.

"Lissianna's husband Greg?" Etienne asked with a confusion equal to Lucian's.

"Yes," she said, suddenly excited. Lucian didn't think that boded well, and was sure of it when Rachel explained, "He's a psychologist. He'll know how best to approach Leigh about it. We should get him over, let him talk to her, get a feel for what she's like and—"

"No," Lucian interrupted firmly.

Rachel blinked in confusion. "Why not?"

Why not, indeed? Lucian thought. The answer was that Gregory Hewitt was even less fond of him than Rachel. The man hadn't yet forgiven him for taunting him into going through the change without drugs. There had been no choice with Leigh, since he hadn't had any drugs available to him on the plane. However, with Greg's turning, there *had* been drugs available, but he'd taunted the man into proving himself by going without them.

In truth, Lucian hadn't expected him to stick to it, but Greg Hewitt had proven himself as stubborn as any of the Argeneau men. Ever since then, however, Greg hadn't been overly fond of his new uncle. It was bad enough having Rachel and Etienne help him with this problem. Lucian didn't think he could bear the humiliation of Lissianna's husband knowing he needed help landing a woman as well.

"I'm sure he'd understand," Rachel said sympathetically, and Lucian growled under his breath as he realized she'd read his mind . . . again.

"In fact, I don't think he's really angry anymore, and reading your thoughts would probably make you two closer. He'd understand—like I now do—that you're a great big marshmallow under all that bluster and crust."

Lucian's eyes widened in horror at this accusation, his mouth working but nothing coming out as he sought for some response strong enough to express his dismay at her altered opinion of him. A marshmallow? He wasn't a damned marshmallow! He was cold, and mean and hard enough to do what had to be done when others faltered. He was a damned warrior, had slain both mortal and immortal down through the ages with sword, knife, mace, spear, lance—

"I think we'd better go now," Etienne said, eyeing his uncle warily as he took Rachel's elbow to lead her quickly up the hall. They were at the stairs before his nephew glanced back to add, "We'll call you later, after we've thought of ways to handle Leigh. And after you've calmed down."

Lucian simply glared as the pair made good their escape.

"Lucian?"

He turned slowly, his anger slipping away as he saw Leigh standing in the door to her room. Her nose had healed and she'd washed her face. She looked about ten years old standing there with no makeup on and in Etienne's clothes.

"Yes?" he asked gruffly.

"I think I'm going to lie down for a while," she said. "I thought I should let you know."

"That's fine," he said at once. "Sleep is the best thing for you at the moment."

Lucian glanced toward the stairs as he heard the front door close behind Rachel and Etienne, then glanced back to add, "I'll be in the library for a while. I have some calls to make, but I'll check on you in a bit."

"There's no need to check on me. I'll probably only sleep for an hour or so," Leigh said with a smile as she turned back into the room, then paused to add, "Bastien asked me to have you call him when you woke up."

"Thank you," Lucian murmured.

The door had barely closed softly behind her when the door to his own room opened next to it and an older woman came out, dragging Marguerite's vacuum behind her.

"Oh, hello," the woman said on spotting him. "You must be Mr. Argeneau."

Lucian stared blankly. He hadn't a clue who the woman was.

Seeming to recognize that by the expression on his face, she smiled wryly and said, "I'm Linda. From Speedy Clean? We—"

"Oh, yes, yes," Lucian said, giving his head a shake. He'd entirely forgotten about the cleaning people.

"I've done all the rooms up here but this one," she announced, approaching the door he stood in front of. "I'll just do it now, then move downstairs."

"There's no need," Lucian said. "This room is fine. Besides, Leigh is sleeping in there now."

"Oh, all right. I'll just head down to help Andrea with the main floor, then."

Lucian watched her head downstairs, then turned to the door before him. He stared at the wooden panel for a moment, then reached out to touch it.

His life mate lay on the other side. Countless millennia alone and now he had a life mate. All he had to do was convince her of it.

Eleven

Leigh slept through the night. She hadn't expected to. It was only afternoon when she'd lain down, but it was early dawn when she woke up . . . *And she was starved.* This time there was no mistaking which hunger. It was both. However, the minute she sat up in bed and saw the little refrigerator, the very thought of the bags inside made her teeth protrude.

She opened the door, lifted one out, then grimaced before popping it to her teeth. The consumption of blood was the one thing she disliked about her new state. It was also the one thing she couldn't change, so she decided not to think about it as she sat waiting for the bag to drain. Determined to fill up and prevent anything like what had happened in the kitchen the day before, she had three bags in a row before crawling out of bed. She'd come far too close to biting that poor cleaning girl and didn't think she could live with that.

Leigh dressed in the clothes she'd worn the day before. She would take a bath or shower later and change into clean clothes—preferably Lissianna's this time—but right then what she wanted more than anything in the world was something to drink. Well, really, she wanted food in her belly, but a cup of tea would have to do for now, she thought as she ran a brush through her hair.

With no makeup to put on, she supposed she was ready and headed for the door. Her tongue ran over her teeth as she went. It would be lovely to be able to brush her teeth again. And soon she would, Leigh assured herself as she left her room. Today she'd be able to go shopping.

Bastien had promised that her bag should show up today, and she was excited at the prospect of having it. It meant she would no longer be so dependent on Lucian and his family. She could make calls on her cell phone rather than run up the long distance charges on Marguerite's phone. She could buy clothes instead of borrow them. Purchase herself the shampoos she liked, some makeup, a toothbrush, toothpaste...

Leigh almost shivered with excitement at the thought of once again having things that were her own. She could buy food too, she realized, an idea almost as attractive as having her own clothes. She'd never made those cookies she'd planned on yesterday, and hadn't eaten in . . . she wasn't even sure how long it had been. She suspected that might be part of the reason she was sleeping so much. From what she could tell, Lucian didn't seem to eat at all and did well enough, but she—and her body—were used to real food, not just liquid nourishment.

Leigh didn't run into anyone on the way to the kitchen, but hearing the television as she passed the closed living room door, she supposed Lucian was in there. After filling the electric teakettle in the kitchen and turning it on, she wandered back to the living room, intending to say good morning.

Lucian was seated on the couch, feet crossed on the coffee table and head hanging back. He was snoring up a storm. She smiled with amusement, then glanced at Julius, splayed out on the couch beside him. The mastiff was flat on his back with his paws up in the air, head shifting against Lucian's leg, making little whimpers of pleasure. He was obviously having doggy dreams.

Chuckling softly, Leigh walked to the TV and shut it off. The lack of sound woke Lucian, and his head snapped up abruptly.

He peered blearily around the room and said, "What?" in a confused voice, as if she'd spoken to him.

"Sorry," Leigh said apologetically. "I just turned off the television."

For a moment Lucian just stared at her, expression blank and body unmoving. Even Julius only stirred himself enough to open one sleepy eye in her direction. Then Lucian forced himself upright on the couch and gave his head a groggy shake. Julius rolled off the couch to the floor as the man said, "That's okay, I wasn't sleeping."

"You weren't, huh?" Leigh said, not hiding her doubt.

"No, I was just thinking with my eyes closed."

"Uh-huh," Leigh murmured, amusement tipping her lips. "Well, you go on and keep thinking. I was just going to make a grocery list."

He blinked with confusion. "A grocery list?"

"For food," she said, then explained, "My purse is supposed to arrive today. I was hoping to go out shopping for clothes and groceries. If that's okay?" she added uncertainly. She didn't need him to take her shopping—she could take a taxi—but wasn't sure if he would think it a good idea for her to go out at all. As she'd learned yesterday, she might not be the safest person to be allowed around mortals at the moment.

Much to her relief, he nodded, "Oh, I see. Yes, that's fine. I'll take you."

"I can take a taxi. You don't have to—"

"I'll take you," Lucian repeated firmly, and got to his feet. "I'll just— Have you fed yet?"

"Three bags," she said quietly.

"Good, good." He turned toward the door. "I'm going to grab a bag and make some calls in the library. Marguerite has a good selection of books if you find yourself bored. Otherwise, give me a shout when the courier arrives."

Leigh watched him go, then glanced down as Julius nudged her hand.

"I bet you're hungry, too, huh boy?" she asked lightly, petting the dog before leading the way to the kitchen. She wasn't surprised to find his food dish empty. Lucian seemed forgetful when it came to things like food.

She had opened a can of dog food and was just straightening from dumping it in Julius's bowl when the kitchen door opened and Lucian stuck his head in.

"Are you hungry?"

Leigh's eyebrows rose in surprise at the question, then she nodded. Her stomach had begun to growl the moment the scent of the dog food hit her nose, and if not for the fact that it was *dog* food, she might have given it a try.

"Right." He nodded. "I'll splash some water on my face, change, and we'll head out for breakfast."

"But the courier—" Leigh began.

"It's not even seven A.M., Leigh. Deliveries don't start until at least eight. We'll be back by then. Just give me ten minutes."

Lucian backed out of the room, feeling guilty about the wide grateful grin that had claimed Leigh's mouth at his words. He wished he deserved it. Unfortunately, breakfast had been Bastien's idea. His nephew was the first call he'd made, catching him just as he'd headed off to bed. They'd spoken briefly, and just before hanging up, Bastien commented, "I don't suppose Mother has much food there for Leigh to eat?"

When Lucian acknowledged there wasn't, Bastien pointed out that Leigh was used to eating and that he might consider taking her out for breakfast. Lucian hung up and decided to forgo the rest of his calls and take Leigh to a local restaurant. He just wished he'd thought of it himself.

He'd have to work on his awareness, he decided as he entered the bathroom. He had to remember to consider more than himself. The needs of others was something he hadn't had to think about for a long, long time, and that lack had made him inconsiderate.

Lucian grimaced as he caught sight of himself in the bathroom mirror. His hair was ruffled and even standing on end in some spots. He didn't want to take the time for a shower, but his head needed sticking under a tap. He'd also shave, he decided, running a hand over his scruffy face. The idea wasn't a cheerful one. He'd left everything in Kansas, including his duffel bag with his razor in it. Mortimer had apparently taken over his room when he learned he wouldn't be returning. He'd found his wallet, keys, and cell phone on the bedside table and sent them off right away by courier. They'd arrived late yesterday while Leigh was sleeping, but the man hadn't thought to send his duffel bag, too, which held both his phone charger and his shaving gear. It meant that for the moment his phone was useless and the only razor available to him was an old, used disposable he'd found in the drawer. It would have to do, he thought unhappily.

"Wow! You're ready and with a minute to spare," Leigh greeted him as he rushed into the kitchen nine minutes later. She then blinked at the sight of him and shook her head. "You should have used the extra minute."

Snatching a tissue from a box on the table, she began breaking off little pieces as she approached, then dotted them over his cuts to stop the bleeding. "Good Lord! What did you use to shave? A weed whacker?"

"I only have the one blade at the moment. It's overused," Lucian said, trying for dignity but fearing he failed miserably. It was hard to be dignified with half a dozen bits of tissue dotting your face.

"Right. Razors and stuff. I'd better add them to the grocery list so we don't forget." She paused, then added, "I'm surprised the nicks weren't healed before you headed downstairs. Shouldn't the nanos be fixing this?"

Lucian shrugged. "They're shallow cuts, not an emergency. The nanos are slower acting on such things. They'll probably be healed by the time you finish pasting me with your bits of tissue."

"Hmm." Finished with her first aid efforts to his face, Leigh moved back to the table to take up a pad and pen she'd apparently been making a grocery list with while he was getting ready.

"Razor blades," she said as she scribbled on the pad. "Is there anything else?"

When Lucian didn't answer right away, she glanced at him, then muttered, "A hairbrush."

As she lowered her head to continue writing, Lucian raised a hand to his head and smoothed down his hair. He hadn't been able to find a comb, so had made do with finger-combing his hair. He gathered it showed.

Finished with her list, they headed out.

They found a restaurant pretty quick considering neither of them knew restaurants in the area. They chose it based on the fact that the parking lot was half full. For that hour in the morning, it was an encouraging sign. It was small, decorated in soothing light blues, and comprised of twelve tables and six booths that lined the front of the restaurant.

Apparently, the booths were popular, Lucian noted as they slid into the last available one.

A short, stick-thin waitress with short black hair was at the table almost immediately, a bright smile on her face and two menus in hand.

"Can I get you coffee while you decide what you want?" she asked.

"Yes, please," Leigh said, smiling widely. Lucian could only guess that the prospect of food pleased her, and kicked himself again for neglecting her needs.

When the waitress glanced his way, he hesitated, then nodded. He had never tasted coffee, but it seemed a popular drink in the movies he saw and books he read.

Leigh had her menu open before the girl turned away from the table. Lucian shrugged, then followed suit just to give himself something to do. His gaze slid over the words and images with curiosity. While he might not know that Alpo was a dog food brand rather than the name of a human food producer, he had heard of some of the dishes on the menu. Omelets, bacon, eggs, toast . . . He'd come across all of them at one time or another, though he'd never eaten them. He was still reading through the offerings when the waitress returned with their coffee.

"Are you ready to order?" she asked, setting the coffees down.

"Thank you," Leigh murmured, reaching for the cup.

"Yes. I'll have the breakfast quiche, a side of sausage, and whole wheat toast, buttered, please."

The waitress didn't bat an eye at the large order. She simply wrote it down with a nod and glanced at Lucian. "And you, sir?"

"I'm not eating," he said automatically.

Nodding, she slid her pen behind her ear, took their menus, and headed away.

"Have you ever had coffee?"

Leigh's question drew his gaze back to her, then he glanced down at his cup. He shook his head.

"Try it," she urged.

Lucian hesitated, picked it up and took a cautious sip, which he promptly spit out with disgust. "*This* is what everyone is so desperate for first thing in the morning?"

Leigh smiled faintly at his horror. "It tastes better with sugar and cream. Would you like me to doctor it for you?"

Lucian nodded, then watched her fix both their coffees, adding a teaspoon of sugar and some cream to each before sliding his back to him.

Lucian tried another sip. It was still bitter on his tongue, but not as bad as it had been the first time.

"It will grow on you," Leigh said with amusement.

Lucian made a face, wondering why he would want it to, then noticed her attention had turned toward the back of the restaurant and the kitchens. She was obviously hungry, one hand absently rubbing her stomach.

"I'm sorry," he said with a frown. When she glanced his way in question, he added, "I meant to get you groceries yesterday, but forgot. I should have taken you out for a meal at least."

Leigh shrugged. "Groceries would have been nice, but

going out probably wouldn't have been. I might have bit the waitress instead of tipping her."

Lucian smiled faintly. "I could have made sure you'd fed well first."

"Made sure I fed well before feeding?" she asked with amusement.

He smiled wryly.

"Here we are."

They both turned to find the waitress had returned with two plates of food, one with a good-sized quiche and sausages, the other smaller plate holding toast.

"That was fast," Leigh commented, her eyes locked on the food being set before her.

"You picked the right dish, honey. Our breakfast quiches are our most popular specialty. We cook a certain number ahead and keep them warm," she explained. "And the cook always has lots of sausage on the go. The only thing you had to wait for was the toast. Enjoy."

Leigh thanked the woman as she left, but it was an absent, distracted murmur. Her attention was wholly focused on the food as she reached for her knife and fork.

Lucian was watching her dig in when the food's smell reached his nose. It was an enticing aroma and stirred his interest. He found himself leaning over the table, following his nose to the plate . . . until a fork gently poked him in the tip of the nose.

Pausing, he blinked and his eyes shot up. Leigh's gaze was amused.

She finished chewing the food in her mouth, swallowed, then said, "You looked like you were about to crawl into my plate."

Lucian straightened in his seat and cleared his throat, muttering, "Sorry, it smelled good."

Leigh tilted her head and considered him briefly. She'd gotten the distinct impression that food wasn't high on his priority list.

"When's the last time you ate?" she asked. There was no food in the house, so she knew he hadn't eaten there since their arrival, but suspected it had been longer than that.

Lucian tipped his head, his expression thoughtful, then said, "At the celebration of Alex and Roxane's marriage."

"Who are Alex and Roxane?" she asked with confusion.

"Alexandros III Philippou Makedonon. They call him Alexander the Great now. He was a—"

"I know who Alexander the Great is," Leigh interrupted, eyes wide. "You're joking right?"

"No."

"But that was two thousand years ago," she protested.

"Two thousand, three hundred and something," Lucian corrected.

"You haven't eaten in two thousand and three hundred years?" she asked carefully.

"That's right." He shrugged. "Actually, I only ate then because he was a good friend and it was a celebration."

Her gaze dropped to his stomach. "Do you even *have* a stomach anymore?"

"Of course," he said with annoyance.

Leigh nodded. "Of course . . . but does it work after all this time?"

"Of course it does." Lucian shifted, feeling suddenly self-conscious; like he'd sprouted a second nose out of his abdomen or something. Frowning, he reminded her, "The nanos keep us in peak condition and all that. They keep it in working order whether we use it or not."

"Right," Leigh said slowly, then shook her head and took another bite of quiche. She couldn't help noting the way Lucian's gaze moved from her mouth to her plate then away, only to follow the same circuit again.

Leigh watched him warily as she ate. Despite the fact that he didn't eat, she saw definite lust in his eyes as they slid over her food. She was almost tempted to put her arm around her plate and growl like a dog to warn him off.

Realizing how rude she was being, she said reluctantly, "I suppose you don't want any."

Much to her alarm, he immediately sat forward.

"Just a bite," Lucian said, and while his voice was nonchalant, his eyes were eager. "To try it. It smells interesting."

Wishing she'd kept her mouth shut, rude or not, Leigh began to cut a small piece of quiche.

Lucian watched her with interest, then asked, "What's that?"

"Quiche," she answered tersely, then raised the piece she'd cut to offer to him, only to blink in surprise when he looked horrified and sat back like a child refusing spinach. Frowning, she asked, "What? I thought you wanted to try."

"Real men don't eat quiche," Lucian informed her dryly.

Leigh blinked in surprise at the old expression, then a laugh burst from her lips.

"Nonsense. That was a stupid book title from way back in the eighties. The truth is *real* men don't feel threatened by quiche."

Realizing she was working to convince him to try it when in fact she had no desire to share the food, she shrugged. "Never mind. You don't have to try it."

She almost had the fork to her mouth when he suddenly said, "All right."

Leigh froze, the bite so close to her lips she could almost taste it, then her shoulders slumped and she held it out for him. She watched his mouth close over the food and pulled the fork free, silently praying he wouldn't like it. She was starved and didn't want to have to be polite and offer him more. With the fork free, Leigh quickly cut another bite for herself and slipped it into her mouth.

"That's delicious."

Leigh stopped chewing, her eyes narrowing on his surprised expression. There was definite lust in his eyes now as he contemplated her plate, and that—combined with his comment—made her fear he might want more.

"Is the sausage good, too?" he asked.

Leigh scowled. "Yes."

"I'll have a bite of that, too," Lucian said, then frowned and corrected himself quickly, "I mean, can I try a bit of that, too?"

Leigh's mouth tightened with displeasure. She'd feared as much. Now he wanted more. She wanted to snarl at him to order his own, but he was buying it for her, after all. She cut a piece of sausage and silently held it out, watching his lips again close over her fork, then their eyes met. For some reason in that moment, Leigh recalled her shower fantasy and felt a shiver run up her spine.

Swallowing, she pulled her hand back and ducked her head to concentrate on her food.

"That's good, too." Lucian's voice had taken on something of a sexy growl, and Leigh felt another shiver run up her back. "Can I have another?"

Leigh's gaze shot up. The resentment that had plagued her over the first two requests was now gone. Instead, she was a mass of confusion. Something had changed in his eyes, the silver had become more prominent, almost molten.

Forcing herself to look away, Leigh cleared her throat and cut another piece of sausage. Her hand was trembling now as she reached across the table to offer it to him. The piece of meat fell off halfway across the table and they both stared at it blankly, then Leigh instinctively reached for it, picking it up between thumb and forefinger to set it on the side of her plate and cut him another piece. However, before she could, Lucian's fingers closed around her wrist and slowly drew her hand to him. Her mouth parted slightly, heat rippling through her stomach as his lips closed around her fingers and slowly drew down, pulling the sausage from her grasp.

Hoping to calm the confusion suddenly rife within her, Leigh closed her eyes. However, the moment she did, images flashed through her brain, quick disjointed pictures of Lucian kissing her, his hand tangled in her hair, his body firm against hers . . . his mouth suckling at her breast, tugging gently but insistently at one excited nipple . . . their naked bodies like entwined marble on black satin sheets . . . cold tile against her back as he drove into her . . . then Lucian suddenly rose up out of his seat, swept the table clear of food and dishes, and lifted her onto it.

"I brought you another fork since it looks like you're going to share."

Leigh's eyes snapped open and she stared at their waitress as she set the fork in front of Lucian. A glance at the table showed that their cups and plates were all still there. It took a moment for her mind to recover enough for her to offer a weak smile.

"Thank you," she murmured.

"Would you like more coffee?" the woman asked.

"Yes," Lucian answered when Leigh just stared, unable to process the question, then he added, "And two more orders of what she has."

Leigh blinked in surprise as much at the husky growl evident in his voice as at the request itself. His eyes, she noted, were sleepy looking and still swirling hot silver, but then he smiled and said, "That way I won't have to steal yours and fear you stabbing me with a fork for my impertinence."

A slow smile spread her lips as the waitress moved off with a chuckle, then Leigh gestured to the extra fork the woman had brought them. "You may as well help me with this."

Lucian smiled and picked up the fork as Leigh shifted her plate to the center of the table and they set to work demolishing it.

They ate in companionable silence, Leigh thinking about the strange experience moments earlier. The images had seemed as real as when she'd fantasized in the shower. In fact, she shouldn't really call them images at all. It was more like flashbacks to that waking wet dream . . . except for the flash of them entwined on black satin sheets. That hadn't been in her shower experience, but had seemed just as real as the rest of it.

She had no idea what happened, but—since she'd never experienced anything like it before Morgan bit her—supposed it must be a result of the nanos. Perhaps senses weren't the only thing changed, they might alter her brain somehow as well.

They had just finished off the breakfast Leigh had ordered when the waitress arrived with the two fresh servings. She took away the empty plates they'd cleaned up and went away.

Now that they no longer had to hunch forward in their seats to reach the plate in the center of the table, Leigh and Lucian both relaxed back in their seats and their moods became more relaxed as well. They'd already eaten half a breakfast each, so were able now to eat at a more leisurely pace, interspersing conversation between bites.

"So, is hunting rogues a paid job or do you have another one?" Leigh asked between bites. The question was both out of curiosity and the concern that he was neglecting his work to look after her.

"Rogue hunters are our enforcers and most of them are paid," Lucian said a tad stiffly. "I'm also on the council."

Leigh blinked at this announcement, her attention turned. "The council? You've mentioned that before. What exactly is the council?"

"The governing body for immortals," he explained. "We act as lawmakers, judges, and basically oversee anything that affects immortals."

"All of them?" Leigh asked, eyes growing wide. It seemed she'd landed herself with a powerful person amongst the immortals. She wasn't sure if that was a good thing or not.

"There aren't that many, really. We've kept our population relatively low."

She peered at him curiously. He was answering questions more easily this morning. It made her wonder how much of his earlier exasperation had been due to sleep deprivation. "How many people are there on the council?"

Lucian shrugged. "It fluctuates. We try to keep at least six on the council, but members serve for a while, then leave as they desire."

"Are Etienne and Rachel on it, too?" she asked curiously.

"Good Lord, no." He looked appalled at the very idea. "They're far too young. Only the oldest immortals can sit on the council."

Leigh's eyebrows arched. "I see ageism is alive and well amongst immortals, too."

He chuckled at her dry tone, but explained, "Older immortals have seen and experienced more. Besides, council members aren't paid, and younger immortals are generally more concerned with making a living and can't give the position the time and attention it deserves."

"And you don't?" she asked dryly, one eyebrow arched.

Lucian shook his head. "I am in the fortunate position of being half-owner of Argeneau Enterprises."

"What's that?" she asked.

"It's a company my brother and I started . . . when was it? The sixteenth century or the seventeenth?" he said thoughtfully, then glanced at her with surprise when she burst out laughing.

"Sorry," Leigh said. "It's just rather odd to hear someone ponder which *century* they— Never mind. So, okay, you and your brother started a company centuries ago. You both had a half?"

Lucian nodded. "His half was split between his children and Marguerite when Jean Claude died."

"Jean Claude is your brother?"

"My twin brother."

Leigh's eyebrows rose, her gaze sliding over him as she pondered the fact that there had once been two such handsome, powerful men in the world.

"Jean Claude and I ran the company at first, but Bastien took it over some time ago and runs it with the help of a board."

"It's hard to believe that I haven't heard of a four- or five-hundred-year-old company," Leigh commented.

"Not at all," Lucian assured her. "It's changed names a couple of times and we don't sell anything that the common person would buy in a store."

"What do you sell?"

"Argeneaus is very diversified. We have a branch that manufactures parts, another handles investments, another buys and sells real estate, and another branch is into medical things," he said vaguely.

"Medical things like what?" Leigh asked curiously.

"Research and development, blood banks and specialized bars."

Leigh blinked. The last part just seemed odd trailing after the first two, and she echoed, "Specialized bars? Why would the branch that handles 'medical things,' as you call it, deal with specialized bars?"

Lucian smiled at her expression. "They're blood bars."

"Blood bars?" Leigh repeated slowly, then her eyes widened. "You mean . . . ?"

"For our people," he acknowledged.

"There are places you can just go in and order a—" She caught herself when he raised a hand, and she realized her voice had risen with her amazement. They weren't supposed to draw attention to themselves, and squealing about blood bars would have done that.

"They have specialty drinks," Lucian said quietly. "Bloody Mary's, Sweet Tooths, Fiery Redheads, Bloody Bibbos, and so on."

Leigh listened, fascinated. She owned a restaurant bar, so this was of interest to her. Before she could ask more, he changed the subject. "You said your parents died when you were ten. How did they die?"

Leigh was silent for a while as her mind shifted gears, then explained, "My parents went out to dinner with my aunt and uncle to celebrate their anniversary. Their car was hit by a drunk driver on the way back. All four of them died."

"And your grandfather took you in," Lucian murmured. "He lived in Kansas City?"

"No." She shook her head. "I was born and raised in McKeesport. It's a small town outside Pittsburgh, Pennsylvania. I lived there until I went away to Harvard."

"Which is when your grandfather died," Lucian murmured.

Leigh nodded, her mouth turning down. "I was away at Harvard when he died. I knew his health was failing and wanted to go to school closer to home, but he wouldn't hear of it."

"Yesterday, you mentioned being married."

Leigh shifted uncomfortably. The subject was taking a turn she didn't care for. She didn't like to think of that time in her life. She'd been weak and pathetic then, to her critical mind. She'd been so dependent emotionally on Kenny that she'd allowed herself to become a victim. She never wanted to be in that position again.

Before she could come up with a way to change the subject, he said, "You suggested your husband was abusive."

A short, harsh laugh slipped from her lips at the understatement, then Leigh shook her head. "It was my own fault." She saw him stiffen and said quickly, "Not his being abusive. That was all him. I'm not that stupid," she added wryly.

"Then what was your fault?"

"Marrying him," she answered, and explained, "We'd only been dating six weeks. I shouldn't have agreed when he asked, but Gramps had just died, and he was supportive and comforting through it all . . ."

Leigh frowned and toyed with her coffee cup, then said, "We were on a trip to Vegas with a bunch of other students. I'd dropped out of school to take care of my grandfather's funeral and grieve, but the trip had been paid for and all the reservations made and Kenny convinced me to go."

"Kenny was your husband?"

The disgust he put in pronouncing the name made her smile faintly. "Yes. He became my husband that weekend. We were there in Vegas, he asked, I said yes . . ." She shrugged. "The die was cast."

"You were lonely, suddenly alone in the world, and he took advantage," Lucian said quietly.

Leigh blinked sudden tears away and shook her head. "I was an adult. I should have known better, should have got to know him better." She frowned and shook her head with confusion. She didn't think Kenny had set out to take advantage of her. "We were both young and foolish."

"Even young predators are very good at picking prey."

Leigh stiffened at the quiet comment. "You mean the weak."

"No. I mean those who are vulnerable. Everyone is vulnerable at one time or another."

"When's the last time you were vulnerable?" she asked doubtfully.

Lucian was silent for a long time, then quietly said, "You would be surprised."

Leigh stared, wondering what he meant by that, then he continued, "They say it takes a year to grieve. How long after your grandfather's death did he ask you to marry him?"

"Three weeks."

"Ahhh," he said with a nod. "You see? Even an idiot would know you were still grieving and not thinking clearly."

Leigh shrugged. She'd like to claim Kenny hadn't been all that bright, but it wasn't true. They didn't let idiots into Harvard, and that's where they'd met.

"He never hit you before the wedding?"

"Good God, no! I never would have married him."

Lucian nodded. "It started with verbal abuse."

Leigh grimaced. "Yes. I was stupid, fat, and so on."

"Hitting on your weak points."

"You say it like it's obvious those would be my weaknesses," she said dryly.

Lucian shrugged. "You said you'd left school when your grandfather died. That means you lost your identity as a student, would be feeling insecure about your abilities."

"And the fat?" she asked, arching an eyebrow.

Lucian looked amused. "Every mortal female thinks she's fat, even if she's stick thin. I had a maid once who thought she was fat. Her husband encouraged it. She was so thin her hips stuck out, and still he told her she had a fat ass, and she believed him."

He shook his head, obviously finding it difficult to understand. Leigh smiled faintly, but said, "You say all mortal women think they're fat. Immortal women don't?"

"How could they?" he asked. "Nanos keep us at our peak health and shape. It's what they do. So every immortal is their perfect shape." He grinned. "Rachel was disappointed that she didn't suddenly turn stick thin, but she wasn't meant to be. Now she is secure in the knowledge that she's a perfect Rachel."

Lucian suddenly grimaced and muttered, "Well, mostly perfect. The nanos don't affect personality, unfortunately."

Leigh chuckled at his words. "I *did* get the feeling that Rachel isn't overly fond of you."

"I do what I have to do to protect my family, my people." There was steel in his voice. "Sometimes that doesn't make me popular."

Leigh nodded slowly. "I can understand. As the owner of Coco's there are things I have to do that I don't like."

"Owner?" Lucian stiffened. "I thought you worked the bar there? Bricker and Mortimer—"

"I do work the bar sometimes at night when someone's sick, but I own the place, too," Leigh said, and explained, "Donny didn't show up all week so I filled in. That's why I was working the bar when Morty and Bricker came in." She tipped her head, curious. "They still eat, obviously? At least Bricker does. Mortimer seemed mostly to pick at his food."

"He was just there to keep Bricker company. Bricker's younger and still eats food."

"So do you," Leigh pointed out with amusement as he finished off the sausage she'd been too full to eat and he'd snatched from her plate.

Lucian's chewing slowed and an odd expression crossed his face. Before she could ask about it, the waitress was at their table.

"Are we all set? Or can I get you anything else?" the woman asked cheerfully.

"We're done," Lucian answered, then glanced at Leigh and added, "We should get back. It's after eight and the couriers start delivering at eight-thirty."

Leigh's eyes brightened with excitement. "Then we can go shopping."

Twelve

"I'm going to go check again."

Lucian glanced up from the notes he was making, his mouth curving with amusement as Leigh tossed aside the book she'd been trying to read and headed for the library door. They'd been home exactly one hour and twenty-one minutes and she'd already gone to look out the front window to see if the courier was coming up the drive at least thirty times. The woman was up and down like a jack-in-the-box.

Shaking his head, Lucian glanced back at the notes he was making for his next conversation with Mortimer and read over what he'd written. He'd decided to give the men a break and not call them while they were sleeping today. Mortimer didn't make much sense when half asleep anyway, and Lucian had a lot of questions to ask, so he was making a list of those questions and any ideas he could think of to help the hunt along.

He made another note and smiled to himself. Oddly enough, he no longer resented not being on the hunt. At the moment, he'd much rather make notes, give them suggestions to follow up, and go shopping with Leigh. But then, he was finding the woman much more exciting than he'd found hunts in a while.

Lucian sat back in his chair and thought back to breakfast. He'd enjoyed that. The food, the company . . . the sex. His mouth curved at the memory of what he'd done at the table. He hadn't meant to . . . or perhaps it was more accurate to say he simply hadn't been able to help himself. There had been something seductive about Leigh feeding him, and when she'd dropped the bit of sausage on the table and reached to pick it up, he hadn't even thought, but simply grabbed her hand and started to pull it to his mouth to take the sausage from her fingers. But then his eyes had found hers as his mouth had closed around her flesh. He'd heard the soft puff of air that slipped from her parting lips, heard the way her breathing accelerated with excitement, and seen the way her eyes drooped to half-mast before closing all the way. He hadn't been able to stop the images that flashed though his own mind of the two of them together . . . in the shower, on his bed, right there in the restaurant. And he'd projected them out at her.

While true life mates couldn't read each other, they *could* send their thoughts to each other once they'd both turned, though usually that kind of bond didn't happen until a couple had been together for a while. But Lucian was positive that Leigh had received the images he'd projected. She'd jerked as if startled, then sat completely still, her breathing becoming more labored, and small sighs and one soft moan slipping from her lips. He had been affected himself, and might have done something silly if the waitress hadn't arrived to throw cold water over the moment.

Lucian glanced toward the door as it opened and Leigh moved unhappily back into the room.

"You're as impatient as a child," he teased as she began to pace, not even pretending to return to her book.

Leigh turned a sharp eye his way and sniffed. "So? You're as grumpy as an old man."

It wasn't the first time he'd been accused of being grumpy, but he didn't think he was at the moment. "I am not grumpy."

Leigh shrugged. "It's all right, I'm used to it." Lucian's eyes narrowed as she went on, "I grew up with my grandfather. He was a grumpy, crusty old soul, too."

His mouth dropped open at being compared to her grandfather, then he caught the sparkle in her eyes and realized she was teasing him. He was debating how to get her back when the telephone rang and he snatched up the receiver.

"Yes?" he barked.

"Uncle Lucian?"

He sat a little straighter at the sound of Bastien's voice. His nephew wouldn't call unless something had happened. Morgan getting caught was the something he was hoping for.

"Yes, Bastien," he said, then glanced toward Leigh as the doorbell rang.

"My purse!" she squealed, and was out the door like a shot, leaving him smiling after her. He'd never seen a woman so excited just to get something of her own back, he thought absently as he listened to her footsteps rush up the hall and heard the front door open. Now, if it were a gift she was getting—like, say, a diamond choker—he'd understand.

That thought made him pause as he considered that Leigh would look lovely in a diamond choker.

"Uncle?" Bastien's voice drew his attention back to the phone.

"Yes," he repeated. "What was that? I missed whatever you said."

"I was just apologizing for forgetting to tell you about Donny. I hadn't had much sleep, and with all the distraction of Leigh and the cleaners and everything that happened yesterday, I just forgot."

"Forgot to tell me what about Donny?" Lucian asked with a frown.

"That when my man went to the restaurant to alter the memories of Leigh's staff, he found out from Milly, the day manager, that Donny had called, asking for Leigh, and she told him that Leigh was visiting friends in Canada."

Lucian's eyebrows flew up at this news.

"I didn't think anything of it at the time," Bastien said, "but now . . ."

"Now what?" Lucian asked.

"But now it looks like Morgan and Donny are heading your way," he answered grimly.

Lucian wasn't terribly surprised at this news. He'd suspected as much when he heard the path they were taking in the rental car, and said so now. "I thought that might be the case, but it seems a stupid move, and just because they were driving north didn't mean they had to be headed this way. I take it they've done something that makes you think they are?" he queried quietly.

"I'm afraid so." Bastien's voice was equally quiet and grim. "Two charges popped up on Stobie's credit card this morning. A gas station in Iowa—"

"He's continuing north," Lucian interrupted to murmur.

"Faster than you think," Bastien said grimly. "The second charge was for two plane tickets from Des Moines to Toronto."

Des Moines to Toronto. The words were still ringing in Lucian's ears when Leigh let out a shriek from the front of the house.

The phone slipped forgotten from his fingers as Lucian lunged to his feet and raced from the room. He exploded into the hall, expecting to find Leigh fighting off Morgan's grasping hands or being dragged from the house by the man and the redheaded Donny. Instead he arrived to see Leigh standing in the ruins of brown wrapping paper and a ripped-open box, a purse clasped to her chest as she did a little dance in the entry and squealed with glee.

Lucian slumped with relief, a small smile tugging at his lips as he watched her do her happy little dance, then his gaze slid to the man standing by the door and his smile morphed to a scowl. The courier was five-ten, well-built and good-looking in the tall, dark, and handsome sort of way women gushed over. He stood grinning at Leigh with an interest that was purely male and vastly annoying to Lucian.

"Man, I love my job," the courier murmured, his eyes glued to Leigh's lightly bouncing chest as she danced around.

Every cell in Lucian's body was screaming out in possessive rage at the man's leering smile as he ogled his woman. While he had the restraint to keep from swooping on the courier and ripping his throat out for the impertinence, he couldn't keep back the low growl that slid from his lips. It was a deep, soft sound of warning. Leigh didn't appear to hear it as she stopped her dancing to open her purse and paw through its contents, but the courier did. Stiffening, the man turned slowly, as if expecting to find himself facing a wild dog. He didn't look much relieved to find himself facing a furious Lucian. Without a word he nodded slowly, as if to acknowledge Lucian's alpha status, then eased backward out of the door before turning to hurry to his waiting truck.

Lucian stalked to the door and closed it, then turned to Leigh, his expression softening as she exclaimed while going through the purse's contents.

"Ooh, a brush. I can brush my hair. And lipstick!"

Feeling the last of the adrenaline slip from his body, Lucian managed a smile and asked, "Is everything there?"

"It looks like it." Leigh glanced up to beam at him, then asked eagerly, "Can we go shopping?"

Lucian's mouth twitched at her expression. Dear God, she was so adorable. No child at Christmas looked as eager as this woman at the prospect of buying toothpaste and other hygiene products. "Yes, of course."

"Wonderful," she exclaimed, and did a little twirl in the middle of the hall.

Lucian shook his head and chuckled under his breath, then realized it wasn't something he did often. He suspected he'd be doing it more often with this woman in his life.

"Oh!" Leigh stopped suddenly, her eyes wide. "I'd better feed before we go."

"That would probably be good."

Turning, she headed for the stairs, no doubt headed for her room and the blood in the refrigerator there. Lucian was about to tell her she needn't go up to get it, that there was some in the kitchen refrigerator now, but before he could, the sound of a car coming up the driveway made him pause.

Leigh apparently also heard it. Stopping at the foot of the stairs, she turned back, eyes wide in question.

"Go upstairs, Leigh," Lucian said grimly, recalling the news that Bastien had dispatched just before Leigh's screams had dragged him from the phone.

Morgan had bought two plane tickets to Canada.

Lucian hadn't managed to learn on what flight or when he might arrive before Leigh's scream had drawn him out here. His first thought as he'd raced from the library had been that the rogue vampire had arrived. It was the first thought that occurred to him now, too, and his immediate response was to keep Leigh out of harm's way. She wasn't cooperating, however. Ignoring his order, something no one else had ever dared do with him, she scampered lightly back to the door and peered out.

"It's Rachel and Etienne," she announced without glancing around to see the scowl on Lucian's face as he rushed protectively to her side. By the time he reached her, she was already pulling the door open.

"My purse just got here!" she announced gleefully by way of greeting, blissfully unaware of the glare Lucian was sending her way.

Rachel and Etienne paused abruptly at the sight of the two of them in the doorway, their worried expressions giving way to relief. Then Rachel managed to force a weary smile as she led Etienne forward to join them in the foyer.

"So you'll be shopping today?" she asked quietly as Etienne pushed the door closed behind them.

"Yes!" Leigh said with excitement. "Do you want to come?"

Rachel shook her head. "It would be fun, but I worked last night and need to sleep. Maybe next time."

"I hope you aren't wearing that t-shirt out shopping," Etienne murmured, slipping an arm around his exhausted wife and pulling her to lean against his chest.

Leigh glanced down at herself, her eyes widening with horror as she saw that she was still wearing his joggers and cyber sex t-shirt.

"Oh, pooh! I forgot to change," she exclaimed with

alarm. "And I was going to shower, too. Ten minutes," she told Lucian, and rushed upstairs, clutching her purse in a death grip.

Lucian watched her go, torn between tender amusement at her excitement and fury that she'd ignored his order to go upstairs earlier.

"I take it Leigh's screaming was just excitement over the arrival of her purse," Etienne said quietly once Leigh had disappeared from sight and they heard her bedroom door bang closed.

Lucian glanced at his nephew with surprise. "Her screaming?"

"Bastien called," Etienne explained. "He was all in a panic. He said he was talking to you on the phone when Leigh started screaming. He said you dropped the phone and took off and he couldn't get through to find out what was happening. He pretty much ordered me to get over here and see that everything was all right."

"Yes. She was just excited about her purse," Lucian admitted, then grimaced apologetically. "I'm sorry you had to come rushing over here. You both look dead on your feet and this is usually your sleeping time."

"It's your usual sleeping time, too. Why don't you look tired?" Rachel asked almost resentfully.

Lucian shrugged. "My hours are all buggered up from sleeping all day yesterday. I napped for an hour or so this morning, too."

"Hmm."

They were all silent before Etienne commented, "So I gather Bastien thinks Morgan is on his way here?"

"It would seem so," Lucian said with a frown, suddenly rethinking this planned shopping trip. "Maybe I shouldn't take Leigh out shopping until this is over and Morgan is caught."

"Oh no," Rachel protested. "Leigh is so excited about it. Besides, you have to at least get her food."

"Rachel's right," Etienne said quietly. "And surely it's safe for now. It will take at least another day or more for him to drive up here, won't it?"

Lucian blinked in surprise at the comment. "Didn't Bastien tell you?"

"Tell me what?" Etienne asked.

Lucian ran a hand through his hair. "Well, it seems Morgan bought two plane tickets from Des Moines to Toronto. He's definitely headed this way, or here already. I didn't get the chance to find out what time the flight was supposed to land."

"Des Moines?" Rachel asked with surprise. "I thought they were in Missouri."

"Bastien told me Iowa," Lucian said with a shrug.

"It could be a red herring," Etienne murmured, and Lucian blinked at him with surprise.

"Why would he buy plane tickets here as a red herring?"

"Well, why would he head here where you are waiting to catch him?" Etienne pointed out, then added, "Besides, it's hard to believe Morgan would fly here, he has a phobia to flying."

"What?" Lucian asked with amazement.

"He and Dad were friends," Etienne reminded him. "And I heard Dad teasing him about it once. I gather he had a bad experience while with someone named . . ." He paused to think and then said uncertainly, "Cayley?"

"George Cayley," Lucian murmured. "He came up with the first fixed-wing aircraft. A glider, really."

"Well, from what I overheard that day, Morgan tested one of his first gliders for him and it didn't go well. He's refused to fly ever since."

Lucian nodded. It fit. Morgan had lived in the Yorkshire area of England several times between 1700 and when he'd caught a ship to America in 1875 and George Cayley had been born, lived, and done his experiments there somewhere in that time. His shoulders began to relax. "Okay, so he wouldn't fly, the tickets are probably a red herring to confuse us, and he probably isn't heading this way at all."

"I wouldn't be so sure," Rachel murmured. "I think Morgan wants Leigh."

Lucian's eyes narrowed. "Why? From the conversation we overheard in the kitchen, it was the redhead, Donny, who wanted her turned in the first place."

"Would Morgan be willing to come up here to get Leigh for this Donny?" Etienne asked with a frown.

Lucian shook his head impatiently. "Morgan won't give a damn what Donny wants."

"I read her thoughts," Rachel said quietly. "I saw that night in her memories. Morgan couldn't completely control her. She seems to have a strong mind. He could control what she *did*, but not what she *thought*. It fascinated him . . . enough that I think he'd come after her."

Etienne frowned, then asked his uncle, "Does Morgan know where you live?"

Lucian grimaced. "As you say, he used to be friends with Jean Claude. He spent a lot of time in the Toronto area for a while and they visited my home together several times."

"But he doesn't know you're here at Marguerite's," Rachel said.

"No. He does know the address, though, and if he gets to my place and finds I'm not there, this would probably be his next stop."

"If he's headed this way anyway, why not have Bricker

and Mortimer fly here and wait for him at the airport?" Rachel suggested.

When both men turned to peer at her, she shrugged. "Well, they know what he looks like. They could catch him when he steps off the plane. What flight were the tickets for?"

"I don't know," Lucian admitted. "Bastien hadn't told me that when Leigh started screaming. For all I know, the flight could have already landed."

Etienne shook his head. "If that were the case, Bastien would have said Morgan was here in Toronto, not that he was headed this way."

"That's true," Rachel agreed, then smiled at Lucian. "Which means you don't have to disappoint Leigh. It should be perfectly safe for you to take her shopping."

Lucian hesitated, part of him not wanting to disappoint Leigh and wanting to be sure she had the things she needed to be comfortable, but the other part telling him he had other responsibilities, too. Finally he shook his head. "I should call Bastien and find out what flight Morgan is booked on and when it should arrive, then arrange for one of the company planes to pick up Mortimer and Bricker and get them up here."

He knew that the flight Morgan had bought tickets for must already have left, otherwise Bastien simply would have arranged for Mortimer and Bricker to get to the airport and catch Morgan and Donny before they boarded the flight. The rogue would be smart enough not to buy the tickets until the last minute. He had to know they would be tracking the credit card. Morgan had been friends with Jean Claude for centuries and had heard the tales of Lucian's exploits in rogue hunting. He knew all the tricks.

"I'm ready."

The trio glanced toward the stairs as Leigh bounded down. She'd showered in record time. Her damp hair was slicked back, and she'd borrowed a pair of Lissianna's jeans that fit her in the hips but were obviously too long. She'd rolled them up to keep from treading on the hems. She was also wearing a red t-shirt with a scooped neck that was a bit tight and emphasized her generous breasts.

She looked mouth-watering to Lucian, and he was embarrassed to note that his brain wasn't the only part of his anatomy that had taken notice. His penis shifted in his jeans as he got a semierection just at the sight of her.

He'd definitely been too long without a woman, if this was how he was going to react, he thought. He didn't even recall being this bad as a hormone-ridden teenager in Atlantis. In fact, he was pretty sure he'd missed that stage. Now, it appeared he was going to suffer it . . . with a vengeance.

Bad timing, Lucian thought grimly. He was supposed to take it slow and sneak up on her, but now that he'd decided to go ahead, it was as if his body had slipped some mental chain he'd placed on it. It was loping around like a panting dog with its tongue hanging out . . . semi stiff.

"We should head out," Rachel announced, and Lucian turned narrowed eyes to her. She'd sounded terribly amused, obvious laughter underscoring her tone. She had read his mind again. And so had Etienne, he realized, as he saw the amusement on his face as well.

Sighing, Lucian waved them on to the door. "Go on then. Leave."

"I'd be happy to make those phone calls for you so you can go shopping," Etienne said as he opened the front door. "Do you want me to?"

Lucian blinked in surprise at the offer. No one had ever offered to help him before.

"You've never seemed to need it," Etienne said, obviously reading his mind once more. "Or asked for it."

"Or wanted it," Rachel added dryly, seeming to suggest he'd been too proud.

Lucian chose to ignore her. They appeared to be getting along well at the moment and he didn't want to ruin that. Gaze firmly on Etienne, Lucian did the hardest thing he'd had to do in a long time and accepted help. "I'd appreciate your making the calls for me. I'd do it, but—"

"But you promised Leigh you'd go shopping." Etienne grinned.

"Is there something you need to do before we go, Lucian?" Leigh asked anxiously, having overheard them as she approached. "If there is, we can put off shopping until you're done."

The offer was sincere and sweet and obviously reluctantly offered. Lucian smiled at her pained expression.

"No," he assured her firmly. "Etienne will make the calls for me."

She looked so relieved he wanted to kiss her.

"We're out of here," Etienne announced, ushering Rachel ahead of him. "I'll call you later."

"Thank you." The words came out stiff and awkward. Lucian wasn't used to having to say them. Shaking his head at himself, he stepped to the door to watch them walk to their car, then closed the door as they drove away.

"Aren't we going shopping?" Leigh asked with surprise as he locked the door.

"Yes," Lucian said patiently. "But I thought you'd rather take the car than walk twenty miles to the nearest mall."

"Oh. Right." She grinned, clearly overjoyed at the prospect of shopping.

Typical woman, he thought with amusement, then promptly took the thought back. There was nothing typical about his Leigh.

Turning, he led her into the kitchen.

"Well, that's new," Leigh said when he opened the refrigerator door to reveal stacks of bagged blood.

"I had it delivered last night after the cleaners left," Lucian explained, retrieving two bags.

"Hmm. Good thing it wasn't there when the cleaners were here."

"That's why I waited to order it," Lucian said wryly as he handed her one of the bags.

She wrinkled her nose at him as he popped his own bag to his teeth.

Leigh hesitated, then her mouth opened and he saw her tongue run over her teeth. It wasn't until then he realized that he'd forgotten that she couldn't yet bring on her own teeth. It was one of the things he had to train her to do. Then he frowned as he realized that the only time he'd helped her bring on her teeth was the first time he'd fed her after she'd awakened. But then he knew her bloody nose in the kitchen had brought them on yesterday afternoon. Her teeth had been showing as she'd rushed past them in the hall on the way upstairs to binge feed on blood.

As for this morning, she said she'd fed, but he had no idea how she'd brought on her teeth. He was thinking he'd have to bring her teeth on for her when he finished his bag when she suddenly relaxed. A second later his eyes widened as he saw them slide down.

Leigh smiled, obviously pleased with herself, then slapped the bag to her mouth.

Lucian stared at her over his own bag, both amazed and impressed that she'd managed to figure out how to control her teeth without any training at all. This was seriously impressive. And Morgan, he reminded himself, hadn't been able to control her completely. According to Rachel, he'd been able to control her actions but not her thoughts. Leigh appeared to have some impressive abilities.

They had three bags each. Leigh would have gone for a fourth, but he assured her it wasn't necessary. They were headed for the door when she stopped with a squeal of, "My purse! I left it up in the room."

"I'll be in the garage," Lucian called after her with a chuckle as she whirled and flew out of the kitchen. His smiled faded, though, as he realized he'd forgotten something himself. Shaking his head, he moved to fetch the portable cooler out of the closet, then quickly filled it with blood from the refrigerator. He was about to take it to the car when scratching at the back door made him stop. Setting the cooler on the table, he moved to the door, opened it and smiled wryly as Julius cantered in. He had put the dog out a few minutes before the phone call from Bastien and forgotten about him.

"Good thing you scratched when you did, buddy, or you'd have been stuck out there while we went shopping."

Lucian gave the dog a scratch under the chin, then patted his back before straightening to collect the cooler.

"Behave while we're gone. No tearing through the house with garbage," he said, then took the cooler out to the car.

He was closing the trunk when Leigh joined him.

"Ready to go?" he asked as he opened the passenger door for her.

"All set." She patted her purse happily and slid into the car.

"So," he said, sliding behind the steering wheel a moment later. "Where do you want to shop? Is a mall all right? Or would you prefer the boutiques in downtown Toronto?"

Lucian reached for the remote on the dashboard of Marguerite's little red sports car to press the button to open the garage door, then started the engine before glancing at Leigh to see why she wasn't answering. He stilled when he saw the disbelieving look on her face.

"What?" he asked with bewilderment.

"Do I look like a boutique kind of girl?" she asked, her voice half dry and half amused.

Lucian let his gaze drop over her, taking in Lissianna's clothes on her curvaceous body, then lifted his eyes back to her heart-shaped face. Her eyes were a pure gold now, and were reflecting light in the dim garage. Her lashes were long, her nose a turned-up little button, her lips full and pouty and sensuous. She didn't have a lick of makeup on but was more beautiful than most women *with* makeup. The gods had been kind when creating her.

"Sure. Why not?" he said finally, and forced himself to turn his gaze forward again before his little Lucian was startled awake. He shifted the car into gear and drove out of the garage, hitting the remote to close the door behind them as he headed up the driveway.

"A mall will be fine. All I need are jeans and t-shirts, really. It's not like I'll be going anywhere," Leigh said quietly, then he sensed her eyes sharp on him as she asked, "Will I?"

"Yes," Lucian said slowly, his mind slipping over the lessons he was to give her over the next few days. "Once you have full control of your teeth, we'll have to go out for you to practice reading minds and then controlling mortals."

"But I don't want to read minds and control people," she said with displeasure.

"I'm afraid you'll have to."

"Why?" She sounded rebellious. "I don't want to take advantage of others just because—"

"It's a skill you'll need," Lucian interrupted.

"Why?" she repeated.

He felt impatience rear inside him, then suddenly relaxed and smiled. She had this effect on him, but even the impatience was better than being emotionally dead.

Shaking his head, he said, "Because should you find yourself in an emergency where you have to feed off the hoof, you'll want to be able to control their minds so they don't suffer pain or recall the event."

Before she could ask why again, Lucian added, "If they recall the event, they'll have to be dealt with."

"You mean killed," Leigh accused.

"No, I mean dealt with," he said patiently. "Their memories erased, or their recollection of the events altered. Death is only ever used as a last resort."

"Oh." Leigh was silent for a moment, then said, "Well, I have no intention of biting anyone, so it won't be necessary for me to learn—"

"I know you don't intend to, or want to, but you might not be able to stop yourself. Remember what you felt in the kitchen with the cleaner?"

"I resisted," Leigh said, but sounded shaken.

"You resisted *this time*. What if you're in an accident? There's blood everywhere. You've been injured and bled a lot before the nanos stopped the bleeding and repaired the damage and you need blood. There's no one around for miles, no blood to be had but for the other driver, and he's bleeding copious amounts, the smell taunting you."

"It sounds like you're describing something that actually happened to you," Leigh said quietly.

Lucian shrugged. "I've been alive a very long time. Many things have happened to me. And many things will happen to you in the coming centuries as well."

"Centuries," she murmured, and shuddered.

Lucian glanced at her as he braked at a red light, then reached out to pat her hand where it lay on her leg. "It's better to have the skill whether you intend to use it or not, than to need it and not have it."

Leigh let out a shaky breath and nodded. "All right. But I'm not going to like it."

Lucian smiled faintly and pressed his foot down on the gas as the light changed, then explained, "Learning it is actually more for their sake than yours. I don't know what you recall of Morgan's biting you, but—"

"I remember it all."

"Did you feel a sudden euphoria or pleasure?" Lucian asked, and catching sight of her blush, he nodded. "Well, that's a trick to veil the pain. We can control their minds so they don't feel anything, or let them feel our pleasure so that all they come away with is a memory of passion, or a planted memory of a talk even. While there are occasions where feeding off the hoof is necessary, there's never any excuse for letting a host suffer."

"Off the hoof," she murmured. "That's the second time you've called it that."

He shrugged. "It's a common term among our people."

"Do you really think of mortals as nothing more than cattle?"

Lucian frowned. He rarely thought of mortals at all, if the truth were told. When he called the cleaners, it wasn't in his thoughts that he would call in the *mortal* cleaners, they were just the cleaners. But there had been a time—before blood banks—when they had fed directly from the source and they'd used such terms to distance themselves emotionally from the fact that they had to dine on their neighbors and sometimes friends. It could be difficult at times living and walking among mortals you needed to feed off of to survive. He tried to explain that to Leigh, and thought from her expression when he finished that she understood.

They'd reached the mall by then and they both fell silent as they got out of the car and made their way through the parking lot to the mall entrance.

"Where to first?" Lucian asked as he followed her inside the bright, bustling building.

Leigh hesitated, then glanced at him uncertainly. "Was there somewhere you wanted to go while I shop? We could meet up in the food court afterward if they have one here."

"No. I'm at your service," he said simply, and noted she looked less than pleased at the news. He fretted over why that might be as he followed her to the first clothing store.

Thirteen

Leigh rifled through the clothes on the rack, but her mind wasn't on what she was doing. She was terribly aware of Lucian standing a couple of feet behind her, patiently waiting. She hadn't considered that he might actually come into the stores with her. He was a man, and men were notorious for hating to shop.

"You'd look good in that."

She glanced at the shirt she'd been blankly sliding along the rod, her eyes narrowing with doubt. A pale pink jersey, it had a cowl neck and flared sleeves. The cowl neck wasn't a style that looked good on her. She was too busty, and it seemed to emphasize that.

"Try it on," Lucian suggested.

She shook her head. "I don't look good in cowl necks."

The next top was a plain, V-necked jersey in off-white. Leigh looked for her size, found it, and took it off the rack, then froze as Lucian reached over her and quickly slid aside several of the pale pink cowl tops until he found one in the same size as the blouse she'd just pulled.

"Try it on," he said firmly, and she was feeling rebellion well up within her when he added, "Please. If it doesn't look good, I won't suggest another thing."

Leigh considered him briefly, then took the top and turned away to head to the dressing room. "Okay. But it won't look good."

"We'll see," he said, following her.

The blonde in charge of the changing room glanced up from where she bent over a note she was making in a book, and smiled widely as Leigh and Lucian stopped at the counter. "Did you want to try that on?"

When Leigh made a face that spoke of her lack of enthusiasm, Lucian answered for her, "Yes, she does."

"Okay." The blonde straightened and stepped around the counter, and Leigh found herself looking up. The girl was an Amazon, almost as tall as Lucian and willowy to boot. Some days Leigh hated being short and rounded. This was one of them.

"If you and your husband would follow me." The girl smiled again and started to lead the way up the row of changing rooms.

"He's not my husband," Leigh said quickly, and felt the flare of embarrassment flushing her cheeks.

"I'll just wait out here," Lucian announced at almost the same moment, and the changing room girl smiled at him with interest over Leigh's head. She felt like the child between two adults.

Grimacing to herself, she followed the girl to the very last of several empty changing rooms and waited as she stepped in to hang the top on the hook.

"There you are," she said cheerfully, stepping back out. "Take your time."

Leigh's eyebrows flew up, but the woman didn't notice; she was moving back up the way they'd come . . . toward Lucian. Leigh couldn't help noticing she walked with a hip-rolling animal grace that spoke of a predator approaching its prey.

Wondering why it bothered her, Leigh slid into the changing room and closed the door. She was out of her borrowed t-shirt and into the cowl-necked jersey in no time, then stood frowning at herself with disgust. As she'd known, she didn't wear cowls well.

Sighing, she opened the door and stepped out into the hall. Lucian stood by the counter at the entrance, his expression bored as he listened to something the changing room girl was saying. He straightened and looked more alive the moment he spotted Leigh.

"See?" she said triumphantly as he moved down the hall to meet her. "I told you I don't—"

She snapped her mouth closed with surprise as he stepped toward her, reached out to catch the wide cowl neck and tug it down off her shoulders. He fussed with it a bit, then turned her to face the full-length mirror on the wall at the end of the aisle. Leigh blinked at herself in amazement. He'd turned the cowl neck into an off-the-shoulder top that showed off her slender neck while showing her figure to good effect.

She touched the collar with amazement. "But it's not supposed to be worn like this, is it?"

"Oh yes. These can be worn either way, though this looks much better on you." The changing room girl was suddenly reflected in the mirror beside them, then she turned to Lucian and said, "You have an eye for fashion."

"I know what I like," he said with a shrug, and turned to head up the aisle. "I'll bring more tops."

Leigh watched him go, the blonde hurrying after him, then she stepped back into her changing room, closed the door, and stared at herself in the mirror. She never would have thought to wear it like this. She hadn't known you *could* wear it like this. It looked good, though.

She had barely slid the top off and reached for her

own t-shirt when the blonde knocked on the door, then slid it open to hand three more tops in to her.

"Lucian said to bring you these. He's finding more for you."

"Oh." Leigh stared at them with surprise, then took the tops and hung them on the hook where she'd just placed the cowl. She supposed she should be surprised at the speed he'd shown in hunting them up, but she wasn't. *I know what I like*, he'd said, and she was now willing to see if what he liked looked good on her.

Leigh spent the next hour trying on clothes Lucian chose. Tops, blouses, sweaters, pants . . . he sent them in, in groups of three. There were colors she never would have thought to try, even styles she'd always assumed wouldn't look good, but every single thing looked good on her. None of them made her taller or less curvy, but they made the height and figure she *did* have look their best. The man really did have an eye for fashion.

By the time she finished, her problem was one she wasn't used to. She generally couldn't find things she liked, but now she liked everything and couldn't decide what to choose.

"How are we doing?" the blonde asked as Leigh staggered up the aisle with her arms full of the clothes she'd tried on.

"Good. Too good. I can't decide what to take and what not to take," she admitted wryly as Lucian and the blonde moved to help unburden her.

"Why not take them all?" Lucian asked.

"Oh, I couldn't," Leigh said, glancing at him askance. When her grandfather took her in, he'd been on a pension and refused to touch her inheritance from her parents, insisting it was for college. She'd gone through her teens with little money and always had to be cautious and sparing in her clothing purchases. It was a habit she hadn't broken in the years since then.

"Why?" Lucian asked, seeming truly bewildered. "If it's money, I could—"

"No, it's not money," Leigh said quickly, and blinked as she realized it was true. She could afford to buy everything here if she liked. Coco's was successful. It did a booming business. She also had investments. She was far from poor and could easily afford the clothes. It was just her conscience and natural caution holding her back.

Raising her chin, she nodded and opened her purse to grab her credit card. "Fine. I want it all."

"How are you feeling?" Lucian asked later, as he led her out of the store, both of them laden with bags.

"Er . . ." She shook her head, trembly and faint as she considered what she'd spent, but she wasn't going to tell him that. It was silly, really.

"You've gone pale," Lucian announced with a frown, then glanced around. "Here, sit down."

Leigh let him lead her to a table in the food court and settled in one of the chairs with a sigh.

"I put a cooler in the car earlier," Lucian announced abruptly as he set her purchases on the empty chairs of the four chair table, then settled in the seat across from her. "After you've rested for a minute, I think we should go out and have a nip."

Leigh was slow to catch on to what he was talking about, and once she did, gave a little laugh. "That isn't the problem. I'm just feeling a little light-headed over spending so much in one shot. I've never done that before."

"Hmm," Lucian said slowly, but asked, "How's your stomach? Are you experiencing any kind of cramping, or almost an acidic biting sensation?"

Leigh blinked. "Well, yes . . . but . . ."

He nodded as if it was what he'd expected. "We'll make a quick nip out. It will only take a minute. Besides, this way we can put the bags in the car so we don't have to carry them around."

"But I only fed just before we left," she protested. "That was only an hour or so ago."

"More than two hours ago," Lucian corrected with a glance at his watch. "And it's a sunny day, you were exposed to the sun for about twenty minutes in the car on the way here, then on the walk across the parking lot. And, as I told you, for the next little while you'll need to feed often."

Leigh frowned, then asked, "Do all new turns have to feed this often?"

Lucian shrugged. "It's different for different people. It just depends on the individual."

Her frown deepened. "How often will I have to feed once the turning is done?"

He considered the question, then shrugged again. "That differs between people, too. Some need to feed every four hours or so, some can have two or three bags when they wake up and not need to feed again until just before they retire for the night. "Of course, those who work jobs where they have to be up and about in the daylight tend to need to feed more."

Leigh smiled faintly. "Then I guess I should be glad I've always been a night owl and like to work the night shift."

Lucian peered at her curiously. "How did you end up owning a bar?"

She smiled faintly at his expression. Most men were surprised she owned it. For some reason, people expected a bar owner to be male . . . or a crusty old broad with pink hair. She had no idea why.

"Leigh?"

"Oh, sorry," she murmured, cleared her throat, opened her mouth to answer his question, then hesitated, unsure where to start. "It's kind of a long story."

"In that case . . ." He stood up and collected his half of the bags again. "Let's go put these in the car, grab a bag, then go to a restaurant for some lunch."

"Lunch?" she asked with surprise as she stood to gather half of the purchases. "It's too early for lunch."

"Brunch, then," Lucian said with a shrug. "I'm hungry."

"I thought you didn't eat," she said with amusement as she walked with him out of the mall.

Lucian shrugged and said, "Things change."

"I guess they do," she agreed wryly, thinking how much her own life had changed in the last few days.

Lucian carried the tray carefully, his nose twitching as he inhaled the scent of the cappuccinos and hot cinnamon buns Leigh had assured him were good. They'd put her purchases in the trunk, sat in the car while Leigh had two bags of blood, then returned to the mall.

Lucian had tried to steer her to a restaurant, but she convinced him they could go to one for a late lunch later if they had a cappuccino and sticky bun now. She'd assured him they were yummy, and he had to admit the bun smelled good, but the cappuccino smelled just like coffee to him, though it was topped with some foamy substance.

"How's this?"

Lucian glanced up to see Leigh had chosen a table amidst a selection of empty ones. They could talk there without anyone overhearing them. He nodded. "Fine."

"Good?" Leigh asked after he'd taken his first bite of the bun.

Lucian nodded. "You were right."

She beamed at the compliment, small though it had been, and he decided that she mustn't have heard many in her life to be so pleased. But then, she'd been in an abusive relationship, Lucian reminded himself. Compliments would have been sparse in her marriage. He'd have to be sure to give her lots of compliments.

Swallowing the bite of bun, he prodded, "So? The bar?"

Leigh nearly choked on her own bun, then swallowed and chuckled. "I was hoping you'd forgotten about that."

"Why?"

"To explain it I have to touch on . . ." She paused and frowned, then simply said, "When I left Kenny, my husband, I had to hide."

Lucian's eyes narrowed. "Why?"

"I—Kenny had always said that if I ran away he'd find me and kill me." Leigh shrugged. "Looking back, I don't know if he really would have or not, but I believed it at the time. It's why I stayed in the marriage as long as I did . . . or maybe I just wasn't ready to be on my own."

Lucian opened his mouth to speak, but she waved him to silence.

"Don't. Let me just tell it. You can speak after."

When he nodded, she relaxed and continued, "Anyway, it took three years to finally make me leave. I woke up in the hospital that last time with a broken arm, several cracked ribs, and a concussion. Kenny was there, going on about how he was sorry, he loved me, and if I just wouldn't make him so angry he wouldn't have to hurt me." She grimaced. "Then the police walked in and asked him to leave so they could talk to me.

"Kenny leaned over to hug me and whispered in my ear that I'd tripped over a shoe and fallen down the stairs, and it was all I remembered . . . or else."

"Bastard," Lucian muttered.

"That's pretty much what I was thinking at the time," Leigh said with a shrug, then continued, "Before he straightened, I slipped a hand in his suit coat pocket and took his wallet. I slid it under the blankets as he turned away. Then I told the police exactly what he told me to say."

"Surely, they didn't believe it," he protested.

"No," Leigh admitted. "I don't think they did, but what could they do?"

Lucian frowned, thinking he'd have taken the man out and beaten the truth out of him.

"I pretended to go to sleep to make them leave, continued pretending when Kenny came back in so he'd go, too, then the minute I heard the door close behind him, I got up, got dressed, and walked out. There was an ATM in the lobby, and I withdrew the limit, then handed the wallet in at the information desk and said I'd found it in the elevator. Then I walked out the front doors and got into one of the row of taxis waiting in front of the hospital. I took it to the bus station." She paused to take a drink of her coffee, then said, "There were three buses leaving within fifteen minutes when I got there. I caught the one to Kansas City."

"Why Kansas City?" Lucian asked.

Leigh shrugged. "Kenny always scorned anything to

do with Kansas, for some reason. I don't know why. I don't think he'd ever even been there, but he considered it the hayseed capital of the world, so that's where I went."

Lucian nodded. It was as good a reason as any.

"I lived under an alias, working under the table to avoid having to give details, always afraid Kenny would find me and make good on his threat. I spent two years looking over my shoulder."

"Would he have really followed you?" Lucian asked. "Surely he had a job?"

"Oh yes, Kenny landed an excellent job right out of college. He was an investment banker. As for his following me . . . He was a sick man, possessive, controlling, jealous. He once told me if I ever left him, he'd hire a private investigator to hunt me down, then I'd hear a knock on the door one night and open it to find him there . . ."

Leigh grimaced. "Actually, I probably would have worried less if I'd thought he'd try to hunt me down himself. With the threat of a P.I. possibly being on my tail, I was worried that they'd be able to track me by my Social Security number, so I was afraid to use it. I was restricted to working jobs under the table for low pay and no benefits."

"It must have been a struggle," Lucian said quietly, wondering where she'd found the strength to live like that.

Leigh just shrugged. "I got by. It got easier when I landed a job at Coco's. Earl—the owner then," she explained, "he was an ex-cop with a heart of gold."

She smiled. "I swear, he seemed to hire only the walking wounded of the world. A lot of his employees were men starting over and women fresh from abusive relationships. He didn't bat an eye when I said I'd rather work under the table. I think he took one look at me and knew I was running from something. Life got a little easier after I started working there, and I relaxed a little.

"I'd been working there for a little less than a year when Kenny's private investigator finally caught up to me."

Lucian stiffened, and she smiled. "It's okay. I was terrified at first when he told me who he was, but then he said I was safe. Kenny was dead. It seems without me around to use as a punching bag, he'd had to find another outlet for his temper. He'd finally chosen the wrong person to punch. He died when his head bounced off the corner of a table in a bar during a brawl."

Lucian thought it served the man right, but Leigh paused and shook her head. "I didn't know what to say. I never wished Kenny dead, I just wanted him to leave me alone."

"If your husband was dead, why was the private detective there?" Lucian asked.

"That's what I asked," Leigh said wryly. "It seems it was a recent death. The private detective had finally traced me to Kansas City the day before. I was living under an assumed name, though, so he apparently took pictures of me and e-mailed them back to Massachusetts to be shown to Kenny, but when he called that morning to find out if Kenny had verified it was me, his partner said Kenny hadn't got the chance to see the photos. He was dead."

"So you were a widow."

"A rich widow," Leigh said dryly. "That was the detective's next bit of news. Kenny had done really well while I was gone, both in investments and business. He was made a junior partner in his company. His father had also died the year before and left him a hefty inheritance."

"And that's how you bought Coco's," Lucian said with a smile.

Leigh nodded, but glanced down. "Coco's is the only reason I took the money."

Lucian frowned. "I don't understand."

Leigh shrugged. "I liked my life. I liked working at the restaurant, liked the people . . . There was nothing for me to go back to Massachusetts for . . . except the money. And the very fact that it was Kenny's tainted it for me whether it was legally mine or not. But after the private investigator left, Earl came around the bar, took my arm and led me to his office. He'd heard every word the detective had said and he could tell I didn't want the money." She grinned. "Earl was really good at reading people."

"He convinced you to take the money," Lucian murmured.

"Yes. Earl wanted to retire to California to be closer to his daughter, but he didn't want to sell unless he was sure whoever bought it would keep on everyone already working there. He was as loyal to us as we all were to him, you see."

Leigh shrugged. "I was on a train back to Massachusetts the next day. Six months after that I was the proud owner of Coco' s." She grinned. "And I've lived happily ever after since then . . . until Donny stopped me on the street the other night."

Lucian stared silently, myriad emotions flowing through him. She'd lost so much in her short life, struggled to be free from abuse and gain independence, probably half-starved during those two years she'd been on the run, but she'd survived and even flourished. However,

Leigh had also cut herself off from people, much as he'd done after the death of his wife and children.

He had his work cut out for him, Lucian realized, and felt his heart sink. He'd never been a very patient person. All he wanted to do right then was take her home and make love to her, and coddle and protect her, make sure she never had another hard moment in her life. Leigh wouldn't take to that well, he knew. She'd fought too hard for her independence to give it up easily. And she wouldn't give her trust easily, he was sure.

"That's it," Leigh said lightly. "Now you know everything about me."

Not everything, Lucian thought. Not what she tasted like, not how she would fit in his arms, not how her hair would feel in his hands, or her skin sliding against his...

"I guess our next stop should be a drugstore."

Lucian blinked his thoughts away to see that Leigh had her list out and was going over it.

"I need shampoo, toothpaste, stuff like that, and you need razors," Leigh reminded him.

"Yes," he agreed. Glancing down, he saw that he'd finished his cappuccino and eaten his cinnamon bun without realizing it while she'd talked. He forced himself to his feet. "I wouldn't mind hitting a bookstore either."

Leigh looked surprised. "With all those books in Marguerite's library?"

"I've read most of them," he said with a shrug as she stood, too.

Leigh hesitated, then offered, "If you tell me what razor blades you need, I can pick them up for you. That way you can go to the bookstore while I go to the drugstore."

"Actually," Lucian said, "I think I'll just stop at home on the way back to Marguerite's and pick up my own razor. Some clothing, too." He grimaced. "Like you, I've been borrowing clothes, and it would be nice to wear some of my own stuff."

Leigh blinked in surprise. "You live around here, too?"

Lucian nodded.

"Then why are we at Marguerite's?"

"The IV was there," he said, rather than admit he'd originally intended on dumping her on his sister-in-law. "And now Julius needs looking after."

"Oh. Yes." She nodded. "Well, why don't you hit the bookstore while I do the drugstore, then we can meet up here again afterward."

Lucian hesitated. He didn't like the idea of leaving her alone if it was possible Morgan had reached the city. On the other hand, Morgan could hardly know they were at the mall. Besides, if everything had gone as planned, Mortimer and Bricker would have been at the airport to meet Morgan's plane.

"I'd really rather shop at the drugstore on my own," Leigh said quietly when he still hesitated. "There are some personal items I'd like to get."

Lucian forced himself to relax and nodded in acquiescence. "Okay, but go straight there and straight back and don't leave the mall without me."

Leigh grinned and sprang to her feet. "Meet here in half an hour, okay?"

She didn't wait for an answer, but swept off. Lucian felt a twinge of anxiety as she disappeared into the crowd, but tried to ignore it. Morgan and Donny couldn't be here at this mall. She would be fine, he assured himself. Still, he decided he'd get his business done quickly to be sure to be back before the half hour was up.

Turning away from the table, he set off at a quick clip. The bookstore was, of course, at the opposite end of the mall, but he covered the area quickly. He had nearly reached the store when he thought of calling Bastien. He'd feel better if he could find out for sure that Mortimer and Bricker had managed to get to the airport before Morgan's flight landed. Unfortunately, he didn't have his cell phone to make the call. It was back at the house, on the dresser with a dead battery. He looked for pay phones then, but didn't pass any before reaching the bookstore.

Anxious and impatient to be done with the task and get to a phone, Lucian decided he needed help and enlisted the aid of the first worker he came across—a tall, skinny kid who couldn't have been more than twenty and who bore a tag stating his name was Carl.

"Yes, sir?" Carl asked when he stopped him. "Can I help you?"

"Yes," Lucian said tersely. "I need books."

Carl's mouth tipped with amusement. "That's what we sell. What kind?"

Lucian hesitated, suddenly embarrassed, then recalled his boast to Rachel that he'd lived too long to be afraid of anyone or anything. Time to prove that. Straightening his shoulders, he said, "Books on how to get girls."

Carl's eyebrows flew up.

Lucian shifted uncomfortably under the kid's suddenly sharp inspection, feeling like an idiot, but this seemed the smartest route to him. If he didn't know something, he bought a book on it. He didn't know how to make Leigh fall in love with him, so he'd get a book on it. A primer on how to get the girl of your dreams. It made perfect sense to him and he thought it was a good idea . . . until he saw the excitement suddenly enter Carl's face and the wide grin that split his lips. A twinge of concern suddenly bloomed in him.

"Oh man! Have I got some books for you. Follow me."

It was as the young man turned away that Lucian spotted the cell phone clipped to his belt. He promptly opened his mouth to ask to use the phone, then caught back the question and simply slipped into the clerk's mind to take control, making Carl give him the phone and then go hunt up the books for him while he made his call.

Without Marguerite's handy speed dial or his own list of contacts, he wasn't able to call Bastien. But he knew the number to Mortimer's cell phone by heart after working with the man for decades, so he called him. Relief coursed through him when the other man answered on the second ring.

"Did you get Morgan?" he asked abruptly, not bothering with a greeting.

"Hello to you, too, Lucian," Mortimer chuckled, then answered the question. "No. I'm afraid not. We got to the airport half an hour before the plane arrived and watched every single person leave the plane, but neither Morgan nor Donny were on it. We think the tickets might have been a red herring to throw us off the track."

Lucian let his breath out slowly as he concentrated on the tone of Mortimer's voice. "You don't sound too sure about that. What's happened?"

"There were a couple of large withdrawals of cash on Stobie's bank account," Mortimer admitted.

Lucian growled under his breath. With cash, Morgan would be harder to track. There might not be recorded transactions at gas stations or restaurants, and tickets could be bought for cash. Morgan could give them the slip . . . or could sneak up on them without warning. Lucian's instincts were still telling him that the man had some interest in Leigh, and Rachel's comments that Morgan hadn't been able to fully control Leigh strengthened his belief that the man might come after her. Lucian found Leigh fascinating himself, but knew even if she weren't his life mate, he would have been fascinated by anyone he couldn't control.

"Where are you?" he finally asked.

"Watching your house," Mortimer answered. "If he *is* headed here, we'll be ready for him. Otherwise, we have to wait until he charges something again, and this is as good a place to wait as any."

Lucian nodded and was about to speak again when he saw the clerk, Carl, staggering toward him carrying a stack of books. His eyes widened incredulously at the sheer volume of titles the lad had found.

"Lucian? Are you still there?" Mortimer asked, and he was recalled to the phone.

"Yes, yes," he muttered with distraction. "I'll be at the house soon."

He snapped the phone closed without saying goodbye and turned his attention to the books Carl had brought him.

Fourteen

Leigh glanced at the clock on the wall as she left the drugstore and cursed under her breath. She'd been hoping to get done and stop to pick up panties, bras, and socks before meeting up with Lucian. The socks, she wouldn't mind buying in his company, but picking out underthings with him peering over her shoulder and—dear God—possibly offering suggestions, as he had with the clothes she'd bought . . . Well, she didn't think she could face that.

Unfortunately, it had taken her longer at the drugstore than she'd intended, thanks mostly to a difficult customer in front of her in the checkout line. Now she wouldn't have time to stop on her own. However, none of the items were optional. She had to buy some, and it looked like it would be in his company.

She spotted Lucian by the food court one moment before she spotted the lingerie shop she was passing. The tense smile of greeting that had started on her face froze as she skidded to a halt.

Five minutes, she thought. *That's all it will take. Five. Four if I just snatch and pay*. It didn't matter what they looked like. Hell, she'd intended to just pick up some cotton undies from the nearest Wal-mart or whatever, but she'd pay the extra money to avoid having to shop for them with Lucian there.

Glancing back to where he stood watching passing customers, she hesitated, then ducked into the lingerie store . . . only to pause inside the door, her eyes flying left, right, then straight ahead, suddenly unsure where to start.

Panties, she told herself firmly. Thanks to the nanos, her breasts seemed to have regained their ability to defy gravity and she could make do without a bra for a day if necessary, but panties, she needed. Having made the decision, Leigh turned toward a table with scads of lacy panties on display and walked over to have a look. A pair of red silk bikini panties caught her eye and she picked them up to check the size.

"Leigh."

Eyes widening, and two red flags in her cheeks, she whirled to find Lucian walking toward her, carrying two large bags bearing a bookstore logo.

"I saw you rush in here and came to see— Oh." Mouth open and eyes widening, he looked at the display she stood in front of, then peered around the shop.

Leigh followed his gaze. Everywhere you looked was silk, satin, and lace. It was definitely not your cotton underwear kind of store, and she knew her cheeks probably matched the red panties she held when his gaze returned to her. But—much to her surprise—Lucian looked more embarrassed and uncomfortable than she was. She hadn't expected that.

"Er . . ." Lucian cleared his throat, his gaze avoiding hers but appearing not to know where to settle. He looked like a man trapped.

"Er . . ." he said again, then muttering something about the food court, he whirled away. Only to come up short when he found his way blocked by a short round woman in a red dress with glasses that hung around her neck from a gold chain.

"Oh, now you can't leave yet, son," the woman said merrily. "You should help your wife pick something you'll like. It's for you, after all."

"I'm not—"

"Now, what do you think of those she's holding? They're our most popular style."

Lucian gaped at the red panties Leigh held and looked like he was about to swallow his own tongue.

"I think he likes them," the little woman assured her, then nudged Lucian. "Don't you, son?"

"Er . . . yes . . ."

Leigh's eyes widened as she saw his eyes flame to life in a swirl of molten silver. She got the feeling he was picturing her in the bit of silk and nothing else, but then decided she must be wrong. She might lust after him, but she wasn't the sort men lusted after.

"I know just the thing!" The woman rushed over to a side display, returning with a black corset with a red and white rosebud trim. "What do you think, son?"

"I . . . er . . . It . . ." Apparently at a loss for words, Lucian turned abruptly and rushed out of the store, growling, "I'll be in the food court."

"Shy fellow, isn't he?" the saleslady commented with amusement.

Leigh bit her lip as she watched him go. In truth, she found it stunning that he was even embarrassed. He'd lived so long, seen so much . . . yet the sight of wisps of silk and satin seemed to embarrass him. Surely he'd seen this sort of thing before? Many, many times, even.

Why, Lucian must have had hundreds, even thousands,

of lovers over the years who had worn such things for him, she thought, and found she didn't care for the idea. In fact, she didn't care for it at all.

"Here, dear, this dark pink set would look lovely on you."

Pushing her thoughts away, Leigh turned her attention to picking out panties.

Once she explained her need for at least half a dozen pairs, as well as bras and socks, and that she was in a bit of a hurry, the woman became a little tornado of activity.

Ten minutes later Leigh was walking out with two bags of silky things.

Lucian hadn't returned to the food court. He was pacing outside the lingerie store like a caged tiger, his expression grim.

Leigh pasted a smile on her face as she approached, searching for something to say to get past the awkward moment. She thought she'd come up with the perfect opener when she asked brightly, "What books did you buy?"

Much to her amazement, her innocuous question made Lucian freeze mid-step and stiffen up like she'd shoved a pole up his backside. While she was still worrying over that, he whirled abruptly toward the exit and said, "Let's go."

Leigh hurried after him, her gaze now curious, on the bag. When she'd asked the question, she hadn't really cared what books he'd bought. Now she did, though. His reaction ensured she would. Unfortunately, she couldn't see through the dark bag to the titles. All she could tell was that he had *a lot* of books.

"We still have to get groceries," he reminded her as

he opened the trunk for them to set the bags inside.

Leigh took one look at the packed trunk and raised an eyebrow.

"I guess there isn't room this trip," he said with a frown, then suggested, "Do you want to take these home and then come back out for groceries?"

"That would be fine," Leigh agreed as he closed the trunk.

"We could stop for lunch on the way home," Lucian suggested, leading her to the passenger door and opening it.

"Okay," she agreed, but shook her head with amusement as he closed her door and walked around to the driver's side. For a man who previously hadn't been interested in food, he'd certainly changed his tune.

They ate at the same restaurant where they'd had breakfast. Leigh ordered a Reuben sandwich and a Coke. Lucian had the same. It was then that she realized that if he hadn't eaten for thousands of years, he'd have no idea what today's food tasted like . . . which was no doubt why he'd simply asked for what she'd ordered. Leigh decided she'd have to make sure she had something different every meal, so he could try different things and see what he liked.

They talked a bit about books and movies while they waited for their food, but Lucian seemed distracted, his gaze constantly moving around the restaurant and examining the parking lot. It was almost a relief when the food arrived and there was no need to try to keep a conversation going. Lucian seemed to like his sandwich and fries. He wasn't as keen on the Coke, saying the bubbles got up his nose.

They headed to his place to pick up some clothes after lunch. Lucian seemed to grow even more tense then, so Leigh left him to whatever was bothering him and spent the ride trying to imagine what sort of place he would live in, and came up with an apartment, modern, all sharp lines and steel.

She got a bit of a shock when he pulled up to the gate of a stone fence. Forget the apartment, he owned an estate. They drove a winding lane through trees that then opened up to reveal a river flowing into a pond on their right, and an arbor on their left. From the outside, the house itself wasn't all that impressive. It was large, its walls red stone, and had lots of windows. If it had been red-painted wood instead of stone, she would have thought it was a renovated barn . . . until she got inside.

Lucian unlocked the old-fashioned metal and wood door and held it open for her. Leigh stepped through, eyes widening and flitting everywhere. Then a little sigh of pleasure slipped from her lips. The inside was beautiful, rustic, and open, so you could see into every room on the ground floor. There was a large living room on the left, and a kitchen/dining area on the right. The floors were a combination of hardwood and stone, the path leading from the doorway to the stairs to the second level was stone, like a cobbled street from England. On either side of that, a light hardwood spread away into the actual living spaces. The outer walls within the house were a red brick similar to the outside, while the inner walls were cream-colored. Along with its many windows and open concept, it gave a light and airy feeling yet a warm rustic feeling. It was a perfect combination. She loved it!

Leigh turned back to find him watching her, and asked, "Can I look upstairs?"

"Of course," he said.

Smiling, she mounted the stairs and discovered they led up to a large open sitting area on the left that ran the length of the house. A row of doors stood to her right, bedrooms and bathrooms, she guessed, and turned into the sitting area to take it in. She ran her hand over the light leather furniture and admired the stone wall, the fireplace, and the thick rug in front of it.

It was all just perfect. She loved it and could hardly wait to see what was behind the closed doors. Leigh turned to do so and nearly ran into the man who had crept up behind her.

Lucian checked the front window again as Leigh headed upstairs, but saw no sign of anyone lurking around. Not even Mortimer and Bricker, who were supposed to be watching the place, but then they were good at their job and would hardly be out in the open.

Turning away from the window, he paced briefly between the door and the stairs. He was eager to get his things and get Leigh out of there in case Morgan did show up. He'd prefer to have her out of harm's way, but didn't think it could hurt to let Leigh have a few minutes upstairs on her own to look around before he hustled her out. He'd seen the reaction he had hoped for on the main floor. She liked his home, which was encouraging. One hurdle crossed.

Lucian paced to the window again, scanning the woods surrounding his home. He didn't see anything, but was growing more impatient by the minute. She'd had enough time, he decided, and turned toward the stairs.

He'd just put his foot on the first step when her scream sliced the air.

Morgan, he thought. Somehow the man had slipped past Mortimer and Bricker and gotten into the house.

He was up the stairs in a heartbeat, ready to rip the bastard's heart out with his bare hands if he'd touched one hair on Leigh's precious head.

What he found was Leigh laughing, slapping Mortimer lightly on the shoulder and then giving him a hug as she gasped, "Dear Lord, you scared me to death! I thought you were Morgan."

Lucian scowled as the adrenaline evaporated. He was glad it wasn't Morgan. On the other hand, Mortimer looked far too happy hugging Leigh. And, she'd never smiled at *him* like that, or hugged *him*, he thought with resentment.

As if hearing his thoughts, Mortimer suddenly stepped back from Leigh and turned to look at him. "Hey, Lucian," he said, the wary smile on his face suggesting to Lucian that his jealousy was showing.

"What are you doing here?" Lucian asked, forcing himself to relax.

"I told you we were watching the house," Mortimer answered mildly.

"Yes, *watching* it. I assumed that meant you were doing so from outside. How did you get in?" Lucian asked as he crossed the room.

"Thomas picked us up at the airport when that turned out to be a bust," Bricker announced. Lucian glanced over his shoulder to see the brunet coming out of a door near the front of the house. His hair was tousled, his face sleep-creased, and he was only wearing a pair of joggers that hung low around his waist. "He had a key. He said he got it from the office."

"Argeneau Enterprises has a key to each of our houses in case of emergency," Lucian said, for Leigh's benefit more than anyone else's, then he scowled at Bricker and added, "That's my room."

"I know. I saw your stuff in there. Great bed." Bricker
grinned widely, then turned his gaze to Leigh and crossed
the sitting area to her side. "Hey there, Leigh. You're
looking pretty darn fine. Much better than when last I
saw you."

"There's been no sign of Morgan yet, and no new
charges on the credit card," Mortimer said, bringing an
end to Lucian's attempt to set Bricker on fire with his
eyes as the younger man paused by Leigh and gave her
a hug.

Lucian grunted, but his attention was on Leigh as she
smiled and hugged Bricker back.

Straightening, Bricker asked her, "How are you feeling? Has Lucian been treating you well, or is he being
his grumpy old self?"

Despite having accused Lucian of being grumpy herself, Leigh smacked Bricker playfully in the stomach and
said, "Lucian isn't grumpy. He's taken very good care
of me. He nursed me through the turning, then today
took me out to breakfast, then shopping for clothes. We
just had a late lunch, and after we pick up some of his
things and drop them off at Marguerite's, we're going
for groceries."

Lucian felt himself stand a little taller at Leigh's praise
and obvious appreciation, until Bricker gasped, "No
way! Not the Argeneau I know. He did all that?"

Leigh made a face. "You guys all go on like he's some
kind of ogre, but he's been nothing but kind to me . . .
well, except for the first day," she allowed. "He was
kind of grumpy then, but I don't think he'd had much
sleep."

Lucian grimaced as Bricker glanced his way with an
arched eyebrow.

"Yeah?" the younger man said, then peered back to

Leigh to ask, "Who are the 'you guys' who are making him out to be an ogre?"

Leigh wrinkled her nose. "Rachel doesn't seem to care for Lucian much."

"Ah," Bricker murmured knowingly, then his expression turned serious as he said, "Well, as it happens, I don't think Lucian's an ogre. I think he's a great guy, a good friend, and cool under fire. You couldn't find anyone better than him for a mate."

Lucian scowled at him as he noted that Leigh was taken aback at the comment. He'd been taking it slow to sneak up on her, and Bricker was openly playing matchmaker. It was obvious someone had been talking, and Bricker knew he couldn't read Leigh.

"Bricker. Shut up," he said, and turned to walk to his room to pack some clothes.

He was in his closet, stuffing clothes into a black duffel bag, when he heard Leigh call out to him. Pausing, he walked to the door between the closet and bedroom and saw her peering curiously into the room.

"Yes?" he asked.

Leigh glanced his way and smiled. "Bricker was just saying that you have no groceries here and he wouldn't mind tagging along with us to get some. Is that okay?"

Lucian grimaced, not at all pleased with the idea, but he nodded with resignation. "Yeah. Tell him he has ten minutes to get ready."

Leigh turned her head and peered at someone outside the room. "You have ten minutes to get ready."

"I told you he'd say yes if *you* asked." Bricker's voice drifted into the room on a laugh.

Leigh just chuckled, then started to turn back to Lucian, her gaze stopping before it reached him. Curious, he glanced to see what had caught her attention. The only thing there was his bed, mussed from Bricker's use.

"Black satin sheets," she murmured with amazement, and Lucian felt his heart trip as he recalled the images he'd sent her that morning. Their bodies entwined on black satin sheets. Eyes widening like a schoolboy caught doing mischief, he turned abruptly and ducked back into the closet.

Lucian almost expected her to follow him into the closet and demand an explanation, but she didn't. After a moment he stepped back to the door and peered warily out. Leigh was still standing in the doorway, staring at the bed, a confused look on her face.

He was debating whether to say anything when Bricker called from somewhere deep in the house, "Hey, Leigh! What do fashionable Canadian men wear grocery shopping?"

Leigh blinked and turned to peer out the door. "How do I know? I'm from Kansas."

"Yeah, but you've at least been shopping today and seen the guys out there."

"Toques and plaid?" she suggested with amusement.

"You're joking!" Bricker squawked.

"Yes, I am." Leigh chuckled as she moved out of the door. "Just wear . . ."

Lucian didn't hear the rest. Letting his shoulders relax, he turned back into the closet. He stuffed a couple more items into his bag, then moved to the en suite bathroom to grab his spare razor and a few other items.

When he stepped out into the sitting area, it was empty, and he followed the murmur of voices downstairs. Leigh and Mortimer were in the kitchen, talking as they waited for the kettle to boil.

"I'm making tea," Mortimer announced as he entered. "You want any?"

"Tea?" Lucian asked with interest. It was something he hadn't yet tried.

Mortimer grabbed a third cup from the cupboard, paused, then took a fourth cup as well. For Bricker, Lucian supposed.

"Are you coming shopping, too?" he asked Mortimer.

"No." The other man picked up the kettle and poured water into each cup as he said, "I'm going to sleep. We were taking turns driving to try to catch up with Morgan. We were driving around the clock, one sleeping while the other drove. My shift was just ending when Bastien called and told us about the plane tickets and that he was sending a plane for us."

Lucian nodded.

"I'll let you each fix your own tea," Mortimer announced as he took the tea bags out. He then took his own cup to the table.

"Ahh, tea," Bricker said, entering the kitchen as they were finishing off their cups several minutes later. He'd changed into faded, holey jeans and a skintight maroon t-shirt. "I'll have one of those, too."

"No time," Lucian announced, getting to his feet. "Your ten minutes are up."

Bricker groaned. "You're a hard man, Lucian."

"Yes, I am. Don't forget it," he said dryly. "If you're coming, then let's go."

Taking Leigh's arm as she got to her feet, Lucian walked her out to the car, noticing the way her eyes ate up the environment he'd had built around his home.

"How much land do you have?" she asked, curious.

"Twenty or thirty acres," he answered, then glanced around and realized she'd only seen the front yard. "The river winds through it, then comes around the house and empties into the pond. "There's a fountain spout in the pond," he added, gesturing to a point just in front a little bridge and pagoda. "I turned it off before heading down to Kansas, though," he explained, then promised, "I'll bring you back in the next couple of days and show you around properly. There's a pool, an outdoor shower, a bunkhouse, and a little studio on its own."

"It's lovely, and I'd love to see more," Leigh told him solemnly.

"Tomorrow," he decided. "I'll bring you back tomorrow."

Lucian opened the front passenger door for her, then closed it and turned, remembering that Bricker was accompanying them. He was standing beside the car, grinning like an idiot. Lucian scowled.

"Get in," he muttered, and walked around to the driver's side.

It occurred to him then that he was acting as out of character around Leigh as the two of them had on the day they brought her back to the hotel. The difference was, he'd been surprised and exasperated by their behavior. His own actions, on the other hand, seemed to be causing Bricker a great deal of amusement. Sighing, Lucian slid behind the wheel and started the car.

They stopped at Marguerite's to drop off their purchases, to make room in the trunk for the groceries, setting them inside the foyer to be put away when they got back. Then they fed Julius before continuing on to the grocery store.

Leigh was an organized shopper, Lucian saw with approval. She had the list she'd made that morning and followed it, placing item after item in the cart he was pushing. Bricker, on the other hand, seemed to throw everything his eyes landed on into his own cart. He also wandered off, got distracted, goofed about, and joked constantly . . . making Leigh laugh, much to Lucian's annoyance. And somehow, with all Bricker's tomfoolery, Leigh ended up pushing his cart for him, at which point the man jumped on the low railing in front of the cart and said, "Push me, Leigh!"

"No," she laughed.

"Ah, come on," Bricker coaxed.

"No. You could get hurt," Leigh said primly, then shook her head and glanced at Lucian to ask, "Why do I feel like we're Mommy and Daddy and he's the spoiled son?"

A smile broke through Lucian's gloom. He'd been growing more depressed as she laughed at Bricker's antics, feeling like the old stogie to Bricker's young stud. But now that Leigh was siding herself with him and saw Bricker as childish, he felt better.

Bricker laughed. "I may be young at heart, but I'm hardly young enough to be your son," he said to Leigh. "In truth, I'm more around the age of your grandfather if he were still alive. Is he still alive?"

She shook her head. "No. None of my grandparents are still alive. Neither are my parents, for that matter." Then she tilted her head and asked him, "How old are you?"

Bricker grinned and admitted, "Ninety-seven."

"Man, I hope I look as young as you at ninety-seven."

"You will," Lucian and Bricker said at the same moment.

Leigh considered that, and a wry expression crossed her face. "I started out cursing Donny, but now I'm starting to think I should be thanking him. Maybe I should send him a thank-you card . . . or flowers."

"Flowers?" Lucian said with amusement.

"Too girly?" she asked, and tipped her head briefly to think before shouting, "I know! Blood-filled chocolates."

Lucian raised his eyebrows at the suggestion, and she said, "You said there are specialty bars. I don't suppose we have specialty chocolates and things like that, too?"

"No." Lucian grinned. "But I'd be willing to be your financial backer if you wanted to start making them. The women might love it."

Leigh shook her head. "It was just a joke. Besides, you really don't have to taste the blood, do you? Not when you feed from a blood bag. I doubt anyone really enjoys the taste of blood."

"You will acquire the taste," Lucian assured her. "You've already acquired enjoyment of the smell."

Leigh blinked in surprise at his claim, then said, "The cleaner."

Lucian nodded.

She frowned, apparently not pleased to acknowledge she'd been attracted to the scent, then her eyes widened with horror and she asked, "Do you mean to say I'm going to begin to actually enjoy the taste of blood?"

"I'm afraid so," he said apologetically, though he wasn't sure why he felt he should apologize.

"Gross," she said with disgust.

Leigh was quiet after that as they finished the last bit of shopping and made their way to the checkout.

They dropped Bricker off at Lucian's house with his groceries, then continued on to Marguerite's with their own.

"Someone's here," Leigh said with surprise as they drove up the driveway.

Lucian frowned as he peered at the three cars in front of the house. He recognized one of them as Rachel and Etienne's. The other looked like Lissianna and Greg's. He had no idea who the third vehicle belonged to and could only wonder what had brought them all there.

He parked in the garage, popped the trunk, and began to pull out bags, his mind taken up with what might have happened to cause his relatives to descend on him. Between himself and Leigh, they managed to grab all of the grocery bags from the trunk, but then, he could carry more than the average man and had six in each hand, while Leigh had only three bags in each.

The door opened as they approached, and Thomas appeared with Julius at his side. His presence told Lucian three things: one, the third car belonged to him; two, whatever was happening couldn't be that serious or the man wouldn't be smiling like an idiot as usual; and three, Thomas hadn't died and so had no excuse for the way he'd been avoiding his phone calls.

Before he could growl at the young man, Thomas announced blithely, "I hear you've been trying to call me. I'm afraid my cell phone broke down. I didn't realize it until just this morning. I had to go pick up another one today. Remind me, and I'll give you the new number before I leave."

With the fire taken out from under him, Lucian merely growled as he passed the younger man and entered the kitchen. He set the groceries down on the counter, started to turn back to take the groceries Leigh carried, only to freeze as he spotted Rachel, Etienne, Lissianna, and Greg all grouped together by the kitchen entrance. Every single one of them was smiling widely.

"What's going on?" he asked warily.

"It's an intervention," Lissianna said with a grin.

"What?" he asked with confusion, but all four of

them just grinned harder and moved forward, gravitating toward Leigh.

Stepping quickly to her side, Lucian took the groceries from her, then gestured to everyone in the room one after the other. "This is my nephew, Thomas. You won't remember him but he picked us up at the airport when we flew in from Kansas City," he explained, then gestured to the other four. "You remember Rachel and Etienne."

When she nodded, he went on, "And that's my niece Lissianna and her husband Gregory Hewitt."

"Hello," Leigh said.

A chorus of hellos answered her, then all five of his nieces and nephews suddenly went into action, taking bags and unloading groceries. Lucian sighed and turned to pick up and begin emptying one of the bags himself. It appeared he'd have to wait to find out what the hell was going on.

Fifteen

"I don't need help," Lucian said, facing his nieces and nephews with irritation.

The groceries were unpacked and Leigh took her purchases upstairs. The moment she left, his family announced they were there to help him "land Leigh."

Thank you, Rachel, he thought with irritation. Honestly, his life had been easier when she'd still been angry with him, and he briefly wondered how to make it happen again.

"It won't happen again. I know you now," Rachel said with amusement, drawing a glare from him.

"Will you stop reading my mind, woman!" he snapped.

Rather than look cowed, the redhead grinned, unrepentant.

He was ruined, Lucian realized with dismay. His reputation as a hardass lay in tatters, and every last one of his nieces and nephews were smiling at him as if he was the cutest damned thing they'd ever seen. It was humiliating.

"I *am* a hardass," Lucian said coldly, as if they had openly disputed it.

"Of course you are, Uncle. And none of us would want

to anger you, or you'd surely prove it," Lissianna said solemnly. She was blond, tall, and normally willowy. Her pregnancy was showing, however, and it alarmed Lucian how big she was. He was afraid if she didn't have this child soon, it would explode from her belly like a stripper out of a cake . . . and probably already walking and talking.

"But at the moment you need our help," Etienne said. He glanced around at the others, then shrugged and added, "And we *want* to help."

"I've taken care of the matter myself. I don't *need* your help," Lucian repeated firmly.

A moment passed as the quintet exchanged glances, then Rachel asked suspiciously, "How have you taken care of it?"

"That's none of your business," he said abruptly, knowing better than to even think about the purchase he'd made that day. If they were reading his mind and he let it even enter his head, they'd know about the books. He didn't want that.

He felt the focus of five pairs of eyes lock on his head, and five minds trying to rifle through his own. He did his damnedest to shut them out and keep them from reading anything.

"You can still lock us out," Rachel said with surprise.

"He's concentrating *real* hard," Etienne commented, then assured them, "He can't keep it up. It will slip out once he relaxes."

Rachel shifted impatiently, and Lucian knew she wasn't pleased with the idea of having to wait. Standing abruptly, she asked, "Would anyone like tea?"

Everyone assented, including Lucian, who then added, "We picked up some almond pastries Leigh assures me are good, if anyone feels like snacking." The five of them turned surprised smiles his way, and he scowled. "So, I'm eating now. I can eat, too. You all do."

"Yes, we do," Greg said soothingly.

"Stop being so defensive, Uncle," Lissianna chided. "Finding your life mate is a wonderful thing. It strengthens you."

"Yeah yeah," Lucian said with a sigh.

"Books!" Rachel said triumphantly, and his head snapped her way.

"You evil little witch, you brought up the offer of tea just to distract me so you could read my mind," he said, but there was little heat behind his words. Rather than anger, Lucian felt admiration. Etienne had himself a clever little gal on his hands.

"Thank you, Uncle Lucian." Rachel grinned, then turned and headed for the door. "I'll go put the tea on."

Lucian watched her go with a sigh, then glanced to Etienne as his nephew spoke.

"I'm glad you two have finally got past that first meeting, Uncle. It's been a bit awkward at times with her so angry at you."

He opened his mouth to answer, then stiffened as they heard a shriek of *"Oh my God!"* from the back of the house. He frowned toward the door, wondering what had made Rachel react like that, and then he knew. Springing to his feet before the others had even processed the sound fully, he sped from the room, nearly tripping over Julius in his haste.

Lucian's heart did a little stutter when he reached the hall and saw the door to the library open. He'd been right. Dammit.

"Rachel!" he snapped, striding into the room to find her pulling books out of the bookstore bags he'd put in there earlier. He'd done it while they were unloading groceries. Remembering that the books were still in the front foyer with Leigh's clothes, he had slid out briefly to move them into the library and out of sight before anyone could see them and comment.

Rachel had found them. Though whether she'd read their whereabouts in his mind or noticed him slipping out, he couldn't say.

"Put those down," Lucian growled.

"What are they?" Etienne asked, and Lucian turned to see that everyone had followed him and were now crowding into the library, eyeing the books curiously.

"His idea of taking care of the matter," Rachel said with disgust and—much to his dismay—began to read the titles as she pulled the books from the bag. *"Understanding Women . . . How to Chat Up Women . . . How to Pick Up Beautiful Women . . . The Complete Asshole's Guide to Handling Chicks?"* Her voice rose at the end in question and she turned to peer at him with disbelief.

Lucian shifted uncomfortably, his voice stiff as he said, "Carl said it has some good tips for non-asshole-type guys, too."

Lucian heard a snicker behind him and turned to glare over his shoulder. Unfortunately, he couldn't tell who it had come from, so he just glared at all of them.

"How to Succeed With Women," Rachel went on. *"Body Language Secrets: A Guide During Courtship and Dating . . . How to Meet The Right Woman?"* Pausing, she shook her head and pointed out, "You've already met her."

"It gives advice on other things. Like stuff to say and what to learn that will impress her . . . like dancing,"

Lucian muttered, struggling to recall what Carl had said about the book.

"*The Rules of the Game . . . The System, How to Get Laid Today?*" Rachel continued, her voice dripping with disgust.

Lucian crossed his arms and glared to the side, refusing to comment or even look at her. Then a soft sound from her drew his gaze back. Rachel had frozen with two new books in hand. Her eyes were wide as she gaped at them.

He stiffened. He didn't need her to read the titles, he knew what they were. They were the only ones left. His humiliation was about to be completed, he realized with a sinking heart.

"What is it?" Thomas asked.

Much to Lucian's surprise, Rachel hesitated, then shoved the books back in the bag and shook her head. "Never mind."

"Oh, no way!" Thomas rushed forward and snatched the bag from her. Pulling out the first book, he gave a little whoop of amusement, then read, "*The Art of Seduction!*"

Lucian struggled to keep his face expressionless, but inside he felt about two inches tall.

Thomas tossed the book on the desk with the others Rachel had pulled out, retrieved the other one and said, "And the last one is . . . *How to Satisfy Her Every Time.*"

Thomas's voice had slowed and become less amused and more quiet with each word. When he closed his mouth, the room fell into a complete and uncomfortable silence. No one seemed to want to look at anyone else.

"It has been a while," Lucian said finally, his voice stiff as he broke the silence.

"And you want to please her," Greg said quietly as he crossed the room. He took the book from Thomas and returned it to the bag. "That's understandable."

"Yeah," Etienne echoed.

"I think it's sweet." Lissianna patted his shoulder.

"But I don't think the book is necessary," Greg added. "I realize that the length of time since you've . . . er . . . indulged in . . . er . . . well . . . you may be feeling inadequate, but—" He paused to ask curiously, "How long has it been?"

Lucian hesitated, then admitted, "I haven't indulged—as you put it—since the Romans left Britain."

Shocked expressions covered every face and silence filled the room, then Greg cleared his throat and said, "That's . . . a long time."

"I know," Lucian said miserably. He'd be lucky if the damn thing worked.

"Well . . ." Greg cleared his throat. "I'm sure it will be fine. It's like riding a bike—"

He stopped abruptly when a burst of laughter slipped from Thomas. Before anyone could comment, Thomas covered his mouth and turned away, muttering, "Sorry."

"You'll remember what to do," Greg finished.

"I *do* remember what to do," Lucian snapped. "I just wanted . . . Carl said they had some tips . . ."

"Who *is* this Carl?" Rachel asked.

"The clerk at the bookstore. He helped me choose the books," Lucian said stiffly.

"The bookstore cashier? What was he? Twelve?" Rachel asked with disgust, then gestured to the books stacked on the desk and said, "These aren't going to help you, Uncle. They're crap."

She picked up one of the books, rifled through it,

paused and snorted, then read aloud, "'Don't buy them a meal until they sleep with you.'"

Lucian frowned. He'd already blown that rule. He'd bought Leigh both breakfast and lunch and a snack in between. He glanced to Rachel as she tossed the book aside and grabbed another.

"Oh this is good. 'Always remain in control,'" she read. "'Of the situation, the date, the relationship, the *woman*'?"

She tsked with disgust, but Lucian relaxed a little. He could do that.

Rachel grabbed another book, but didn't even bother to open it. She just held it up and said, "*The Layguide*, Uncle?"

"He's supposed to be an expert," Lucian argued.

"An expert? He's probably single," she derided. "Besides, sleeping with a handful of women doesn't make you an expert on them. I sleep with Etienne all the time and still don't know a damned thing about men. None of you make sense to me. Why would you think these books could help you?"

"She's right, Uncle," Etienne said. "These books are all about how a man can get some action. Not on how to get a mate."

"Exactly," Rachel agreed. "And trust me. The only expert on a woman is another woman. You guys don't even think like we do, your brains are built completely differently."

"Don't be ridiculous," Lucian disparaged

"Oh no?" Rachel asked. "What is the first thing you do when you get lost on a road trip?"

"I don't get lost," Lucian said dryly.

"Right." She rolled her eyes. "But if you did?"

"You *can't* get lost," Lucian explained dryly. "If

you have even a basic idea of where you're headed—north, south, east, west—you just keep going in the direction—"

"Exactly," Rachel said dryly as if he'd just proven her point. "A woman doesn't think like that."

"She'd stop the moment she realized she was lost and ask for directions," Lissianna announced.

"Ask for directions? Well, that's . . ." Lucian muttered under his breath, then said, "This isn't about directions, it's about getting a woman."

"No," Greg said quietly. "It's about winning *Leigh*."

"And these books are about *getting laid*," Rachel said, waving to them again. Then she peered at him solemnly and said, "Trust me, any guy can get laid any day of the week. This is the twenty-first century, there are willing women everywhere. Every night, men around the world get lucky because some drunk female is lonely and thinks he looks a bit like Jude Law or some other actor. It's only an idiot who thinks it's his technique and his *taking control*. News flash! The man is never in control. The woman is the gateway. She says yes or no . . . unless it's rape. And then he isn't *getting* any, he's *taking* it. That's why they call rape a power crime."

"Yes," Lucian said. "But these books teach you how to be charming and—"

"You already *are* charming," Rachel said, and the room went silent as the others turned toward her with disbelief. Blinking as she realized what she'd said, Rachel frowned. "Well, maybe not charming exactly, but you're fair and you care about your family and love them and . . ."

She seemed at a loss, then rallied and said, "Look, these won't help you. Frankly, I suspect all these books really teach a man is how to avoid women they aren't likely to get into bed, and to move on to the ones who *are* interested."

"Well, Leigh doesn't seem interested in me at all," Lucian muttered.

"Of course not. Once bitten, twice shy. Kenny hurt her. You need to show her you would never do that. You need to show her that you can be gentle and caring."

"Rachel's saying you should be yourself," Greg added quietly. "You should be who you are, not act like some book says you should."

"But what if she doesn't like who I am?" Lucian asked with frustration.

Silence filled the room and they all stared at him wide-eyed.

"She's going to love you, Uncle Lucian," Lissianna said quietly, moving to his side to rub his back, as if she thought he needed soothing.

"Yeah," Thomas agreed. "You have the life mate thing going for you, Uncle."

"You're meant to be together," Rachel reminded him. "You just have to show her that."

Lucian shifted. It wasn't the first time they'd said that, but they hadn't told him *how* to show her that he was gentle and caring and they were meant to be together. Maybe he should just read the books and see if they had any tips about—

"Please trust me, Lucian," Rachel said, interrupting his thoughts. "Those books have nothing to do with proving you're gentle and caring."

"Well, then what am I supposed to do? I took her to breakfast today, then shopping, and helped her pick out clothes. I enjoyed it and thought she did, too, but . . ."

"But?"

"But then we stopped at my place to pick up clothes,

and Bricker and Mortimer were there and she hugged them both and laughed with *them* and they were flirting like crazy. She doesn't flirt with me, or hug me, or anything."

"Maybe it's easier to flirt with Bricker and Mortimer because she doesn't care for them," Greg suggested, then shrugged and added, "Some people can't flirt with someone they're attracted to."

"And she *is* attracted to you," Etienne assured him.

"How do you know?" Lucian asked.

"You're not the only one we can read. Her mind's an open book," Rachel said, rolling her eyes. "Half-naked images of you kept popping into her head while we were talking to her. It was really quite alarming."

"Leigh seems to think you have a fine ass," Etienne informed him. "She kept seeing your butt in tight black jeans in her mind's eye over and over."

"Yeah?" Lucian asked with interest. He had the sudden urge to go look at his butt in a mirror to see what she liked about it, but restrained himself. He'd done quite enough to look like an idiot in the eyes of these young people today. He then recalled that they could all read his mind and realized that he'd just made himself look like an ass again.

"She likes your chest, too," Rachel announced, passing up the opportunity to make fun of him. "She thinks it's hunky."

"Hunky?" Lucian glanced down at his chest and flexed his muscles a little.

"I think what we need to do is get the two of you into a more relaxed, social atmosphere," Greg announced.

Lucian glanced at him with interest. "Like?"

"The Night Club."

"The Night Club?" he echoed with a frown.

"You could both relax, dance—"

"I don't dance," Lucian announced.

"Surely for Leigh . . . ?"

"I don't know *how* to dance," he said more specifically.

"Oh." There was silence as everyone glanced at each other, then Rachel stood.

"Okay, you boys teach him how to dance, and Lissianna and I will go get Leigh ready for the night ahead."

Lucian opened his mouth to protest, and Rachel said, "Do you want Leigh? Even that book of yours said learning to dance would be good."

He closed his mouth, unable to argue with that logic, then watched unhappily as the two women left.

"So? Who's going to be the girl for these dance lessons?" Thomas asked, and Lucian turned to stare at him with horror.

"I think you just volunteered," Etienne announced. "What do you think, Greg?"

"Sounded like it to me," Greg agreed.

"Oh, no way—" Thomas began.

"Thomas, I've always wondered why it is that you're all 'dude' and 'man' when Lucern and Bastien are here, but not around the rest of us. Why is that?" Greg asked, then added, "And do they know this?"

"That's blackmail!" Thomas cried.

"Yeah." Greg grinned, then turned to Lucian and suggested, "Just imagine him in a skirt."

"How do I look?" Leigh peered nervously in the mirror, her eyes on the two women reflected beside her. Lissianna was on her left; tall, blond, beautiful, and very, very pregnant. Rachel stood on her right in the reflection; also tall, at least taller than she was, red-haired and gorgeous. Then there was herself in the middle; shorter, but looking pretty darned hot if she said so herself. Well, hot for her.

Lissianna and Rachel had insisted she wear the pink, off-the-shoulder cowl and a pair of cream-colored suede pants. Her hair was in the bob she'd worn for the last two years, but it shone and almost glowed with life, as did her skin. The only makeup she had on was lipstick and eye shadow, and she looked better than she ever had with foundation and blush and all that gunk. She didn't need it. The nanos made her look like a million bucks without it.

"You look lovely," Lissianna said, and gave her a quick hug.

Rachel nodded and said, "You're gonna knock him dead."

Leigh made a face in the mirror at the prediction. Lissianna and Rachel had just spent several hours enlightening her about things that Lucian neglected to mention. None of it was anything she blamed him for bypassing.

Considering his discomfort at finding himself in the women's lingerie shop, she wasn't surprised that he couldn't bring himself to explain the differences she would find in female topics like monthlies or pregnancies. If he even knew what those were, she thought with amusement. But she was also terribly grateful that he hadn't told her about life mates, and explained the signs of them and what they meant.

Leigh had listened to Lissianna and Rachel rhapsodize about how wonderful it was to have a life mate, someone meant just for you, who couldn't read your mind and use it against you, but could project thoughts to you and you could project thoughts back to. Apparently, this was a skill Greg and Lissianna had just begun to develop between them and one Rachel couldn't wait to have.

Leigh even felt a touch of envy as the women expressed their happiness and pleasure in their relationships, explaining the difference in sex, how powerful it was, how it was the rare time when the minds could merge and that they shared their pleasure, mirroring it between them and bouncing it back and forth, stronger and stronger until it was almost unbearable. It sounded like a wondrous relationship, and she couldn't wait for it to happen. Then Rachel said, "It already has."

She had listened blankly as Rachel reminded her that Lucian couldn't read her, the first and main sign of a life mate. She'd then gone on to touch on things that Leigh hadn't realized, but that Rachel had worked out from reading both her and Lucian. It seemed her shower sex fantasy had been transmitted to Lucian while he slept . . . another sign. She was busy being embarrassed hearing that he knew what she'd been fantasizing, when Rachel informed her she hadn't had it alone, that once pulled into it, Lucian had joined in and taken control. Did she remember a point when her "fantasy lover" had done something unexpected and seemed to have a mind of his own? Well, Rachel told her, that's because he had.

That's when her envy and confusion gave way to fear. It was too soon; she hardly knew Lucian. Dear God, she'd married Kenny after dating for only six weeks, and look what a mistake that had been! She'd only know Lucian for a matter of days. Two, that she'd been conscious. That thought had shocked her. Two days? It felt like a lifetime. Lissianna had offered the solution.

Just because they were life mates didn't mean they had to rush off and get married right away. They could date and get to know each other better until she felt secure in the relationship.

Leigh felt as if a huge mountain of pressure had slid from her shoulders then. Dating. Seeing each other. Going out for dinner, to movies, dancing . . . She could handle that. And heck, she lived in Kansas and Lucian in Canada. It would even be long distance dating. She could cope with that. Feeling better, she'd allowed them to help her dress herself up to go out to the Night Club.

Now, Leigh peered in the mirror at the two women framing her. They were watching her silently, probably listening to her thoughts as they patiently waited for her to decide she was ready.

Giving a nod, she turned from the mirror and moved toward the door, saying, "Let's go."

"It will be fun," Lissianna assured her. "It will give you two a chance to relax and have fun together."

Leigh murmured something that might have been taken as agreement and tried to squelch the nervousness bubbling toward the surface. Lissianna and Rachel had spent a good deal of time trying to tell her Lucian's good points and how wonderful he was while they'd helped her get ready, trying to build him up in her mind, but Kenny's family had thought he was the cat's meow, too. They hadn't had a clue. How a man would act as a son or brother or uncle just wasn't the same as how he would behave as a husband. She'd learned that the hard way.

"They were in the library when we came upstairs," Lissianna announced as they reached the bottom of the stairs, and Leigh turned that way, heading up the hall.

In the lead as she was, Leigh was the one to open the door. She then froze, her eyes going wide.

The men were in the center of the library, Lucian holding Thomas in the classic dance style and Greg holding Etienne in the same way as the two "couples" rotated around the room. Greg was humming some waltz or other, and Lucian was murmuring "One two three, one two three" as he watched his feet and woodenly steered a miserable-looking Thomas around the room.

Sixteen

"I can't believe you guys were teaching him to waltz."

Rachel's words brought the memory to the front of Leigh's mind, making her smile with amusement. She'd done a lot of smiling in the three hours since they arrived at the Night Club, she realized as she looked around. In her opinion, it was a surprisingly pedestrian dance/lounge bar. It wasn't that she'd expected stuffed bats on the walls or posters of Bela Lugosi everywhere, but she had expected something unusual to mark it as a vampire bar.

Oops, immortal bar, she corrected herself.

Anyway, there wasn't any of that. It was made up of two rooms: this lounge area, with the music at a level where they could actually talk and hear each other; and a larger room with a dance floor surrounded by booths, where the music was several decibels louder. The two bars were separated by a swinging door, but the walls between them were soundproofed glass. Leigh and the others had chosen to sit in the lounge, but made forays into the dance area when a good song came on and someone felt like dancing.

All the men had taken a turn or two on the dance

floor, but only Thomas went every time the girls went. Lucian had proven himself a pretty capable dancer for someone the men had thought they should teach. He seemed to have a natural sense of rhythm.

Her gaze slid to the bar, where Lucian, Etienne, and Greg were gathered around Bricker and Mortimer. The women and Thomas had returned from their last excursion to the dance floor to find the men had abandoned their table for the bar.

"Seriously," Lissianna said, smacking Thomas in the arm. "What were you thinking? They don't waltz here."

"I was thinking I didn't want my uncle clasping my butt, and our chests rubbing together as he stepped on my feet while trying to shuffle me around the floor," Thomas answered dryly.

Leigh nearly choked on her drink as she burst out laughing at the image he'd just put in their minds.

"Yeah . . . laugh," Thomas said. "You weren't the one dancing with him. You have my sympathies, Leigh," he teased, reaching out to pat her hand.

"He dances just fine," she said firmly, then scowled and added, "Now will you guys stop that."

"Stop what?" Thomas asked with genuine confusion.

"Stop talking like Lucian and I are a couple."

"You are."

"We've just met," Leigh protested, but he just shrugged as if that meant nothing.

"Doesn't matter whether you've known him five minutes or five millennia, you're life mates. He's yours and you're his. The only question now is when the two of you will get past your fears and claim each other."

Leigh arched an eyebrow. "What if I don't want to claim him?"

"Forever is a long time to be alone," Thomas said

quietly. "Hell, two hundred years is a long time. Trust me. I know."

"Yeah, well, I could choose to be with someone else," she pointed out. "I might find contentment, at least, with someone else."

Thomas's eyes widened incredulously, then he turned to Lissianna and Rachel. "Before we went over tonight, you two said you were going to get Leigh alone and tell her everything. Didn't you do that?"

"Of course we did," Rachel began, then stopped when she saw Lissianna's wide eyes. Frowning, she asked, "What did we forget?"

"I think we just neglected to clarify something," Lissianna said with a sigh, and turned to Leigh. "Do you remember the tale of my mother and father?"

Leigh nodded. Marguerite Argeneau and her husband Jean Claude had, apparently, not been true life mates. He'd been able to read and control her . . . and had. It made for a miserable marriage for both of them. Marguerite had been little better than a puppet that he posed and did with as he willed. Even worse, she'd been aware of it, but unable to stop it, much as Leigh had been aware and able to think, but unable to stop Morgan from controlling her own body and actions. Marguerite had—understandably—resented Jean Claude for it.

"Well," Lissianna said, "any other relationship, but Lucian, would be like that for you. You won't be happy with anyone else."

Leigh shook her head firmly. "I would never do what your father did."

"Do you think my father intended to when he turned and married her?" Lissianna asked quietly. "Do you really think he didn't feel guilt and self-loathing over it?

Why do you think he became an alcoholic and ended up burned to death? It was as good as suicide."

"Besides, who says you'd have the stronger mind?" Rachel pointed out. "Whoever you choose for a mate might do it to you."

"What?" She stiffened.

"Father was stronger minded because he was so old," Lissianna said. "But there are new turns who have displayed stronger minds than most immortals have. Greg, for instance."

"Lucian's old, too," Leigh said with alarm. "Could he—"

"He can't even read you," Rachel pointed out. "He couldn't control you. It's why you'd make perfect life mates."

They fell silent as the waitress arrived with the drinks Thomas had ordered. He immediately leapt to his feet to help her distribute the cocktails, then thanked and tipped her.

"That looks familiar." Rachel suspiciously eyed the glass Thomas placed in front of Leigh.

Leigh smiled at the red umbrella sticking out of her glass. Shifting it aside, she removed the candy heart on the little plastic sword that had been laid across the top of the glass and ate it.

She had tried several drinks tonight, and much to her dismay, enjoyed them all. She liked the energy drinks especially. So much for her belief that she'd never care for the taste of blood. As had happened with the scent smelling as sweet to her as perfume, blood now had an entirely different taste to her, and she wondered how the nanos managed that.

Leigh picked up her glass to try this latest drink, only to find it snatched from her hand by Rachel as the other woman turned a glare on Thomas. "It's a Sweet Ecstasy!" she said accusingly.

"Yes," Leigh said, confused. "Thomas said it was good."

"Oh, yeah?" Rachel continued to glare at him. "If it's so good, why don't you drink it, Thomas?"

He made a face. "I don't know what your problem is. It worked for you and Etienne. It'll work here to speed things up, too."

"I don't understand. What's going on?" Leigh asked. "What exactly is a Sweet Ecstasy?"

"It's chock full of the pheromones and hormones of sexually excited mortals."

Leigh raised her eyebrows.

"You've heard of Spanish Fly?" Rachel asked.

"Yes," she said with a frown.

"Well, I don't know if *that* really exists, but this is the immortal version, and I can guarantee you it *does* work."

Leigh turned a horrified gaze on Thomas, and he quickly said in his own defense, "I was just trying to heat things up for you."

She gave a short burst of disbelieving laughter. "Well geez, Thomas, I don't need that. I'm already having waking wet dreams. Give it to Lucian instead." She snapped her mouth closed on the last word as she realized what she'd said, turned on Thomas herself and said accusingly, "I thought you said there wasn't much alcohol in those drinks."

"You won't have the same tolerance you used to have," Lissianna explained soothingly. "And don't be embarrassed about what you said. It's all right, Leigh. We've all been through the madness of finding a life mate and all said or done stupid things in the midst of it. Well, Rachel and I have."

Thomas almost seemed to flinch at her words, and Leigh realized he wished for a life mate of his own. Lissianna seemed to realize it as well, for she patted his shoulder and added, "And Thomas will soon enough, too."

"Right." Thomas didn't sound as if he were likely to hold his breath waiting for it. Then he snatched the drink from Rachel and said, "But Leigh's right. I'll give it to Lucian instead."

Getting to his feet, he turned away to cross to the bar before anyone could speak.

"He won't really?" Leigh asked with alarm.

Neither woman answered. They all watched Thomas approach the bar and tap Lucian on the shoulder. When his uncle turned, the younger man said something and gestured back toward their table. The moment Lucian looked their way, Thomas traded the glass he held for the one that sat on the bar in front of Lucian.

"Oh God, he did it," Leigh said with dismay.

"He certainly did," Rachel agreed dryly, then added, "You're in for an interesting night."

"No, I'm not," Leigh said firmly. "I couldn't possibly take advantage of Lucian that way."

"Considering the thoughts I've seen floating through his head, I don't think you could call it taking advantage," Lissianna assured her with a small smile.

"The men are coming back," Rachel announced. "And they're looking pretty serious. Bricker and Mortimer must not have had good news."

Leigh noted that Lucian's face did indeed look grim. He'd told her on the way to the club that they suspected Morgan and Donny were headed north to Canada, following her. She found that hard to believe. If they'd thought it was because of Donny, she might have agreed it was possible, since Donny was the one who'd wanted her turned, and he'd gone on about being eternally happy and so on. But they seemed to think Morgan wanted her, which made no sense to her at all. She wasn't some great beauty who could enslave men with a smile. She was the kind you found attractive as you got to know her better, and Morgan hadn't known her more than a matter of minutes.

"What did Mortimer and Bricker say?" Lissianna asked as the men reclaimed their seats.

"Morgan and Donny may be here somewhere after all," Lucian answered. "A second credit card from another one of Morgan's victims at the house was activated at a hotel in Iowa. As soon as he was informed, Bastien sent Pimms and Anders there. They were two of my men who were in the area," he explained to Leigh, before continuing, "When they raided the room that had been rented, they rounded up a young couple who had apparently escaped with Morgan and Donny the morning we hit the house."

"So four of them escaped that morning?" Rachel asked with a frown.

"Six," Lucian corrected. "There were two other men with Morgan and Donny. Apparently, they're the ones who flew up on the plane from Des Moines, new turns that Mortimer and Bricker wouldn't have recognized."

"Morgan sent two up on the plane?" Lissianna asked with surprise. "Why didn't they all fly up?"

"Morgan has a phobia to flying," Etienne answered, then added, "Apparently, while he was tired of the long drive with the seven of them crammed in the van, he didn't want to put all his eggs in one basket. He sent two of the men on the plane, gave the second credit card to the couple Pimms and Anders caught and told them to take turns driving, travel straight through without stopping, and meet him here in Toronto."

"But they stopped at a hotel and got caught for disobeying him," Rachel said.

"The van broke down," Greg explained quietly. "They took a room to sleep in while it was being repaired."

"But where are Donny and Morgan?" Leigh asked with a frown.

Lucian hesitated, but reluctantly admitted, "Morgan had the couple drop him and Donny at the train station. They bought tickets to Toronto with cash."

Leigh stilled, alarm coursing through her. "How long does it take to get here by train?"

When the men exchanged grim glances but didn't rush to answer the question, her eyes widened and she said with dread, "They're already here, aren't they?"

"They could be," Etienne admitted solemnly. "And if not, they will be soon. Unfortunately, they paid cash and didn't buy the tickets in their own names, so we don't know exactly which trains and transfers they took and when they'll arrive."

"If it's possible they're already here, shouldn't Mortimer and Bricker be at the house watching for them?" Lissianna asked.

"Pimms and Anders flew straight here after handling the couple in Iowa. They're at the house now," Greg assured her. "Two more men are watching the train station here in Toronto, though we suspect it's too late to catch them there. Mortimer and Bricker are here to watch the bar. Morgan apparently planned for everyone to meet up here tonight, so he may show up at some point."

Leigh glanced around, suddenly feeling uncomfortable. It looked like she'd been wrong and Donny and Morgan *were* headed her way. She found it hard to believe, but apparently they were.

"We should call it a night," Greg said quietly.

The women all nodded in agreement and started to gather their things.

"We also think Uncle Lucian and Leigh should go stay in a hotel. Just to be safe," Etienne added.

Leigh stiffened, her eyes shooting to Lucian. His face was expressionless, no upset showing, but she was sure he would be. He'd had to leave the hunt for Morgan in Kansas to bring her north and oversee her turning. Now Morgan was on his home turf, and rather than be able to stand and fight, Lucian had to rush her to safety. He had to resent it.

Leigh's unhappy thoughts were interrupted when Etienne added, "There's a slim possibility that Morgan was already here in Toronto and watching Uncle Lucian's house when they swung by to pick up his things this afternoon." He turned his gaze to Leigh and continued, "They may have followed you back to Marguerite's and are waiting until you're alone to do anything. We all think you should head straight to the hotel from here rather than stop there and risk running into him."

"But Julius is at the house. We can't leave him alone without food or water," Leigh said with concern, then her eyes widened and she asked, "Morgan wouldn't hurt Julius, would he?"

The men all exchanged glances, then Greg said, "We could take Julius for a couple days."

"Or we could," Etienne added, then hesitated. "But it might be better if he stays with Lucian and Leigh. He'd be added protection."

Lucian nodded. "We'll pick him up on the way out of town."

"But you can't," Lissianna reminded him. "You shouldn't go to the house by yourselves. Besides, what hotel takes dogs? Especially Julius-sized dogs?"

There was silence as everyone considered the matter, then Rachel sat forward.

"Okay, here's an idea," she said. "Greg and Etienne head over to get Julius. The rest of us go to our place to wait for them. Then, when the guys bring Julius back, Leigh and Lucian take my car and head out of town."

"Why your car?" Etienne asked.

"In case Morgan is already here somewhere watching. If he follows us to the house, all he'll see is a car leaving the garage. The windows are darkened. Lucian's car will still be there, and hopefully he won't think it's them leaving."

"That's good, but there's still the problem of a hotel that will take dogs," Lissianna pointed out.

Everyone frowned, then Thomas sprung upright. "The cottage."

"The cottage?" Leigh asked with confusion.

"I have a cottage on the lake," he explained. "It's about two and a half hours south of here. You guys could go there with Julius. Morgan couldn't possibly know about it."

They were all silent, then Greg nodded. "Sounds like a plan."

Leigh remained silent as everyone stood and began to make their way out of the club. She waited until she and Lucian were outside and walking a little behind the others before saying, "You don't have to do this."

He slowed to a stop and turned to peer at her in confusion. "Do what?"

Leigh bit her lip. "I realize you probably want to be in on catching Morgan. I appreciate that you gave up the hunt to look after me during the turn, but it seems unfair that you'll have to give it up again when he's come to your own hometown. You don't have to take me to a hotel. I can go by myself, maybe take Julius just in case, and you could stay and be in on the hunt."

A soft smile curved Lucian's lips and he raised a hand to brush it gently down her cheek as he shook his head. "Leigh, your safety is my top priority."

She peered up at him uncertainly. "You aren't going to resent me for—"

"Of course not," he assured her as if she were being silly. When she still looked uncertain, he said, "Leigh, I've been alive thousands of years, and been a warrior for most of that time. I've hunted and brought in more rogues than I can count. I have nothing to prove, no burning desire to chase him down and bring him in myself. You're my main concern. If Morgan's after you, I want to make sure you're well out of the way and he can't get his hands on you. I don't mind leaving the actual catching of him to others. Besides, there will always be another hunt."

When Leigh let her shoulders relax, a small, relieved smile pulling at her lips, Lucian smiled back and took her hand to urge her after the others.

"You can turn your windshield wipers off. The rain has stopped."

Leigh ground her teeth together and flicked the switch to turn off the wipers. They'd been on the road for two hours. Julius had finally stopped drooling over her shoulder about half an hour ago and gone to sleep in the back. She wished Lucian would do the same in the front seat. He was driving her crazy.

Everything had gone according to plan except one thing. They'd gotten to the house, Greg and Etienne had shown up with Julius, they talked for several hours, going over what to do if there was a problem and so on, then piled into the attached garage of Rachel and Etienne's home. That was when things stopped going according to plan. Lucian got into the driver's seat, stopped in surprise and cursed. Rachel's car was a stick shift. Much to Leigh's surprise, Lucian didn't drive stick. It seemed that until they'd invented automatic cars, he'd had a driver, and so never bothered to learn.

Foolishly, Leigh had said it wasn't a problem, she drove stick. She'd been regretting it for almost every minute of the last two hours. Lucian was a backseat driver. "You're going too fast. You're going too slow. Turn up your defroster. Turn off your wipers. You should have turned your blinker on sooner to give anyone following more time to slow down . . ." Never mind that they were the only idiots on the road at three o'clock in the morning!

If they were going to survive as life mates without her wringing his neck, she would have to never drive again, Leigh decided, then blinked at her own thoughts. It was the closest she'd come to acknowledging that all the arguments and persuading Thomas, Lissianna, and Rachel had done that night were beginning to work. Sort of. Maybe. She wasn't ready to jump in feet first or anything, but they could date for a while, see how it went . . . then, maybe, down the road—say in a year or two, if they got along—they could consider this whole life mate thing. She had jumped into her first marriage and regretted it. She wasn't jumping again.

"Turn right," Lucian said suddenly, and Leigh blinked her thoughts away.

She flicked on her blinker and turned, hoping they were almost there. Thomas had said the cottage was two and a half hours away on the lake, but that would have been at a normal speed limit. With the roads empty and Lucian driving her crazy, she'd sped up whenever he wasn't looking at the speedometer, hoping to shorten the trip before she drove into a passing tree just to end it herself. Not that it would actually end anything, she supposed.

"There it is. Slow down."

Leigh ground her jaws together, pressed her foot down on the brakes and wondered if they could take a bus back when all this was over. Or a taxi. Anything to avoid another drive like the one she'd just suffered.

"There," Lucian said with a sigh as she pulled to a stop in front of the "cottage."

Leigh stared at the chalet style house. She should have known the Argeneau idea of a cottage wouldn't be her idea of a cottage. To her, a cottage was a two or three room shack with the basic necessities. This was bigger than most people's homes. It was also gorgeous.

Grateful to see the end of the trip, she turned off the car and opened her door, nearly tripping over her feet in her haste to get out. A bark from Julius told her the dog was awake, and she opened the back door of the car as Lucian moved to the trunk. Julius leapt out of the backseat, trailing his leash behind him. Leigh caught it and drew him to a halt, grimacing when she found it wet.

"Can you pop the—" Lucian's request died as Leigh hit the button on the remote to open the trunk. He leaned in to retrieve their bags and the cooler they'd brought. Once again they were without their own clothes and personal items, but the men had brought Julius's dog food with them, and Rachel had filled bags with food and drink and some clothes for them both from her own home. She'd also packed a cooler with enough blood to last a couple days.

Lucian managed to gather everything in one trip, shaking his head when Leigh offered to help. Shrugging, she followed him to the door of the cottage, leading Julius. The mastiff was well-trained. He walked at her side, then sat down on his haunches when she paused on the wooden deck at the front door. Leigh patted him absently for the good behavior as Lucian stubbornly struggled with everything and tried to open the door at the same time.

After a moment she lost her patience, stepped up to his side and snatched away the keys he was fumbling with.

"You need to learn to accept help," she said impatiently as she sorted through the keys, looking for the one she assumed would open the cottage. "You can't do everything and control everything yourself. Even Superman needed his Lois Lane and Jimmy."

Lucian's mouth tightened and he followed her stiffly inside when she got the door open.

Leigh went to close the door behind them, then realized Julius was still outside. She'd dropped the leash to take the keys from Lucian, and the dog was now dragging it around the yard, jerking at it when it caught on things as he ran around, leaving his mark everywhere. Once satisfied that he'd staked out his territory, the dog trotted inside and stood patiently while Leigh removed the leash.

"Good doggy," she murmured, patting his head. Julius gave her hand a swipe with his tongue, then padded off into the cottage, leaving her to close and lock the door.

Leigh surveyed their temporary new home with disbelief as she followed. The ground floor was one large living room with a small corner set off for a kitchen. The wall facing out on the lake was all glass, and there was lots of wood and light colors. It was beautiful, of course. These people didn't appear to do anything by halves.

Ignoring Lucian in the kitchen, Leigh picked up the bag with their clothes in it and set it on the stairs leading to the second level. She knew it must be where the bedrooms were, and didn't want to forget to take it up with her when she went to investigate. For now, she was content to take in the main floor.

Leigh peered over the comfortable looking furniture and glass and wood tables, then walked to the wall of glass and peered out at the lake. It was a calm night, no wind in sight, and the moonlight glinting off the placid surface looked so inviting she wondered if she'd be able to find a swimsuit around here. It was late fall but had been warm the last few nights, and the water should be beautiful.

Her thoughts were disturbed by a glass of wine appearing suddenly before her. Leigh followed the hand holding it, up the arm, then to Lucian's face.

"I'm sorry."

It was obvious Lucian wasn't used to apologizing. He muttered the two words with the attitude of a six-year-old ordered by his mother to apologize, and her tension slid away as a laugh bubbled from her lips.

Lucian immediately relaxed, a wry smile claiming his lips.

"I guess that wasn't the most gracious apology," he admitted. "Thank you for not throwing it back in my face."

"Which? The wine or the apology?" Leigh asked as she finally took the glass.

"Either," Lucian said with a grin, then added sincerely,

"I really am sorry. I know I was being a bit of a backseat driver in the car and—"

"A bit?" she asked pointedly.

"And you're right," he continued, ignoring her interruption. "I should learn to accept help better. It's something I'm just learning."

Leigh nodded and sipped her wine, watching as he drank his own, then turned to peer out the window at the lake.

"It's beautiful here," Lucian commented with a surprise that made Leigh's eyebrows rise.

"Haven't you been here before?"

Lucian shook his head. "The kids come down here some weekends in the summer to kick back and relax. Even Marguerite comes once in a while, but I—" He shrugged. "They've invited me, but . . ."

He left the sentence unfinished and stared out at the water with a frown, then glanced down to see the amusement on her face and asked, "What's so funny?"

"Nothing . . . us. Here I've always wanted family, and you've got it, but shun yours."

Lucian frowned. "It's not that I shun them. I just don't feel I belong most of the time. I had a family and lost them and—"

He stopped abruptly, and Leigh said, "I know about your family. I'm sorry."

"It was a long time ago," he said quietly.

"But it still hurts you."

Lucian stared at the water, then said, "I loved my family, Leigh. But it was a long, long time ago. Sometimes I can't even remember their faces anymore . . . but I remember what it was like having them and being a part of a family. I can hear their laughter, the girls' giggles, and remember how good it felt just to have a family of your own, people who loved you and you belonged with."

"Lissianna and the others love you," Leigh said quietly.

"Yes, but . . ." He struggled briefly, then tried to explain. "Jean Claude married Marguerite and they had the kids, and I was a part of their family, but on the outside."

"Like a fifth wheel," Leigh said with understanding. She'd been a fifth wheel often enough at the Christmases and celebrations of friends and their families.

Lucian nodded, then shrugged. "Now, the kids are pretty much grown up and starting families of their own."

Leigh blinked at the "pretty much grown up" bit. She knew the oldest son, Lucern, was over six hundred years old, and Lissianna over two hundred. How old did they have to be before they were fully grown up? Dear God, she thought. If Lissianna was only "pretty much grown up" in his eyes at two hundred, how did he see her?

Troubled by the idea that Lucian might see her as a child, she downed her wine and moved to set the glass down on the wood and glass coffee table, then started up the stairs. "I'm going to see if I can find a bathing suit."

"Why bother? There's no one around for miles and it's dark out."

Leigh paused at the challenge in his voice. She peered at him, but Lucian had turned away, staring out at the water. Her gaze followed his out to the lake. It was dark, but not dark enough to make her invisible. *He* would be able to see her.

As she hesitated, Lucian finished his wine, set it next to her empty glass, then straightened and peered at her as he began to undo the buttons of his shirt. Leigh watched one button after another slip through their holes, then swallowed and turned to the stairs. "I'll just—"

"Coward." The soft word slid through the air between them, and she turned back as he asked, "Have you ever been skinny dipping in the moonlight?"

Her eyes traced the contours of his chest as he shrugged the shirt off, tossing it over the end of the couch. Leigh licked her lips and shook her head.

"The water's like a caress. The moon like a kiss. The sand as soft as a bed."

Her mind suddenly filled with images, but not of the water caressing her, or the moon kissing her. It was Lucian. She closed her eyes as the images assaulted her, aware that her breathing was becoming shallow and her body reacting to both his words and the ideas in her head. When she blinked her eyes open a moment later, Lucian was standing before her. With her on the first step, and he on the floor, they were almost the same height.

His gaze meeting hers, Lucian lifted a finger and ran it lightly along the collar of the off-the-shoulder top he'd chosen. His voice was husky as he offered, "I could help you with this."

Without meaning to, hardly aware she was doing it, Leigh swayed forward, her mouth parting. In the next instant, Lucian's arms were around her, his mouth claiming hers. In her fantasy in the shower, his kisses had been hot and deep and all-consuming. They were more so in reality. Her world tilted and spun as his tongue slid into her. She had to clutch at his shoulders to remain upright.

He tasted of wine, sweet and strong, and she moaned into his mouth with pleasure as his tongue lashed her own. As if the sound were permission given, Lucian abruptly broke the kiss, his mouth trailing down her neck.

Leigh shivered and let her head drop back as he nibbled at the base of her throat where it met her shoulder. Then she gasped and tangled one hand in his short hair as his lips dipped to trace the line of her collar.

With a tug, he pulled on her collar, and Leigh peered down as the pink cloth slipped lower to reveal one naked breast. She was glad this shirt didn't allow bras as his mouth immediately moved to claim the already erect nipple that was revealed. She thought she was ready for it, but still jerked and clutched at his hair as his lips closed hot and wet over the small nub and began to suckle, sending shock waves of pleasure and excitement rippling through her body.

Lucian was still pushing down on her top, and she made a sound of protest as her arms were forced down with it, trapping them at her sides. He left off her breast then and raised his head to kiss her again, but continued to push the top down until Leigh could free her hands from the cloth. She immediately ran them over his chest, sighing at the feel of him. He was so big, so strong...

Her pleasure was distracted by the knowledge that he was still pushing the material downward and her pants were now going with it. Somehow, while she was distracted by his kisses, Lucian had undone the suede pants without her being aware of it, and now they were slipping over her hips with her pink top.

Leigh didn't care. He was like a fire in her blood, so much so that she could almost believe *she'd* drunk the Sweet Ecstasy that Thomas had intended to give her and—

She froze abruptly as she recalled the Sweet Ecstasy. She hadn't drunk it. Rachel had stopped her before she could. But Lucian had.

She could have wept. All this passion, all this

excitement—at least on his side—was all because of some immortal Spanish Fly Lucian had been fed.

Apparently sensing the change in her response, Lucian broke the kiss. Pulling back slightly, he peered at her with concern.

"What is it?" he asked breathlessly. They were both panting like dogs after a run, both as tense as bowstrings, both flush with passion; but only hers was real, she thought.

Leigh leaned her forehead against his shoulder and struggled with herself. If he weren't under the influence, she'd push him to the floor and ride him like a cowgirl that very minute. Unfortunately, her conscience was battling with her desires and *ruining* everything.

"Leigh?" Lucian asked uncertainly.

"I . . ." She hesitated, at a loss as to what to say to explain her stopping him. She didn't want to tell him what Thomas had done for fear he'd be angry at the man. She'd been raised not to tattle. But what could she say?

Movement over Lucian's shoulder caught her eye, and Leigh saw Julius pawing at the bag with the dog food in it, then looking their way and whimpering before pawing it again.

"Julius is hungry," she said. The moment Lucian turned to glance over his shoulder, Leigh whirled away, snatching up the bag of clothes as she turned. Holding them in one hand, she used the other to pull her pants back up over her hips as she rushed upstairs.

Leigh waited until she reached the top step before announcing, "I have a headache. I'm going to bed."

Seventeen

Grateful that Lucian didn't chase after her or press her for explanations, Leigh paused once off the stairs and took a moment to gather herself. Her body was tingling, her heart still racing, and she truly wished it hadn't been that drink Thomas gave Lucian that made him act as he had. Then she wouldn't have had to stop him, and she wished she hadn't had to stop him.

She took a deep breath, held it for a moment, then let it out and tried to distract herself from her body's aching by taking in her surroundings. The second floor of the "cottage" was half the size of the lower floor. It was a loft. There was no wall at the end overlooking the first floor, just a railing.

Leigh had expected two or maybe three bedrooms up here, but it was one large room with an en suite bathroom she could see through the open door on the far wall.

There was a huge bed in the very center of the floor, and then a sound system, television, and the door to the bathroom along the wall on her left. Two sets of drawers rested beneath a row of windows on the far wall, and a closet ran the length of the wall on her right, its surface made up of mirrors. Where a fourth wall would have been, there was the railing; a small table and chairs, as well as a couch and matching chairs, were arranged in front of it.

Though she tried to ignore it, her gaze kept returning to the big red bed. She'd never seen one so huge. Or one that was round, for that matter. It had to be custom made. The sheets must have been, too. It was giving her a whole new perspective on Thomas.

The murmur of Lucian's voice reached her ears, and Leigh stepped closer to the railing to see that he was leading Julius into the kitchen. She quickly moved back when he glanced up, hoping he hadn't seen her, then unzipped the bag she held and began riffling through it in search of the clothes Rachel had promised.

A nightgown was the first thing she touched, and she tugged it out and pulled it over her head without even looking at it, eager to cover her nakedness in case Lucian came up after all. Her top was pooled around her waist, so she simply pushed it off over her hips with her pants, wondering if the cowl neckline of the top would bounce back or forever be ruined.

That worry was forgotten when she noticed how short the nightgown was, and then the two slits in the front that rose all the way up to the bottom of each breast . . . and that it was see-through. She could see her own damn nipples.

Mouth falling open, Leigh ran forward and dropped the bag on the bed as she peered at herself in the mirrors on the closet doors.

"Lord above," she breathed with something between shock and horror as she regarded herself. She looked like . . . well, this was . . . She couldn't believe Rachel would—

The crash of breaking glass made her jump. Tearing

her eyes away from her reflection, she turned to see Lucian standing at the top of the stairs, a broken tray at his feet.

"I brought you some aspirin and water." His voice cracked as he stared at her. His eyes were eating her alive, and all the excitement and desire she had been battling since recalling the drink he'd had came rushing back up through her as she let her gaze drift from his swirling silver eyes, to his still naked chest, then finally to the obvious bulge in the front of his tight jeans.

Leigh wondered if he would be as big in real life as he'd been in her fantasy, and shivered with anticipation. She knew her eyes were as hungry as his own when she lifted them to meet his gaze, but couldn't seem to help herself.

A growl slipping from his lips, Lucian stepped over the tray and broken glass on the floor and started toward her. A little frisson of panic sliced up her back, and she began to back away around the bed.

"We can't, Lucian."

"You want me."

"Yes, but—" Wrong answer, she realized when he rushed toward her. Whirling, Leigh hurried around the bed to keep him from touching her. If he did, she knew all her good intentions would be lost.

"We can't!" she cried, glancing over her shoulder to see that he'd stopped. Then stopping herself, to keep from running around the bed and into him, she eyed him warily.

"Why?" Lucian began to pad after her again, moving slowly, eyes narrowed, a hunter after his prey.

Leigh swallowed and began to back away around the bed. "You don't understand."

"What don't I understand?" His voice was halfway between whisper and growl and brushed over every nerve in her body like a caress.

"This isn't you. You don't want me," Leigh said, glancing over her shoulder to be sure she didn't trip over anything.

"Oh yes, I want you," Lucian assured her grimly. "I've wanted you since the first night. I wanted you on the plane when you lay there so pale and beautiful, I wanted you in the shower, I wanted you in the restaurant. I wanted you downstairs, and I want you now."

Leigh stopped backing away. "Really?"

Lucian halted. They were now facing each other across the bed. "Really."

Leigh hesitated. If he'd wanted her before the drink, maybe the drink didn't matter. Maybe it just increased what he'd already been feeling.

"You don't have a headache," Lucian said. It wasn't a question, but Leigh shook her head anyway, and he asked, "Why did you lie?"

"Thomas gave you a Sweet Ecstasy, and I was afraid you were under the influence," she blurted quickly, silently apologizing to Thomas for tattling.

A slow smile spread over Lucian's face. "You were trying to protect me from myself."

Leigh nodded, then gasped as he suddenly lunged across the bed. Lucian was before her on his knees on the side of the bed in a blink. One more blink and he'd caught her around the waist and tugged her down, tucking her under him on the red satin surface.

"I didn't drink the drink Thomas gave me," Lucian announced, peering down at her solemnly as his hand slipped under the short nightie and slid up along her stomach.

"You didn't?" Leigh asked in a squeak as his caress sent her stomach rippling.

Lucian shook his head as he used his legs to shift hers apart. He settled one leg between hers, pressing it against her as he added, "I saw him make the switch out of the corner of my eye, and even if I hadn't, I would have recognized it for what it was. He didn't think to remove the red umbrella. Only Sweet Ecstasies have red umbrellas at the Night Club."

"Oh," she breathed shakily, then gasped as he bent his head to tongue her nipple through the sheer material of the nightie. "I—"

"Leigh," Lucian murmured around what he was doing.

"Yes?" she asked vaguely.

He lifted his head and opened his mouth to speak, then paused, his eyes sliding over her before he breathed, "You're beautiful."

"Thank you," she said softly, then noticed the frown that touched the edges of his mouth.

"But pale."

"Pale?"

"Hmmm. You need blood. I don't want you biting me. At least, not for the wrong reason." Suddenly he was off the bed and striding to the stairs.

Leigh sat up and stared after him with amazement, then sighed and slowly slid off the bed as he bent to collect the tray he'd dropped. Most of what he'd been bringing had stayed on the tray, she saw as she approached. Still, there were a couple of bits of glass and spots of water on the floor.

"Watch your feet," he ordered gruffly as he straightened with the tray. He peered down at the floor, suddenly stepped up to her and bent to catch her around the hips with one arm, then straightened.

"Hey!" she cried as she fell forward over his shoulder.

"I don't want you to cut your feet," he explained, but she could hear the amusement in his voice, felt his breath on her hip as he spoke, and knew he was looking at her behind. Then she felt his hand slide over one butt cheek.

"Lucian!" she squawked, pushing against his back.

"Don't squirm, you'll make me drop the tray," he said, and Leigh definitely heard laughter in his voice. His hand was now taking great liberty with her vulnerable position; sliding, squeezing, caressing...

She bit her lip and tried not to squirm under his touch as he started toward the stairs.

"There's no glass here, you can set me down," she pointed out as soon as Lucian started down the stairs.

"Too dangerous here. Better wait till I get to the ground floor," he said lightly, pinching one cheek.

Leigh growled and pinched his butt in retribution as she watched the stairs slide by beneath her.

Lucian didn't set her down until they reached the kitchen, then placed the tray on the table first before setting her down on the counter.

"Stay," he ordered, and turned away to the refrigerator.

"Yes, master," Leigh muttered, scowling at his back.

Lucian chuckled. "I like the sound of that. Master. It has a nice ring."

"Hmmm." Leigh grimaced. "If I thought you really meant that, I'd kick you in the butt."

"You could try," he allowed, turning back from the refrigerator with two bags of blood. He popped one to her teeth as she opened her mouth to respond to his challenge. He then popped the other to his own mouth, his eyes traveling over her in the indecent nightie as his teeth drained the bag. Neither of them could speak, but he didn't have to speak for her to know what he was thinking as his gaze shifted over her body. The man's eyes were going white silver, swirling with the molten color she was beginning to recognize. His eyes were hungry.

Uncomfortable sitting up there on display, Leigh pushed him back and slid off the counter. Lucian tried to catch her with his free hand, but she managed to evade his grasping hand and slid from the kitchen area, to move to the glass wall. Lucian followed, as she'd expected he would, stopping so close behind her she felt his heat along her back as she stared out at the lake.

When his hand slid around her waist, Leigh leaned back into him, then blinked in surprise as she saw their reflection in the window. She took in the picture of herself with him at her back, then raised her eyes to his to find them staring back. She drew her eyes from his and glanced at their bodies as his hand slid up toward her breast. She watched the reflection with fascination as his hand closed around the soft mound. She saw her body arch, pushing her breast invitingly into the caress before she even realized she was doing it.

When his other hand suddenly appeared in front of her face, she blinked at it with confusion, then glanced up to their reflected faces to see that his blood bag was gone and her own—while still in her mouth—was empty. Leigh took the bag out of her mouth and let him take it, glancing to the side as he tossed it on the coffee table next to his own.

She started to turn toward him then, but his hand tightened on her breast, the other going to her shoulder to hold her in place and keep her facing their image in the glass.

Stilling, she watched as he brushed the hair away from her neck and bent to press a kiss there as his hand loosened on her breast and continued to caress her.

Leigh had never thought of herself as an exhibitionist, but there was something erotic about seeing Lucian's taller, wider body framing hers from behind. There was also something exciting about watching his hands and mouth move on her as he bent his head to her neck. She swallowed hard, her bottom pressing back against him as her back arched, pressing her breast into his hand.

Lucian raised his head and met her gaze in the mirror for the briefest moment, then shifted to watch himself as he pulled one strap of the naughty little nightgown off her shoulder. The triangle of gossamer cloth covering her breast dropped away, and even in their faded ghost-like image, she could see how hard and erect her nipple was, revealed to the cool air.

She expected Lucian to touch her bare skin, to toy with the nipple now revealed, as he was doing to the cloth-covered breast, but he didn't. Instead, his hand drifted down her stomach, then pressed the fine net of the nightie between her legs as he cupped her.

Leigh groaned, her eyes trying to droop closed, but she forced them open, watching with fascination as her body responded, writhing and pushing and shifting as it came alive to his touch. Her legs shifted farther apart of their own accord, giving him better access and allowing him to push the cloth to the very heart of her, and she gasped and bucked against the caress. Then Lucian pinched the nipple of her still cloth-covered breast, and her eyes shot up to watch what he was doing there. It was only then that she realized she was panting. She could see her chest rising and falling quickly in the window, see her arms reaching back as she grabbed at him with her hands, both of them only able to reach the side seams of his black jeans. They were tight and there was no give in the material, but she still managed to dig her fingers in, forming handholds for herself, which she tugged at as he continued his caressing ministrations.

Exciting as it was, it was frustrating, too. Leigh wanted to kiss him, wanted to touch him, wanted . . . After an unbearable moment, she released one hand from his jeans and raised it to catch him behind the head. She pulled it down, then turned her head, offering her lips to him, silently begging for a kiss.

Lucian complied, his mouth closing over hers, but they were at an awkward angle. She wanted more. She wanted a proper kiss and tried to turn again, but was even more trapped by his caresses.

When Leigh dug her nails into the back of his skull in frustration, Lucian abruptly shifted, taking her in his arms and kissing her as she wanted to be kissed, his tongue thrusting into her mouth and staking its claim.

Leigh moaned, her body singing as he cupped her behind and lifted her, pressing her against him. She could feel the hardness of him grinding against her tender flesh, and wanted to wrap her legs around his hips and rub herself against him.

Even as she had that thought, Lucian tipped her back, his mouth pulling from hers and dropping to claim the little roseate pearl jutting out from her exposed breast. Leigh cried out, her hands clutching at his head and shoulders with excitement, then he turned his mouth to the other breast and did the same thing, this time through the cloth, and she blinked her eyes open in surprise at the sensation. Were he to ask her then which she preferred, she would have been hard-pressed to know. But then, at that moment she would have been hard-pressed to know her name.

Feeling the floor beneath her feet again, Leigh blinked her eyes open with surprise, immediately finding their reflection in the glass. Lucian had dropped to his knees, setting her back on the floor as he went. His wide back was a marble sculpture in the glass, half hiding her body, then he dropped to his haunches and her upper body was fully exposed. Leigh lowered her head, then stiffened and gasped as he lifted the short skirt of her nightie and pressed a kiss to the curls there.

When Lucian caught her upper legs in each hand and opened her up to his attentions like a book, she cried out and started to fall, but there wasn't far to go. While he'd held her off the ground, he'd backed her up to the couch. She sagged against it as his head dipped between her legs.

Leigh's mind went on hiatus. All ability to think died. All she was aware of was need. The need he was creating . . . and that seemed to swamp her . . . and then other needs that clamored to be heard. Her hands were fisted, nails digging into tender flesh, needing something to touch and hold onto. But there was only his head, and she was afraid she'd pull his hair hard and dig her claws into his scalp and hurt him, so refused herself that contact. Her lips wanted attention, too, wanting to open under his. If she'd had a pillow, she would have bitten it, but there was nothing near enough to bite.

Her frustrations built with her excitement as his mouth and tongue moved over her, then he suddenly pushed a finger up inside her and white light exploded behind her eyes. Her body was wracked with jolt after jolt of raw pleasure, and Leigh screamed, the sound piercing in her

own head. It was echoed by Lucian as his teeth sank into
her flesh. Then, like a supernova, the light went out and
she felt herself falling.

Lucian woke with a start. He felt the cold floor hard
under his back and the warm body splayed on his chest,
and smiled, his eyes still closed. Leigh. His gift from God.
His future. He would wake to find her warm by his side
every morning from now on. They were life mates.

The knowledge left a warm fuzzy feeling in his chest,
and he slowly opened his eyes to look at her.

Her cheek was plastered to his chest, her mouth open
and drool slipping from one corner. Her hair was a tangle
of snakes around her head . . . and she was perfect. She
was also pale again, he thought with sudden concern.

He'd bitten her, Lucian recalled. It hadn't been inten-
tional. As he'd pleasured her, their minds had merged
and he'd experienced what she felt. Every lick, every
nibble, every caress had resonated through him, guiding
him in his efforts and rewarding them as well.

He had forgotten that aspect of having a life mate.
Knowing their pleasure, sharing it, bouncing it back so
they experienced it anew, and then your own pleasure
on top of that. Their mind then bounced it back again. It
went back and forth, stronger each time, until the mind
couldn't handle it anymore and the mutual orgasm was
mind-numbing.

In that moment, as the world shattered and dissolved
around him, he had instinctively sunk his teeth into
Leigh's tender flesh. It happened on occasion, however—
not being a newbie—he'd had enough sense to pull back
before he consumed too much blood.

He had a vague recollection of falling back on the floor
then, Leigh sliding down with him, then he'd blacked

out. That wasn't unusual either, although it was more common for a new turn who wasn't used to the extremes of pleasure immortals could experience. Lucian wasn't a newbie, but it had been so long since he'd enjoyed the pleasures of the body that he was practically a born again virgin. Fortunately, Greg had been right and his body had known what to do. It looked like he hadn't needed those books after all. He knew without a doubt he'd satisfied Leigh.

A soft murmur from her drew his gaze back down, and Lucian once again noted her pallor. He might not have taken much blood, but between her turning and the exertion, Leigh needed to feed anyway. So did he, Lucian realized.

Easing out from under her, he grabbed an afghan off the couch, covered her with it, then got to his feet and went to the kitchen to fetch blood from the refrigerator. He consumed two bags there, then retrieved two more and returned to the living room.

Leigh hadn't moved a muscle since he'd left her side, and Lucian smiled at her limp state. Kneeling beside her, he slid an arm under her and lifted her up so her head lay over his arm, her mouth dropping open. Of course, her teeth weren't there, and he hesitated, then leaned down and breathed by her nose, hoping the scent of blood on his breath would be enough to bring them on. It worked, and Lucian relaxed as he watched her teeth slide out, then popped a bag of blood to her fangs and held her while she fed.

The second bag was to her mouth and almost empty when Leigh started to wake. She blinked her eyes open and murmured something unintelligible around the bag, and Lucian smiled. It was only a moment before the bag was empty, and he removed it.

"Good morning," Leigh said huskily as soon as she could speak.

"We didn't sleep that long," Lucian told her quietly. "I think we were only out for ten minutes or so."

Leigh shrugged. "It's still morning."

Lucian glanced over his shoulder to see it was true. The sky was lightening, the sun sending streaks of light ahead to warn of its approach.

"What are we going to do about the windows?" she asked, glancing around at the wall of glass.

"They're specially treated," Lucian assured her. "The UVs can't get through. It's safe."

"Oh."

He glanced back to see her smiling shyly, then she dropped her gaze, cleared her throat and murmured, "Thank you for . . . I'm sorry I didn't—I'm not usually so selfish in—I mean, you didn't get to—I should have—"

Lucian chuckled and silenced her stumbling apologies for what she thought had been a one-sided activity with a kiss. The passion immediately leapt back to life between them, but he broke it off before he could get carried away and forget to say what he wanted to. He responded to each of her stumbling attempts at apology one after the other.

"You're welcome. I did. You weren't selfish, and I did get to . . ."

When Leigh blinked at him with confusion, he explained, "We merged, Leigh. I experienced everything you felt—including the orgasm—as my own."

"You did?" she asked with surprise.

Lucian chuckled and nodded. "I'm not surprised you didn't realize it. The first time is overwhelming. You'll be able to tell next time."

"So there will be a next time?" she asked shyly.

"I certainly hope so," he said solemnly, brushing one finger lightly down her cheek and drawing her face up. "Right now if you like. I want to make love to you as the sun rises and burns away the night."

Leigh gave a little shiver, then slid her arms around his neck and pressed up to rub her breasts across his chest.

"I'd like that," she whispered against his mouth, then Lucian kissed her.

She was heat and life in his arms, her body soft to his hard, delicate against his strength. Growling into her mouth, Lucian eased her back on the rug in front of the couch, and lay on his side next to her as he kissed and caressed her. Her skin felt like warm velvet under his fingertips, but it was alive, muscles and flesh rippling as his palm slid over her stomach. He closed his hand over one breast and kneaded it gently as he thrust his tongue into her.

Leigh gasped into his kiss, her body arching upward as her own hands began to move up his arms, then down his chest, and then she opened for him, her mind merging with his, and he knew her desire to caress him and kiss every inch of him, and he smiled around their kiss. She felt perfect, tasted perfect, smelled perfect, was perfect for him.

Lucian rolled forward and slid one leg between hers, urging them apart as his thigh rubbed against her. He felt one of her small hands drift down his stomach, and his abdomen rippled in anticipation, then stilled on an indrawn breath as she closed her fingers around his hardness.

Leigh murmured her pleasure into his mouth and tightened her clasp on him, then drew her fingers down his length. Lucian bucked under the caress and felt her own hips buck in response as she experienced his pleasure.

Unable to concentrate on their kiss anymore, he tore his mouth away and shifted to suck mindlessly at any flesh he could find; her neck, her shoulder, her breast. His fingers were kneading the flesh of her breast with mindless excitement as he suckled her, his hips continuing to move under her caress. It was too much, it had been too long, and the earlier round had barely taken the edge off. If they continued like this, he knew he would spill himself in her hand and would not get to make love to her properly, their bodies merging like their minds and becoming one.

"Yes," Leigh gasped, now as aware of his needs as he of hers. She shifted her legs farther apart and tugged at his erection, urging him to enter her, but Lucian resisted. Instead, he slid a hand down between her legs and brushed his fingers lightly over the folds there. She was wet and ready for him, but still he resisted, taking the time to torture them both just a little bit more as his fingers slid between the folds and caressed the hard nub at the center of her desire.

Leigh cried out, her hand tightening around him and her hips bucking, and Lucian was hard-pressed not to bite down into the flesh of her breast as his own body was washed with waves of need, both hers and his own. Giving up any attempt to draw it out, he shifted abruptly, settling between her legs as her hand dropped away and moved to clutch at his shoulders.

Lucian paused there, above her, and peered down into her face. Her cheeks were flushed with excitement, her eyes spilling golden fire, and her mouth was open as she gasped with desire. He suddenly wished he was a painter and could paint her just like this, then he bent to cover her mouth with his own and drove into her.

Leigh was tight and hot, her body gloving him and squeezing around his flesh as if to keep him there as she thrust her own hips up to meet him and they both groaned at the shared feeling. Then he slowly withdrew, only to thrust back in again, this time shifting forward as he did, so he rubbed against her sensitive nub. The result was electrifying for them both, and Leigh clutched at his shoulders, urging him on.

Laughing breathlessly into her mouth, Lucian withdrew once more, and did it again and again, the excitement becoming more unbearable with each movement. Leigh's nails scored his skin and she tore her mouth from his, pressing it to his shoulder instead as her legs wrapped around him, changing the angle again, then he drove into her once more and stiffened, his head rearing back and a roar slipping out to match the scream ripped from her throat as the pleasure snapped, consuming them.

When it finally rippled away, Lucian's body went limp and he rolled to his side, taking her with him so that she lay splayed across his chest, her head on his heart. His last sight as his eyes closed was Leigh's face framed in the sunlight spilling through the window.

Something wet and rough slid along her cheek.

Leigh scowled and opened one eye to discover she was lying on the rug on the living room floor, an afghan tucked around her and Julius standing over her, giving her wet doggy kisses.

"Ewww, Julius. You have doggy breath," she muttered, and pushed his head away. Unoffended by her comment, he gave her face one more lick, then turned and trotted out of sight around the couch. Leigh lay still for a minute, frowning as she woke up enough to realize she was alone there on the floor. Lucian was gone. Then she became aware of the sound of spattering grease and someone humming.

She sat up and glanced toward the kitchen, eyebrows rising at the sight of Lucian in an apron and nothing else as he puttered around by the stove. She could smell food.

Leaning forward, Leigh snagged his shirt from the end of the couch, where it landed when he'd discarded it last night, and shrugged into it as she got to her feet. She only did up two buttons, since it was large enough to drape over her without needing more done up, and followed her nose into the kitchen area on silent feet.

Despite her silence, Lucian heard her and turned to glance over his shoulder as she crossed to his side.

"Good morning." His voice was a growl as he slid his eyes over her, then his left arm snaked around her waist and pulled her close for a kiss. When it ended, he eased his hold and peered down at her. "You look much better in my shirt than I do."

"You think so?" She slipped her arm around his back and leaned into him as he slid a hand through the undone front and ran his fingers lightly over her belly.

"Are you hungry?"

Leigh grinned cheekily, her hand slipping down over his bottom, but then she made herself behave. He was talking food. It was obvious he'd been cooking. Besides, now that he mentioned it, she *was* hungry. Turning, she peered into the frying pan and blinked.

"What—" She snapped her mouth closed on asking exactly what he was cooking as she stared at the blackened mess in the pan. Clearing her throat, she said instead, "I'm surprised there was food here. Surely they don't keep food here all the time in case someone comes around?"

Lucian shook his head and turned back to scrape some of the charred mess off the bottom of the pan and move it around. "It was delivered about half an hour, forty-five minutes ago."

"Delivered?" She glanced at him with surprise. "I didn't hear anyone."

"You were dead to the world," he said with a grin, then added wryly, "Actually, I was, too. I think he must have been knocking awhile before it roused me and I answered . . . naked."

When Leigh's eyebrows rose, he smiled and shrugged. "I guess I wasn't that awake yet. Gave the delivery guy quite a start."

Leigh smiled, but asked, "Did you order the groceries when we arrived last night?"

Lucian shook his head. "Bastien. He's the plan man. Etienne called him last night after we left and let him know what was going on. He apparently called and ordered both food and blood to be delivered."

"Ah." Leigh nodded and ran her hand up and down his back, but her gaze slid back to the pan. Lucian sighed beside her.

"I was hoping to make you breakfast, but it appears I'm a failure as a cook," he admitted, his expression unhappy as he contemplated the mess. Then he frowned with frustration and said, "I don't know what I did wrong. I kept turning it and turning it and still it burned."

"Ah . . . well . . ." Leigh reached to the stove and lowered the heat from high to medium. "This is the temperature best for cooking. Or lower."

"Halfway?" he asked with doubt. "Wouldn't that make it cook more slowly?"

"Yes. But it also doesn't burn."

"Oh." He frowned.

"It's all right," she said with a shrug as she reached out and turned off the burner. "We can make some more. I'll cook."

"There *is* no more."

Leigh peered down at the pan. She thought it might be two charred eggs and three strips of bacon curled up in their black death. There was something else, but she didn't recognize it at all, except to know it wasn't bacon.

"They delivered only three strips of bacon?" she asked with disbelief.

"Well . . . no," Lucian admitted with a frown. "This is the fourth batch I've tried to cook. They all kept burning up, though, so I threw them out and tried again, and again . . ." He gave her an apologetic smile. "Sorry."

Leigh smiled, a slow, soft smile, and leaned up to kiss him softly on the lips. "You're so sweet."

Lucian blinked in surprise, then slid his arms around her and kissed her properly.

"Mmm," she sighed as they broke the kiss. "I'm starved. Let's go out for breakfast. I'll buy."

"I'll buy," Lucian growled, scooping her up into his arms and starting across the floor.

"We'll flip for it," Leigh countered as she slid her arms around his neck.

"Hmm," was all he said, and she kissed the corner of his mouth again, chasing his scowl away.

"Did I tell you what Etienne told me about the bed in the loft?" Lucian asked as he started upstairs with her in his arms.

Her eyebrows rose. "No."

"He said there are straps on it."

"Straps?" Leigh asked with confusion.

"Hmmm. The satin sheets are slippery and there's no headboard to brace yourself against, so Thomas had straps put on the bed to hold onto . . . or to tie someone down with." Lucian grinned wickedly as her eyes widened. "How hungry are you?"

Leigh considered, a slow smile drawing her lips wide. "Well, I *am* hungry, but I think I can wait a bit. What did you have in mind?"

"Dessert first."

"And what are we having for dessert?" she teased as they reached the top of the stairs and he carried her toward the bed.

"Well, I don't know what you're having, but I'm having a little Leigh." He then dropped her on the bed and came down on top of her.

 Eighteen

Lucian opened his eyes when Leigh shifted sleepily against him. He'd blacked out again, but just for a
heartbeat this time, he was sure. Leigh, however, was
still under. He didn't mind. It meant he got the chance
just to lay here, holding her and planning their future.
The years stretched away in his mind, full of happiness
and laughter.

Leigh liked his house, which was good. There'd
be little to do to accommodate her there, though he
thought they should get a bed like this big round one
of Thomas's. A smile crept over his face as he recalled
all that they'd done, and all that they could still do on
a bed like this.

Of course, he realized, they couldn't stay at his house
all the time. She had a business in Kansas City she'd
want to oversee, but perhaps he could persuade her to
hire more help and spend less time there. He'd have to
see. He wanted her happy.

Lucian toyed with a strand of her hair and wondered
what her own house was like. He was imagining it small
and cozy, full of overstuffed furniture and comfy pillows. He supposed he'd find out soon enough. They'd

head down there once Morgan and Donny were caught and out of the way.

Leigh murmured sleepily again, rubbing her head on his chest like a cat, and Lucian smiled. Releasing her hair, he let his hand run down her warm skin, caressing her back, his smile widening as she murmured and cuddled against him while arching into the touch. He loved touching her. He loved how she responded. He loved her.

The thought didn't surprise him. Their minds had merged while they'd made love, and he'd caught glimpses into her. Leigh had a quick, intelligent brain, a kind and loving heart, and she cared for others before herself. She was also as alone and lonely as he was. A kindred spirit.

Unfortunately, she also had a passel of fears bundled up inside her. He had only touched on them, but knew there were some things to get past before their future could be pursued. But for the most part, he felt sure everything was fine.

"Hello. How long did I sleep?"

Lucian glanced down and smiled at the sexy, sleepy look on Leigh's face.

"Not long. Are you ready for a shower and breakfast?" he asked, though it was going to be more like a late lunch. It had been past lunchtime when he'd tried to cook. Now the clock on the dresser said it was close to three in the afternoon.

"Oh yes," Leigh moaned, then gasped with surprise as Lucian suddenly shifted and swung her up in his arms as he slid off the bed.

"Mmm," she purred, slipping her arms around his neck. "You'd better watch it, Argeneau. What with you feeding me, then carting me about . . . you'll spoil me with all this care, and I'll come to expect it."

"And so you should. A smart man treats his life mate as the jewel she is," Lucian said softly, and Leigh's smile faded, a flicker of concern drifting through her eyes.

"What is it?" he asked, but she glanced away, then cleared her throat as she saw he'd carried her into the bathroom.

"Ooh, this is nice," she murmured, peering around the huge room with its sunken sauna and stand-up shower that could fit four, maybe five people. "Thomas certainly has luxurious taste."

"He can afford it," Lucian said with a shrug, setting her on her feet as she began to wiggle. He felt her absence as she moved to the shower and opened the door.

"Are we sharing?" Leigh asked, tossing him a smile over her shoulder.

"Water conservation is always a good idea," he said with feigned solemnity.

Leigh chuckled as she stepped into the shower and moved to adjust the water taps. "Yes, well, that's all well and good, but you behave yourself. I *am* hungry, and if you start something, we'll never get out to breakfast."

"I think it will actually have to be brunch," Lucian admitted as he stepped into the shower stall with her.

Leigh was fiddling with the selection of knobs on the wall, trying to sort out what would start the shower. Lucian found the curve of her back irresistible and stepped up behind her, his hands catching her waist as he pulled her back against him.

"Lucian," she said in warning.

"What?" he asked innocently, pressing his semierection against her backside, then he squawked and jumped back as cold water shot out of the shower head.

Leigh laughed and quickly began turning knobs, trying to adjust the spray.

"Sorry." She turned toward him once she finally got it at the proper temperature. "I couldn't figure out the—"

Her words ended on a gasp as he kissed her. Leigh allowed it for a moment, then pushed at his chest.

"Food," she said, her voice husky.

"I have to soap you up. There's no reason I can't kiss you while I do it," Lucian said mildly, and reached for the soap, then put his arms around her to lather behind her back as he bent to her lips again.

Leigh sighed into his mouth, her arms slipping around his neck as he kissed her. Then she shifted and sighed again when he broke their kiss and turned her out of the water, blocking it with his own body as he ran his soapy hands over her back.

"You're like a cat wanting stroking," he growled by her ear as his hands drifted lower.

"Cats don't like water," Leigh reminded him, pressing against his erection as his hands now slid up her arms, then under them and around to cover her breasts in lather.

"Mmm," she murmured, and covered his hands, her head lolling against his chest, her bottom pushing back to rub against his now full erection as he caressed her soapy body.

"Where have you been all my life?" she asked on a sigh, and groaned as he dipped one soapy hand between her legs.

Lucian smiled and kissed the side of her neck, then nibbled at her ear before whispering, "Waiting for you," as he slid one finger inside her. Leigh gasped, and stiffened as he withdrew his hand.

"Food," Lucian taunted when she groaned in protest and caught at his hand, urging it back.

"Food can wait," she assured him, one hand sliding back between their bodies and closing over his erection.

Lucian held strong and turned her into the water, rinsing her and wetting her hair at the same time.

"Tease," she grumbled under her breath, but quit trying to touch him and let him wash her hair. Little sighs of pleasure slipped from her lips as he massaged her scalp. Despite his words, Lucian had gone hard as a rock. Her body kept brushing his in the shower with teasing, fleeting caresses of skin, and he was hard-pressed not to finish what he'd started. But she was hungry, and he actually was, too, and she needed food.

"This is a big shower," she commented on a little sigh as he moved her back under the water so she could rinse the soap from her hair. While she did that, he quickly shampooed his own hair.

"Yes." He glanced toward the walls as he massaged the shampoo into his scalp, thinking he'd like to make love to her here as he had in the dream of her shower. "Maybe we should put one in at the house. We could arrange to have it done while we were in Kansas so we wouldn't have to put up with the inconvenience and noise of the workmen."

Lucian felt her still, and glanced back to find her eyes open, that same troubled look in their depths. He raised an eyebrow. "What is it?"

"I— You keep talking like we're—" Leigh frowned, then said gently, "Lucian, I don't want to rush into anything."

"What does that mean?" he asked slowly.

She hesitated, then said, "I mean, I'm willing to give it a try and date you, but—"

"Date?" he squawked with amazement. "Leigh, you're my life mate. We aren't dating. We're—"

"If we aren't dating, we aren't anything," she interrupted, and suddenly stepped out of the shower. He watched dumbfounded as she snatched a towel off the rack and began to dry herself, then he turned and stepped under the water to rinse the soap away before following.

"Leigh, last night—"

"Last night was lovely, but—"

"Lovely?" he echoed sharply. "Flowers are lovely, cinnamon buns are lovely. What we shared was incredible, dynamite . . . *rare*. Our minds merged, Leigh. We *are* life mates."

"Yes," she agreed. "It was all of that and I still want to just date for a while." She stomped out of the bathroom.

"So, you sleep with everyone you date?" Lucian asked, following to find her pulling on her clothes. "It meant nothing to you?"

"No, I don't sleep with everyone I date." She frowned, then said on a sigh, "You're angry."

"You're damned right I am. I offer you my heart, my body, my life, and you say let's just date?" Lucian stopped abruptly as he noticed the fear that had entered her eyes and the way she'd flinched as he'd gestured with his hand. Leigh had thought he was going to hit her, he realized with shock, and suddenly understood what this was all about. Kenny. The abusive and, fortunately for him, dead ex-husband. She'd dated him six weeks, married him, and only found out then that he liked to talk with his fists. Leigh had only known him a matter of days and—life mate or no life mate—feared making another mistake. This was where the proving he would never hurt her part came in, he realized.

Shoulders slumping with defeat, he sighed. "Okay."

Leigh blinked. "Okay?" she asked with surprise.

"Sure." Lucian made himself shrug, turned to find his own clothes, and started drawing them on. "If you need time to adjust and reassure yourself that I won't start beating you, then so be it. I've waited thousands of years for you, what's a little more time?"

"It's not that I'm afraid you'll become abusive," Leigh began, but fell silent when he turned to stare at her with disbelief.

"If it isn't that, what do you think it is?" he asked quietly. "Aside from the whole life mate thing, we're very compatible. We have similar taste in food, homes, and clothing. We enjoy each other's company and laugh a lot together. From the talk we had at lunch yesterday, I know we both like to read and have similar taste in movies. And we're more than compatible sexually."

Leigh frowned and opened her mouth, but he spoke first, saying, "And I like you, Leigh. I truly like you. Long after the passions are spent and the lust has waned—which will happen in two or three thousand years—I know you'll still be my best friend. You've made me laugh again. I love you, Leigh. And you like and love me."

She opened her mouth, but afraid she'd deny his words, Lucian said, "Our minds merged, Leigh. I know your heart. Whether you'll admit it to yourself or not, you *do* care for me. So the only thing left is trust."

Her shoulders slumped as a sigh slid from her lips. "I don't—"

"No." He forced a smile. "It's okay. I've fought Romans, Scots, Spaniards, and Germans, among others over the millennia. I'll help you fight your fears." His smile turned wry. "I just wish I could do it with a sword. Unfortunately, this is one of those things that take time, and with all the years I've lived, I still hate waiting."

Finished dressing, Lucian turned and headed for the stairs. "Hurry up. The faster you're dressed, the sooner we can get to a restaurant. I'll feed Julius while you finish getting ready."

Leigh's mind was running in circles as she dressed, Lucian's words circling through her head over and over. They liked the same foods, the same clothes, the same movies and books. They were compatible and laughed a lot...

She realized as she tied her shoes that he was right. The only thing holding her back was trust. She didn't trust him...

That thought didn't feel quite right. She knew herself well enough to know that she wouldn't have slept with him and given herself to him if she hadn't trusted him. Perhaps the truth was that she didn't trust herself, her own judgment. While she didn't think Lucian would ever lift a finger to her in anger, she hadn't thought Kenny would become a wife-beater when they'd married either. How was she to know she was right this time, when she'd made such a mess of things before?

Sighing, Leigh finished tying her laces and stood to move to the stairs. Lucian seemed to think it would take time, and he was probably right, but she wished there was a way to do it faster. Despite his outward acceptance, she knew he was hurt by her insistence on keeping their relationship to just dating for now.

"Stupid dog, cut that out."

Leigh glanced around the main floor as she descended the stairs, finding Lucian and Julius in the kitchen area.

At first she thought they were wrestling. Lucian was lying on his side on the hardwood floor with his legs wrapped around the big dog's body as he tried to pry his mouth open. Unfortunately, Julius was not cooperating. Squirming and pawing and clawing, the dog was doing all he could to escape.

"It's for your own good," Lucian told him firmly, readjusting his grip and trying again to pry his mouth open.

"What . . .?" Leigh said in bewilderment as Lucian managed to pop a little colored pill in the dog's mouth. He immediately forced Julius's mouth closed and massaged his throat to get him to swallow.

His medicine, Leigh realized. Marguerite had mentioned something about an infection in that first phone call. She'd forgotten about it. She had never seen Lucian try to give it to the beast before. It looked like he had, though.

"There. You're done. Go." Apparently sure Julius had swallowed the medicine, Lucian let go of him. The mutt was instantly on his feet and shaking himself, then leaned over and gave Lucian's cheek a lick as if in apology for being difficult.

"Yeah yeah," Lucian muttered, pushing the huge head away as he got to his feet. "Go eat or something and get the taste out of your mouth."

Leigh smiled faintly at the order as Lucian moved to the sink, then frowned as she saw the blood dripping from the hand he lifted to put under the tap.

"He bit you," she said with surprise, hurrying to his side. "Are you okay?"

"It'll heal," Lucian said with a shrug as the water washed the blood away.

Leigh hardly heard the words, she was staring at his

hand. It was a good bite and must have hurt, but Lucian didn't sound particularly angry and hadn't been rough with the dog when she'd come down.

"It's my own fault anyway. I haven't a clue what I'm doing, and think I'm doing it wrong. And he's just as dumb as me and doesn't understand it's for his own good," Lucian added dryly. "He thinks I'm trying to choke him or something."

Leigh lifted her gaze to his face. Kenny would have kicked the dog and blamed him for everything. Lucian was taking the fault on himself.

"There's probably an easier way to do it," Lucian muttered, pulling his hand out to see how it was healing. "I'm sure Marguerite and Maria know how to do it without getting bit."

"They probably put it in his dog food," Leigh murmured, peering at his hand. It was healing quickly, she noted. There wouldn't even be a scar in an hour or so.

A curse from Lucian drew her gaze up to see him rolling his eyes. "Of course! In his dog food. You're brilliant! I'll try that tomorrow. Thanks."

He leaned to kiss her on the cheek, then grabbed a paper towel to dry his hand, and Leigh turned to peer at Julius. The mastiff was contentedly lapping up dog food Lucian had set out for him, the trauma over for the day. She could almost believe it hadn't happened. Julius wasn't keeping one wary eye on Lucian or anything that would indicate...

Leigh paused as she realized what she was thinking. The scene here had reminded Leigh of an incident with Kenny and his parents' dog, Dolly, before they'd married. A border collie, Dolly had been friendly with everyone but Kenny. She'd shied away from him, cowering and flinching whenever he raised his voice or moved too suddenly. Leigh hadn't noticed it until later, after they were married and she started doing the same thing.

The incident she was thinking of at the moment, however, was when they'd gone to his parents' house for a Sunday dinner. Dolly, asleep in the living room, was startled awake when Kenny clumsily stepped on her paw in passing. Coming awake with a squeal, the collie's head shot around instinctively to snap at him. She only snapped at the air by his foot, but Kenny kicked out at Dolly in retribution, missing her only because she'd been quicker than him.

Kenny had said "Stupid dog" then, as Lucian often did, but there wasn't a drop of affection in the words, just dislike. That incident had always bothered her. She'd only realized how telling it was after the wedding, though. Kenny had treated her the same way he treated Dolly, blaming her for his own clumsiness and inadequacies and striking out at her for them. She had often wished that she'd paid more attention to how the dog had reacted to him before agreeing to the marriage.

Her gaze slid over Julius, and she considered his reactions to Lucian. The dog never cowered or flinched around him, whether Lucian raised his voice or moved suddenly, or not.

"Ready to go?"

Leigh glanced around to Lucian to see his hand was mostly healed. Pushing herself away from the counter, she nodded. "Yes."

"Good." He slid his arm around her waist, kissing her lightly before urging her toward the door. "You look nice."

Leigh chuckled wryly at the compliment. Her hair was still damp and slicked back off her face, she had no makeup on and was wearing the suede pants again and a t-shirt she'd found in the drawers upstairs. She was hardly a fashion plate.

"I hope Thomas won't mind, but I borrowed one of his t-shirts. The collar of the pink top is kind of stretched out. I'm hoping a run through the washer will fix it, but in the meantime, the only clothes Rachel packed was the nightie," she explained as they reached the front door.

"Nightwear is really a most important consideration," Lucian said with a grin, allowing his hand to slide over her bottom as he opened the front door for her to walk outside. Then he added, "I shall have to thank Rachel for her thoughtfulness when we get back."

"Oh, she'll love that," Leigh chuckled as she waited for him to lock the door, then she frowned and said, "Rachel said you threatened to have her terminated when you first met."

Lucian stiffened, then finished at the door and turned to face her, his expression solemn. "I protect my people, Leigh. It's what I do. I protect my people from discovery, and protect mortals from any of my people who have gone bad. Rachel was threatening the welfare of us all by stubbornly refusing to go along with a plan we hoped would end another threat. I had to shake her up and get her on board."

"Yes, I know," Leigh murmured, then asked what she really wanted to know, the reason she'd brought the topic up again. "Would you have killed her?"

Lucian hesitated, and she could see the battle in his eyes and knew he wanted to say no to reassure her, but in the end he offered her the truth.

"If there were no other way to handle the matter, yes."

Leigh nodded thoughtfully. She could tell by his expression that he feared his honesty might have hurt his efforts to gain her trust, but the opposite was the case. He'd been honest with her. She'd already known the answer before he spoke it. Lucian did what he had to do to protect his people, even if it meant killing someone. She'd already figured that out.

"Leigh, I . . ." He paused, apparently at a loss, and she leaned up and kissed him on the corner of the mouth as she took his hand.

"It's okay. Let's go, I'm hungry," she said, and turned to lead him toward the car, her steps slowing as she realized she'd have to drive.

"I won't say a single solitary thing the whole ride," Lucian assured her, apparently picking up on her reaction and zeroing in at once on the reason for it. "I promise."

"Yeah, right." Leigh laughed and got into the car. She started it as he walked around, then shifted into reverse to back out of the driveway once he was in.

Lucian was true to his word and didn't say a thing, but he sure had to do a lot of lip biting on the way. He also sat with hands clenched and foot occasionally slapping the floor as if searching for brakes. But he did keep his promise.

Leigh thought about that and other things as they laughed and chatted over their late lunch. One of the other things was that Lucian was taking her decision to go slow and just date very well. He wasn't sulking or angry with her for the choice. Kenny had sulked, she remembered. They were in Vegas, he'd suggested getting married, and she had shied like a mare who spots a snake in the road. Kenny had sulked. He'd pouted, then turned cold to her afterward, and it scared her. She'd felt abandoned, and it reminded her of how alone she was, leaving her afraid he'd break up with her and she would have absolutely nobody. It was why she'd given in and agreed to the marriage.

Lucian wasn't doing any of that. If anything, he was more affectionate than he'd previously been, constantly reaching out to touch her or take her hand, rubbing his own hand over her back, kissing her on the cheek, neck, or lips at every opportunity. Of course, part of that was because they were now lovers. He'd touched her a lot before last night, but then it had been more mundane touches like taking her arm to walk her places, or a hand at her back as he followed her through a door. But he wasn't treating her coolly as punishment for putting him off. He wasn't another Kenny.

"Do you want to go for a swim?" Lucian asked as they headed back to the cottage.

Leigh glanced over, smiling with amusement as she saw that he had discovered the "Oh shit" bar over the door and was holding it as if his life depended on it. She was only going the speed limit. "A swim sounds nice."

"Maybe we could barbecue some steaks later," Lucian suggested, sounding a little more relaxed as she turned into the dirt lane to the cottage.

"That sounds good, too," she admitted, her gaze moving over the woods they were driving through. It had been after four by the time they'd reached the restaurant. Now, on their way back, it was after six and the sky was darkening overhead. It had been gray and dim while they were on the road, but here in the cover of the trees it was almost dark. She had to resist the urge to turn the car's headlights on.

"Geez, what is it with you guys and people?" Leigh said abruptly.

"What do you mean?" Lucian asked.

"I mean Marguerite's house, your house, and this

'cottage' are all surrounded by forest. I presume that's because you don't want neighbors."

"It's more because we don't like to move."

"Move?" she asked.

Lucian nodded, then pointed out, "We don't age, Leigh. If you have neighbors, they tend to notice that after a while and you end up moving every ten years or so to avoid troublesome questions. This way, no one really knows who lives in the house. They never see you coming or going, so unless you're foolish enough to go knocking on their door, you can live here as long as you like."

"Oh," Leigh breathed as she recognized the sense of his words, then her eyes widened. "They'll notice I'm not aging at work."

"I'm afraid so," he said quietly. "It's not something to worry about right away, but eventually you'll have to stop running it yourself, or sell it and start somewhere else."

Leigh frowned at this news. She loved Coco's. It had been her salvation years ago. Her whole life revolved around the restaurant/bar. Or had, she realized, and then frowned as it occurred to her that she hadn't called Milly in a couple days to check and make sure everything was running smoothly. That had to be the first time since she'd owned the bar that she hadn't been in contact with the restaurant once a day. Even when she was in the hospital with pneumonia two years ago, she'd called to check on the place.

"You could always start an immortal bar," Lucian said, and she glanced at him with surprise.

"Well, you can run those forever without raising the eyebrows of your customers or employees. You just have someone else deal with the delivery guys and so on," Lucian pointed out, then reached over and patted her hand. "Don't worry. Everything will sort itself out eventually. By the time your not aging becomes a worry, you might have grown tired of the whole bar scene and decided to do something else."

Leigh managed a smile. "What? Like help you kick rogue butt?"

Lucian chuckled at the suggestion as she parked the car.

"You don't think I could?" she challenged as she turned off the engine. "I learned my lesson with Kenny and took some self-defense classes after I left."

"I'm sure you did, and you're probably very . . . competent."

"Ohh, competent. That sounds like humoring the little woman, Argeneau," Leigh said with amusement as she got out of the car.

"Not at all," he assured her. "I just—"

"Yeah yeah," she interrupted with a laugh. "You just wait. Before we go swimming, I'll throw you around the beach a bit."

"Hmmm," he almost purred. "That sounds promising. Almost kinky."

"Honestly." She laughed as she opened the front door and walked into the house. "The only things you seem to think about are food and sex."

"Leigh." Lucian grabbed her arm.

She turned back. There was a frozen look on his face as he peered at the door she'd just opened.

"You locked that, didn't you?" she said quietly, fear slipping up her back and setting the hair at the nape of her neck prickling.

"He did," someone said mildly behind her.

Lucian's hand tightened on her arm as Leigh slowly

turned to peer into the living area. At first she didn't see anything, but then Morgan sat up on the couch and peered at them over the back of it.

Smiling, he added, "Fortunately, Donny has a certain skill with locks. It's one of the talents I'm sure he didn't bother to mention on his application for a job in your Coco's."

Nineteen

Leigh stared at Morgan, her mind slow to accept that he
had somehow found them. The rogue vampire looked
just as he had the last time she'd seen him: long greasy
hair, pale sharp-angled face, and in need of a good scrubbing. She doubted he'd bathed, or changed his clothes,
since she'd first met him.

She glanced back at Lucian, her mouth opening to
speak then snapping closed as two men filled the doorway behind them. Neither man was as tall as Lucian, but
they were both brawny, wide and strong. Musclemen.
One had a long wicked knife strapped to his thigh, the
other had a sword in hand. Both had the metallic eyes
of immortals and looked oddly familiar. Leigh narrowed
her eyes as she tried to place where she'd seen them before.

Lucian followed her gaze over his shoulder. His expression was void of any emotion when he turned back.
"What did you do, Morgan? Raid a gym?"

"Actually, both Brad and Martin happen to be personal trainers. Or they were back in Kansas before they
were turned," Morgan admitted with amusement, then
his gaze slid to Leigh and he grinned briefly, enjoying the
game before he turned back to Lucian and commented,

"Leigh's wracking her mind trying to remember where she's seen them before. But you recognized them at once, didn't you, Lucian? You've always had a good memory. Help her out, won't you?"

"The Night Club," Lucian growled, sounding bored.

The moment he said it, Leigh remembered the two men sitting at the table next to theirs. They'd been close enough to touch the night before . . . close enough to hear everything they'd said.

"Yes, they heard everything—that Lucian's men caught my little lovebirds when they ran into car trouble in Iowa, that you planned to leave town and come to the cottage," Morgan murmured, obviously reading her thoughts. His gaze shifted to Lucian again and he grimaced. "Do come in and join us. I'm getting a crick in my neck from sitting like this."

Leigh started to walk when Lucian put his hand on her elbow and urged her forward. The sound of footsteps behind them told her that Morgan's two men, Brad and Martin, had followed them inside. She heard the door shut as it closed behind them. It was a soft click, but in her head had as much power as a prison cell clanging closed. She stiffened in response, and Lucian shifted his hand to her back to rub it soothingly, then said, "Join *us*?"

"Donny's here," Morgan announced just before they walked around the couch and spotted him.

Leigh gasped in shock at her first sight of the man. The redhead was hunched on the floor in front of the couch, dried blood on his face, arm, and chest from very fresh injuries that were already healing. He was also pale, emaciated, and obviously suffering terrible pain from a need to feed.

"Donny's been a bad boy," Morgan explained. "He disobeyed me and had to be punished."

"You told me to take care of the dog, and I did," Donny muttered.

Leigh stiffened. Until then she'd been too distracted to realize that Julius wasn't about. Now she glanced around the main floor with alarm.

"I told you to *kill* him," Morgan said harshly.

"There was no need," Donny argued grimly. "He's locked in the bathroom."

Leigh relaxed at this news, but Morgan wasn't as pleased. He gave a tsk of disgust and cuffed him.

"Donny looks hungry," Lucian commented. "Yet the rest of you look well fed."

"You have friendly neighbors. Well . . . had," Morgan corrected himself with a mean smile. "As for Donny, he can feed when he's ready to kill to do it." He glared at the redhead and added, "If he'd killed the dog as I ordered, he'd be fed by now. Unfortunately, Donny has a problem killing *anything*. If it weren't for his talent with locks, I'd have killed him. As it is, I need him to teach the skill to one of the other men."

"And then?" Lucian asked, his tone suggesting he knew the answer.

"And then I'll kill him," Morgan said simply.

Leigh stiffened. She and Donny had been friends once, and the redhead hadn't killed Julius, or anyone else from the sound of it. Besides, she wasn't angry with him anymore for dragging her into this mess. If he hadn't, she wouldn't have met Lucian.

Donny's head rose, eyes burning a bright silver blue as he glared at Morgan. "You—"

"A vampire who won't kill is of no use to me," Morgan snapped. "The dog should be dead. Not being dead means he could still be a problem. What if he breaks out?"

"I hope he does," Donny muttered, and received another cuffing for his trouble.

Straightening from hitting him, Morgan spotted the expression on Leigh's face and sighed. "Oh, don't look so upset. By the time I kill Donny, he'll be glad for it, I promise. He'll welcome the respite from the agony he's suffering."

"It looks like you picked a man with a conscience," Lucian said with amusement, drawing the attention back to himself. "You should've checked his morals before turning him. Not everyone makes a good rogue, Morgan."

"Yes, yes. I know that *now*," Morgan said impatiently. "Unfortunately, some things can't be tested until the moment arrives. Thank you for the advice, though, Lucian. I shall keep it in mind in future." He paused and tilted his head. "Speaking of futures, yours isn't looking very bright."

Lucian smiled. "Better men than you have tried to kill me, Morgan. I'm still here."

"Perhaps," he allowed. "But those men didn't have the advantage I do."

"Oh?" Lucian asked warily. "What would that be?"

Morgan merely smiled, then turned to Leigh. The next moment, her body began to move forward. She instinctively tried to stop herself and felt her footsteps falter, but then quickly ceded the control she'd briefly had. It appeared she might be able to fight his hold over her now that she was an immortal. But there was no sense letting Morgan know that until it would be of some use.

Recalling that Morgan could read her thoughts, she forced her mind blank, not wanting to give anything away as she allowed her body to do his bidding. Rebellion reared in her, however, when her feet took her right up between his legs, then turned her and sat her down in his lap, but she gritted her teeth and did nothing. For now. It was hard, though. In her mind, this felt much the same as Kenny's abuse. Her dead husband had used fear and his fists to control her. Morgan was using his mind. Both were still all about control.

"Surely it isn't as bad as all that." Morgan said, sounding amused. "Comparing my small liberties to your dead husband's abuses is rather harsh. Don't you think?"

"I think only a sick mind enjoys controlling others," Leigh muttered.

"You have a sharp mouth on you," he commented. "But lovely for all that. I hadn't realized how lovely until this morning."

"This morning?" Lucian growled, and Leigh glanced his way to see that his face was still expressionless, but anger and suspicion were growing in his eyes.

"Yes, this morning," Morgan said, sounding like he was enjoying himself as he added, "I watched you together."

Leigh's gaze shot to Morgan, a seed of horror bursting to life in her mind. Surely he didn't mean . . . ?

"The little episode on the stairs was quite appetizing," he announced, and she closed her eyes as she realized exactly what he'd meant. He continued, "I was sorry when it ended partway through and Leigh fled upstairs."

"You were here then?" Lucian's question was sharp.

"Yes," Morgan answered easily. "Donny and I arrived at the Night Club just in time to see you and Jean Claude's brood enter. I decided it was prudent to wait for Brad and Martin outside. When they arrived, I sent them in to see if they couldn't find out what was going on. They heard most of what you said, that you'd be taking Rachel's car and going to some cottage, but they didn't catch where. So we drove over to Rachel and Etienne's and waited for you to leave."

"And followed us here last night," Lucian said.

Morgan nodded. "When you stopped, Donald and I stayed to keep an eye on you, while Brad and Martin looked for somewhere nearby to take shelter during the day. We watched through the front window as you made love to Leigh on the steps . . . Well, at least until she fled upstairs."

Leigh turned her head and peered at the front window beside the door. Like the rest of the house, it had no curtains. But then why should it? No one could see in unless they crept up to the house and played voyeur . . . as Morgan and Donny had. And they'd seen them on the stairs, she thought, embarrassment making her angry.

"I'm sorry, Leigh," Donny said miserably. "I'm sorry about everything. I—"

"Shut up, Donald," Morgan snapped. "Just shut up. I'm sick to death of your mealy-mouthed, spineless, whining ways. *You* were the one who wanted her turned in the first place, then you refused to watch them on the stairs like some goody two shoes little—" He cut himself off sharply and took a deep breath. He turned back to Leigh and Lucian to continue, "Brad returned shortly after that to tell us they'd located an inhabited cottage nearby."

He shrugged. "The show was over, and you two appeared to be settled in for the night, so we went next door to feed and wait out the worst of daylight."

Leigh first felt rage at what the unknown neighbors must have suffered, and then a grim satisfaction that his disgusting actions had at least made him miss the show he'd wanted to see. And he would have had a fine seat since it had taken place right here on the floor in front of the glass wall.

When the rogue vampire's mouth tightened with sudden displeasure, she knew he'd read her thoughts again.

"So we missed the big show after all," he said, sounding angry again.

"I'm afraid so," Leigh said with pleasure.

"No you're not," Morgan countered. "But I am. It's a long time since I've felt the passion and beauty of life mates joining. I could have slipped into your mind and experienced it with you."

Leigh shuddered at the very idea. She was glad he hadn't and thought he was a disgusting little man for even considering it.

"Oh, now, Leigh," he chided. "Surely you wouldn't begrudge me? Not one who has lost his own life mate? It would be good to feel alive again."

"Lost your life mate?" Lucian asked with obvious shock. "I didn't know you'd found a life mate."

"Oh yes." Morgan released a breath, then said bitterly, "But she wouldn't allow me to turn her. She was very religious and thought it would be a sin against God. Pious little—" He choked on whatever else he would have said, then added, "I had to watch her age and grow frail, watch time take its toll . . . Only at the end when she realized she was going to die did she agree to let me turn her, but it was too late then. She was eighty-two and ailing. Her heart gave out while the nanos were trying to reverse it all. She died in my arms."

There was real pain on his face, but more bitterness, and it quickly turned to rage. "The stupid bitch! If she'd just—" He cut himself off, then glanced at Lucian. "I wasn't willing to wait for another life mate, as you have.

I don't have the patience. I have no family. Jean Claude was my only friend and he's now dead. I don't *want* to be alone for thousands of years in the hopes that someday, maybe, another life mate will come. I'd rather end it."

Leigh blinked. He'd as good as just admitted—at least in her mind—that his going rogue was just another form of suicide.

"Well why didn't you, then?" she asked with amazement. "Why harm so many people and take them with you?"

"Because there's still pleasures to be had." Morgan said it as though she were stupid not to realize it. "I thought I'd give some of them a try."

He ran his hand down her arm once more. "Perhaps you could make me smile again."

"What he really means is that he's too cowardly to kill himself, and selfish enough that he wants to take others with him," Lucian said dryly.

"I'm afraid so," Morgan admitted without shame. "Why go alone when I can make so many others miserable, too?"

Lucian snorted with disgust, but merely said, "So I suppose you intend to begin a new nest with these three?"

Morgan glanced at Donny, then at the other two men, before returning his gaze back to Lucian and saying, "Four."

He smiled at Lucian as he ran his hand down Leigh's back, adding, "And the many more I shall turn. A smart man could make himself an army. There are lots of them to choose from. If there's one thing mortals can be counted on for, it's that they breed like bunnies. In truth, it's *all* they're really good for."

"That and for you to feed on," Leigh pointed out sarcastically.

Morgan shrugged. "You feed on them, too. You couldn't survive without it now."

"I use bagged blood from a blood blank," Leigh snapped. "I don't attack and maul people."

"We can feed from blood banks?" Donny perked up with interest.

"Yes." Leigh frowned as she realized he hadn't known that. Of course, Morgan wouldn't have told him, it would have weakened his control.

"No," Morgan said grimly. "It weakens you, takes away your freedom. The Argeneaus control you through their blood banks."

"Oh please. He's not stupid enough to fall for that." Leigh rolled her eyes, then turned to Donny. "He's been feeding you crap, Donny. You *can* feed on bagged blood. And you don't have to stay out of daylight, or sleep in a coffin."

"But he said daylight could kill us," Donny said with confusion.

"Of course he did. It helps him control you. It's still daylight now, barely," she added, looking out the window to see the setting sun. "How did you get into the house? You weren't here when we left, it was daylight then, and still daylight now. You must have come out into the sun."

"It was overcast and he said the long-sleeve clothes helped."

Leigh shook her head. "I've been out today in daylight. Full-on daylight when we left for the restaurant for lunch," she pointed out. "It didn't burn me. I'm alive and well."

"Shut up," Morgan snapped, but Leigh ignored him.

"We're not soulless either. It's not a curse, it's nanos."

"Nanos?" Donny asked with bewilderment.

"Shut up!" Morgan caught Leigh by the hair, jerking her head back cruelly in an effort to silence her.

"You're starting to piss me off, Morgan," Leigh said grimly. "This move is rather like something Kenny used to do."

"How unfortunate," he snarled. "Get used to it."

Leigh felt anger build within her. She'd sworn never to be manhandled again. Never to be under another's control. Fury and rage from years of Kenny's abuse reared up in her, but she stamped down on it.

"Are you going to hiss and spit like a kitten?" Morgan asked with interest, tugging her head farther back.

"Keep it up and you'll find out," she answered grimly.

Her eyes sought Lucian. He was stiff and still, a statue of furious stone. She wasn't the only one to notice the way he'd tensed. The two men on either side of him had stepped closer, weapons turned his way.

"Let her go!"

Leigh glanced to Donny, not so much surprised by the anger in his voice as by his courage in voicing it and sticking up for her.

Fortunately for Donny, rather than angered by it, Morgan gave a little laugh and reminded him with glee, "You wanted her turned. She's only here because of you."

"It was a mistake. She was my best friend. I didn't want to lose her. I was wrong. I should have just accepted my fate and left her out of it. You like to hurt people. You—"

"Yes, yes, I'm the big bad wolf," Morgan said dryly. "And you've seen the error of your ways and regret everything." He turned to Leigh. "Don't you find inde-cisive men annoying?"

"Mostly, I find men who lie and cheat to keep others in their control annoying," Leigh said, scowling, then added, "And don't blame Donny for my being here now. You obviously don't care what he wants. He isn't why you're here." Frowning, she asked, "Why *are* you here? What do you want with me?"

His hold on her hair eased and Morgan stared at her a long time. So long, in fact, Leigh was positive he wouldn't answer, but then he said, "You're the first mortal I haven't been able to fully control since my life mate died. You fascinate me. Why can't I control you? I could control your body before, but not your mind, and now . . ." His eyes narrowed on her face and she felt that ruffling again, then he shook his head. "Now I don't even have full control over your body anymore."

When she stiffened, he admitted, "I felt you resist when I first brought you to me. I know you're just letting me think I'm controlling you and can take it back any time. And you're speaking. You shouldn't be speaking."

So much for the element of surprise, Leigh thought on an inward sigh. It seemed all those years of martial arts training she'd taken since leaving Kenny were going to come in handy after all. The classes had been expensive, especially the first two years while she was on the run and money had been so short. It appeared now, how-ever, that those lessons would be put to good use.

A grunt drew her attention to Lucian in time to see him drive his elbow into the stomach of the immor-tal with the sword. Leigh didn't wait to see any more. Without even thinking about it, she snapped her own arm down, slamming it into Morgan's throat. The man's eyes went wide with shock and pain and his hold on her hair loosened abruptly.

While he was still stunned, Leigh turned on his lap and drove a thumb into his eye, grimacing at the sensation as the wet orb gave way, but that was as far as she got.

Morgan's survival instinct kicked in and he lunged to his feet with a roar, dumping her to the ground. Leigh instinctively rolled away and out of kicking distance, then glanced back warily. Much to her surprise, Morgan wasn't following her. He couldn't. Donny had launched himself at the man. The two were now struggling in front of the couch. Her gaze shot to Lucian.

He was doing quite well on his own, and she found herself admiring the way his body shifted and rippled as he fought. He really was beautiful. Lucian glanced over his shoulder and shouted something, but Leigh couldn't hear him over the yelling and grunting going on in the room and the barking that had suddenly erupted from the bathroom in the loft. Julius sounded frantic to get out. She could hear the repeated thud of something hitting the bathroom door upstairs, interspersed with the barking, and could imagine the animal hurtling himself at the door. It appeared Morgan had been right to be concerned—at this rate, the dog would be through the door and downstairs within minutes.

A scream from behind drew Leigh's attention. Donny was on the hardwood floor, blood pouring from his arm and his head though she wasn't sure how exactly he'd been wounded. Morgan's eye was a mess, but it didn't look like Donny had added to his injuries. In truth, Donny appeared to have just kept him busy.

She'd have to give Donny self-defense lessons when this was over, she thought as she crawled to her feet. He fought like an untrained girl, hands flying every which way, his face turned away to protect it. He seemed to think he was having a bitch-slapping session rather than the life and death struggle it was. Morgan was suicidal, but he was also afraid to die, otherwise he'd have killed himself rather than drag in the countless numbers of people he'd pulled into this mess to get the council set on himself.

Honestly, people drove her crazy. How much easier would it have been had he just killed himself and left everyone else out of it? On the other hand, then she never would have met Lucian and fallen in love and—

Well hell, Leigh thought with amazement, *this was a fine time to*—

A scream from Donny caught her attention, and she saw that Morgan had pulled a knife from somewhere on his person and was trying to cut through Donny's throat. Geez. The guy might be suicidal, but his survival instinct was still strong. She hurried forward and lunged onto Morgan's back, then reached around to put her hands over his on the knife. She pulled, trying to get it away from Donny's throat, but Morgan was very strong. Brute strength wasn't going to work here.

Pulling herself off of him, she kicked, slamming the toe of her running shoe into his throat. Much to her satisfaction, Morgan made a choked sound and grabbed for his throat as he rolled off Donny.

"Thanks," the redhead muttered, wiping the blood from his face.

Nodding, Leigh turned to see how Lucian was doing. He was weaponless, and ducking and feinting with one man with a sword while trying to avoid the other man's knife. Actually, his ability to do so was quite impressive. But Leigh was afraid he'd get hurt. She hesitated briefly, eyes widening as Lucian carried out a move that suddenly put the man with the knife between himself and the man with the sword as he swung at Lucian. Unable to stop himself, the man thrust his sword through the heart of his comrade and all three men froze.

It was then that Leigh made her move. The swordsman's sword was temporarily out of commission, so she approached from the side and slammed her foot into the immortal's knee. Leigh grimaced as it snapped, then shot her hand out, catching him in the nose with the heel of her hand. There was a disgusting crunch and the man hit the floor with a thud. *Geez, they should warn you about how gross this could all be*, she thought, then gave a start when Lucian gave her a quick hard kiss.

"Thank you," he said as he released her. Then he turned and snatched the sword from the other man and handed it to her. "Keep an eye on these two. I'll go after Morgan."

"Go after—" Leigh turned to see that in the few seconds when she hadn't been looking, Morgan had regained himself, seen that his side was losing the battle, and was now fleeing for the front door.

Leigh's gaze swung to Donny, who was struggling to his feet to give chase. Lucian saw him, too, and faltered, turning on him.

"Lucian no!" she cried. "Donny hasn't killed anyone. He didn't ask to be turned. He helped us."

Lucian hesitated. "He's fed on mortals, Leigh."

"But he didn't know any better. He hasn't killed anyone, and he certainly hasn't fed well. You heard what Morgan said."

Lucian's eyes narrowed on Donny, and Leigh suspected he was rifling through the redhead's thoughts. She sagged with relief when he nodded and turned to go after Morgan. Sighing, she eyed the two men on the floor and frowned, seeing how quickly they were healing. The one who had been caught by the sword had stopped bleeding and the wound was smaller than it had been. The other was no longer holding his leg, but watching her with a predatory gaze.

Leigh's mouth tightened and she raised the sword as the two men began to get to their feet. The one whose knee she'd broken staggered and winced as he gained his feet, but stayed upright. The other was holding his side, but they were both mobile.

"Leigh, they're fast," Donny warned. "Back up a little."

She stepped back, her eyes darting to the side in time to see Donny pick up the knife the second man had dropped. Gripping it firmly, he moved to Leigh's side and eyed the men warily.

The shorter of the men, the one with the sword wound, smiled. Leigh didn't think that was a good sign.

"You're on your own, little girl. Can you handle two of us?"

"She has me," Donny said through gritted teeth, and the man sneered at him.

"You haven't fed in days. You're useless," he said. "Nope. She's on her own."

Leigh frowned, afraid it was true. Donny would try, but he'd been weak to begin with, and after the blood lost during the struggle with Morgan, was now swaying on his feet.

The other man began to limp to the side. He ground his teeth as he put weight on his leg and said, "You're going to pay for that."

Leigh raised the sword and braced her feet, then glanced sharply over her shoulder as a crash came from upstairs. She'd forgotten all about Julius. His barking and banging had become background noise that she'd hardly paid attention to as the battle unfolded. Now she remembered, and smiled as he appeared at the top of the stairs.

Julius wasn't immortal, but he was two hundred pounds of rabid fury barreling down the stairs. The way the jowls of his silly wrinkly face swung back and forth as he charged didn't seem amusing now, not with his teeth bared in preparation of attack.

"Looks like I'm not alone after all," Leigh commented, and turned back just in time to see the two immortals slip out the sliding glass door and slam it closed before running off down the sand.

"Damn." Donny sighed wearily at the prospect of a chase, then moved resolutely to open the door. Julius didn't even slow down. He leapt from the stairs, crossed to the door in three strides, and raced through the door the redhead had just opened, charging after the two men.

Leigh moved to follow as Donny stepped out behind the dog, then she paused and caught Donny's arm with a frown as the sound of a rotor caught her ear. Glancing skyward, she saw a helicopter dropping out of the sky toward the beach in front of the cottage. The air was suddenly aswirl with sand. It whirled in tornadolike clouds.

As Leigh raised a hand to shield her eyes, she saw the two immortals throw their arms over their faces and drop to the sand. She also saw Julius turn on his heel and charge back toward them. Leigh and Donny rushed back into the cottage, waited for Julius to gallop back in behind them, then slammed the door shut with relief.

"Who are they?" Donny asked with amazement as

four men leapt from the helicopter the moment it set down on the sand.

"Lucian's men," Leigh said with surprise, recognizing the two in the lead as Mortimer and Bricker. She presumed the other two were either Pimms and Anders, or the two men who had been watching the train station.

Leigh ran an absent hand over Julius's back as they watched the immortals being dragged back to the helicopter by the two men Leigh didn't know. Then Mortimer and Bricker headed toward the cottage, only to pause and move to the side as Lucian appeared with Morgan in tow. He shoved the man at them and stopped to talk.

"Good. Then it's finally over," Donny sighed. "Morgan was an evil bastard."

"How did you get involved with him?" Leigh asked curiously.

Donny shook his head. "They were in the bar the Thursday before my night off. I served them. On Friday night I went out with friends and ran into them at another bar. They recognized me and invited me back to the house."

He grimaced. "I was stupid. He sold me all this 'live forever, never age, have you with me' bunk . . ." Donny sighed and ran a hand through his hair. "And I fell for it like a sucker. I didn't realize it would mean his controlling everything and trying to make me hurt and kill people."

He let his hand drop to his side. "I'm really sorry, Leigh."

She frowned. He looked horrible, and lines of pain were becoming permanent around his eyes. He'd been stupid, but he knew it, and the stupidity had brought her Lucian. And a huge family, if she had the courage to take Lucian on and stop dragging her feet like the coward she was acting like.

Leigh glanced out at the men on the beach, her attention focusing on Lucian.

"It's okay," she said at last. "Don't worry about it. It's done now."

"But—"

Leigh shook her head and repeated, "It's over. There's blood in the refrigerator in the kitchen. Go feed before you fall over."

Donny hesitated, then turned and shuffled to the kitchen.

Leigh was setting the sword beside the chair when he called, "How do I eat this?"

"Slap the bag to your teeth," she instructed. "And have as much as you need."

Her gaze slid outside to see that the men had finished talking. Mortimer and Bricker were dragging Morgan to the helicopter while Lucian walked to the cottage.

The helicopter rotors hadn't stopped, and Leigh grimaced and stepped back as Lucian opened the door to enter. He was quick, though, and little sand got in with him. She heard the door slam shut, but before she could blink her eyes back open, his arms were sliding around her.

"Have I told you I love you?" he whispered against her mouth as she slid her own arms around him.

"If you did, I don't mind hearing it again," Leigh said with a slow smile.

Lucian chuckled, then pressed a kiss to her mouth and said, "I do love you."

"I love you, too," she admitted, and he squeezed her tight.

"Thank you," he murmured finally, then eased his

hold enough to raise one hand and caress her cheek. "Are we still dating?"

Leigh smiled at the way he winced as he asked the question, but said solemnly, "I think we've moved beyond dating. We're life mates."

"Oh, thank God." Lucian kissed her properly, his mouth claiming her as his own until Donny's voice intruded.

"So, does my still being alive and not on that helicopter mean you're not going to kill me?"

Lucian lifted his head to spear the man with a glare and growled, "Only if you don't interrupt us again."

"Right," Donny said slowly. "I'll go . . ." He glanced around, at a loss. "Walk the dog?"

"Sounds like a good idea, Donald," Lucian said dryly as he turned back to peer down at Leigh.

"Call me Donny," the redhead murmured, then patted his leg and moved toward the door, saying, "Come on . . . dog."

"His name's Julius," Leigh sighed as Lucian pressed kisses along her neck.

"Right. Julius," Donny said, and slid out of the house.

"Leigh?" Lucian murmured, pulling the t-shirt from her pants and pushing it up her stomach.

"Hmmm?" she asked, beginning to tug at his clothes.

"You know how I laughed at the idea of your kicking bad guy butt?"

"Yeah."

"You did good."

"Yeah?" Leigh asked, pausing.

"Yeah. Want to work for the council with me? You could be my secret weapon."

"Are you serious?" she asked, surprised.

"Leigh, honey, most of the rogues don't know crap about fighting. They count on the fact that they're immortals and stronger than mortals to get them through. You could really kick some butt with your skills."

She smiled faintly. "You have that much faith in me after one small skirmish?"

"Yes I do," Lucian said solemnly. "Besides, I'd have your back."

"And I'd have yours," Leigh said quietly, then chuckled, and suddenly dropped to her knees before him.

"What are you doing?" Lucian asked with amazement as she unbuckled his belt and began to undo his pants.

"I thought I'd see in what other areas I have talents." She raised her eyes and smiled wickedly. "It seems only fair. You showed me a skill or two."

God, I love this woman, Lucian thought with a smile, then noticed the way she had stilled, a frown crossing her face. "What is it?"

Leigh glanced up with uncertainty, then back to his groin with a sort of horrified fascination. "Well, um . . . is there something about immortals you haven't told me?"

"What? What do you mean?" he asked with bewilderment.

Leigh shook her head, then leaned forward and said "Hello?" to his groin, only to stiffen again and jerk back as if it had hissed at her.

"Are you talking to my penis?" Lucian asked with disbelief.

"It talked to me first," she said defensively, and frowned. "You didn't mention this little skill."

Lucian decided she must be joking and laughed. "So, what did it say?"

"It said, 'Lucian? Lucian, are you there?'"

He blinked. "Why would it say that?"

"I don't know. It's *your* penis."

That's when he recalled the cell phone in his pocket. A laugh bursting from his lips, Lucian reached in his pocket to retrieve the phone. "I punched in Bastien's number when we first came in. I figured, if nothing else, it would get you help eventually if anything happened to me. That's why the cavalry arrived in the helicopter. Bastien rallied the troops and sent them the minute he answered the phone and heard us talking to Morgan. I guess he's still on the line."

"Oh." Leigh slumped back on her heels, obvious relief on her face.

Shaking his head, Lucian lifted the phone to his ear.

 *Epilogue*

"Oh, look, she's smiling." Leigh glanced up from the baby she held toward Lucian. "Isn't your grandniece beautiful?"

"Yes." He smiled at the baby in Leigh's arms, then slid his arm around her, drew her to his side for a kiss and whispered, "But not as beautiful as her aunt."

"Hush, she'll hear you and you'll give her a complex before she's even teething," Leigh said with affection as she kissed him on the cheek.

"Give her back to me," Lissianna said firmly, but an indulgent smile softened the words. "You're so wrapped up in each other, you're going to drop her."

"Never," Leigh assured her, but handed the baby back, knowing Lissianna just wanted to hold her.

Lissianna and Greg peered down at the child they'd created and smiled, then Greg glanced up and asked, "So how are the wedding arrangements going?"

"Great," Leigh said with amusement. "Bastien is taking care of everything."

"Bastien?" Lissianna said with amazement. "You're letting him handle your wedding arrangements?"

"And the honeymoon," Leigh said with a laugh. "He insisted I was too busy, what with running back and forth between Kansas and Toronto trying to get everything in order."

"And her pregnancy," Lucian murmured, rubbing one hand lightly over Leigh's still flat belly. He liked to bring it up at every opportunity. He was very pleased that she was pregnant and liked to rub it in the faces of his nephews at every turn. He'd gotten her pregnant the first night. Leigh suspected it had something to do with the fact that they all knew he hadn't had a lover in years before her, and he saw the pregnancy as some sort of proof of his virility. Men could be so cute in a pain-in-the-butt kind of way, she thought affectionately.

"Yes, but *Bastien*?" Lissianna asked. "He's supposed to be arranging his own wedding to Terri. He—"

"Yes. He says it makes it easier, they just double up on everything," Leigh said with a grin, then added, "And Thomas and Donny are helping him."

"Dear God," Greg breathed. "It's going to be a surfer dude/gangsta wedding."

Leigh burst out laughing at the suggestion. "Don't be silly. It'll be fine. Bastien is riding heel on them. Besides, those two aren't as bad as you think. Donny is really quite sweet now that he's away from Morgan. Actually, he always was quite sweet. And he's grown up a lot since Lucian took over his training. Donny wants to be a hunter for the council when he grows up."

Lucian rolled his eyes at her comment. Leigh was very protective of, and doted on, the little twerp. She was right, though, Donny wasn't a bad lad, just a bit misguided. He hadn't set a foot down wrong since that day in the cottage. Though, truthfully, he hadn't done more than bite mortals before that. He'd refused to kill, much to Morgan's displeasure. It was the reason he'd been allowed to live. Donny had been misled by Morgan and bullied by him, and still refused to kill even a dog. The council decided to give him a second chance. But if he blew it . . . Lucian sincerely hoped he didn't. Leigh would be very hurt, and then he'd have to hunt him down personally for doing it. Morgan and the others hadn't received a second chance.

"Have you heard from Marguerite?" Leigh asked, drawing Lucian's attention back to the people around him.

Lissianna shook her head and frowned. "Actually, I'm really starting to worry. It isn't like Mom to stay out of contact this long. Especially with my being pregnant and everything."

Lucian frowned, too. It really *wasn't* like Marguerite, but he said, "I'm sure she's fine. Maria and Vittorio would call if anything had happened."

"If they could. We haven't been able to reach them either. They've checked out of the hotel and not left a forwarding address, or number, or anything. That just isn't like Mom."

Lucian frowned, then squeezed Leigh to his side. "Have you ever been to Europe?"

Leigh blinked. "No. I've never been out of the U.S.... Well, besides Toronto, I mean," she added wryly.

"Hmmm . . . How do you feel about croissants for breakfast?" he asked.

Leigh smiled slowly. "You mean *real* French croissants from France?"

Lucian nodded. "We could grab a company plane, hop over, check on Marguerite and tell her she's a grandmother." He grinned at the word. "Grandmother. That ought to freak her out a bit."

"You're a cruel man, Lucian," Leigh said solemnly, and he grinned.

"Actually," Greg commented, "I think she went to Italy."

"Italy?" Lucian said with surprise.

Greg nodded. "The guy she's working for is named Christian Notte. I'm sure it was Italy."

"Notte," Lucian said slowly, and frowned as something twigged in his memory.

Leigh eyed him curiously, then said, "Italy sounds good, too. It might be fun to try real pizza from Italy. Or— Oh! Gelatos!"

"Gelatos?" Lucian asked.

"Italian ice cream. It's supposed to be *very* good."

"Yeah?" he asked with interest.

Leigh nodded.

"Okay, Italy it is," he announced, and glanced at Lissianna. "Stop worrying. You're a new mother, you have enough to worry about. Besides, you'll produce sour milk and give the baby a stomachache."

"I'm pretty sure that's an old wives' tale," Lissianna said with amusement.

"Well, old wives ought to know, right?" he said. "So stop worrying. Leigh and I will head to Italy and find your mother and tell her she's a grandma. She'll be back here on the next plane."

"I need to go down to Kansas before we go, Lucian," Leigh said as he steered her toward the door. "I have to make sure Milly—"

He silenced her with a kiss and asked, "Have I told you I love you today?"

She shook her head.

"Well I do. You brighten up my life and make me laugh, Leigh. I love you."

"I love you too, Lucian," she murmured, and rested her head against his chest as they walked along the hall.

They had reached the elevator when she suddenly asked, "Do they have bidets in Italy? I've always wanted to try one of those."

"Can I watch?" Lucian asked with a lascivious grin, and Leigh smacked him in the arm.

"God! All you think about is food and sex," she accused as they stepped onto the elevator. She then turned into his arms and kissed him lightly on the lips before murmuring, "And I wouldn't have it any other way."

Celebrate the new year and get started
on a fresh batch of romance novels
to rejuvenate the soul and
rekindle the passion!

Want unforgettable romances
and amazing authors?
Then look no further
than these four
Romance Superleaders.

Not Another New Year's

Christie Ridgway
Coming January 2007

USA Today **bestselling author Christie Ridgway taps into all that New Year's pressure in her fun and sexy new book. Hannah Davis has made a resolution—she's going to have a memorable New Year's Eve! At a bar on December 31, she picks up ex-Secret Service Agent Tanner Hart, a gloomy good-looker, and lets him take her to bed. She was feeling great until the next morning, when a woman bursts in on them and a bleary-eyed Hannah realizes that the man she's in bed with is more complicated than she bargained for.**

♡

*W*omen had always been a weakness of his, Tanner Hart admitted to himself, looking down at the flushed, long-legged beauty in his lap. When he'd spied her careening toward him out of the crowd, he'd had a gut-churning moment of foreboding when he thought she was his bad luck charm, Desirée, but one breath of her scent, one second of her resting in the cradle of his body, and he'd known she was someone else entirely.

Funny, though. The foreboding wasn't fully gone.

And because of that, and because he'd given his vow, he knew he should set her back on her feet.

But hell, it was New Year's Eve and how could one little kiss hurt? He was just drunk enough to forget that it was one little kiss that had fried his ass in hellfire to begin with.

So Tanner bent his head toward her, his gaze on her lips, flushed such a pretty red. He smiled a little, appreciating the passionate color. In his experience, a woman's mouth reddened to the exact same shade as her ni—

"Here's your drinks," a no-nonsense voice grated out.

Tanner's head jerked up. His eyes met those of his brother, Troy, as the other man clacked down another beer and some girly drink on the table.

"I was this close to tossing her butt out," Troy said, nodding toward the figure in his arms.

That was Troy, all right, out to save Tanner, his Marine medals always invisibly pinned to his T-shirt.

"But now I realize . . ." His brother's voice trailed off.

"Yeah," Tanner agreed, reading Troy's mind. His arms tightened possessively on the flushed beauty, even though he figured the other man's presence had ruined the moment.

Now that most of the midnight kissing in the bar was complete, his chance of getting a second shot at the dark-haired female he held was probably remote. Too bad, he thought, but it was probably for the best. After all, he *was* sworn off the opposite sex until he got his career problems straightened out and his life back under his control.

"She's not her," he told Troy. She's . . ." He tilted his head to study the woman in his arms. While her hair was silky darkness like his bad luck charm's, and what he could tell of her body claimed the same stellar curves, instead of possessing the slight exotic cast of the big D's features, this woman's were of the apple-cheeked, cute-nosed variety.

Lovely in the extreme, but one hundred percent American rose. Long-stemmed. Dewy. Velvety. Sweet.

In that paper crown, she looked like a princess who should be reigning over the American Legion's parade float on the Fourth of July.

" . . . definitely not Desirée," he finished.

The girl's face flushed deeper and the inside points of her arched brows slammed together. Her big brown eyes went from soft to stone. "Why is everyone saying that?" she hissed.

Tanner glanced at Troy for help. "Uh . . ."

The strange woman scooped up the girly drink and jerked straight in his lap.

Tanner bit back a yelp as her offended tailbone connected with the bone on his body that had reacted like a pointer's tail on the opening day of duck hunting season the instant the American rose had landed against him. And okay, so the dog metaphor fit, because yes, he was already hard. Horny.

Sue him. He'd been celibate for eleven months and counting. It was supposed to make him a better person, maybe not a bona fide white hat like the other men in his famous family, but at least someone who could be known for something other than screwing up.

The girl tossed back the booze, slammed the glass to the table again, and glared at him. Then she grabbed the sides of his hair and yanked his face close.

Kissed him.

Desirée had done that once too.

Except American Rose didn't taste like Desirée. Well, he couldn't remember *what* damn Desirée had tasted like. But certainly not tangy-sweet like this, with a little bite of mint. Mojito, he thought. Mojito and her own unique flavor.

He liked it. He liked it a hell of a lot.

Now she really went after the kiss, mashing her lips against his, more function than form, and he drew back, not just because he could sense her desperation, but because it was surging weirdly through him too.

"Whoa," he said, fighting her pull on the ends of his hair and trying to sound amused and casual and not hornier than ever. "Whoa whoa whoa. Where's the fire, sweetheart?"

Troy snickered and walked off, while American Rose froze. Then her hands dropped, her shoulders slumped, and a long sigh fluttered the ends of his hair. He thought she might cry.

"God," she moaned instead. "I read *this* all wrong too, didn't I? You don't want me either, do you?"

Maybe they were both a little tipsy, because she continued to sit on his thighs, though wilted now. "I haven't looked at a man in four years," she continued. "And then I have to be attracted to one who doesn't find me—"

She broke off, brightened a little. "Are you by any chance gay?"

Definitely both tipsy, he decided, not just because she'd asked such a question, but because he felt so instantly compelled to answer it.

With his mouth against hers.

Bending to her again, he licked his tongue across her pillowy bottom lip. Once. Twice. Felt her startled sip of air and the way her belly tensed against his inner forearm.

"Sweetheart, does that seem like gay to you?" he whispered, letting the words play across her wet mouth.

Bite Me If You Can

Lynsay Sands
Coming February 2007

USA Today bestselling author Lynsay Sands continues with her popular vampire series starring the Argeneau family. Lucian Argeneau may be a vampire, but he's also a bit of a grump. Hundreds of years spent hunting rogue immortals will do that to a man. The last thing he expects to find is a reluctant vampire who's having a bit of a tough time adjusting to her new life. Lucian hasn't had to interact with a woman this closely for thousands of years, and he has no intention of starting now. But the best laid plans . . .

♡

*L*ucian jerked his hand back and waited. The door only opened halfway before the brunette named Leigh slid through and took a cautious step into the kitchen.

As he stared in amazement, her head slowly turned and she blinked at the sight of him. Lucian saw fear leap into her eyes and moved quickly, clasping one hand over her mouth and drawing her silently away from the door so that her back was pressed hard to his chest.

Her body briefly tensed, as if preparing to struggle, then she suddenly went still. When Lucian glanced down, he saw that her wide eyes were on Mortimer and Bricker on the other side of the door. Both men were giving her what he supposed were reassuring smiles. They just looked like a pair of idiots to him, but it apparently worked on Leigh. As he watched, Bricker placed one finger to his mouth to warn her to be quiet, while Mortimer stared at her with a concentration that suggested he was sending her reassuring thoughts and perhaps the silent warning to stay quiet. The brunette relaxed against Lucian and he found himself responding as her body molded to his, her bottom unintentionally nestling his groin.

"I had just fallen asleep, Donald. I don't appreciate being woken up for this."

Lucian stiffened as that voice floated up the stairs, aware that Leigh had gone still. She was actually holding her breath, he realized, and found he disliked that she was so afraid.

"I'm sorry, sire," someone—presumably Donald—responded, but in truth he sounded more resentful than apologetic. "But I've searched the basement and she—"

"Because she's not going to hide in the basement. She's going to run, you idiot!" Morgan's angry voice snapped back.

"But why? Why isn't she willing?" Donald's voice had turned frustrated and even whiney.

"Not everyone wants to be a child of the night. I warned you of that. I told you, you couldn't turn your back on her for a moment until we have control over her. Not for a damned moment! I *told* you that! She isn't a willing turn. Until she accepts me as master, she'll try to run."

"I just left her alone for a minute. I—"

"You shouldn't have left her alone at all. Get her back and—"

"But what if she's outside? The sun's coming up!"

"You wanted her. She's—"

The words stopped short and Lucian felt himself stiffen further. The voices had drawn closer with each passing moment and by his guess the speakers were at the bottom of the steps now. The sudden silence seemed to suggest something had given away their presence.

Lucian glanced at Mortimer and Bricker, but he was sure neither man could be seen from below. He let his gaze drop over the woman before him, and spotted the problem at once. Lucian hadn't pulled Leigh far enough back. She was short, barely the top of her head reaching his throat, but she was generously proportioned, and part of her generous proportions were protruding past the edge of the door in her bright white blouse.

"Is that a boob?" Donald's voice suddenly asked and Lucian closed his eyes.

The ensuing silence was so long, he just knew that Morgan was seeking out Leigh's mind and searching for information on the situation at the top of the stairs. Lucian supposed it would have been too much to hope the man would just assume she was a bimbo bartender too stupid to leave the house, and she was standing up here contemplating her navel. No. Morgan suspected something was up.

Knowing their surprise approach was now over, Lucian shifted Leigh so that he could lean forward and peer around the edge of the door. On the other side, Mortimer did the same thing, and they found themselves staring at two men frozen at the bottom of the wooden steps. Then all hell broke loose.

Morgan and Donald suddenly spun and sped up the dark hall below, breaking into a run as they slipped out of sight. Bricker and Mortimer charged after them, and Lucian pulled Leigh away from the door, pushing her into a chair at the kitchen table.

"Stay," he hissed, then paused briefly, his gaze sliding over her face as he got his first close-up of her. She was a beautiful woman, with glossy chestnut waves of hair framing large, almond-shaped eyes, a straight nose, and high cheekbones in an oval face. She was also terribly pale and swaying in the seat he'd placed her in, so that he wondered just how much blood she'd lost.

Lucian would have asked, but a burst of gunfire from below reminded him of more urgent matters and, instead, he left her there and turned away to hurry downstairs after his comrades.

Warrior Angel
Margaret and Lizz Weis
Coming March 2007

New York Times bestselling author Margaret Weis teams up with her daughter for a paranormal romance series featuring good but flawed Guardian Angels striving to protect their mortal charges, never expecting to fall in love. Derek is a fallen angel, formerly of the Knights Templar. Disillusioned with God and His grand plan, he chooses to remain forever in Limbo, fighting against the Dark Angels, rather than enter into Heaven. But then news of impending war between the forces of good and evil sends Derek to save mankind—and a tempting woman named Rachel Duncan.

♡

*R*achel left her apartment and rode the elevator down to the lobby. A car usually picked her up for work. She owned her own car—a Volkswagen Passat—and she drove it around town. But the parking fees at the Merc were insanely high and it was cheaper for her to hire a car service. Only the car wasn't there yet.

She looked at her watch. She was on time. Mildly irritated that the car was late, Rachel stood tapping her foot impatiently inside the entrance, keeping out of the wind that came roaring off Lake Michigan. She suddenly felt the hair on the back of her neck prickle, like she was standing beneath an air-conditioner blowing cold air on her. Only there was no air-conditioner. Someone was staring at her.

Rachel turned to say, "Good morning, Alex—"

She stopped mid-sentence. The man wearing the livery of the doorman was definitely not Alex. This man was handsome—really, really handsome—devastatingly handsome. He was maybe thirty, with a body that went to the gym, yet didn't brag about it. He had blond hair, crystal blue eyes, and a strong, take-it-on-the-chin jaw. And this handsome man was scowling at her like she'd done something to offend him.

"Oh, I'm sorry. You're obviously not Alex," said Rachel, taken aback. "You must be new. I'm not quite awake yet, I guess.... I'm Rachel Duncan. I'm in apartment 2215. I guess maybe Alex's wife had the baby . . ." She realized she was babbling like a schoolgirl and she made herself shut up.

The new guy didn't say anything. He stood there glaring at her in complete and utter silence. Was he mad that she'd mistaken him for someone else? If so, he could let it go, for heaven's sake! Rachel felt her neck prickle again, this time in hot embarrassment. She was suddenly annoyed that he wouldn't say a word to ease her obvious discomfort.

What a jerk!

Fortunately her car pulled up in front of the building. She turned and gave the doorman The Look. Then she shifted her gaze to the door and stood there, waiting. He didn't seem to get it at first. He just stood there like a bump on a log.

She looked back at him. "You're a doorman," she said coldly. "You're paid to open doors. Right?"

He grudgingly walked over to the glass door and held it open. She breezed past him without a glance. She hoped he froze to death in the backlash of the arctic chill she sent his direction as she walked by.

The nerve of some people. She'd at least tried to apologize for calling him by the wrong name. But what was his right name? Damn, she hadn't thought to look at his name tag. And why was he giving her that awful look, as if he resented her for something she'd done to him, and she'd never even seen him before? She was sure of that much, at least. She would have remembered him.

Damn! Was he ever good-looking, she thought as she settled back into the black leather seat of the car. Six foot three, she guessed. Sandy blond hair that just kissed the collar at the back of his uniform. And icy-blue eyes. Cold and hard on the surface, though. They weren't the eyes of a nice man. No, that look and those eyes weren't nice at all. But there was something underneath the ice, something smoldering. Fire and ice . . .

And he had to be one of the best-looking men Rachel Duncan had ever seen in her life.

The Secret Passion of Simon Blackwell

Samantha James
Coming April 2007

From *New York Times* Extended and *USA Today* bestselling author Samantha James comes a powerful and sweeping romance in which a tortured hero has a second chance at love. Simon Blackwell tragically lost his wife and sons six years earlier in a fire and has simply been going through the motions of life, until he meets the alluring Annabel, who soon finds herself falling for the handsome and brooding widower. But for Simon, to love so completely, only to lose everything—is not something he's willing to risk again.

A nne was in the habit of walking daily. Even at Gleneden, when the Scottish winds blustered and squalled, only the fiercest of weather kept her indoors. If she was not walking, she was riding. Admittedly, as she ambled toward Hyde Park, the notion of crossing paths with Simon Blackwell again cropped up in her mind. But that was silly. She wouldn't allow anyone to keep her from her pleasure, certainly not him.

The day was not as hot as previously, but it was still very warm. Anne rested her parasol on her shoulder, quite enjoying her stroll. She passed a man angling in the Serpentine—and then she saw him.

Oh, no. It could not be. It simply could not be.

Their eyes tangled. He stopped short—or was it she?

Anne had the oddest sense he didn't know what to do as well, or what to say. But it appeared there was no help for it.

"Well, well, my lady, I see your dilemma. You are uncertain whether to acknowledge me or ignore me."

His bluntness took her aback, but only for an instant. "And I see you're as eager to see me as I am to see you."

He accorded her a faint bow. "I trust you've quite recovered from your headache?"

His tone was politeness itself. He knew, damn him, he knew it had been a lie!

They eyed each other. The oddest thought shot through Anne's mind. He was dressed entirely in severe black. No one would ever accuse him of being a peacock, that was for certain. And just as last night, she sensed power and strength beneath the clothing.

Her heart was pounding oddly as well. Anne swallowed. "There is no one present," she said. "We need not stand on pretense as we did last night."

"Pretense? Is that what it was?"

His gaze had sharpened along with his tone.

"The truth is, I didn't expect that you would come to supper last night." The confession emerged before she could stop it.

"My dear Lady Anne, I was invited."

"So you were."

"And if I hadn't come, would that have made me a coward in your eyes?"

"Of course not," she stated shortly. "It would simply indicate that you've a mind of your own."

There was a sudden glint in his eye. "Some might take that as a challenge, my lady."